# Scarlet Wave

a story in the
## RomantiSea Serenades
series

J.D. Harbor

Ebook ISBN: 979-8-9921213-8-4
Paperback ISBN: 979-8-9921213-4-6

Cover Design: J.D. Harbor
Editing and Proofreading: Nicole Kincaid, Naughty Nook PR
Formatting: Nicole Kincaid, Naughty Nook PR

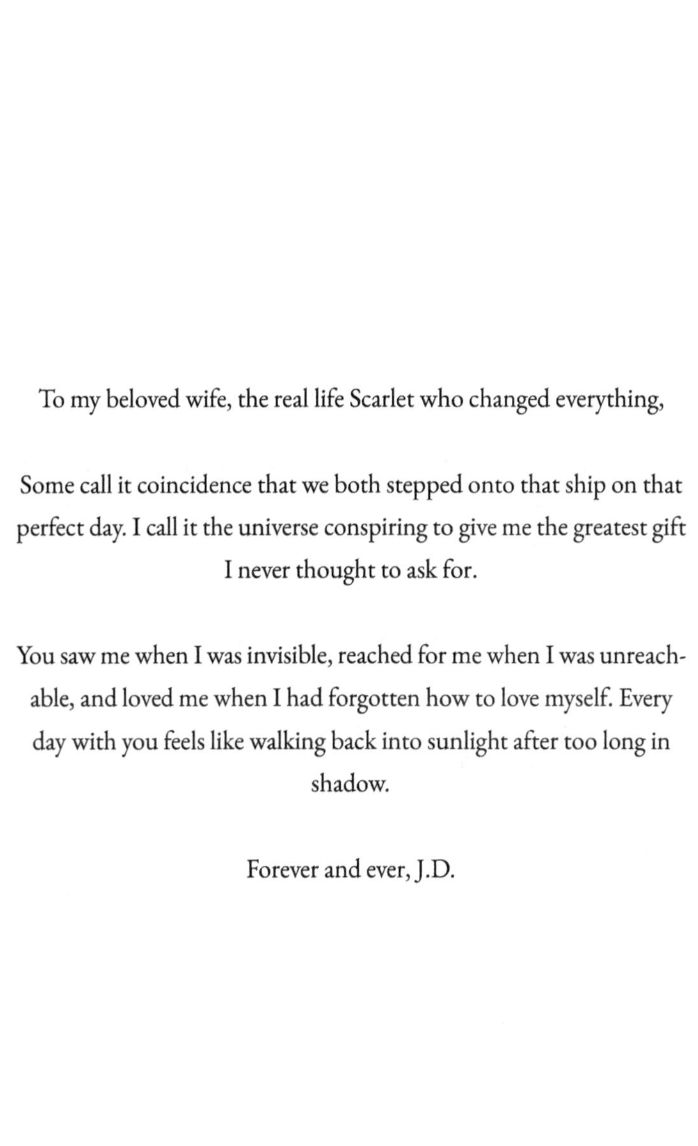

To my beloved wife, the real life Scarlet who changed everything,

Some call it coincidence that we both stepped onto that ship on that perfect day. I call it the universe conspiring to give me the greatest gift I never thought to ask for.

You saw me when I was invisible, reached for me when I was unreachable, and loved me when I had forgotten how to love myself. Every day with you feels like walking back into sunlight after too long in shadow.

Forever and ever, J.D.

# Preface

This story is about learning to release perfection, step away from performance, and surrender the belief that love must be earned by keeping everything and everyone intact.

It's about learning to want again, even after disappointment. About building something new from the pieces you thought were too broken to matter.

While *Scarlet Wave* is at its heart a love story, it also explores themes that may be emotionally complex for some readers.

Even with these heavier elements, I wanted this story to feel like a breath of ocean air.

So alongside the ache, there's laughter. There's rooftop dancing, cruise ship cocktails, chaotic family brunches, fiercely loyal friendships, and a redhead who refuses to settle for less than real love.

This book was written for anyone who's ever felt too much, asked too little, or wondered if they were allowed to want more.

Here's your permission.

Welcome aboard.

**Content considerations include:**

- Past miscarriage and unspoken grief (referenced gently but centrally important)

- Navigating neurodivergence and disability in parenting and caregiving roles

- Emotional burnout and fear of vulnerability

- Military deployment and the strain of long-distance relationships

- Family pressure, work identity, and rediscovering self-worth

# Prologue

S carlet claimed her usual seat at the edge of the aquarium-like meeting room, pen hovering for show above an untouched notebook.

She already knew the rhythm: performative check-ins, recycled buzzwords, and Eric's misguided pep rally, delivered with all the earnestness of a man who thought charisma was the same as leadership.

He was mid-stance now, sleeves rolled in a move that suggested effort.

Maybe he'd broken a sweat arguing with a pie chart.

His voice rang out with that smooth, overconfident cadence she'd come to recognize as his version of sincerity.

"Before we close out," Eric said, "I've got something special. A little surprise. In fact, the person I'm talking about doesn't even know this is coming."

That caught her attention.

Scarlet's fingers flexed around her pen. Her gaze flicked up from her closed notebook, careful not to move too fast. Hope didn't look good on her. It clashed with reality.

The room collectively leaned in. So did she, against her better judgment.

"I want to take a second to recognize someone who's been quietly instrumental. She's been holding things together, stepping up on tough accounts, and consistently delivering real results."

Scarlet's throat tightened. She sat just a touch straighter, legs crossed at the ankle, expression composed but suddenly very aware of every inch of her posture.

He didn't mean her. He never meant her. And yet. He *could*, right?

"She's brought fresh energy, strong instincts, and a real commitment to team culture."

Scarlet blinked. Once. Her pulse tapped gently at her collarbone. *Could be me. But probably not.*

Her inner voice was already shifting gears, rehearsing a gracious smile, mentally rerouting herself toward another quiet disappointment. Still ... just for a second, she let herself believe.

Eric's grin widened as he gestured toward the head of the table. "That's why we're thrilled to announce Maya's promotion to Associate Director of Client Strategy!"

Applause erupted. Someone let out a too-loud whoop that bounced off the glass walls, as if enthusiasm at volume equaled sincerity.

Scarlet smiled. Automatically. Two polite claps, evenly spaced. Just enough to register as supportive, not enough to betray the hollow pit forming beneath her ribs.

Of course. Of course it was Maya.

Maya, who color-coded her social calendar but missed half her deadlines. Who dazzled clients with buzzwords and big energy, then left the backend details in disarray. Details Scarlet always cleaned up. Who had been here two years and somehow became indispensable by simply being impossible to ignore.

Scarlet's pen hadn't moved. Her notebook remained blank. But her stomach? That had dropped three floors and landed somewhere near her knees.

She wasn't surprised. Not really. But it still landed with that particular sting reserved for the not-quite-unexpected. Like checking the mailbox for a letter you know isn't coming, but hoping maybe this time would be different.

It wasn't the lack of praise that got her. Scarlet didn't care for the spotlight. She'd spent most of her career excelling just outside its edge. It was the principle. The track record. The pattern. She'd built a life so tightly wound around achievement, there was no room for the ache she refused to name. Better to be irreplaceable than to be cracked open.

This was the third time she'd been passed over in eighteen months, each time for someone newer, louder, more performative.

As if the work itself didn't matter unless it came wrapped in glitter.

Movement in the hallway caught her eye. Through the frosted glass, Scarlet saw the HR parade approaching. Balloons bounced, a sheet cake sagged under pink gel icing, and someone gripped a Bluetooth speaker triumphantly like it was the Stanley Cup.

She blinked slowly. The irony was sharp enough to sting: the clichéd surprise, the cheap cake, the overly eager interns giggling like they were delivering a sweepstakes prize. Of course this was how it went. Of course the promotion announcement had a soundtrack.

And of course Scarlet, seated at the far end near the door, just happened to be in the perfect spot to "help."

She stood, careful not to draw attention, and stepped toward the door with the kind of pleasant efficiency she was known for. "Let me get that," she said lightly, all professional polish.

As the HR manager and two overzealous interns funneled into the room with their arms full of celebration clichés, Scarlet held the door just long enough for the chaos to pass her.

Then, as if camouflaged by helium and frosting, she slipped out behind them, moving quiet and seamless and unnoticed.

Someone cranked the volume behind her, and the tinny opening bars of "Celebration" chased her down the hallway.

At her desk, the glow of her monitor cast a faint bluish hue across the now-vacant row of cubicles, all eerily still and fluorescent-lit. The overhead lights buzzed with just enough voltage to remind her how unnatural they were. The office was trying to feel alive while the celebration roared down the hall.

Her inbox sat open, a parade of unread messages stacked like laundry in a basket you keep meaning to fold. A spreadsheet blinked in the background, half-populated cells like confessions left unfinished.

From the conference room, the sound of laughter carried down the corridor, muffled only slightly by the glass walls. Someone shouted Maya's name. A second later, a round of applause broke out again, followed by the unmistakable clink of plastic forks against paper plates. Frosting and fanfare.

Scarlet didn't move. She clicked into a file that didn't require thought and stared at a half-finished line item until the numbers started to soften at the edges, slipping into each other like wet ink.

Her computer pinged with a Teams notification.

Simon

**Hey. You good?**

Scarlet didn't respond. She wasn't in the mood for pity dressed as professionalism.

Twenty minutes later, Simon appeared beside her desk, walking like someone trying not to intrude, but definitely still intruding. He was balancing a paper plate with a small piece of cake and a plastic fork stuck dead center like a sad little flag.

"I come bearing peace," he said, setting it down beside her keyboard. "Best I could do. They were protective of the edges."

Scarlet finally looked up, one brow arched. "So not even an edge slice? Wow. And here I thought we were friends."

Simon cracked a small smile, the kind he always wore when unsure if she was joking.

"It was this or frosting crumbs."

She tilted her head, assessing the tiny slab of fluff and icing. "So ... pink sugar and disappointment. How on-brand."

Simon leaned against the desk beside hers. "You know, Maya didn't even know the promotion was coming."

Scarlet nodded once, a clipped gesture. "Of course she didn't. The best part about glitter is that it doesn't need context; it just sparkles." He sighed. "Look, I know it doesn't feel great right now, but your time will come."

Scarlet's smile was tight and practiced, the kind you could hang a marketing strategy off of. "Sure. Just like the budget will balance itself and Eric will stop saying 'pivot' in meetings."

Simon winced, maybe at her tone, maybe at the truth in it.

"You're not invisible, Scarlet."

She didn't answer that. Not directly.

Just then, her inbox dinged. Another email. Another ask. It was from Eric with the subject line: Quick favor before the weekend?

Hey Scarlet,

Hate to ask this late, but could you run this quick batch of reports before EOD? I need to pull Maya for another project. I know I can always count on you.

Really appreciate it.

—Eric

Scarlet stared at the message. Then at the cake. Then back at the screen.

That phrase, *I know I can always count on you*, landed like a sigh too deep to fully exhale. The kind that settled into your bones and made itself comfortable.

Of course he could. That was the problem.

"I should get on this," she said, voice flat but not unfriendly. Just ... done.

Simon nodded and pushed off the desk. "Yeah. I figured."

He didn't try to stop her. That wasn't how their friendship worked. They shared proximity, understanding, and the occasional eye roll across a meeting table. But he knew better than to linger when her armor went up.

Scarlet turned back to her screen, adjusted her posture, and placed both hands on the keyboard.

And just like that, her mask was back on. She did the work.

By 5:15, the office was empty.

The laughter and clatter of plastic forks had long faded, replaced by the low hum of the weekend cleaning crew. Somewhere in the distance, a vacuum whirred as it sucked up the last of the confetti.

Scarlet closed her laptop with a soft, final *snap*.

Her shoulders cracked when she rolled them back, stiff from hours of thankless work no one would remember by Monday. She reached for her water bottle, then froze.

The cake.

Still sitting there. Uncut. Untouched. A lopsided square of pink frosting now reduced to a lukewarm slouch, the icing sliding lazily down the side like it couldn't even be bothered to hold its form anymore.

She stared at it. One beat. Then another.

Then, with sharp precision, she scooped up the plate and flung it into the trash. The smack of plastic against plastic was oddly satisfying. A thick smear of frosting splattered against the inside wall of the bin: bright, artificial, defeated.

Scarlet didn't flinch.

She straightened her skirt, grabbed her bag, and walked toward the elevator. Her heels echoed in the silence like punctuation.

She paused at the call button. Pulled out her phone and without hesitation sent a quick text message to her sister.

# One

The moment Scarlet stepped into the taqueria, the scent hit her: grilled meat, lime, and warm tortillas wrapping around her like muscle memory. She hadn't come for comfort, but it found her anyway.

The place buzzed with energy. Low lights, string bulbs drooping from exposed beams, lime walls cluttered with faded lucha posters and beach prints that had seen too many summers. The air smelled like fryer oil, citrus, and ambition giving way to tequila.

At the bar, three guys in flip-flops laughed like they'd never had a bad day. A toddler shrieked from a corner booth, churro sugar on her cheeks, palms slapping the table like applause. Her mom didn't blink, too busy with her margarita and maybe-date. Scarlet looked, but only for a second. Not at him. At the kid. Something about the curls, the chaos. She looked away before the thought formed.

A waitress with neon braids floated past, tray stacked with fajitas, moving like this wasn't her first rodeo. Probably not even her worst.

Cami and Jade were in their usual spot at the corner booth by the window, napkins fluttering under the fan. Cami, back to the brick, sunglasses in her braids, crunching a chip like royalty. Jade, barefoot under the table, laughing at whatever was on her phone.

Scarlet skipped hello. She reached for her perfectly crafted margarita, complete with salted rim and properly positioned lime wedge, and took a long, grounding sip.

"Oh, thank God," she breathed, sinking into the seat. The tequila cut clean through her. "I'm off duty."

Cami smirked. "That kind of day?"

"Let me finish the drink before you start diagnosing," Scarlet said, flicking her eyes to the ceiling fan like it owed her peace.

Cami held up her hands in mock surrender but didn't lose the gleam in her eyes. "Fine. I'll stall with a distraction. Allow me to introduce: today's eligible bachelor."

Scarlet groaned, already regretting everything. "Stop. Remember Rick? Or Carlos? Or what about crooked hat guy?"

"Crooked hat guy?" Jade repeated, pulling her attention away from her phone.

"Yeah, crooked hat guy," Scarlet said, waving vaguely in the air like she was trying to swat away the memory. "I don't remember his name. I just remember his stupid hat. Slightly off-center. Like his morals and his conversational skills."

"Mike!" Cami reminded her, pointing a chip in Scarlet's direction. "Mike was his name. He's friends with my brother."

Scarlet gave her a long, unimpressed blink. "Exactly. And you're officially zero for five on matchmaking attempts. At some point, you have to accept the data."

Cami rolled her eyes. "You're impossible."

"I'm selective," Scarlet corrected. "There's a difference."

"Well, this one is different," Cami insisted, leaning in with a conspiratorial grin. "He's tall, a little older, and has a great jawline. I mean, objectively great. Defined but not try-hard. He's got a good job, wears real clothes instead of tech-bro fleece, and actually seems like he has his act together."

Scarlet raised her glass to her lips again, sighing dramatically before taking another slow sip. "No. I'm too tired to argue with you. Just ... no. You'd have better luck convincing me if you waited until Sunday brunch. At least then I'd be halfway through my third mimosa and emotionally compromised."

"Give it a chance," Jade chimed in, siding with Cami without missing a beat. "You never know, he could be hung like a rocket."

"Jade! What the hell?" Scarlet choked, nearly snorting tequila. She set her glass down and gestured wildly, fingers in full air-quote mode. "'Rocket'? I do *not* need a rocket."

Jade just smirked. "I'm saying, if you're gonna break the dry spell, make it count."

Cami leaned in, chin propped on one hand. "Seriously, when was the last time you got laid?"

Scarlet stared at the salt crusted on her glass. Fair question. Annoying, but fair.

"It's been a minute," she muttered. "Work's been ... a lot."

That didn't even cover it. Between the late nights, the spreadsheets, and the expectation to hold everything together, dating had slipped below even *"clean the pantry"* and *"buy that emergency kit she didn't actually own."*

Cami and Jade leaned in, synchronized sharks, grinning like they smelled gossip.

Scarlet groaned. "Don't even—"

"Who was the last guy you slept with?" Cami asked, eyes gleaming.

Scarlet held up a single finger. "Boundaries."

"Was it crooked hat guy?" Jade asked, already laughing.

All three of them cracked up.

"Absolutely not," Scarlet said, shaking her head.

"Rick?" Cami guessed.

"Carlos?" Jade added.

"Jimmy? Wes? Victor?" Cami rattled them off like a failed fantasy football draft.

Scarlet just kept sipping, unimpressed. "No. None of them. Not even close."

She held her glass midair, then smiled without humor. "That includes the bedroom."

Jade sighed theatrically. "You *do* remember that casual sex exists, right?"

Scarlet glanced sideways. "Is that clinical advice or personal wisdom?"

"Neither. Target's home decor aisle. Surprisingly profound."

Cami gave her a look. "How long?"

Scarlet rubbed her temples. "Too long. Like ... my vibrator's getting clingy. It tried to spoon me last night."

She sat back, exasperated. "Also, why is this suddenly *my* intervention? You're both out here flying solo too."

"Well ..." Jade said, stretching the word with dangerous intent.

Cami and Scarlet both turned.

"What is that tone?" Cami asked slowly. "You sound like you're about to drop a bomb."

"Is this guy-related?" Scarlet asked, brows knitting.

Jade's expression wobbled, teetering somewhere between a grin and a breakdown.

Cami gasped. "Wait. You're not ... are you *pregnant?*"

Scarlet choked on her margarita. "You've got to be kidding."

Jade burst into laughter, holding up her glass. "Would I be throwing back tequila with a baby on board?"

Scarlet blinked. "You've made worse decisions."

"Touché," Jade said, still laughing. "But no. Not that."

"Then what?" Cami asked, practically vibrating. "Spit it out."

Jade reached into her purse with a dramatic pause.

Cami leaned in like a hawk.

Jade pulled out a dainty gold ring with a champagne diamond that caught the light like it had secrets to tell.

Cami gasped. "*Engaged?*"

Jade nodded. "Yep. I didn't wear it because I knew you'd clock it before the queso hit the table."

Scarlet blinked, completely thrown. "Wait! To who? Or should I ask, which John?"

It *was* a valid question. Jade called every guy she dated "John." The habit became strategy after she walked in on her high school sweetheart and college roommate mid-betrayal. Since then, no real names. No emotional real estate. Just Johns.

Cami leaned forward, fully in gossip mode. "Was it Rancher John? No ... wait, Officer John. He had handcuffs."

Scarlet glanced toward the bar. "Just please don't say it's Bartender John. Henry has emotional investment in our guacamole."

Cami purred. "What about Stripper John? The one with the kangaroo tattoo? I've *never* recovered from that Snapchat."

Jade laughed, waving them off. "None of those. But Stripper John *could* help Scarlet out. Might knock the dust off."

"Thanks, but I'm not interested in your sparkle-stained seconds," Scarlet said, deadpan.

Cami wheezed. "You sure?"

"I'm not desperate. Just thirsty," she replied, finishing her drink. "Now talk. Who's this new John?"

Jade smiled and raised her hand, tapping the gold ring, diamond catching the glow like a firefly. "First off, his name's Lucas."

Scarlet stared for a beat, then turned to the bar. "Henry, cancel my restraint and bring another round. Extra tequila. I'm going to need it."

Cami leaned in, eyes bright. "Oooh, we're getting the real name. This is serious."

Scarlet turned back to her sister, now fully engaged. "Okay, spill. Who is Lucas? Where have you been hiding him? And how the hell did he make it out of the John Zone alive?"

Jade twisted the ring slightly on her finger, her smile almost shy now. "We've actually been seeing each other for a while. Things are ... solid."

"*Solid?* That's what you're going with?" Scarlet raised an eyebrow. "You're engaged, not submitting a quarterly report. How long is 'a while,' exactly?"

Jade paused, visibly bracing. "A year and a half. We met at a Halloween party last year, not this year's."

Scarlet recoiled. "Hold up. *That* Halloween?"

"*Banana John?!*" she and Cami shrieked in perfect sync, loud enough to startle the table behind them.

Jade slapped her hands over her face. "God, yes. I know. Terrible branding."

Cami wheezed. "You gave your future husband a smoothie name."

Scarlet leaned on the table, wide-eyed. "The dude who asked if you were 'ripe for the picking'?"

Jade peeked out, eyes sparkling. "What can I say? He's been … *fruitful.*"

Scarlet shook her head, smiling despite herself. "So you've been hiding an actual boyfriend for *eighteen months* and just casually drop the engagement bomb over fajitas?"

"I was going to tell you," Jade said with a shrug. "Eventually. I just … wanted to be sure."

Scarlet's expression shifted, the humor thinning just a touch. "Why didn't you say anything sooner? Christmas? Mom's birthday?"

Jade shrugged. "I don't know. I didn't want to jinx it. Or have to explain it before I was ready."

"Are you happy?" Cami asked, stepping in gently, her voice cutting through the moment.

Jade nodded without hesitation. "Very much so."

Scarlet stood and circled the table, pulling her sister into a warm hug. "If you're happy, then I'm excited for you. I can't wait to meet him."

"I hope you're bringing him to brunch on Sunday," Cami added, raising her glass.

Jade gave a sheepish smile. "Can't. We're moving into our new place this weekend."

Scarlet and Cami let out a synchronized squeal, loud enough to make the bartender glance over.

"So next weekend," Scarlet said firmly, reclaiming her seat. "You're both coming to Mom's. No excuses."

"Absolutely," Jade said, clinking her glass against Cami's.

Scarlet leaned back, letting it all settle: the ring, the name, the fact that her sister had been quietly, actually *happy* for a while now. It felt like catching up to a train she hadn't realized she'd missed.

"Well, hell," she said. "Good for Banana John."

"To Lucas," Cami said, lifting her glass again.

"To the first John with a name," Scarlet added.

The gentle chime of their toast barely rose above the warm noise around them.

Scarlet felt an unexpected rush: proud, startled, and shadowed by a feeling she didn't dare define.

They lingered for a while, laughing, grazing on crumbs, placing half-joking bets on Lucas's future playlist. But eventually, the night faded. Laughter gave way to fatigue, and they peeled off toward their own corners of life.

At home, the warmth of the evening faded into something gentler.

Scarlet kicked off her heels, the soft thud of them landing on the tile louder than expected in the hush of her apartment. Storm appeared instantly, tail flicking, purring like she'd abandoned him for days instead of hours.

She bent down and scooped him up, his body warm and familiar, pressing close as if he could sense the unravel of something inside her.

"Miss me?" she murmured, rubbing her cheek against his fur as she made her way to the couch.

Storm didn't dignify her with a meow, just curled against her the second she sank into her favorite corner, limbs folding beneath her. His heartbeat tapped against her ribs like a second clock.

Scarlet let out a long, slow breath.

The apartment was still. Predictable. Safe.

But it felt different tonight, somehow just a shade emptier, a little too neat. Like something had been removed and she hadn't noticed until now.

She'd told herself for years that healing meant order, control, the absence of chaos. But sometimes it just felt like proof that nothing had taken root since.

She reached for her phone out of habit, thumb hovering before her brain caught up. No urgent emails. No missed calls. Just one unread text, timestamped somewhere between the second and third margarita.

The words lit up her screen with Simon's signature mix of blunt encouragement and quiet loyalty. Scarlet stared at the message, her thumb grazing the glass. She could almost hear his voice, firm and practical, with that thread of warmth he always kept tucked beneath the professionalism.

She sighed, locked the phone, and set it aside on the armrest.

Scratching behind Storm's ears, she murmured to her feline companion, "I've heard that story over and over again. When am I finally going to learn?"

Storm blinked up at her, unimpressed, then stretched out a paw across her stomach as if claiming a patch of territory, her stillness included.

Scarlet let her head fall back against the cushions, her eyes drifting toward the window where the city lights shimmered in scattered gold. Somewhere, a car alarm chirped lazily. Down the hall, someone laughed.

Life continued on outside. Noisy, careless, full.

Her apartment, by contrast, held a stillness. Not empty. Just suspended.

This was a pause with purpose. A breath between chapters.

She shut her eyes, drawing in the hush like a slow tide.

Come Monday, she'd return. Polished. Precise. Unyielding.

They'd remember why she was their anchor, and before long, that title would be hers.

Maybe not today. Maybe not this month.

But she hadn't made it this far just to be overlooked forever.

# Two

Tucked into Coral Gables like a storybook secret, the Bellari home basked in its terracotta skin and sun-warmed charm. Scarlet eased her Mazda behind her father's weathered Camry, stole a glance in the mirror to check that her hair was in place and her face composed, bracing for whatever her sister had staged.

The front door gave easily under her hand, and the scent hit her. Sofrito, golden and alive, made up of onions, peppers, garlic, all singing in oil. The smell pressed pause on her posture.

Inside, the house glowed. Sunlight spilled through open windows, scattering dust into slow-motion waltzes above a parade of photographs.

Three decades of Bellari history smiled back at her from every surface. Snapshots of sunburned shoulders, frosted cakes, tassels mid-flight, each moment honored with a frame, just as her mother insisted they should be.

"Mija!" Her mother's voice carried from the kitchen, warm and knowing. Elisa appeared in the doorway, wooden spoon in hand, flour dusting one cheek. "You're early."

Scarlet held up a bag of pastries. "Thought I'd help set up."

Elisa's eyes narrowed slightly. They were the same hazel as Scarlet's but softer around the edges. She wiped her hands on her apron and cupped Scarlet's face, studying her like a familiar passage with a new footnote.

"You look tired," she said, the observation gentle but unavoidable.

"I'm fine," Scarlet replied automatically. "Just work. The usual."

From the living room, her father's voice boomed over pre-game commentary. "Is that my responsible daughter or my wild child stepchild?"

"It's the one who remembers to call," Scarlet called back, slipping past her mother with a quick kiss on the cheek.

Leo Bellari sat in his designated armchair, the leather worn to a perfect impression of his frame. He muted the TV and extended an arm for a hug.

"Flying solo today?" he asked, rising slightly to embrace her.

Scarlet smiled. "Oh, I'm always solo, Papa. You know I only have room in my heart for you."

He nodded, not asking the questions his eyes held. That was the dance they'd perfected, affection without interrogation.

"Well," he said, squeezing her shoulder once before releasing her, "more food for the rest of us."

Back in the kitchen, Elisa had already claimed the pastries, arranging them on a blue ceramic platter that had survived three decades of Sunday gatherings.

"Your sister says she's bringing someone," Elisa mentioned, too casually.

Scarlet focused on washing her hands. "Is she?"

"A boyfriend." Elisa's tone lifted with restrained curiosity. "She's been very ... secretive."

Scarlet bit back a smile. "Has she?"

"First time she's bringing anyone home since ... well." Elisa's hands stilled briefly over the fruit she was slicing. "You know."

Scarlet did know. Jade hadn't brought anyone home since high school. Not since Ryan, who had shattered her heart so thoroughly that she'd renamed every man who followed. The John Era, as Scarlet privately called it, had lasted nearly a decade.

"I haven't met him either," Scarlet offered, grabbing a knife to help with the mangoes.

Elisa's eyebrows lifted. "Not even you? She usually tells you everything."

Scarlet hedged. "Only through texts. Says he's different. And you know how Jade edits reality."

The front door swung open with a familiar creak, followed by the jingle of bracelets and Cami's unmistakable laughter. She swept into the kitchen like a summer storm, arms laden with a bottle of champagne and what looked like homemade flan.

"Bellari family!" she announced, setting her offerings on the counter. "Your favorite has arrived!"

Leo's laugh echoed from the living room. "That's a funny way to pronounce 'loudest,' Camellia!"

Cami blew a kiss in his direction before enfolding Elisa in a hug. "Mama B, whatever you're cooking needs to be illegal. I could smell it from the driveway."

Elisa beamed, patting Cami's cheek. "You're too skinny. Sit down, I'll fix you a plate."

"Thank you," Cami replied, preening slightly. "Finally someone appreciating my metabolism. And yes, I'm starving."

"She just got here, Mom," Scarlet said, amused.

"And I'm hungry," Cami countered, stealing a slice of mango. "Oh … Maude's parking. She insisted on bringing her famous sangria."

Elisa brightened. "Perfect! I was hoping she'd join us."

Scarlet exchanged a glance with Cami, arching an eyebrow. Cami's grin was unrepentant.

"What?" Cami said, popping another mango slice into her mouth. "As if Maude would miss Jade's big debut."

"So you invited her," Scarlet said flatly.

"Of course I invited her. It's Maude." Cami stole a third piece of fruit. "Besides, something tells me this Lucas guy is going to be worth meeting."

Elisa lit up. "Have you met him already?"

"Not yet," Cami said, shrugging. "But if he managed to get Jade to use his actual name instead of calling him John like all the others, he must be … something."

The front door opened again, and Maude's serene voice floated in. "Hello, beautiful souls!"

She appeared in the kitchen doorway, a large glass pitcher of ruby-red sangria in her hands, fresh fruit suspended like jewels. Leo emerged from the living room, remote still in hand.

"Maude," he greeted her warmly. "Gorgeous day, isn't it?"

"Even better now," she replied with her melodic laugh, setting the sangria on the counter. She embraced Elisa, who immediately launched into Spanish, hands flying as she detailed her hopes for Jade's mystery man.

Maude responded gently, her own Spanish accented but fluent, clearly tempering expectations with wisdom.

Scarlet seized the moment to pull Cami aside. "I didn't know you invited Maude. This is supposed to be just family."

"We are family," Cami shot back, unbothered. "Besides, Maude has that ... way about her. She'll know if this guy is the real deal or just another John with a fancier name."

Before Scarlet could respond, the front door burst open, followed by Jade's unmistakable voice: bright, slightly too loud, nervous energy vibrating beneath.

"Familia! We're here!"

Elisa wiped her hands hurriedly on her apron, smoothing her hair. "Mija! In the kitchen!"

There was a suspended moment of rustling shoes being removed and murmured instructions. Then Jade appeared in the doorway, radiant in a yellow sundress. Behind her stood a tall man with perfect teeth and artfully tousled hair, his smile practiced and dazzling.

"Everyone," Jade said, her voice uncharacteristically soft, "this is Lucas."

Lucas stepped forward with confident grace, hand extended toward Leo first. "Mr. Bellari. It's an honor to finally meet you."

Leo's handshake was firm, his eyes narrowing slightly before crinkling at the corners. "So. You're the one who finally earned a real name."

Lucas laughed, the sound easy and perhaps a touch rehearsed. "I'm still working on living up to it, sir."

Elisa moved forward, embracing Jade before turning to Lucas with an appraising look that only mothers could master. "Welcome, Luis. We've heard ... well, almost nothing about you!"

"Lucas, Mami," Jade corrected quietly, a flicker of something crossing her face. Embarrassment? Concern?

"Yes, of course, Lucas," Elisa amended, patting his arm. "Come, come eat. Tell us everything."

They settled into the living room like chess pieces, and Leo launched into his classic interrogation about profession, heritage, and sports.

Lucas responded with polished ease: pediatric physical therapist, a multicultural household with three sisters, and college-level basketball skills that sounded suspiciously embellished.

There was something in the details that didn't quite align. His Miami neighborhood stories felt lifted from someone else's life. And when he listed his favorite Cuban foods, they read more like the sampler platter at a chain restaurant.

Yet somehow, by the time they were out on the patio and Lucas's hand had found its place at Jade's waist, even Leo was in stitches.

"So, Luis, how did you and Jade meet?" Elisa asked, setting down a steaming platter of ropa vieja.

"Lucas, Mami," Jade reminded her, a slight edge to her voice now.

"Dios mío, I'm sorry," Elisa said, genuinely contrite. "Lucas."

Lucas waved it off with practiced grace. "My mother does the same thing with my sisters' boyfriends. It took her three years to remember my brother-in-law's name."

He launched into the story of meeting Jade at a charity gala and how he'd had to work for weeks just to get her to agree to coffee. Scarlet couldn't recall Jade ever attending such events, but she kept that observation to herself.

"She kept calling me John," he said, squeezing Jade's shoulder. "It became our little joke."

Cami caught Scarlet's eye across the table, one eyebrow slightly raised. That didn't sound like Jade's joke, which had always been something private between the sisters and Cami.

Brunch shifted into a languid afternoon feast, the table groaning under the weight of Elisa's cooking. Conversation flowed easily, Lucas fitting into their dynamic with practiced ease. He remembered everyone's drinks, complimented Elisa's cooking with specific observations, and somehow knew the exact questions to ask Leo about his contracting business.

Between second helpings and Maude's potent sangria, the announcement finally came.

"So," Jade said, clearing her throat and reaching for Lucas's hand. "We actually have some news."

Elisa leaned forward, eyes sparkling. Leo maintained his practiced poker face.

"Lucas and I are engaged," Jade said, her voice steadier than Scarlet had expected. She held up her left hand, the delicate ring catching sunlight.

The reactions came fast and full-bodied: Elisa's joyful sobs, Leo's half-hug and half-remembered name, Cami gasping loud enough for the neighbors to hear.

Only Maude stayed quiet, observing from the edge. Her smile was gracious, but her eyes told another story. Curious, weighing.

Later, as they cleared dishes, conversation turned to wedding plans.

"Nothing big," Jade was saying. "Maybe something beachside. Simple."

"You could do it on a cruise," Cami suggested, waggling her eyebrows at Maude. "Maude could help coordinate."

Maude smiled. "I've witnessed enough shipboard romances to know how to throw a lovely ceremony."

"Any good stories from your latest voyage?" Leo asked, refilling glasses.

"Actually, I just got back from a wedding," Maude replied. "In the northern Georgia mountains. Beautiful ceremony."

"One of your success stories?" Elisa asked, intrigued.

Maude nodded. "Met on one of my cruises last year."

"Oh, another one of those cruise flings that will fizzle out in under a year," Scarlet said, unable to resist.

"I truly think this one will work out," Maude replied, not rising to the bait. "They're both a bit free-spirited, but it works for them."

Cami snorted. "Unlike someone we know who has a five-year plan color-coded by fiscal quarter."

"I'm spontaneous," Scarlet protested.

The table erupted in laughter.

"Mija," Elisa said gently, "you iron your t-shirts."

"Only the work ones!" Scarlet fired back, but she was smiling too.

"The beauty of these cruises isn't about finding love," Maude said, her voice cutting through the laughter with soft authority. "It's about disconnecting to find yourself."

Scarlet looked up, catching Maude's gaze. Something about her words landed differently than all her previous cruise pitches. The part about finding yourself, specifically.

Lucas checked his watch discreetly, then whispered something in Jade's ear. She nodded, her smile never wavering.

"We should probably head out," Jade announced. "Lucas has an early meeting tomorrow."

"On a Monday?" Leo asked, brow furrowing. "What kind of physical therapist has meetings at dawn?"

"Hospital administration," Lucas replied smoothly. "Budget reviews. The glamorous side of healthcare."

He stood, helping Jade with her chair in a gesture that seemed both gallant and slightly performative.

The goodbyes shifted to the front door, a chaotic swirl of hugs and promises to call. When Lucas embraced Elisa, he whispered something that made her beam. With Leo, he shook hands like they were sealing a deal.

When he reached Scarlet, his smile remained perfect, but his eyes held something calculating. "Looking forward to getting to know you better, Scarlet. Jade says you're the family rock."

His grip lingered a half-second too long, his cologne just a touch too strong.

With dusk pressing at the windows and the last guests departing, Scarlet stood elbow to elbow with Maude, stacking dishes with quiet efficiency.

"What do you think of him?" Scarlet asked, voice low.

Maude's smile was gentle. "I think your sister is glowing."

"That's not what I asked."

Maude handed her another dish. "Time reveals character, Scarlet. And sometimes, distance provides clarity."

"Speaking of distance," Scarlet said, rinsing a plate, "you've been trying to get me on one of your cruises for what, two years now?"

"Two and a half. But who's counting?"

"And yet you never push. Why is that?"

Maude's eyes caught the kitchen light. "Because it's not about the cruise, Scarlet. It's about being ready for what the cruise offers."

"Which is?"

"Space," Maude said simply. "Space from expectations. From schedules. From being the responsible one everyone can count on."

Scarlet's hands stilled under the running water.

"You keep waiting to be chosen, whether at work or in love. For someone to finally see your worth," Maude continued softly. "But the sea doesn't wait, Scarlet. It moves. It changes everything it touches."

Before Scarlet could respond, Cami appeared in the doorway, car keys jingling. "Earth to Scarlet! I'm heading out."

The moment broke, but Maude's words lingered.

Later that night, in her quiet apartment, Scarlet scrolled through her sister's newly posted engagement photos, likes already numbering in the hundreds. Storm curled against her leg, a warm, purring anchor.

Her phone pinged with a text from Cami.

Cami

Next cruise sails in about two months. You can bunk with me. Just saying.

Scarlet set the phone down, not answering. But she didn't delete the message either.

# Three

The spreadsheet mocked her, cells blurring under her exhausted gaze. Scarlet blinked hard, refocusing on the monitor where numbers refused to align no matter how many times she adjusted the formula.

It was barely 10 a.m. on Tuesday, and she'd already hit the wall. That invisible, unforgiving barrier between capability and collapse had been creeping closer for months.

She'd arrived late after hitting snooze three times. It was a cardinal sin in her personal gospel of professionalism.

Now she sat at her desk, inbox overflowing with red-flagged messages, each one screaming priority that defied the laws of logic and time management.

Her phone buzzed with an app notification: the team thread. She tapped it automatically, then immediately regretted it.

Eric

Huge thanks to Maya for the stellar Denison report! Client just called, and they're thrilled with the insights. This is exactly the kind of strategic thinking that elevates our entire team.

Maya

Thanks, but Scarlet really helped pull everything together. She stayed late to finalize it.

Eric

Great teamwork then! Maya, I'd like you to present the approach at Friday's all-hands.

Scarlet's jaw tightened. She'd stayed until 9 p.m. last Thursday finishing that report, cross-checking Maya's spotty data, rebuilding the visuals, and polishing the conclusions into something approaching coherence. Maya had walked out at 5:30, tossing a casual "Can you just look it over?" over her shoulder like she was asking Scarlet to water a plant. The small attempt at credit-sharing meant nothing when Eric clearly hadn't even registered it.

On her desk, a cup of premium coffee sat waiting. Not the breakroom sludge, but the good stuff from the café downstairs that Maya must have left sometime before Scarlet arrived. Probably a peace offering or attempt to smooth things over. Scarlet had ignored it, brewing her own coffee out of principle.

She set her phone down and pulled up her calendar. Three back-to-back meetings this afternoon, a client call she hadn't prepared for, and somehow, Eric had managed to add a "quick sync" right over her lunch break.

Her inbox pinged again. Another email from Eric had arrived, forwarded with just two words above it: Your take?

She opened it and scrolled through a lengthy chain about the Walker account, specifically, the mess Maya had made of their quarterly forecast. The client was unhappy. The numbers didn't make sense. Someone needed to fix it before Thursday's presentation.

Three guesses who that someone would be.

Scarlet hadn't even touched her coffee yet. She reached for it now, desperate for caffeine, and knocked it with her elbow. The lid popped off, and dark liquid splashed across her keyboard and onto her cream-colored blouse.

"Perfect," she muttered, grabbing tissues from her desk drawer. "Just ... perfect."

As she blotted at the spreading stain, her spreadsheet chose that exact moment to freeze, the rainbow wheel spinning mockingly. The computer fan whirred aggressively, like it too had reached its limit.

Her phone buzzed again. A text this time. Cami.

Cami

Hey. Just checking in. Maude says she needs to release the room soon. I know you weren't feeling it before, but this is one last shot if you wanna join us. No pressure.

Scarlet stared at the message, tissue still pressed to her blouse. The cruise. That floating escape capsule filled with singles trying too hard and drinks that cost more than her hourly rate.

She didn't reply. Instead, she set her phone down and attacked her keyboard with fresh tissues, as if she could wipe away the morning's cascade of failures along with the coffee.

"Rough start?"

Simon stood beside her desk, sleeves rolled up, expression neutral but eyes concerned. He held out a stack of napkins from the break room.

"Just Tuesday being Tuesday," Scarlet replied, accepting the napkins with a tight smile.

Simon leaned against the edge of her desk. "Saw Eric's message about the Walker account."

"Of course you did." She dabbed at her blouse. "Apparently it's my problem now."

"Because you're the only one who doesn't fumble the handoff," Simon said, his voice quiet enough that only she could hear. "Doesn't mean you have to carry it all alone, though."

Scarlet looked up, momentarily disarmed by the simple truth in his words. Simon had been at the firm even longer than she had. He understood the unspoken hierarchies, the invisible labor, the carefully maintained façades.

"I'm fine," she said automatically, straightening her posture. "Just need more coffee and maybe a time machine."

Simon didn't push. He never did. Just nodded and said, "Let me know if you need backup on Walker. I've got the data from last quarter if it helps."

"Thanks," she replied, her voice softer than she intended.

As Simon walked away, her computer unfroze, only to display an error message. The spreadsheet had crashed, taking an hour's work with it.

In the same moment, her inbox pinged again. Eric, again.

Eric

Any thoughts on that Walker situation?
Client's pressing. We need a fix ASAP.

Something inside Scarlet finally snapped. A thread pulled too tight for too long. With stained blouse, crashed spreadsheet, and emptied coffee, she'd hit her limit.

She picked up her phone and typed a quick response to Cami.

Scarlet

Maybe … talk later?

Then she stared at the error message on her screen, a bitter laugh caught in her throat. If only people came with error messages too. At least then you'd know when you'd pushed them beyond capacity.

When Scarlet finally pushed open her apartment door, she was greeted by Storm's theatrical meows. A one-cat opera of suffering and neglect. He stood in the center of the hallway, tail flicking with indignation, eyes wide with accusation.

"I know, I know," she said, dropping her keys in the bowl by the door. "I'm a monster who starves innocent cats."

Storm circled her ankles once, then dramatically collapsed onto his side, paws splayed, as if the mere effort of expressing his displeasure had drained his last reserves of energy. He let out a long, mournful sound that seemed to say, "I've been waiting for hours, wasting away to nothing."

Scarlet rolled her eyes. "You have an automatic feeder. I saw you hit the button this morning."

Storm rolled onto his back, belly exposed, eyes half-closed, looking like the picture of feline martyrdom.

"The Academy Awards called," she told him, stepping over his prone form to kick off her heels. "They want their performance back."

The relief was immediate and physical as she freed her feet from their professional prison. She'd spent the rest of the workday in autopilot mode, fixing problems, attending meetings, rebuilding the spreadsheet, all with a coffee stain blooming across her blouse like a Rorschach test of professional failure.

Storm, realizing his theatrics weren't having the desired effect, abandoned his dying act and trotted ahead of her toward the kitchen, tail held high like a furry metronome of impatience.

Scarlet changed into leggings and an oversized t-shirt, feeling herself begin to decompress. The tension that had been building between her shoulder blades all day began to ease as she followed Storm to the kitchen.

"At least you're honest about what you want," she told him, scratching behind his ears as she filled his bowl with the gourmet food he pretended was barely adequate.

She poured herself a generous glass of wine and sank onto the couch, letting the silence wash over her. After a day of constant demands and expectations, the emptiness felt almost decadent.

Her phone sat on the coffee table, the notification from Cami still unacknowledged. Scarlet took a long sip of wine, then picked it up, opening the message thread.

*Still holding that room?* she typed, surprising herself with the question.

Cami's response was immediate, as if she'd been waiting.

Cami

> Maude said she can hold it for 48 hours. You curious?

Scarlet's lips quirked.





Scarlet hesitated, wine glass poised midair. What was she doing? She didn't do impulsive. She didn't do singles cruises with theme nights and forced mingling.

But what if she did? Just once?



Moments later, her phone pinged with a link. Scarlet set it aside and took another sip of wine, Storm now curled against her thigh, his earlier drama forgotten as he purred contentedly, his warmth a comforting weight.

For a long moment, she just stared at her phone, as if it might bite. Then, slowly, she reached for her laptop.

The Mingle at Sea website practically sparkled with seaside fantasies and forced fun. Pop-up music played automatically, something breezy with steel drums that made Scarlet wince, and the text glittered with phrases like "Your next adventure is just a wave away!" and "New places, new faces, endless possibilities!"

She almost closed the tab right then. But behind the marketing gloss, the photos caught her attention. Azure waters stretching to the horizon, the elegant curve of the ship against a sunset sky, people laughing on sundrenched decks with the kind of abandon she'd forgotten was possible.

Scarlet scrolled past the cheesy testimonials like "I found my soul-mate in the karaoke lounge!" to the practical details. Seven days aboard the Elysian Serenade, stopping at tropical ports, with various "exclusive Mingle events" peppered throughout, whatever those were.

She clicked through the various room types, the accountant in her immediately comparing amenities and prices with detached interest. The room Maude was holding for her was a balcony stateroom. Not the cheapest option, but not extravagant either. It looked ... nice. Peaceful. Private, but with a view of the horizon.

Maude's words from Sunday brunch floated back to her: "The sea doesn't wait, Scarlet. It moves. It changes everything it touches."

Then Simon's quiet observation: "You're the one who keeps it all running."

That was the problem, wasn't it? She kept everything running. The reports, the clients, the family gatherings, the careful balance of her ordered life. But when was the last time she'd let something run through her? When had she allowed herself to be moved instead of being the mover?

Scarlet set the laptop aside and walked to her bedroom. From the nightstand drawer, she pulled out her passport. It had been untouched since a business trip to Toronto last year. She flipped it open, her own face staring back with the blank expression of someone who didn't expect adventure.

Back on the couch, she reopened the laptop. Storm had claimed the warm spot she'd vacated, watching with suspicious eyes as she scrolled through more photos of the ship.

There was no dramatic swell of music, no moment of profound clarity. Just the quiet of her apartment, the weight of a day spent going unnoticed, and the glowing promise of seven days where no one needed anything from her.

Storm shifted on the couch, suddenly alert as if he sensed her thoughts turning toward departure. He gave her a look of pure betrayal, eyes wide and accusatory.

"What do you think?" she asked him. "Terrible idea?"

His eyes widened with what could only be described as feline horror, giving her a look that clearly said, "Don't you dare leave me. I'll starve to death."

Scarlet laughed softly. "Don't worry. Grandma and Aunt Jade will come visit while I'm away. You'll probably get more treats than you know what to do with."

She closed the laptop and took a deep breath. Then, with a decisiveness that surprised her, she picked up her phone and sent a simple text to Cami.

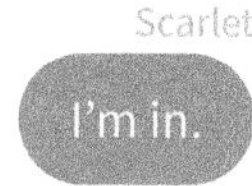

# Four

Storm slid across the sill, a ribbon of smoke with ears. He landed without a sound, nose twitching at the clutter: sandals cast like debris from a tide, swimsuits in soft collisions of color, and a sequined romper winking in the low light.

"If you get glitter in my underwear drawer again, I'm renaming you Tax Season," Scarlet warned, tugging a sheer cover-up over her head.

Cami, half-buried in pillows and plantain chips, wiggled her toes to the music. "He's offering moral support. That thing needs all it can get."

Scarlet twisted sideways with a grimace. "I look like a piña colada left out in the sun."

"You look like foreplay on a cruise ship. Own it."

"I look like a lawsuit in slow motion."

"Then sue me," Cami said, chip in midair, one eyebrow arched. "But that's boarding with us."

With a sigh, Scarlet stripped back down to her unofficial packing uniform: black sports bra and boyshorts. She turned to her closet, hands on hips. "Why did I say yes to this?"

"Let's see …" Cami began counting on fingers stained orange with chip dust, "there was the spreadsheet swinger, the guy who came with a parental chaperone, and your spiritual content king. You need a full reboot."

"I need therapy."

"You need an ocean breeze and at least one bad decision that doesn't involve crypto bros or fitness cults."

Storm jumped onto the bed, sniffed the chips, then dramatically sneezed on the romper before curling up on a white linen dress.

"Perfect," Scarlet muttered. "He's claimed the only thing I packed that doesn't make me look like a backup dancer on Dancing With the Stars: Resort Edition."

Cami swung her legs off the bed. "Pause. We need refills."

She padded to the kitchen, hips swaying to the breezy pop song thumping from Scarlet's speaker that made the room feel like it was already offshore.

Scarlet adjusted a strappy sundress. "So … this cruise isn't just an elaborate trap to get me drunk and married to someone who wears shark-tooth necklaces?"

"Only if you're lucky," Cami shouted back.

She returned with two very full glasses of Pinot Grigio. "Drink up. The judgment fades after glass three."

"I'm on glass two."

"Then pace yourself. We still have theme night outfits to discuss."

Scarlet took a sip. "How many theme nights again?"

"Oh honey," Cami said, rolling onto her stomach. "There's an entire itinerary of flirtation-fueled pageantry. Neon night. All-white party. Tropical masquerade. Also, karaoke, which I already put your name down for."

Scarlet choked. "You what?"

"Don't worry. You're doing Norah Jones." Cami warbled an off-key "Come Away With Me" to a throw pillow.

"I will Norah your corpse."

"You're welcome."

They sipped in silence. Storm stretched, rolled onto his back, and let out a noise that sounded suspiciously like judgment.

Cami lifted her glass in his direction. "To Storm, our grumpy emotional support feline."

"To Storm," Scarlet echoed. "May he ruin only half my outfits."

Cami grew serious as her bouncing reduced to a gentle sway. "Look. I know you're not looking for some epic romance. I know you're still haunted by that human paper towel you dated for seven years."

"Eight," Scarlet corrected with a grimace, counting the years down with her fingers.

"Right. But this cruise isn't about falling in love."

"Then what is it about?"

Cami leaned in, voice soft but bright. "It's about remembering you're allowed to flirt. To feel beautiful. To say yes to things without knowing the return on investment. It's about choosing yourself."

Scarlet looked down, fingering the edge of a teal wrap dress in her suitcase. "What if I forgot how?"

"You didn't," Cami said. "You're just rusty. One hot tub, two cocktails, and a compliment from a man who can hold eye contact without checking your LinkedIn? You'll be right back in it."

Scarlet sat back on her heels, staring into the half-open drawer beside her bed. She hadn't reached for the red lace teddy in over a year, not since... well. Some things she'd boxed up so tightly, she barely remembered the shape of them anymore. Only the ache that flared when she reached for something soft, like wanting, like worthiness, and found nothing but hesitation.

It was still beautiful. Still bold. And something in her wanted to feel that way again.

Before she could second-guess herself, she slipped it into the suitcase.

Then—

"Bitch, what the fuck is that?" Cami's voice hit a decibel typically reserved for fire alarms.

Scarlet froze, hand still inside the suitcase. Her cheeks flushed with heat she hadn't felt in years.

Cami was watching her now, body utterly still like a predator sensing blood.

Scarlet sighed and held up the lingerie. "It's called preparedness, Cami."

Cami let out a cackle that rattled the walls. "Preparedness?! For what, Scarlet the Responsible? Did you suddenly decide casual sin is on your cruise itinerary?"

"It's just in case."

"Just in case what? You 'accidentally' fall onto a dick?" She mimed a pratfall so dramatic it sent chips flying.

Scarlet raised her wine glass like a shield. "I hate you."

"I love that you think you're being subtle."

Scarlet took a long sip as Cami announced, "Try it on."

"Absolutely not."

"Try. It. On." Cami bounced with each syllable.

"Are you going to keep screaming until I do?"

"I absolutely am."

"Jesus Christ." Scarlet grabbed the teddy and stormed into the bathroom.

She struggled into it, wondering why these things had so many straps, twisting her arms at impossible angles. One strap caught in her hair, another twisted around her waist.

"Are you having a medical emergency in there?" Cami called. "Because it sounds like you're wrestling an octopus."

"I'm fine," Scarlet hissed back.

After several minutes of fabric origami, she finally got everything in place. And had to admit ... it was a problem. A good problem.

She stepped out of the bathroom, arms crossed tightly over her chest. Her face flamed with heat. "Happy now?"

Cami's mouth dropped open. A chip fell forgotten from her fingers.

Scarlet felt self-consciousness wash over her. She started to back up. "Never mind, this is ridic—"

"Holy mother of—" Cami finally managed. "You look—" She made a chef's kiss gesture followed by an explosion motion.

Scarlet laughed despite herself, tugging at the teddy's hem. "You are deranged."

Cami whipped out her phone. "I'm taking a picture!"

Scarlet lunged across the room. "No you are not!"

They wrestled on the bed, Scarlet trying to snatch the phone while Cami held it aloft. As the teddy rode up alarmingly high, Scarlet yelped, "Delete those!"

"Never! These are going in a shrine to your rebirth as a sexual being!"

Storm fled the room in protest as Scarlet grabbed a pillow and whacked Cami across the face with it.

As the pillow fight escalated, the teddy shifted into increasingly awkward configurations. One strap slipped down Scarlet's shoulder, making her gasp and clutch at it.

"Victory!" Cami shouted, snapping three more photos.

"I hate everything," Scarlet groaned, grabbing another pillow to cover herself.

When she emerged from the bathroom in sweats again, Cami was calmly scrolling on her phone.

"You better have deleted those," Scarlet muttered, trying to flatten her disaster hair.

"Already made them my lockscreen," Cami replied, dodging a sock flung at her head.

"Okay, your turn," Scarlet huffed, plopping next to her.

"Oh, baby," Cami grinned. "Let me educate you."

She flipped through past Mingle at Sea photos: glamorous deck parties, extravagant drinks, a very flirty encounter with a French bartender.

Swipe. A photo of Cami and three women laughing in a hot tub.

Swipe. Cami dancing with a six-foot-four problem who looked like he knew what he was doing.

Swipe. A sunset shot over the infinity pool.

"You really lived your best life on these cruises."

"Oh honey, I majored in best life," Cami purred. "You? You're about to get your PhD."

Swipe. Cami, sucking face with a man whose hands were on her ass.

Swipe. And then ...

Oh. OH.

Scarlet's brain short-circuited.

There, full-screen, was a bald man mid-mission with his face buried between Cami's thighs, bikini bottoms yanked aside, his head haloed by deck lighting.

Scarlet dropped her wineglass. "What. The. Actual. Fuck."

Cami screamed, launching the phone across the room. "No! Why?! I forgot that was even in my camera roll!"

"Why would you take a picture of that?!"

"I didn't mean to!" Cami faceplanted into a pillow. "It was a horny night! The moon was glowing! I thought it looked artistic!"

"Artistic?! Girl, that was a crime scene."

"Please delete me from planet Earth."

Scarlet clutched her chest. "It was on the deck?!"

"It was late! I thought we were alone!"

"You need Jesus."

Cami groaned. "I hate everything."

"That photo's going in your wedding slideshow."

"I'm going to burn your soul."

They lost it all over again, occasionally making eye contact only to dissolve into fresh peals of laughter.

After a full minute of recovery, Cami fixed Scarlet with a devious grin. "So. Are you excited for the cruise now?"

Scarlet stared at her, wine-stained and breathless.

Then, without breaking eye contact, she grabbed the red lace teddy and shoved it deeper into the suitcase, pushing it down with both hands.

Cami shrieked, launching herself onto her knees. "That's right, bitch. We comin'."

Scarlet shook her head, laughing. "This is gonna be a disaster."

Cami smirked. "It's gonna be legendary."

# Five

The atrium doors glided open like a velvet curtain, revealing the ship's heart in full dramatic splendor. Light poured in from above, catching on polished surfaces and refracted crystal until the whole space shimmered like a mirage made real.

Scarlet paused at the threshold, the air conditioning brushing cool against her bare legs as her eyes scanned the room with the practiced detachment of someone professionally trained to find flaws in even the prettiest picture. She adjusted the strap of her crossbody bag and shifted her weight in a pair of sleek white sneakers. They were comfortably broken-in, chosen specifically to save her feet for later battles with heels and formalwear.

"Okay," she muttered under her breath, barely loud enough to rise above the ambient murmur of curated luxury. "This is ... excessive."

The Elysian Serenade's grand atrium stretched upward like an architectural love letter to decadence, featuring three soaring stories of creamy marble and cascading light. Multiple chandeliers, more than any reasonable space should need, dripped from the domed ceiling like frozen constellations, each one catching the light and throwing it back in delicate, shimmering shards. Giant palms stood at attention along the perimeter, casting graceful shadows that looked suspiciously intentional.

"Excessive?" Cami gasped, looping her arm through Scarlet's as she stepped forward, her sundress catching the filtered sunlight like she was auditioning for a commercial. "Babe, this is luxury reincarnated with a cocktail menu."

She spun slowly in place like a runway model and pointed skyward. "See that chandelier? New as of last season. The crystals shift color with the sun. Watch."

Scarlet tilted her head up, squinting against the filtered glow. Sure enough, the facets flickered from gold to rose to clear again, like they were catching and releasing sunset in real time.

Annoyingly stunning. Of course they were. Even the lighting had a flair for drama on this ship.

"And the marble," Cami continued, already a few paces ahead. "They softened the finish. Mixed in something to take the chill out. Like barefoot spa vibes meets billionaire foyer."

Scarlet stepped cautiously across the floor, feeling the unexpected warmth beneath her soles. It didn't have that sterile, over-waxed gleam she expected. She reached out and ran her fingers along the nearest brass railing. It was smooth, cool, and somehow still inviting. Not just expensive. Designed to feel like ease.

"They've kept the best parts," Cami said, planting one hand on her hip as she surveyed the space like it belonged to her. "But it feels different. Less 'Vegas casino,' more 'Mediterranean villa that comes with a masseuse and a private yacht.'"

Soft music floated down from an alcove above. Live strings, thoughtfully arranged, created a backdrop that was baroque but approachable, just enough edge to suggest class without becoming pretentious. Scarlet glanced up and spotted them perched on a mezzanine balcony, playing with elegant ease.

Of course there was live music. Of course it was perfectly tuned to hit the brain's luxury receptors. Scarlet could practically hear the focus group reports: *Guests respond 27% more favorably to live classical music when paired with floral notes and champagne signage.*

And then ..."Cami! Scarlet!"

Maude's voice carried across the space with the clarity of someone who knew exactly how to project in grand architectural settings. She stood at the far edge of the atrium, finishing what appeared to be a professional consultation with a tall man in a crisp security uniform. He nodded at something she said, his posture radiating the kind of steady authority that didn't need to prove itself.

As they approached, Scarlet studied the contrast. Maude moved like water through familiar channels, her linen wrap floating behind her in practiced elegance. The security officer remained still and observant. He wasn't scanning for threats so much as ensuring his domain ran smoothly.

"Graham," Maude said, turning to include them in the conversation with seamless social grace, "I believe you know Cami, but let me introduce you to our newest Mingle at Sea member, Scarlet."

The man turned to face them fully. His dark eyes took them in with professional assessment that somehow avoided feeling invasive. "Welcome aboard," he said, voice modulated to carry without demanding attention.

"This is Graham Everett," Maude explained. "He oversees ship security. Keeps us all safe while we're finding love."

"Or losing our minds," Cami added with her characteristic laugh.

The corner of Graham's mouth twitched. It was almost a smile, but contained, as if humor had to pass inspection before being released. "If you'll excuse me," he said, giving a small nod to each of them. "I should return to my rounds. Enjoy your voyage." To Maude, he added, "We'll touch base about the deck 5 situation later."

He departed with quiet efficiency, leaving Scarlet with the impression of someone who noticed everything but commented on little. The kind of person whose presence you'd feel more in his absence.

"Now then," Maude said, turning to them with the full warmth of her attention, "let me get a proper look at you both." Her smile carried the genuine pleasure of someone reuniting with cherished friends. "Scarlet, you look lovely. The sea air is going to agree with you, I can tell."

"Thank you," Scarlet replied, some of her usual guardedness softening under Maude's sincerity.

Maude's eyes twinkled as she turned to Cami. "And you, my dear, are practically glowing. That dress was made for this light."

Before Scarlet could respond, Cami was already scanning the atrium's population. "Okay, who else is here for Mingle? I'm seeing at least three definite candidates by the bar, and oh, is that Rebecca? From two cruises ago?"

Maude followed her gaze with practiced subtlety. "Indeed it is. On her fifth voyage with us, actually. You'll find she's mellowed considerably since you last met. Much less aggressive with the karaoke microphone."

"Thank God," Cami muttered. "Last time she tried to make 'My Heart Will Go On' happen at 3 a.m."

Scarlet let their voices drift around her, a soft cocoon of noise while she observed in silence. The Elysian Serenade felt engineered down to the air, with everything cool but never cold, sound-tracked to suggest luxury without intruding on it, dotted with seating designed to be just cozy enough to rest, not nest.

She was halfway through her internal audit when her eyes locked onto something that didn't match the algorithm.

He stood near the curve of the grand staircase, still and quiet while everyone else buzzed around him. As if the ship were a carousel and he'd opted out of the ride.

He was handsome, which Scarlet noticed first because it was obvious, but it was the way he held himself that kept her looking.

Like someone waiting for a different kind of cue.

His scan of the room was too efficient, too quiet. He wasn't browsing the architecture. He was reading the room for danger, the way muscle memory never really fades.

He didn't fidget. He didn't sigh. He just ... held.

Held tension. Held stillness. Held space in a way that said *don't test me.*

And when his eyes met hers, it was like striking glass.

Not flirtation. Not disinterest.

A flicker of recognition. Maybe even respect.

She stared back, her curiosity blooming into something weightier.

She couldn't say why, but her heart thudded like she'd just been seen for real.

"Scarlet?" Cami's voice pulled her back. "You zoning out already? We haven't even gotten to the good stuff yet."

The man's attention shifted slightly, breaking the connection. Not abruptly, not in retreat, but with the careful deliberation of someone putting down something fragile.

"Sorry," Scarlet said, shaking off the moment. "Just taking it all in."

"Well, take it all in while walking," Cami urged, tugging at her arm. "We should let Maude get back to her hosting duties. I want to show you the pool deck before check-in. They've added these cabanas that—"

"Of course, go explore," Maude interrupted with a knowing smile, her eyes scanning the entrance where more guests were beginning to arrive. "I have a few more single sailors to welcome into our fold." She squeezed Scarlet's hand briefly. "The welcome mixer is at seven in the Topaz Lounge. Don't be late."

"Wouldn't dream of it," Cami promised, already turning toward the elevators. "I'll make sure our girl is presentable and punctual."

Maude's laugh carried the warmth of private knowledge. "Just make sure she's present, dear. The rest will take care of itself."

As they walked toward the elevators, Scarlet caught herself glancing back. The man was gone, probably just another passenger blending into the blur.

Still, the moment stuck.

Not because of how he looked, but because of the tension he carried. Though his face would definitely end up in Cami's gossip log.

That flash of something wary. Unsettled.

She knew the feeling. Had known it for years. That was the problem.

And yet, it anchored her.

Like she wasn't the only one who hadn't shown up to this floating paradise in vacation mode.

The elevator arrived with a soft chime. Cami didn't miss a beat, already halfway through a monologue about themed nights and sunburnt regrets.

Scarlet followed her in, nodding, but her mind lingered on the man and the unspoken understanding they'd shared.

By the time the elevator doors opened on the pool deck, Cami was practically glowing. "Okay, we're officially on island time. But make it slutty."

Scarlet snorted. "You're one coconut drink away from coining a lifestyle brand."

"Don't tempt me. Cami Co. is absolutely something I'd trademark after two daiquiris."

They stepped onto the open-air pool deck, where the early boarding crowd had already started to claim loungers and flirt with the idea of day drinking. The sound of splashing mingled with a tropical house remix of something vaguely familiar. Palm trees in giant planters lined the perimeter, swaying just enough to sell the fantasy.

Cami zeroed in on the pool bar like it owed her money. "Come on, pre-unpacking cocktail. It's tradition."

They slipped onto a pair of high stools, the bar already manned by a mixologist in a linen vest and a pirate tattoo sleeve. Scarlet watched him finish torching a pineapple slice with a handheld flame before she even looked at the menu.

"Okay," Cami murmured, scanning the deck behind her sunglasses. "Shirtless with tribal tattoo: 7.5. Dad bod with confidence: solid 8.

That one?" She nodded discreetly toward a man in aviators sipping from a coconut. "I mean ... come on. That jawline's a vacation in itself."

Scarlet glanced over, unimpressed. "You do realize this group is, what, 150 people?"

"A curated 150," Cami corrected, giving a mock-snooty toss of her hair.

"Which probably breaks down to, maybe, fifty single men?" Scarlet continued. "Subtract the ones who think cargo shorts are a personality. Subtract the ones who already found their soulmate in the airport terminal. You're down to a dozen options, max."

"Scarlet," Cami said with mock patience, "You are underestimating two very important things: my charm, and my endurance."

Scarlet raised a brow. "You're also ogling guys who are almost certainly married. Or honeymooning. Or at the very least, traveling with someone who would object to your kind of flirtation."

"Not my fault they didn't spring for matching shirts." Cami nodded toward a man lifting his tank top to apply sunscreen. "Besides, I'm not looking for permanence. Just possibilities."

"That should be your epitaph."

Cami grinned. "If that's how I go, bury me in SPF 30 and pearls."

The bartender slid two drinks toward them. One was garnished with a flaming lime, the other served in a coconut with a straw shaped like a flamingo. Cami lit up like a child on Christmas morning. Scarlet looked mildly concerned.

"What is this?" Scarlet asked, picking up the coconut like it might detonate.

"That is happiness with a rum floater," the bartender said without missing a beat.

"Or a lawsuit waiting to happen," Scarlet muttered, taking a tentative sip. It was aggressively sweet, deceptively strong, and unfortunately delicious.

Cami clinked their drinks together. "To tropical regrets and strategic mingling."

Scarlet smirked. "And to not making eye contact with anyone wearing a gold chain and Crocs."

They drank, the sun warming their shoulders as the pool scene played on around them. And for the first time since stepping onboard, Scarlet didn't feel like she was bracing herself against something. Just ... taking it in.

Even if she'd never admit it to Cami, the view didn't suck.

# Six

Scarlet stood in front of the cabin mirror, running her fingertips over the drape of her green wrap dress. The fabric caught the light with each slight movement, a subtle shimmer against her skin. She rarely wore this shade, a deep emerald that made her hazel eyes flash gold. It wasn't practical for the office, too formal for casual outings, too subtle for parties. But tonight it felt right.

"So," she called over her shoulder to Cami, who was sprawled across one of the twin beds, scrolling through her phone. "Remind me again why we're rushing to this mixer when we could be enjoying room service and an ocean view?"

Cami snorted, not looking up. "Because you didn't book a cruise to hide in your cabin like some kind of aquatic hermit."

"Maybe I did. Maybe that's exactly what I need. A floating cave with turndown service."

"And maybe I'll join a convent." Cami finally glanced up, her eyes narrowing as she took in Scarlet's appearance. A slow, knowing grin spread across her face. "Oh, I see what's happening."

Scarlet turned, arching an eyebrow. "What?"

"You're *trying*." Cami sat up, delighted. "That's the good dress. The one you packed 'just in case,' which is Scarlet-speak for 'I might want to feel pretty but I'm not admitting it.'"

"I'm not—" Scarlet started, then caught herself. "Fine. I didn't want to look like I crawled out of a suitcase. Professional habit."

"Mmhmm." Cami stood, smoothing her own outfit. The cream-colored wide-leg trousers and cropped coral halter made her skin glow like she'd invented sunlight. "And it has nothing to do with making a good first impression on our fellow single sailors?"Scarlet busied herself with her minimal makeup, dabbing a touch of tinted gloss on her lips. "I just don't want to embarrass you in front of your cruise friends."

"As if you could." Cami checked her watch, a delicate gold time-piece that had been a gift from her grandmother. "I need to head down early. Maude probably wants help making sure everything's perfect."

"You're leaving me?" Scarlet tried to hide the hint of panic in her voice.

Cami's smile softened. "Just for a few minutes. You know the way to the Topaz Lounge. Deck 6, forward starboard. Follow the sound of awkward first-date energy and top-shelf liquor."

"Lovely."

"You'll be fine." Cami squeezed her shoulder as she passed. "Fash-ionably late is still late. Don't make me come find you."

The cabin door clicked shut, and Scarlet exhaled, finally alone with her thoughts. She turned back to the mirror, studying her reflection with the same critical eye she used on balance sheets. Hair: soft copper waves falling just past her shoulders, less rigid than her usual office style. Dress: elegant but not trying too hard. Expression ... well, that was still a work in progress.

That was the problem. Her face held a tautness she couldn't quite shake, a wariness that betrayed her.

*This isn't about meeting someone*, she reminded herself. *This is about not disappearing in your own life.*

The phrase had become a mantra since booking the cruise, not a desperate search for love, but a quiet refusal to keep shrinking herself into smaller and smaller spaces. Nine years with a man who barely saw her. A career that used her without promoting her. This trip wasn't about finding another half. It was about being whole on her own terms.

With one final glance in the mirror, she grabbed her small purse, slipped on a pair of low sandals with just enough heel to feel intentional, and left the cabin.

The corridor was quiet, most passengers already at dinner or the welcome events. Her footsteps seemed amplified against the tasteful carpeting, the soft hum of the ship's engines a gentle reminder that they were in motion as they headed somewhere new, even while standing still.

By the time she reached the Topaz Lounge, the knot in her stomach had begun to loosen. Instead of pounding club bass, jazzy and mellow music drifted through the closed doors, inviting without demanding. She paused outside, watching a young couple take a selfie by the ornate sign. They were dressed like they'd coordinated outfits, their matching white ensembles practically screaming "honeymoon."

It wasn't jealousy exactly ... more like a quiet awareness.

She used to picture herself in that role: coordinated clothes, staged smiles.

But that version of life never arrived, and now she wasn't sure she ever really wanted it.

Taking a breath, she pushed through the doors and approached the welcome table. Maude sat behind it, her silver-streaked chestnut hair tied back with a colorful scarf, radiating the same calm authority Scarlet had always admired.

"Scarlet!" Maude called out, her eyes lighting with genuine warmth. "Glad you made it. Here's your bracelet. Have fun tonight."

And that's when Scarlet saw him again. She recognized the man from the atrium immediately: tall, broad-shouldered, with short dark hair and that same steadiness that had caught her attention earlier. He stood beside a shorter, more animated man, examining a bracelet in his palm like it was some kind of coded message.

The recognition was instant, electric.

She accepted the bracelet with a quick "thanks," her focus already pulling in his direction. He turned at Maude's greeting, and their eyes locked immediately. A flicker of recognition passed over his face; he remembered her too.

Something flickered low and steady, but it wasn't desire, though he was undeniably easy to look at.

It was recognition. Like catching the hum of a familiar tune in a room filled with noise.

"You know," she said, unable to help the slight smile that curved her lips, "I thought I was being fashionably late. But I guess my timing's perfect."

The man's face shifted from recognition to something like short-circuit. His mouth opened, closed, then finally managed: "Oh. Uh, yeah. You did. That. I mean, you're ... just in time. Or early. Not early. Definitely not too late."

He blinked rapidly. "Perfect timing. Is what I meant. That's ... what I was going to say."

Scarlet felt her smile widen. There was something endearing in his fumble, not the awkward posturing she'd grown used to from men trying to impress her, but genuine, slightly flustered humanity. It disarmed her more effectively than any smooth line could have.

His friend stepped in smoothly. He was shorter and wiry, with an energy that probably never dimmed. "MacIntyre. Just Mac. And this smooth talker here is Jerry Duncan, who usually has a vocabulary."

*Jerry.* The name fit him ... solid, unpretentious.

She laughed, extending her hand. "Scarlet Bellari. But Scarlet's fine." She shook Mac's hand first, then turned back to Jerry, holding the contact a beat longer than necessary.

She watched him visibly recalibrate, exhaling before trying again.

"It's nice to meet you. Scarlet. You. I mean ... nice to meet you, Scarlet."

Something about his struggle to find equilibrium made her feel steadier than she had since boarding. His awkwardness wasn't calculated; it was refreshingly genuine.

"It's nice to meet you too, Jerry." She slipped the bracelet onto her wrist, the woven gold cord somehow both delicate and substantial against her skin. Glancing toward the lounge doors, she couldn't resist a gentle tease. "Shall we go in before you run out of sentence fragments?"

That earned her a real laugh from him, his smile warming his entire face. The tension in his shoulders eased slightly. "Lead the way."

As they moved toward the entrance, she caught a whispered exchange behind her.

"Admit it ... you're glad you wore the good shirt," Mac murmured.

"Please stop talking," Jerry groaned.

Scarlet glanced back over her shoulder, feeling a spark of playfulness she hadn't expected. "I think it's a great shirt, for the record."

And it was. Simple navy cotton that fit his broad shoulders like it had been tailored, with none of the flashy patterns or logos that seemed to dominate the cruise fashion landscape. It wasn't trying too hard, much like the man himself.

"Told you," Mac said smugly.

A faint blush touched his ears as he shrugged. Scarlet caught herself noticing something unexpected about the gesture, a subtle quality that proved surprisingly hard to ignore.

She turned and pushed open the doors to the Topaz Lounge.

The space enveloped them in warm, amber light. Deep navy walls with gold inlay caught the glow from crystal sconces and soft ceiling panels that mimicked twilight. The room smelled of citrus and polished wood, with a hint of vanilla from fresh orchids placed in strategic corners. From a stage across the room, piano jazz floated at the perfect volume, calibrated with the same precision as everything else on this ship.

Mac immediately set off toward a group across the room, drawn to the social gravity like a moth to flame. Scarlet watched him go, impressed by his natural ability to insert himself anywhere.

"Your friend's a bit of a social butterfly, huh?" she observed.

Jerry snorted beside her, his posture still a bit stiff but less awkward than before. "More like a party shark. Always moving. Always smiling. Usually circling the bar."

The analogy was so spot-on it made her laugh. "Shall we circle the bar then?"

His relief was palpable. "Lead the way."

They found two empty seats at the crescent-shaped bar, its polished surface glowing from subtle underlighting. A bartender approached, towel slung over his shoulder.

"I'll take a mojito, please," Scarlet said without hesitation. "Extra lime. Real mint, not the syrupy shortcut stuff." She had no trouble knowing what she wanted when it came to drinks, even if other decisions proved more complicated.

The bartender nodded appreciatively. "Fresh all the way. Coming right up."

Beside her, Jerry barely glanced at the menu. "Uh ... rum and Coke," he said, a touch sheepish. "Canned Coke's fine. Doesn't have to be fancy."

Scarlet felt her estimation of him tick upward. No craft cocktail posturing, no pretending to know more than he did. Just honest preference without apology.

Their drinks arrived quickly. Scarlet swirled hers, the fresh mint leaves catching in the straw. The gold bracelet caught the light as she moved, the little helm charm cool against her skin.

"Cami's probably going to find us in about ten seconds," she said, smiling knowingly. "Just warning you. She's my best friend and unofficial cruise fairy godmother. Also the person who signed me up for this."

Jerry's eyebrow arched in curiosity. "So you got recruited, too?"

The question made her relax further. Common ground. "Oh, full-on ambushed," she admitted. "Cami and one of our friends teamed up, insisted I needed a week of quote-unquote joyful debauchery." She took a long sip, the lime slice cool against her lips. "Still not sure what that means exactly."

Jerry laughed, the sound softer than she expected from someone his size. He took a sip of his own drink, something in his posture finally surrendering to the moment. "Mac had his own intervention plan. Told me if I didn't get out of town soon, he was going to fake a medical emergency just to get me a leave form."

She caught the phrase that made everything click. Leave form. Of course he was military. It explained the posture, the watchfulness, the economy of movement.

She tilted her glass toward his. "Sounds like our friends should never meet."

"Too late," Jerry said, gesturing out toward the crowd where Mac was already holding court. "They already have a ten-minute head start."

She raised her glass higher. "To pushy friends."

His smile deepened, the tension in his shoulders visibly easing. "And slightly less pushy strangers."

The gentle clink of their glasses created a moment of honest connection amid all the polished performance around them.

Scarlet took a sip, the mojito bright with lime and brisk with mint, slicing through the evening's heaviness like a cool wind.

And then, like a hurricane announcing itself, Cami appeared.

"There you are, Scarlet. Hiding at the bar, huh?"

Scarlet turned to find her best friend making a full dazzle entrance. Cami looked tall and radiant in her cream and coral ensemble, micro braids swinging with each confident step, oversized sun-shaped earrings catching the light. She moved like she owned the ship and everyone on it.

"Jerry, this is Cami Delgado, my co-conspirator." Scarlet said, gesturing between them, "Cami, meet Jerry Duncan."

Cami gave Jerry a slow, deliberate once-over, her lips curving into a smirk. "Well damn. Who let this finely sculpted excuse for a man onto a singles cruise without a warning label?"

Scarlet bit back a laugh at Jerry's deer-in-headlights expression.

"Uh ... hi?" he managed.

Cami laughed, the sound rich and unrestrained as she extended her hand. "Relax, soldier. Your friend Mac told me to come over here and make you uncomfortable."

Jerry glanced across the room, and Scarlet followed his gaze to where Mac was lounging against a wall, drink in hand and smug grin firmly in place.

"Yeah, that checks out," Jerry muttered.

Scarlet couldn't resist. "Told you this group was a full-contact sport."

"And here I thought I was easing into this cruise," Jerry said, raising his glass in mock surrender.

"Oh honey, there's no easing. Just cannonballs," Cami replied with feigned sympathy.

Before the banter could continue, the lights shifted across the lounge. A small platform near the center brightened, and conversations quieted as if by collective agreement.

Maude stepped onto the platform with effortless grace. Her sea-blue dress moved like water as she lifted her glass in subtle greeting.

"Good evening, sailors," she said, her voice carrying without strain. "Welcome aboard the Elysian Serenade."

Scarlet watched her with familiar affection. She'd known Maude for years through Cami, and the woman had an uncanny knack for saying exactly what people needed to hear before they knew they needed it.

"You're here for different reasons," Maude continued. "Some of you came for something new. Some of you are looking for something you lost. And some of you, well, don't even know why you're here yet. That's okay. This week isn't about having all the answers. It's about being open enough to ask the questions."

The room gave a few polite laughs before settling into stillness again.

Scarlet glanced at Jerry. He was watching Maude with the kind of focus that came from genuine interest.

A faint tension showed in his brow, but it wasn't defensive. Just present. Open.

"You don't have to be charming. You don't have to be brave. You just have to show up."

The words landed harder than they should have. *Just show up.*

Lately, Scarlet had been present in body alone, disengaged and paused mid-step, hiding in the lull of routine.

Maude raised her glass higher. "To new beginnings."

The room echoed her words. "To new beginnings."

As Maude stepped down from the platform, she glanced across the lounge and offered a small wave and knowing smile in their direction. Scarlet caught it, the warmth of recognition washing over her. Beside her, Jerry blinked in confusion, clearly unsure if the gesture was meant for him.

Cami downed the last of her drink and stood with theatrical flair. "Well, that's my cue."

"Your cue?" Jerry asked, still watching Maude.

"Captain Maude just called for her first mate." Cami hugged Scarlet quickly, then turned to Jerry with sparkling eyes. "Try not to fall in love while I'm gone. I'm still assessing your long-term viability."

With that parting shot, she sauntered away toward Maude, leaving Scarlet and Jerry in a momentary silence that wasn't entirely uncomfortable.

"Okay ... so she really knows the cruise director," Jerry said, a hint of bemusement in his voice.

Scarlet smiled into her glass. "Maude's kind of a legend on these sailings. Cami's sailed with her before. I've known her a while too. She's not just the hostess. She's like the emotional anchor of the whole thing."

Jerry's expression shifted to skeptical. "An emotional anchor?"

"She's got a knack for saying exactly what you need to hear, exactly when you need to hear it." Scarlet shrugged, but her voice carried genuine affection. "She's good people. A little ... nautical sage. But solid."

Scarlet watched Maude and Cami across the room, already deep in animated conversation that looked half-reunion, half conspiracy.

Jerry's gaze drifted further. "They're off to a strong start."

Following his line of sight, Scarlet spotted Mac charming a small circle of new acquaintances, his arm already draped casually around someone's shoulders. She grinned. "Fast-track to partner swaps by day three."

"Subtle foursome forming," Jerry replied, matching her tone.

The observation surprised a laugh out of her, less for its humor than for how unexpectedly perceptive it was. He'd quickly grasped the social dynamics at play, reading the room with the same quiet observation she'd noticed in the atrium.

She lifted her glass again. "To conspirators and coincidental chemistry."

As they clinked glasses and drank, Scarlet felt something shift in the air between them. Nothing dramatic or loud, just a subtle realignment that reminded her of planets adjusting their orbits to accommodate each other's gravity.

She studied him over the rim of her glass. Jerry Duncan with his steady presence and careful words. Not trying to impress her. Not performing or posturing. Just ... present. It was disconcerting how refreshing that felt.

Across the room, Mac caught their eye and raised his glass in a silent toast. Jerry gave a small headshake that Scarlet suspected contained volumes of brotherly communication.

"So," she said, setting her glass down. "What does Jerry Duncan do when he's not being ambushed onto singles cruises?"

He hesitated just a moment. "Army. Staff Sergeant. I'm stationed at Fort Cavazos. In Texas."

"Texas," she echoed. "That explains the accent. Slight, but it's there, especially on the vowels."

He looked surprised, then smiled. "Most people don't catch that."

"I notice details," she said simply. "It's sort of my job."

"And what job is that?"

"Senior accountant at Brickell & Shore. We're a boutique firm in Miami, specializing in tax strategy and consulting."

His eyebrows lifted. "Numbers person. I should've guessed."

"Oh? What gave it away?"

He gestured vaguely. "The way you scan the room. It's ... methodical. Like you're taking inventory."

Now it was her turn to be surprised. Most people didn't notice how she noticed. It was oddly validating.

"Fair enough," she conceded. "Though I'd argue your situational awareness isn't exactly casual tourist behavior either. You've checked every exit twice since we sat down."

Instead of denying it, he just nodded, a half-smile playing at his lips. "Occupational hazard."

"Same," she agreed, feeling an unexpected kinship. "So what's your actual job in the Army? Or is that classified?" The last bit was teasing, but genuinely curious.

"Nothing that exciting. Platoon leader. And photographer."

"Photographer?" That caught her off guard. "Like ... combat photography?"

He nodded. "Sometimes. Sometimes just documenting operations, training. Visual record-keeping, basically."

"That's ... not what I expected."

"No?"

"You seem more like the direct action type. Not that I'm an expert," she added quickly.

He shrugged, and something about the gesture suggested a story he wasn't sharing. "I like being behind the lens. Gives me a different perspective."

Before she could probe further, a commotion near the stage caught their attention. The jazz trio had taken a break, and someone had commandeered the microphone to make an announcement about tomorrow's first port excursion.

As the crowd's attention shifted, Scarlet caught sight of Mac and Cami again by one of the lounge's arched windows. They were deep in conversation, their body language radiating immediate chemistry. Cami's head was tilted back in laughter, and Mac's animated gestures punctuated whatever story he was telling.

"I think our friends have found their sea legs," she observed.

Jerry followed her gaze and chuckled. "Mac works fast. But he means well."

"Cami too. She's like a hurricane, but one that helps rebuild after it passes."

They shared a moment of comfortable silence that usually took much longer to achieve with someone new. Scarlet couldn't quite explain it, but something about Jerry's presence felt ... steadying. Like finding solid ground after too long at sea.

She still didn't particularly believe in the manufactured romance of cruises like this. But maybe real connections could emerge from all the pretense, like quiet, unexpected anchors in a sea of performance.

When Jerry asked if she'd like another drink, she said yes without hesitation. Not because she needed the alcohol, but because she wasn't ready to end the conversation.

# Seven

Sunlight spilled through the balcony curtains, drawing a warm path across the stateroom floor. For a moment, she simply lay there, savoring the unfamiliar luxury of waking without alarms, without emails demanding immediate attention, without looming deadlines. Just the gentle rocking of the ship and the distant hum of its engines.

She glanced at her watch. 6:47 a.m. Even on vacation, her body refused to sleep past dawn. Some habits were too deeply ingrained to break.

Sliding out of bed, she padded across the cool floor to the balcony door and slipped outside. The morning air carried the tang of salt and possibility. Below, the ocean stretched to the horizon, an endless mosaic of blues that shifted with each passing cloud.

"Not Miami," she whispered to herself, the corner of her mouth lifting.

Back home, it was rooftops and high-rises. This? Something else entirely. A blank canvas of water and sky.

Behind her, Cami was still buried under a mountain of pillows and blankets, the occasional soft snore confirming her deep sleep. After last night's cocktails, Scarlet wasn't surprised.

"Cami," she called softly, returning to the cabin. "Wake up. It's a new day."

Cami groaned and rolled over, peeking out from under her pillow with one bloodshot eye. "It's too early," she mumbled. "What time is it, anyway?"

"Almost seven," Scarlet replied, already pulling workout clothes from her suitcase. "The perfect time to start the day."

"On what planet?" Cami pulled the covers over her head. "This is vacation, not tax season."

Scarlet grabbed her running shoes, tying them with practiced efficiency. "I'm going for a run. Back in an hour, and then we're getting breakfast."

"Make it two hours," came the muffled reply. "And bring coffee when you return. A lot of coffee."

"Done." Scarlet tucked her key card into the small zippered pocket of her shorts, grabbed her earbuds, and slipped out the door.

The ship was quiet at this hour. A few early risers were heading to breakfast, crew members preparing for the day. Scarlet made her way up to the jogging track on the top deck, taking in the views as she climbed each flight of stairs.

At the track, she found a handful of dedicated runners already making their rounds. She plugged in her earbuds, queued up her running playlist, and began her stretching routine. The first notes of Taylor Swift kicked in as she leaned into her hamstring stretch, the familiar rhythm already quickening her pulse.

With a practiced exhale, she pushed off, finding her stride along the track that circled the ship's perimeter. The views stretched spectacularly in every direction, nothing but ocean beneath a sky painted in strokes of gold and coral by the rising sun.

Despite her determination to maintain her routines, Scarlet couldn't help but feel something loosen within her with each step. That ceaseless pressure between her shoulder blades, so familiar from her Miami life, seemed to dissolve into the sea air. By her third lap, she was smiling without realizing it.

On her fourth lap, as she rounded the stern, Scarlet spotted Mac in the middle of his warm-up stretches, completely focused on his routine. She slowed slightly, pulling out one earbud.

"Morning," she called. "Fancy meeting you here."

Mac looked up, grinning. "Hey, Red! Early bird, huh?"

"Always," she said. "Mind if I join you?"

"Be my guest," he said, straightening. "Fair warning, I'm training for a half marathon."

"I do five miles every morning. I'll manage."

They settled into an easy rhythm, adjusting their pace to match. The track wasn't crowded, giving them room to run side by side.

"So," Mac said after a few minutes, "how's Cami this morning?"

Scarlet laughed. "Still unconscious. Those cocktails hit hard."

"She seems like she can handle her liquor."

"She can. Doesn't make mornings easier."

Mac chuckled. "Jerry's probably out cold, too. Sleeping in for once."

"He's not a late sleeper?"

Mac snorted. "Guy doesn't even know how. Five a.m.'s a habit, even on weekends."

"Military life?"

"Partly. But he never really switches off, you know? Always on duty whether he's supposed to be or not. Runs himself ragged if no one stops him."

"Sounds like someone I know," Scarlet said with a half-smile.

"You the responsible type too?"

"My boss uses my vacation days to remind others they have them. Last time I took a long weekend, the admin thought I quit."

Mac laughed. "You and Jerry would get along. He runs on check-lists and caffeine."

"Definitely familiar. Drives Cami nuts."

"Same here. That's why I dragged him on this cruise. He hasn't had a real break in years."

The conversation flowed more easily than Scarlet expected. Mac's straightforward warmth made it easy to open up. By their fifth lap, she'd shared more than she usually did with new acquaintances.

"So, brunch?" Mac asked as they slowed to a walk. "Main dining room in ninety minutes? I'll drag Jerry out of hibernation."

"Perfect," Scarlet said. "I'll need that long to resurrect Cami."

"Deal." He grinned, wiping sweat from his brow. "See you then."

Back in the cabin, Scarlet found Cami still buried under the covers like a shapeless lump, now sprawled diagonally across the bed. With a smirk, Scarlet placed a large coffee on the nightstand, the rich aroma filling the small space.

"Rise and shine, sleeping beauty," she singsonged, nudging the bed. "I come bearing gifts."

One eye opened, narrowing in suspicion. "Is that ..."

"Triple shot Americano? Yes. Now up."

Cami groaned but shifted into a semi-upright position, reaching for the cup with the desperation of a drowning woman. "You're an angel. A loud, morning-person angel, but still."

Scarlet disappeared into the bathroom, stripping off her sweaty workout clothes. Under the hot spray of the shower, she let her mind drift back to the previous night's mixer. Jerry's awkward introduction. The easy flow of their conversation. The way his eyes crinkled when he smiled.

She caught herself and refocused on washing her hair. One pleasant interaction didn't mean anything. She'd had plenty of those over the years that led precisely nowhere.

When she emerged wrapped in a towel, Cami was scrolling through her phone, coffee cup already half-empty.

"I made brunch plans," Scarlet announced, rifling through her suitcase for something appropriate. She pulled out a casual sundress in a soft sage color.

"Let me guess ... that Army guy and his friend?" Cami's voice was knowing, a hint of amusement coloring her words.

Scarlet glanced up, arching an eyebrow. "I ran into Mac this morning. He suggested brunch."

"And his hot friend just happens to be coming too?" Cami pressed, her grin widening.

"His name is Jerry," Scarlet corrected, ignoring the flutter in her stomach. "And yes, apparently he'll be there."

"Good thing I packed my hangover concealer." Cami swung her legs over the side of the bed with exaggerated effort. "Can't have you being the only pretty one at the table."

Scarlet rolled her eyes but couldn't quite suppress her smile. "I saw something on the daily schedule about a 'Mingle Roundtable' this afternoon. Any idea what that is?"

"Oh, the famous Mingle at Sea roundtable!" Cami's eyes lit up mischievously. "Basically a chance to parade down the beefcake buffet line and scope out all the available merchandise without committing to a full-course meal."

Scarlet raised an eyebrow. "That sounds ... horrifying."

"Relax, accountant," Cami laughed. "It's actually more wholesome than my description. It's just a casual meet-and-greet where everyone rotates seats every few minutes. They don't even separate the men and women, so it's not that kind of speed dating. Just a chance to meet other people in the group without awkward bar approaches."

"So, no beefcake buffet line?" Scarlet asked dryly.

Cami shrugged. "Well, that part's still true if you want it to be. But technically, it's for making connections of all kinds. Friendships, activity partners, whatever."

"That actually doesn't sound terrible," Scarlet admitted, considering it. "Quick, efficient social interaction with a clear end time if someone's boring."

"Trust you to make human connection sound like a quarterly review," Cami snorted. "But yes, exactly. Very methodical, very organized. Actually, it's probably the most Scarlet-friendly social event on the entire ship."

Scarlet couldn't help but smile. "When you put it that way, it does sound right up my alley."

An hour later, they made their way to the main dining room, Cami now looking remarkably refreshed despite her earlier zombie state. The dining room was bathed in natural light from floor-to-ceiling windows, the space elegant without being stuffy. White linens and fresh flowers adorned each table, and the room hummed with the pleasant buzz of conversation.

Near the windows, Mac gestured animatedly while Jerry listened, his posture unguarded, a quiet ease in his frame.

With the sea shimmering behind him, he seemed almost otherworldly. Scarlet felt a quiet pull take root, something soft yet startling in its clarity. "There's our guys," Cami murmured. "Ready to make an entrance?"

Before Scarlet could answer, Mac looked up and waved them over. Her traitorous heart skipped as Jerry turned, his eyes meeting hers with a flicker of recognition that felt too much like genuine pleasure.

"Hey there," she called, approaching the table. "Mind if we join you?"

Mac jumped up, pulling out chairs with an exaggerated formality that made her smile. "Of course, wouldn't want to enjoy this feast without some beautiful company."

Jerry's smile was more reserved but no less genuine. When Scarlet settled into the seat beside him, his scent reached her, a blend of clean soap and something warmer, like coffee and sunshine.

"Sleep well?" he asked, his voice lower than she remembered.

"Like a rock," she replied honestly. "First vacation in ages. You?"

"Best sleep I've had in years," he admitted. "Weird what happens when no one wakes you up at 5 a.m. demanding emergency drills."

Mac busied himself pouring mimosas for everyone, making a show of filling Cami's glass extra full. The waiter appeared, and they all studied their menus in comfortable silence. Scarlet's eyes drifted over the offerings, her stomach growling in response.

"I think I'll go for the omelet with a side of pancakes," she announced, closing her menu. "Can't resist a bit of sweet and savory."

Jerry looked up, a hint of a smile tugging at his lips. "Solid choice. I think I'll do the same thing. Can't beat the classics."

Something impulsive fluttered through her. "How about you get the pancakes and I'll order the omelet, then we'll split them both to share?" she suggested. "I don't think I could eat all that food if I ordered it."

The words left her mouth before she had a chance to reel them in, and heat crept up her neck almost instantly.

Had she really just offered to share breakfast with someone she hardly knew?

It was such a minor gesture, yet as soon as it was out there, it seemed she'd nudged the moment into something more.

God, what was she thinking? This wasn't a date. This was brunch with cruise acquaintances. Sharing food belonged in boyfriend territory, the kind of thing you did after weeks of dating, not after one cocktail conversation. He was probably going to think she was being presumptuous or, worse, trying too hard. She could practically feel her cheeks warming as the seconds stretched between her suggestion and his response.

"I like that idea," Jerry agreed, his eyes warming.

The simple acceptance sent a wave of relief through her, followed by a ridiculous flutter of pleasure. She hadn't overstepped. He'd understood the gesture for what it was. Practical and friendly, nothing more. And yet ...

From across the table, Scarlet caught Cami and Mac exchanging a knowing look that she chose to ignore.

"What do you think, Mac?" Cami asked, leaning over with exaggerated formality and a playful smirk. "You get the steak and eggs while I get the French toast, and we too can split?"

Mac's eyes widened with mock horror, clutching his menu protectively to his chest. "And deny myself half my breakfast? Not a chance!" He grinned, patting his stomach. "I was already planning to order both of those for myself alone. I worked up quite an appetite with my morning workout today. But you can order whatever your heart desires, beautiful."

Cami rolled her eyes good-naturedly. "And they say chivalry is dead."

"Chivalry says nothing about sharing perfectly good steak," Mac countered with a wink.

Scarlet bit back a smile as the waiter took their orders. When their food arrived, the simple exchange of Jerry cutting his stack of pancakes in half and sliding them onto her plate while she did the same with her omelet felt oddly meaningful. There was something intimate about sharing food, about the basic trust of mutual provision.

The conversation flowed easily as they ate. Scarlet couldn't remember the last time she'd engaged in small talk that didn't feel like a burden, topics like favorite foods, worst travel disasters, the ridiculous names of the ship's signature cocktails. Nothing important, nothing stressful, just the gentle current of human connection washing over her.

"So, any plans for the rest of the day?" Mac asked, draining his mimosa.

Scarlet shrugged, feeling a small bubble of mischief rise within her. "Well, I heard there's a roundtable event happening this afternoon. Thought I might give it a try."

"Roundtable?" Jerry asked, his tone casual though something flickered in his eyes.

"It's not exactly speed dating," Cami explained, reaching for the carafe to refill her glass. "More like a casual way to meet people on the ship. You rotate every few minutes and chat with different folks."

Without overthinking it, Scarlet met Jerry's eyes. "You should come too ... both of you. Could be fun."

Jerry hesitated, the internal debate playing across his features. He wasn't one for small talk, that much was clear. But curiosity seemed to win out over his reservations.

"Sure," he said finally. "Why not?"

Mac's smug expression wasn't lost on Scarlet, but she chose to focus on her pancakes instead, savoring the fluffy texture against the tang of maple syrup. The brunch stretched longer than she'd expected, each of them reluctant to break the easy flow of conversation.

It was past noon when they finally left the dining room, agreeing to meet at the roundtable event just a short while later. As Scarlet and Cami made their way back to their cabin to freshen up, Cami nudged her with a knowing grin.

"So," she drawled, "Jerry seems nice."

"He does," Scarlet agreed, keeping her tone neutral.

"And you're not interested at all?"

Scarlet rolled her eyes. "I just met him."

"That's not an answer, counselor."

"There's nothing to answer," Scarlet replied, even as a pleasant spark lingered at the memory of Jerry's smile. "It's just cruise culture. Everyone's nice."

"Mmhmm," Cami hummed, clearly unconvinced. "And you suggested sharing food because … ?"

"Because I didn't want a full stack of pancakes," Scarlet replied, ignoring the heat creeping up her neck.

Cami just smirked. "Whatever you say, Scarlet."

The speed meeting was held in the Topaz Lounge, the elegant space now transformed into organized circles of chairs. Scarlet and Cami arrived just as the event coordinator, a cheerful woman named Mary, was explaining the format.

"Welcome, sailors!" Mary announced with infectious enthusiasm. "Today's speed meeting is all about connections. Not just romantic ones, but friendships too. You'll have five minutes with each person before rotating."

Scarlet and Cami drew spots in the outer ring, while Mac and Jerry ended up scattered across the inner circle. As everyone settled into their assigned seats, Scarlet took a place beside Cami, facing an elderly man named Harold for the first rotation.

The conversations passed in a blur. Harold, a retired professor, shared vivid stories from his travels. Next came Eliza, a pediatric nurse with a passion for photography. Then Ryan, a software developer from Seattle, who spent most of their five minutes explaining cryptocurrency.

But Scarlet's attention kept drifting. Her eyes sought out Jerry across the circle, watching as he engaged with each new partner. He maintained polite but guarded body language that softened only in brief flashes when something genuinely caught his interest.

Four rotations in, she spotted him seated across from a brunette who leaned in with animated laughter, her hand brushing his arm more than once. Something cold twisted low in Scarlet's stomach.

"You okay?" the man across from her asked, noticing her distraction.

Fine," she said quickly, forcing a smile. "You were saying about your dental practice?"

But her focus slipped again, drawn back to Jerry and the woman sitting across from him. Stacy, her name tag read even from this distance, laughed often, touched his arm more than once, and leaned in with the kind of interest that felt just a little too practiced.

*She's too loud,* Scarlet thought, surprised by the pettiness. *That laugh? Definitely forced.*

The judgment startled her. Since when did she care how another woman laughed?

"Time to rotate!" Mary called, and Scarlet stood with quiet relief.

The pattern continued. She smiled, nodded, made polite conversation with each new partner, but her attention kept flicking toward Jerry. Her eyes tracked his rotations with unconscious precision, her frustration mounting as each new match brought him everywhere but to her.

By the final rotation, she'd stopped pretending to care.

With the room emptying, Scarlet caught Stacy drifting back to Jerry.

They stood close, her fingers grazing his arm like it was second nature.

The feeling hit Scarlet suddenly. Tight, intrusive, immediate. She didn't know what it was, only that it wasn't neutral.

"That was fun," Cami remarked, appearing at her side. "Meet anyone interesting?"

"A few," Scarlet replied absently, still watching as Stacy said something that made Jerry smile.

Mary's voice cut through the chatter, bright and confident. "Don't forget about this afternoon's Battle of the Sexes event! It's a fun, fast-paced showdown of wits, skills, and maybe a little bit of sabotage. Ladies, you're riding a hot streak with thirty-nine straight sailings. The men are desperate to stop you from making it an even forty. No sign-ups needed, just show up and bring your A-game!"

As they made their way toward the exit, Scarlet couldn't help herself. "Who was that woman talking to Jerry?" she asked, aiming for casual and missing by a mile.

Cami followed her gaze, then broke into a grin. "Why, Scarlet Bellari, are you jealous?"

"No," she said too quickly. "Just curious."

"Uh-huh." Cami's expression was pure skepticism. "You're not ... twitterpated, are you? Has it really been that long that you're ready to throw yourself at the first guy you have breakfast with?"

"No, no," Scarlet protested, stumbling over her words. "It's not that, I promise. I don't know what it is."

"Besides," she added with more conviction, "I've been on numerous dates that you've set me up on, and I never threw myself at any of them. Did I?"

"No, you're right," Cami acknowledged with a laugh. "You successfully crushed anyone that I tried to set you up with." She draped an arm around Scarlet's shoulders as they left the lounge. "Come on, let's go get a frozen drink."

# Eight

Scarlet swirled the last of her mojito, the soft clink of melting ice marking the rhythm of Cami's beach-body commentary. The piano bar buzzed with arrivals for the Battle of the Sexes, and though she rarely went in for anything labeled "fun," she had to admit: she was actually looking forward to this.

"And you're not even listening," Cami said, bumping Scarlet's shoulder.

"Sorry. Just strategizing."

"It's a silly cruise game, not the Olympics." Cami's eyes narrowed. "Though you've got that same look you had before you destroyed everyone at the holiday party charades."

"I have no idea what you're talking about," Scarlet replied primly, but couldn't stop the small smile tugging at her lips. She had indeed practiced charades for two weeks before that party.

Cami's attention suddenly shifted over Scarlet's shoulder, her lips curving into a knowing smile. "Don't look now, but your military man just arrived with his friend. And three, two, one … yep, Stacy's already on the attack."

Scarlet turned, hoping to look unfazed. She wasn't.

Jerry and Mac stepped into the room, and Jerry's eyes swept across it with intent: no wasted motion, no idle glances. He was tracking.

The sharpness of it sent a thrum of energy through her.

They found a spot near the back wall, Jerry instinctively angling himself to face the door.

And then Stacy was there. Again. Her hand landed on his arm and slid beneath his sleeve like she was picking up where they'd left off.

A bolt of heat shot through Scarlet. Not quite jealousy, not quite nothing.

Cami gave a knowing look. "That glass isn't going to refill itself."

"Definitely," Scarlet agreed, suddenly feeling the need for liquid courage. "One more before the competition starts sounds perfect."

They made their way to the bar, but Scarlet's eyes kept drifting back to where Stacy leaned in close to Jerry, laughing at something he said. The bartender handed them fresh mojitos just as Maude swept into the center of the room, her flowing caftan glittering in the stage lights.

"Welcome aboard our nautical battle of wits, sailors! Tonight we'll see if the men can finally get their sea legs or if they'll continue to flounder in our wake!"

The women around Scarlet erupted in cheers, and she joined in, her usual reserve slipping.

Whether it was the buzz in the room or the lingering image of Stacy's hand on Jerry's arm, suddenly Scarlet didn't just want to play.

She wanted to win.

"It's time to dive into the most wave-making competition on the seven seas … Battle of the Sexes!" Maude continued, explaining the four-round format.

Scarlet mentally assessed the setup. It was structured like those corporate team-building exercises Simon arranged every quarter, the kind of competitive challenges designed to foster camaraderie while revealing who had the strongest skills. She'd always excelled at those, approaching each task with the same methodical precision she applied to financial audits.

As the women gathered on their side of the room, Scarlet positioned herself with a clear view of both Maude and, incidentally, Jerry. Strategic positioning, she told herself. Know your competition. But she couldn't deny the small thrill when their eyes briefly met across the divide.

Round One began with Opposite Knowledge Trivia. The men fumbled through questions about fashion designers and romantic comedies while the women tackled sports statistics with varying degrees of success. Scarlet answered her questions with the same concise clarity she used in client presentations, earning approving nods from her teammates.

When Maude asked the men about menstrual cycles, Scarlet expected the usual awkward shuffling and incorrect guesses. Instead, Jerry raised his hand and answered correctly: "Twenty-eight days, on average."

His male teammates turned to stare at him in surprise.

"My money's on sisters," Cami whispered. "Or ex-girlfriends with educational tendencies."

Scarlet felt her cheeks warm slightly at the implication. "Or basic biology," she countered.

"Mmm, that blush suggests you're imagining the practical application," Cami teased.

"I am not—"

"Scarlet!" Maude's voice cut through her denial. "Which team won the Super Bowl in 2022? Patriots, Chiefs, Rams, or Buccaneers?"

"Rams," Scarlet answered automatically, grateful for the distraction. From across the room, she caught Jerry watching her with what looked like mild surprise. She lifted her chin slightly, irrationally pleased to have impressed him.

Her satisfaction was short-lived.

"Bet he's good with his hands," Stacy whispered to someone just behind her, the words light but unmistakable.

The other woman gave a quiet chuckle, and Scarlet felt her pulse tick up.

She kept her gaze fixed forward. She could pretend not to hear, pretend it hadn't landed squarely between her ribs.

By the end of Round One, the scores were close, with the women slightly ahead. As Maude announced the Role Reversal challenge, Scarlet's competitive instinct fully engaged. Each contestant would need to demonstrate or explain a task typically associated with the opposite gender.

One of the men went first, stammering through a painfully incorrect explanation of makeup application that had the room cringing and laughing in equal measure.

When Maude asked for a volunteer from the women's team, Scarlet stepped forward before she could overthink it.

"Excellent! Our corporate warrior steps into the fray," Maude declared. "Scarlet, please explain how to change a tire."

Scarlet nodded, slipping into the composed rhythm she knew best. "First, make sure the car's on level ground with the emergency brake engaged."

Her hands moved with practiced ease as her fingers mimed the turn of a wrench, the placement of a jack, the steady lift.

"Tighten the lug nuts in a star pattern," she said, tracing the motion with quiet certainty.

When she glanced up, she found Jerry watching her. His expression was focused and unreadable at first, but then something shifted.

No polite smile. No feigned interest. Just recognition, clear and direct.

Scarlet felt her shoulders settle.

Across the room, Stacy had gone quiet.

Cami didn't say a word, but when she pressed a second drink into Scarlet's hand, her grin said everything.

The moment broke when Maude asked for the next male volunteer and Stacy called out, "Jerry should go next!" Her voice carried a suggestive lilt that made Scarlet's jaw tighten.

Jerry stepped forward, and Maude handed him a mascara wand. "Demonstrate proper mascara application," she instructed with a mischievous smile.

To Scarlet's surprise, Jerry didn't falter. He explained the technique with unexpected accuracy, demonstrating the gentle zigzag motion and warning about clumping. "You always do the bottom lashes more lightly," he added, "otherwise it gets messy."

"I had a friend in high school who needed help before prom," he explained, noticing the surprised looks. "Her arm was in a cast. You learn to be useful."

Something about his matter-of-fact kindness caught Scarlet off guard. The finance bros she usually dated treated feminine topics with either awkward discomfort or exaggerated tolerance. Jerry's simple competence, devoid of either, was unexpectedly attractive.

"I'd let you do my makeup any day!" Stacy called out, her friends dissolving into giggles.

The Lightning Round approached, and Scarlet's determination intensified. Each team needed to select representatives, and Maude called for volunteers.

"I'll go first for the ladies!" Stacy's hand shot up immediately, her smile wide and confident as she stepped forward. Her eyes found Jerry in the crowd, making sure he was watching her.

Without hesitation, Scarlet raised her hand. "I'd like to try too." She moved to stand right beside Stacy, aware of the hint of surprise that crossed the other woman's face.

"Wonderful! We have Stacy and Scarlet," Maude said. "And we need one more brave sailor."

Stacy handled her questions with enthusiastic confidence, making a show of each correct answer. Her eyes repeatedly found Jerry in the crowd, clearly performing for his benefit. When her twenty seconds ended, she caught Jerry's eye and mouthed, "Beat that," though he didn't seem to notice.

When it was Scarlet's turn, she approached the podium with the same mindset as a client meeting, focused and prepared and precise. The rapid-fire questions came, and she answered each with cool efficiency, no wasted words or movements. She was vaguely aware of her teammates cheering, but her focus remained absolute. This wasn't just about the game anymore. She wanted to win, and more specifically, she wanted Jerry to see her win.

As the final scores were tallied, Maude's eyebrows shot up in surprise. "Well, shiver me timbers! For the first time in thirty-nine cruises, we have a tie going into the final challenge! This calls for our ultimate tiebreaker. The Diaper Disaster Relay!"

Maude explained the final challenge: one representative from each team would race to change a teddy bear's diaper and dispose of it properly.

"The women's team will need to select their champion," Maude declared. "Choose wisely, ladies!"

From the corner of her eye, Scarlet saw Stacy beginning to raise her hand, lips parting to volunteer. Without hesitation, Scarlet stepped forward. "I'll do it."

"Scarlet!" The women's team cheered in unison.

"Our precision specialist," someone called out. "You've got this!"

Stacy's obvious disappointment gave Scarlet a petty moment of satisfaction that she immediately tried to dismiss. She wasn't competing for Jerry's attention. She was competing because ... well, because she always competed to win. That was all.

"And for the gentlemen?" Maude asked.

"Jerry," the entire men's team responded without hesitation.

Scarlet took her mark. Across from her, Jerry stood with arms loose and eyes full of mischief, and she couldn't stop the grin that tugged at her lips.

Each of them had a teddy bear in place, but this wasn't about plush toys.

This was about pride.

And maybe flirting while absolutely destroying him.

"Alright pretty boy, you're going down," she said, the playful challenge surprising even herself.

His response was immediate and unthinking: "Maybe down on you later."

The words hung between them, and she watched color flood his face as he realized what he'd said. His mortified expression was almost endearing. Here was the confident soldier, suddenly flustered by his own accidental innuendo.

Feeling suddenly bold, Scarlet leaned closer, pulse quickening. "Buy me a drink first, then we'll talk," she whispered, just loudly enough for him to hear.

The surprise in his eyes gave way to something warmer, a flash of humor and interest that made her stomach flip.

Maude returned with the teddy bears, each wearing innocent-looking diapers. "Meet Ted and Beary Manilow," she announced. "Your task is simple. Change their diapers and dispose of them in the bins at the far side of the room!"

The whistle blew, and Scarlet lunged forward, determined to win. She grabbed her bear and ripped open the diaper with efficient haste. What she got was an explosion of chocolate pudding that sprayed across her shirt and splattered spectators three rows deep.

A unified shriek erupted from the victims of the pudding blast, followed immediately by horrified laughter.

"What the ..." Scarlet gasped, staring down at the mess in shock.

The mess was real, but so was her response. She contained the pudding, sanitized the bear, wrapped an expert diaper, and then she was moving. Jerry was already ahead, the smug bastard, making it look easy. She didn't know what his secret was, but she was determined to close the gap.

They were neck and neck when Jerry gave her a playful bump with his hip. Not enough to knock her over, just enough to throw her slightly off balance. That split second was all he needed to hit the buzzer first.

The men's team erupted in cheers, rushing forward to celebrate their victory.

"Man overboard! The streak is broken!" Maude announced dramatically. "After thirty-nine consecutive victories, the women's ship has finally sunk!"

Pudding splattered across her front, Scarlet aimed a mock glare squarely at Jerry and stood tall. Sticky, but tall.

The laugh came easily, unexpected and real.

She couldn't recall the last time defeat had tasted this ridiculous … or this sweet.

Their eyes met across the room, and Jerry gave her an unapologetic shrug.

"Dirty tricks, Sergeant!" she called out, shaking her head.

"Nothing dirtier than a diaper cleanup," he replied with a grin that made her stomach do another unexpected flip.

Stacy pushed through the crowd, catching Jerry by the arm. "That was impressive," she said, pressing closer than necessary. "We're having drinks in the Topaz Lounge to commiserate our loss. You should join us." Her hand trailed possessively down his arm.

Jerry's expression shifted, revealing a subtle withdrawal that Scarlet might have missed if she hadn't been watching so closely. Mac appeared beside him, positioning himself between Jerry and the crowd in what seemed like a practiced move.

"You okay?" Cami asked, appearing at Scarlet's side with a handful of napkins.

"Besides being covered in chocolate pudding? I'm great," Scarlet replied, dabbing ineffectually at her shirt.

Cami studied her face. "You like him," she stated simply.

Heat rushed to Scarlet's cheeks. "I need a drink and a shower," she deflected quickly. "I have chocolate pudding in places I didn't know existed."

"Mmmhmm," Cami hummed knowingly, but didn't press further. "I'm heading to the casino with that guy from Montreal. You interested in joining later?"

"I think I'm done for the night," Scarlet said, still watching as Mac helped Jerry extract himself from Stacy's attention. "I'll see you back at the cabin."

Fresh from a shower and dressed in something dry, Scarlet still couldn't shake the restless buzz.

None of the usual options tempted her. Not bars, not shows, not noise.

On a whim, she grabbed her swimsuit and a towel, making her way to the upper deck.

If luck was on her side, she'd have a hot tub all to herself.

The night air was cool against her skin as she stepped onto the deck. Stars glittered overhead, unobscured by Miami's usual light pollution, creating a canopy of silver against the black velvet sky. The only sounds were the gentle hum of the ship's engines and the splash of waves far below.

As she approached the hot tub, she discovered she wasn't the only one seeking solitude. Jerry sat alone, eyes closed, head tilted back as if absorbing the peace. For a moment, she considered turning back, but something held her in place.

"Mind if I join you?" she asked, instantly regretting the slight wobble in her voice.

Jerry's eyes snapped open, and he straightened suddenly, sending water sloshing over the edge of the tub. "I, uh," he stammered, then seemed to collect himself. "Yes. I mean, no. I don't mind."

She raised an eyebrow, enjoying his momentary fluster. There was something endearing about his occasional awkwardness, so different from the calculated smoothness she'd grown accustomed to in men.

"There's room," he clarified, gesturing at the empty space beside him. "Plenty of it. Room, I mean."

Scarlet stepped in carefully, settling into the bubbling water with a contented sigh. The warmth immediately began working at her shoulder tension. Not the kind from chocolate pudding disasters, but the deeper strain that came from emails like Eric's.

"This feels amazing after all that chaos," she said.

Jerry nodded, seeming to regain his composure. "Nothing like pudding warfare to make you appreciate hot water."

Scarlet laughed, the sound blending with the gentle splash of water. "I can't believe the mess I made. I'm usually more ... coordinated."

"The element of surprise will do that," he replied. "I've seen tougher people than you taken down by unexpected substances."

"Speaking from experience?" she asked, curious.

He nodded without elaborating, a shadow crossing his expression that made her wonder what memories she'd unintentionally stirred.

Sensing his hesitation, she smoothly changed the subject. "So about that bump during the race," she said, trying to recapture the earlier playfulness. "Was that a tactical move, Sergeant?"

The shadow lifted as Jerry's eyes warmed with humor. "Would you believe me if I said it was an accident?"

"Not a chance," she replied with a grin.

"Worth a shot." He smiled back. "Consider it payback for that comeback that nearly made me lose focus completely."

Heat crept up Scarlet's neck at the reminder of her boldness. "Fair enough."

She leaned her head back against the edge of the tub, letting the tension of the day dissolve in the warm water as she gazed up at the stars. "God, you can actually see them out here. In Miami, there's too much light pollution."

"That's one of the things I miss most during deployment," Jerry said quietly. "The night sky in the desert is incredible, but you never get to just ... enjoy it."

Scarlet turned to look at him, surprised by the personal admission. "How long have you been in the military?"

"Twelve years," he replied. "Joined right out of high school."

"And you've been deployed?"

"Three times. Iraq, mostly." He shifted slightly, the water rippling around his movements. "Not my favorite topic."

Scarlet nodded, respecting the boundary. "So what is your favorite topic?" she asked instead.

Jerry considered this. "Honestly? Other people," he said after a moment. "Their stories, what makes them tick. Used to play a lot of poker in the barracks, got pretty good at reading tells, the little things people do when they're bluffing or excited."

"That sounds dangerous," Scarlet said, both intrigued and slightly unnerved by the idea of being read so easily. She prided herself on her professional poker face.

"It can be," he admitted with a half-smile. "You learn things people don't always mean to share. But everyone's got a story worth hearing if you pay attention."

"So you're studying me right now?" She raised an eyebrow, half joking.

"Hard not to notice things," Jerry said, his voice softening. "Like how you tap your thumb against your fingers when you're thinking about what to say next. Or how your eyes get sharper when someone challenges you, like during the competition."

Scarlet's eyes widened slightly, her hand stilling in the water where she'd been unconsciously doing exactly what he described. "I didn't realize I was so transparent."

"You're not," Jerry assured her. "Most people wouldn't catch it. I just ... notice."

Being truly seen for who she was rather than her professional achievements or carefully cultivated image left Scarlet feeling both exposed and oddly comforted. She couldn't remember the last time someone had paid such careful attention to her unconscious habits.

"Sounds like a useful skill," she managed.

"Sometimes," he said. "Makes it easier to understand people, harder to misread situations. Comes in handy with …" He caught himself, pausing before continuing more carefully. "In a lot of contexts.

"What about you?" Jerry asked, shifting the focus. "What do you do when you're not crushing diaper-changing competitions?"

"I'm an accountant," she said, falling back on her standard answer. "Senior accounts specialist at a boutique firm in Miami."

"That's right, you told me that already," Jerry reached up to massage the back of his neck as if he had just recalled their conversation from the night prior. "You enjoy it?"

The simple question caught her off guard. People usually asked about her clients or her income or made jokes about number-crunching. They rarely asked if she actually liked her work.

"It's challenging," she said finally. "Keeps me busy."

She could tell by his expression that he'd noted the deflection, but he didn't press. Their conversation flowed easily after that, covering everything from favorite movies to the best meals they'd had on the ship.

"We dock at Grand Turk tomorrow, right?" Scarlet asked eventually. "Any plans?"

"Actually, yeah," Jerry replied, a hint of enthusiasm entering his voice. "I'm going paddleboarding. The water there is supposed to be incredible, crystal clear and calm, perfect conditions."

"Paddleboarding?" She looked intrigued. "I've never tried that."

"It's easier than it looks," Jerry said. "You just stand on a board and use a paddle to move around. Great way to see the coastline, maybe spot some fish."

"Sounds fun," she said, feeling a wistful pull toward the simple pleasure he described.

Jerry hesitated, rubbing the back of his neck. "You could, uh …" he started, then stopped. "I mean, if you wanted to … you know …" He cleared his throat. "What I'm trying to say is, you should, uhm, you could join me. If you want."

The words hung suspended, like a ripple on still water.

She couldn't recall the last time company alone had felt like an unfolding promise. "Really?" she asked, unable to keep the pleasure from her voice. "I'd like that."

"You would?" Jerry looked genuinely surprised, then quickly composed himself. "I mean, great. That's … great."

"Fair warning though, I'm pretty good at it," he added with mock seriousness. "So don't expect to win this competition."

"Oh, it's a competition now?" She raised an eyebrow, enjoying the easy banter. "You're on, Sergeant. But I expect proper instruction before you start keeping score."

"Deal," Jerry said, something in his expression making her heart beat a little faster. "We can rent boards at the beach. I'll show you the basics."

"It's a date," she replied, then quickly added, "I mean, not a date-date, just a …"

"Yeah, no … I mean, yeah, I get what you meant," Jerry assured her, though something in his eyes made her wonder if maybe it was a date after all. The thought sent another thrill through her that she wasn't quite ready to examine.

They fell silent for a moment, the only sounds the bubbling of the hot tub and the distant hum of music from somewhere below deck. The silence felt comfortable in a way Scarlet rarely experienced.

"I should probably head back," she said eventually, though she felt oddly reluctant to leave. "Early day tomorrow."

Jerry nodded. "Meet at the gangway around nine? The ship docks at eight."

"Perfect." She stood up, water cascading off her shoulders. "Thanks for the invite. And for not gloating too much."

Jerry replied with a smile that reached his eyes. "I might still work it into conversation tomorrow."

Scarlet laughed as she stepped out of the hot tub, wrapping her towel around her waist. "Goodnight, Jerry."

"Goodnight, Scarlet."

As she walked away, Scarlet caught herself smiling. Really smiling, not wearing the polished professional expression she used like armor. For the first time in longer than she could remember, she wasn't analyzing an interaction or calculating its implications for future goals.

She was just ... happy. Simple as that.

# Nine

Scarlet woke before her alarm, the room still dark around her. Five years of 5:30 a.m. alarms had permanently rewired her brain, and the cruise had done nothing to change her internal clock.

She slipped from bed quietly, careful not to wake Cami, who was sprawled across her mattress in blissful oblivion. The cabin door clicked softly behind her as she stepped onto their private balcony, coffee in hand.

The horizon was just beginning to glow, a thin line of gold separating sea from sky. Grand Turk was a dark silhouette in the distance, growing more distinct with each passing minute. The rising sun gradually revealed the island's details: sandy beaches, low vegetation, small buildings clustered near the port.

She sipped her coffee, letting the warm liquid combat the morning chill. Her thoughts drifted to Jerry and their plans for the day. Was this a date? The question had plagued her since their conversation in the hot tub. She'd said it wasn't a "date-date," but the distinction felt increasingly meaningless.

Back in the cabin, she opened her suitcase with unusual indecision. Her usual ruthless efficiency with clothing choices had abandoned her. No pre-planned outfits, no quick decisions. Today felt different.

After sorting through several options, she settled on her rust-red halter swimsuit with its semi-sheer tropical print overlay. The soft, molded cups with their subtle knotted tie detail offered just the right balance of support and femininity, while the asymmetrical handkerchief skirt gave it an elegant, flowing quality that set it apart from standard one-pieces.

"Oh my God, the mom-suit makes an appearance," Cami mumbled from her nest of blankets, one eye cracked open. "Already trying to be a mom before you even are one."

"It's not a mom-suit," Scarlet protested, adjusting the tie detail at the bust. "It's practical for water activities."

"You have a black bikini that would make Army Guy's eyes pop out of his head," Cami retorted with a sleepy grin. "But sure, go with the one that screams 'I'm responsible and make good decisions.'"

Scarlet paused, her fingers still toying with the swimsuit tie. "Maybe I want to be a mom someday," she said quietly. Both the admission and the ache it stirred caught her off guard. A flicker of something old and fragile rose up, uninvited. She pushed it back down before it could take shape. "Not anytime soon, but ... eventually."

Cami's teasing expression softened. "You'd be an amazing mom. Terrifying, but amazing. Your kids would have color-coded schedules and perfect attendance records."

"You say that like it's a bad thing," Scarlet replied, but she was smiling.

"So where are you meeting the hot soldier?" Cami asked, bundling the covers around her. "I'm planning to lie by the pool all day and work on evening out these ridiculous tan lines."

"Jerry," Scarlet corrected automatically, "is meeting me at the beach. We're going paddleboarding."

"Jerry, right." Cami's voice took on a sing-song quality. "The guy you were flirting with during the competition? The one you disappeared with after I went to the casino?"

Scarlet felt heat rise to her cheeks. "We just talked."

"In the hot tub. At midnight. Alone."

"It wasn't—"

"Save it for someone who hasn't known you since freshman accounting," Cami said, flopping back onto her pillow. "Go have fun with your not-date in your mom-suit. I'll be here, doing absolutely nothing productive, as God intended for vacation."

At the vanity, Scarlet went for simplicity with her makeup, choosing only waterproof mascara and tinted sunscreen. She twisted her hair into a messy bun, secured with the elastic from around her wrist. The woman in the mirror looked back at her, flushed and somehow younger than the polished professional who'd boarded this ship days ago.

*This is silly*, she thought. *It's just paddleboarding with someone I barely know.*

Yet the flutter in her stomach told a different story.

The beach was already alive with cruise passengers when Scarlet stepped onto the warm sand. Children built castles near the waterline while couples strolled hand-in-hand, pointing at the horizon. She scanned the area, searching for Jerry among the growing crowd.

She spotted him near a rental shack, two paddleboards propped beside him. He stood barefoot and shirtless in navy swim trunks, the morning light turning his skin to warm gold against the deep blue of the ocean behind him. She paused, taking in the sight of him unobserved.

Jerry wasn't built like the fitness influencers she passed on the way to the juice bar. He looked more like someone who used his body, not displayed it.

His frame showed strength in the broad shoulders and steady arms, but also a softness around the edges, the kind that came from eating full meals and getting things done instead of chasing a gym aesthetic.

It grounded him. Made him feel tangible in a world obsessed with polish.

Small scars marked his skin, quiet details of a life lived at full tilt. One near his collarbone shimmered as he bent to lift the board, his movements efficient, unfussy, like everything about him.

His touch was careful, each sweep of sand deliberate, like the board deserved his full attention.

That quiet intent drew her in.

She wasn't just thinking about his arms around her.

She was thinking about the lives they'd held, the things they'd shielded, the weight they'd borne beyond the battlefield.

Before she could reconsider, Jerry looked up, his expression brightening when he saw her. His eyes widened slightly, and he straightened his posture, suddenly more alert. She noticed his throat work as he swallowed before raising his hand in greeting.

"Hey there!" she called, waving as she approached.

Jerry's smile widened, and he started to wave back with both hands, forgetting he was still holding the flotation vests. They flapped comically in the breeze like awkward orange wings. He fumbled them, nearly dropping one before catching it against his chest.

"Good morning!" he called, a hint of color rising in his cheeks. His eyes did a quick sweep of her figure before returning to her face. "You look ... wow. You look stunning."

The compliment caught her off guard, genuine and unpolished. "Thanks," she replied, a bashful chuckle escaping her. "What's with the kiddy vests?"

Jerry seemed to regain his composure, holding up the bright orange life vests with an exaggerated formality. "I thought these vests would be a perfect match for your bathing suit," he teased, his voice steadier now. "I think they'll really enhance your overall outfit on the water."

Scarlet laughed, grateful for the moment of levity that diffused her nervousness. "Oh, is that so? I wasn't aware I needed to accessorize for paddleboarding. I'll take your word for it."

"Absolutely," Jerry replied with a wink. "Nothing like being fashion-forward while you're balancing on a board."

"Ready to give it a try?" He motioned toward the boards staged near the shoreline, his earlier fluster replaced by the quiet confidence she'd come to appreciate.

Scarlet nodded, excitement replacing her earlier anxiety. "Definitely. I've never been paddleboarding before, so I'm looking forward to it."

Jerry handed her a vest and started putting on his own. "It's pretty straightforward. I'll give you a quick rundown before we hit the water. And don't worry, I'll be right there with you."

Something about his manner disarmed her. He was confident without arrogance, knowledgeable without condescension. It was miles away from the men she dealt with in finance who wielded their expertise like weapons.

They waded into the water together, the gentle waves lapping at her thighs. The lightweight chiffon overlay of her swimsuit billowed around her legs, the vibrant teal and coral palm leaves dancing in the current like tropical fish.

"Just a heads-up," Jerry called back with a reassuring smile. "Don't try to stand until we're a bit further from shore. It's a lot easier once we're out of the shallows." He demonstrated, mounting his board with a fluid grace that spoke of practice. "Start by lying on your stomach, then swing your legs over like you're getting on a horse, and finally, sit up."

"I've never ridden a horse either," Scarlet confessed, focusing intently on mimicking his movements. She took a steadying breath and attempted to straddle the board, but the shifting surface threw her off balance. Before she could fully sit down, she wobbled and, with a surprised yelp, tumbled into the water.

She surfaced, salt water streaming down her face, to find Jerry watching with barely contained amusement.

"That was quite the graceful dive!" he said, paddling closer.

"Guess I got a bit too eager," she replied, pushing wet hair from her eyes. The perfectionist in her bristled at the failure, but something about Jerry's easy manner made it hard to stay frustrated.

He hopped off his board and extended a hand toward her. "No worries at all," he said with a reassuring smile. "It's all part of the learning curve. Let's give it another shot."

His hand was warm and solid against hers, steadying her as she climbed back onto the board. The handkerchief hem of her swimsuit clung to her legs, heavy with water.

"Take your time," he encouraged. "Remember, the water's not going anywhere. We'll have you paddling like a pro in no time."

Scarlet wasn't used to being bad at things. In her world, competence was currency. Every misstep got noted, every failure got remembered. Yet here, with only blue ocean as witness, the stakes felt wonderfully, gloriously low.

With Jerry's guidance, she managed to sit stably on the board. The initial wobble gave way to a precarious balance that improved with each passing minute. When Jerry suggested she try standing, however, she hesitated.

"I don't know," she said, eyeing the water beneath her. "I'm just getting comfortable sitting."

"You don't have to," Jerry assured her. "But I think you can do it. Here—" He paddled closer, positioning his board parallel to hers. "I'll help steady you."

With his hand on her board for support, Scarlet slowly shifted to her knees. Her muscle memory betrayed her, bringing that sudden awareness of limbs that usually obeyed without question. It made her grimace.

"I hate being a beginner," she admitted, frustration bleeding into her voice. "I'm not good at it."

"No one is," Jerry replied, his tone matter-of-fact rather than placating. "That's kind of the definition of 'beginner.' But you're doing great."

There was something in his calm that uncoiled her nerves.

Scarlet paused, gathered herself. *No need for flawless—just fun.*

With deliberate care, she slid one foot forward, then the other. Wild wobbling gave way to steady balance.

She was up.

"I did it!" Scarlet exclaimed, a childlike pride bursting through her usual composure.

"You did," Jerry confirmed, his smile matching hers. "Now the real fun begins."

For the next hour, they paddled along the coast, keeping close to the shore. Scarlet fell twice more, but each time, the shock of failure lessened. By the third dunking, she was laughing as she surfaced, accepting Jerry's hand without the flush of embarrassment that had colored her earlier falls.

As they rounded a bend in the shoreline, Jerry pointed ahead. "Check out that secluded spot up ahead. It looks perfect for a break."

Scarlet followed his gaze to a small cove, protected from view by rocky outcroppings. The beach was empty, offering a rare moment of privacy away from the crowds.

"That looks perfect," she agreed, already feeling the pleasant burn in her shoulders from paddling. "And a break sounds wonderful. I could definitely use some time off the board."

Jerry navigated his paddleboard expertly toward the shore, using the momentum to beach it gently on the sand. He hopped off, securing his board before turning to assist Scarlet as she paddled in.

"Careful now, no more surprise splashes," he teased, offering a steadying hand.

Scarlet laughed, gratefully accepting his help. "Thanks. This place really is stunning."

Boards propped in the sand, they stretched out next to each other, sun warming limbs gone loose with fatigue.

The cruise ship was a speck now, barely clinging to the horizon.

Scarlet let the rhythm of surf and the press of earth under her fingertips hold her fully, quietly present.

As they settled into a comfortable silence, Scarlet noticed Jerry absently rubbing the tattoo on his bicep. The gesture seemed almost unconscious, like a habitual comfort.

"Does it have a meaning?" she asked, nodding toward the green and rainbow design on his arm. "Your tattoo, I mean."

Jerry's hand stilled. He shifted slightly, fidgeting with a small pile of sand beside him. "Um, yeah," he said, his confidence from the paddleboarding lesson suddenly absent. "It does."

Scarlet watched as he seemed to debate with himself, his fingers tapping an irregular rhythm against his thigh. His eyes met hers briefly, then darted away to scan the horizon as if checking who might overhear, despite the beach being deserted.

After a moment, he took a breath and glanced down at the tattoo: His fingers traced the outline of a green wheelchair symbol intertwined with a rainbow infinity logo.

"It's for my boys," he said simply, though his voice had a careful quality to it, as if testing the words.

Scarlet blinked, processing the unexpected information. "Your ... boys?"

Jerry nodded, his posture rigid despite his casual position on the sand. "Yeah, I've got two sons at home," he explained, his voice warming with obvious pride even as he continued to fidget with the sand beside him. "Marty's eight, and Emmett's six. The green wheelchair is for Marty. He has cerebral palsy. And the infinity symbol with the rainbow is for Emmett. It's the symbol for autism awareness."

"Marty and Emmett?" Scarlet couldn't help the small snicker that escaped. "Like Back to the Future?"

Jerry's face relaxed into a sheepish grin. "Yeah, exactly. I'm a big fan of the movies. Their mom wasn't thrilled about it, but she let me choose their names."

The thought drifted in with surprising ease.

Hours ago, she'd been musing with Cami about maybe having kids someday.

Now, here she was, ankle-deep in surf beside a man who had already become a father twice over.

Not fear. Not doubt. Just a quiet pull toward the unexpected rhythm of it all, something that had once felt impossible to imagine again. Not after everything.

*No. Not here. Not now.* But the softness in her chest was real. And it didn't feel like grief. It felt like possibility.

"I had no idea," she said softly, her mind racing. "You have children. You're a father."

As Jerry responded, Scarlet's lens shifted.

The body she'd casually admired now told a different story.

His belly wasn't just soft; it spoke of priorities that favored bedtime over barbells.

The scars? They might have come from a life filled with sharp corners and small hands.

His shoulders looked like they'd supported more than just weight, as if they'd steadied others when the world tilted.

The strength in his arms wasn't aesthetic anymore.

It was earned in moments of lifting, catching, carrying—living.

"Yeah. They're staying with my mom while I'm away," Jerry continued, a mix of pride and something like apology crossing his features. "This is actually the first real break I've had in years. Mac practically forced me onto this cruise. Said I needed time to just be Jerry, not just Dad or Sergeant Duncan."

Scarlet studied his face, seeing him in a new light. This morning's idle musings about motherhood suddenly felt weightless compared to Jerry's reality. She noticed the faint lines at the corners of his eyes, the weariness beneath his tan, all signs of responsibility she hadn't recognized before.

"That explains a lot, actually," she said finally, adjusting the tie at the top of her swimsuit as she absorbed this new information.

"Like what?" Jerry asked, curious.

"The way you helped me on the paddleboard, so patient but never condescending. Your comfort with the diaper challenge." She smiled. "You've had practice."

Jerry laughed softly. "I guess I have. Though changing teddy bears is considerably easier than changing actual babies."

"Tell me about them," Scarlet said, genuinely interested. "Your kiddos; Marty and Emmett."

When he began to speak, something shifted in him, a change that moved like a tide rolling in.

The restlessness fell away, replaced by wide gestures and a spark of something honest and unfiltered.

He seemed to grow lighter, more open, as if talking about his children let him step fully into himself.

"Marty's amazing. Despite the challenges with cerebral palsy, he's the happiest kid you'll ever meet. He can't communicate verbally, but his smile says everything he needs to say. He lights up any room and instantly makes everything seem a little bit brighter."

Scarlet listened, drawn in by the love in Jerry's voice. Her morning conversation with Cami echoed in her mind, and her casual musing about motherhood someday seemed so abstract compared to Jerry's vivid, lived reality.

"And Emmett," Jerry continued, "even though he's younger than his brother, he has this strong big brother quality about him. He takes his role seriously, always helping out Marty and making sure he's okay. We spend a lot of time in the kitchen together, and cooking is one of our favorite things to do."

She tried to picture Jerry in a kitchen with a six-year-old, teaching him to stir pancake batter or flip eggs. The image was surprisingly easy to conjure, fitting perfectly with the patient man who'd just taught her to paddleboard.

As he spoke, Scarlet realized she was seeing Jerry differently now. He wasn't just the attractive man from the cruise who'd flirted over diaper races and hot tub conversations, but someone whose life held profound responsibilities. The tattoo wasn't just ink; it was a permanent commitment to his children, etched into his skin as surely as they were etched into his heart.

"They sound wonderful," she said sincerely, adjusting the tie detail at the top of her swimsuit as she shifted to face him more directly. "Back to the Future boys who clearly hit the dad jackpot. You must miss them terribly."

"I do," Jerry admitted. "But this break has been good for all of us. My mom loves having them, and it's given me a chance to ..." He paused, his eyes meeting hers briefly before glancing away. "To reconnect with myself, I guess. To remember there's more to me than just being Dad."

Scarlet nodded, understanding more than she expected. "It's easy to get lost in a role, isn't it? To become so defined by what you do that you forget who you are."

"Exactly," Jerry said, looking grateful for her understanding. "Don't get me wrong, being their dad is the most important thing in my life. But sometimes I need to remember I'm still me, too."

Scarlet glanced at him, wondering about the pieces of his story still hidden from view.

The question hovered, obvious and loaded.

She wavered, unsure whether crossing that line would bring them closer together or push too far into his private world.

"If you don't mind my asking ..." she began tentatively, her fingers tracing circles in the sand. "What about their mother? Is she ... ?" She let the question hang, giving him space to answer or deflect.

Jerry's expression closed slightly, the animation draining from his features. His fingers returned to that nervous fidgeting with the sand. "I don't really want to get into it much," he replied, his voice more reserved. "I'll just say that she's not really in the picture anymore."

"Oh God, I'm sorry," Scarlet said quickly, heat rushing to her face. "That was so inappropriate of me. I shouldn't have. I mean … we just met, and here I am asking personal questions about your …" She shook her head, pressing her palm into the sand. "Just forget I asked. Seriously."

"No, no, it's okay," Jerry assured her, though the tension in his shoulders suggested otherwise. "You didn't know. I just … prefer to talk about some happier subjects." He shifted slightly, turning the conversation. "So, tell me about your story."

Scarlet took a deep breath, her eyes drifting out to the horizon. She traced patterns in the sand with her finger, organizing her thoughts into neat rows and columns.

"Well, I guess you could say I'm on this cruise for a mental break," she began slowly. "Cami practically had to drag me here. She thought I needed to … reconnect with actual humans, I guess."

"As opposed to?" Jerry asked, his attention fully focused on her.

Scarlet laughed softly. "As opposed to my Netflix account and takeout delivery guys. Dating in Miami is …" She shook her head, searching for the right words. "It's a wasteland. Seriously. It's like there are only two types of guys left: the finance bros who never outgrew their frat phase, or thirty-five-year-olds who still live with their parents and work 'flexible hours.'"

Jerry chuckled. "Sounds rough."

"You have no idea," Scarlet continued, smoothing the handkerchief hem of her swimsuit. "The last guy I went out with spent the entire dinner talking about his cryptocurrency investments and then suggested we 'split the check down to the penny.' Another one showed up thirty minutes late and then spent the whole date texting someone else."

She sighed, surprised by her own candor. "It just feels like all the decent ones got snatched up years ago, you know? By thirty-one, the dating pool is basically a puddle, and it's not even a clean puddle. It's one of those gross ones with cigarette butts floating in it."

Jerry laughed, the tension from their earlier conversation dissolving.

"I needed a break from the constant disappointment," she admitted. "I wasn't looking to meet anyone on this cruise. I just wanted to float in a pool with a drink in my hand without having to fend off pickup lines about my 'vibe' or whatever." She glanced at Jerry, allowing a small smile. "But meeting you has been nice. Different."

Jerry's expression was understanding, free from judgment. "I get it. Sometimes it's just ... too much. Too many bad dates, too many disappointments. You need to reset."

Scarlet nodded, drawing her knees up to her chest and wrapping her arms around them. "Exactly. I just needed a chance to breathe, to remember what it feels like to enjoy the moment without analyzing whether it's going anywhere."

As she spoke, Scarlet realized the truth in her words. When had she last just enjoyed someone's company without mentally calculating compatibility or planning the next three dates in advance?

"This," she gestured around them at the tranquil beach, "this has been a good reminder of what it means to just be present."

Jerry smiled, a connection deepening between them. "Well, for what it's worth, I'm glad we both ended up on this ridiculous singles cruise. Seems like we needed it for completely different reasons."

Scarlet returned his smile, feeling lighter than she had in months. "Yeah, me too," she said softly. "It's been nice to just ... talk. No expectations, no pressure."

Jerry glanced at his watch and sighed. "Speaking of which, we should probably start heading back to the main port area. Mac will never let me hear the end of it if we're late."

"Right," Scarlet laughed, getting to her feet and brushing sand from her swimsuit. "Cami's probably wondering where I am, too ... or she's still passed out by the pool."

As they stepped into the surf again, the day's purpose sharpened in her mind.

This wasn't only about trying something new.

It was about leaning into the unpolished edges, about showing up as she was, not as she thought she should be.

The trip back to the main beach felt easier this time, her muscles finally understanding what was expected of them.

Scarlet kept pace with Jerry without effort, their boards carving twin arcs across the water.

She noticed Jerry had grown quiet, his expression thoughtful as they paddled side by side.

"You're quiet," she observed, surprising herself with her boldness. "Penny for your thoughts?"

Jerry smiled, as if caught in some private deliberation. "Just thinking about how much has changed in a few days."

"Good change?" she asked, immediately wishing she could retract the question. She wasn't usually one to seek reassurance so transparently.

"Definitely good," he replied without hesitation.

The cruise ship loomed larger as they approached, a glittering re-minder of the world they would soon rejoin. The main beach was now crowded with fellow passengers, sunbathing and splashing in the shallows. Their peaceful interlude was coming to an end.

An impulsive thought struck her, one so unlike her usual calculated approach that she nearly laughed at herself.

"Race you to shore?" she challenged, flashing a playful grin that felt foreign on her face.

Jerry laughed, his earlier pensiveness dissolving. "You're on."

Scarlet didn't need to make sense of it.

She wasn't measuring potential or forecasting outcomes.

She would hold what she had with Jerry with gratitude, regardless of whether it ended with the trip or continued beyond it.

# Cami

"Save it for someone who hasn't known you since freshman accounting," Cami said, flopping back onto her pillow as Scarlet fussed with her "practical" swimsuit. "Go have fun with your not-date in your mom-suit. I'll be here, doing absolutely nothing productive, as God intended for vacation."

When the cabin door clicked shut behind Scarlet, Cami stretched across her bed. Credit where credit was due: Scarlet Bellari, the woman who color-coded her tax documents and alphabetized her spice rack, was actually letting her hair down. It had only taken three days at sea and one hot military guy to accomplish what Cami had been attempting for years.

After a quick shower, Cami slipped into her favorite turquoise bikini and sheer white cover-up. Unlike Scarlet, she had no qualms about showcasing what she'd worked hard to maintain. By the pool, she settled with coffee and her latest romance novel, enjoying the relative quiet of the deck as most passengers had disembarked to explore Grand Turk.

"Well, look who's up early," came a familiar voice. "I didn't know bookworms liked to sunbathe."

Looking up, Cami found Mac standing over her, plate piled impossibly high with breakfast foods.

"That's original," she replied flatly. "Did you come up with that all by yourself?"

"Ouch. Harsh this early in the morning. Mind if I join you, or is that against bookworm protocol?"

Cami sighed audibly. "Go ahead. I suppose I can tolerate your presence for a little while."

Mac sat across from her and immediately took an oversized bite of his doughnut. "So, what's on your agenda for the day?" he asked, still chewing.

"You know, you could chew first," Cami pointed out. "I haven't decided yet. What about you?"

"Well, Jerry and I were talking about meeting for lunch on the beach. There's a snack shack that's supposed to have good local food. What do you think?"

Cami raised an eyebrow. "A double date? Really?"

"No, not a date," Mac quickly clarified. "Just a casual hangout."

"Alright, fine. But, just so we're clear, I'm not into the whole double date thing. You and I, this is not a thing."

Mac chuckled. "Oh, I am very aware. I'd need a silver spear if I wanted any chance to pierce that hardened heart of yours. However, Jerry agreed to buying the first round."

"Fine. If there's rum involved, maybe I can tolerate your company for another hour," Cami replied. "But if this turns into some cheesy couples' thing, I'm out."

"Deal," Mac agreed, raising his coffee mug. "To a drama-free lunch with good food and decent company."

Cami clinked her mug against his. "So, what did you do before the military?" she asked, genuinely curious despite herself.

"College baseball scholarship that went nowhere," Mac replied with surprising candor. "Turns out I wasn't as good as my high school coach thought. You?"

"Public relations for a record label. Too many late nights and entitled rock stars," Cami said. "Now I run social media for a boutique hotel chain. Less glamorous, way more sane."

Mac whistled. "I can see you handling entitled rock stars. You've got that don't-mess-with-me vibe down pat."

"You should see me with entitled hotel guests," Cami replied. "I'm even scarier."

"I don't doubt it," Mac said, his eyes lingering a moment too long. "That confidence looks good on you, by the way."

Cami's expression cooled instantly. "Don't even try, playboy. Your charm might work on the ship's dance instructor, but I'm immune."

Mac raised his hands in surrender, though his smile remained. "Just stating facts. No ulterior motives."

"Mmhmm," Cami hummed skeptically. "I've heard that one before."

After a few hours by the pool, where Cami read while Mac chatted with various passengers, it was time to head ashore to rescue Scarlet from whatever trouble she'd gotten herself into with Army Boy. Cami gathered her beach bag as Mac returned from his cabin freshly changed into swim trunks and a faded military-themed t-shirt.

Grand Turk's beach looked like a postcard come to life, all white sand and impossibly blue water with just enough breeze to take the edge off the Caribbean heat. After leaving the cruise terminal, Cami and Mac walked along the shoreline, bypassing the crowded tourist trap restaurant where most passengers congregated.

"Jack's Shack should be just up ahead," Mac said, pointing to a weathered tiki structure in the distance.

"Try to keep up," Cami replied, quickening her pace as her sandals dangled from her fingers. "Just because I agreed to lunch doesn't mean I'm thrilled about it."

As they approached, Cami immediately understood why Mac had suggested the place. Unlike the commercialized atmosphere of the cruise terminal, Jack's Shack exuded authentic island charm. Beach chairs scattered across the sand, a volleyball net swayed in the breeze, and the open-air structure with its thatched roof looked like it had weathered many a storm.

Cami's eyes landed on Scarlet and Jerry tucked into a corner table, vibrant cocktails between them.

Their closeness was easy to note, but what gave Cami pause was Scarlet's expression, softened and unguarded.

It had been a while since she'd seen that kind of calm on her friend's face.

"Well, well, the lovebirds found their nest," Cami announced as they approached.

Scarlet's head snapped up, a flash of self-consciousness crossing her features. "We just got here a few minutes ago," she explained quickly. "The paddleboarding was amazing."

A golden retriever trotted over to their table, sniffing curiously at the newcomers. Mac immediately dropped to a knee. "Who's this guy?"

"That's Topher," Jerry explained. "The unofficial mascot."

Cami settled into a chair, studying Scarlet with the practiced eye of a longtime friend. Something was different.

A server in a faded Jack's Shack t-shirt approached. "What can I get you folks? Ready to order?"

"Jerk chicken spring rolls and conch fritters to start," Jerry said. "And I'll have the jerk chicken plate with a Turk's Head lager."

"Make it two on the beer," Mac chimed in. "And I'll take the loaded burger."

"I'll try the rum punch," Scarlet decided. "And the grilled mahi-mahi."

"Rum punch for me too," Cami added. "With the conch fritter platter."

As the server departed, Cami leaned forward. "So, details. How was paddleboarding?"

As Scarlet chatted about the crystal-clear water and tropical fish, Cami tuned out the words and zeroed in on the body language.

The subtle brush of Scarlet's hand against Jerry's arm.

The way she leaned in just a bit when he spoke.

Hold on, was that her foot grazing his under the table?

Cami lifted her menu, hiding a grin.

Their drinks arrived quickly, followed by the appetizers. The spring rolls were exceptional, the spicy-sweet jerk seasoning perfectly complementing the tender chicken inside. Conversation flowed easily as they shared the food, moving from cruise experiences to favorite vacation spots.

"I need to use the restroom," Cami announced after finishing her rum punch. "Scarlet, come with me?"

"I'm fine, actually." Scarlet began.

"Now," Cami insisted, already standing.

Inside the small bathroom, Cami turned on her friend. "Spill it. What happened out there today? And don't say 'nothing' because your foot has been playing footsie with Army Boy's leg for the last twenty minutes."

Scarlet's cheeks flushed instantly. "I wasn't. I mean ... was it that obvious?"

"Only to someone who's known you for a decade," Cami replied. "So? How was it really?"

"We just had a really nice time," Scarlet said, clearly downplaying. "The water was beautiful, and he was patient when I kept falling off the board."

"Uh-huh. And that's why you're glowing like you swallowed a lightbulb?"

"I am not glowing," Scarlet protested, though her smile betrayed her. "He's just ... nice. Different from the guys in Miami."

"Different how?"

"He listens. Really listens," Scarlet said, twisting a loose strand of hair. Cami recognized the nervous habit from college, one she hadn't seen in years. "And he's funny, in this quiet way. Not trying too hard, you know?"

Cami studied her friend. "Just be careful, okay? We're only three days into this cruise. Don't go falling for the first guy who remembers your drink order."

"I'm not falling for anyone," Scarlet insisted, though her eyes slid away. "It's just fun. Vacation fun."

"Mmhmm," Cami hummed skeptically. "Well, vacation fun or not, you might want to tone down the under-table action unless you want the boys to catch on."

"Oh God," Scarlet groaned. "Was it really that obvious?"

"To me? Yes. To them? Who knows. Men can be oblivious to the most obvious signals." Cami reapplied her lip gloss. "Come on, let's get back before they think we're plotting something."

"Aren't we?" Scarlet asked with a small laugh.

"Always," Cami winked.

When they returned to the table, their main courses had arrived. Mac was in the middle of an elaborate story, his hands gesturing wildly as Jerry shook with silent laughter.

"Everything okay?" Jerry asked as they sat back down.

"Just girl talk," Cami replied smoothly.

The rest of lunch passed pleasantly, with food that exceeded expectations and conversation that flowed easily. Cami continued her covert observation of Scarlet. Her friend kept finding little excuses to touch Jerry, whether passing the salt, reaching for her drink, or pointing out something on the beach. And Jerry, for his part, seemed to unconsciously lean toward Scarlet whenever she spoke, his attention completely absorbed by her despite the distractions around them.

As they finished their meal, Topher returned to their table, flopping dramatically at Jerry's feet.

"I think he's adopted you," Scarlet observed, smiling.

"Story of my life," Jerry replied with a soft laugh. "I seem to collect strays."

The afternoon sun was beginning its descent as they paid their bill and gathered their belongings. Jerry and Scarlet walked slightly ahead on the beach, their conversation too quiet for Cami to hear.

"So," Mac said, falling into step beside her, "mission accomplished? Your friend seems happy."

Cami watched Scarlet laugh at something Jerry said, her hand briefly touching his arm. "Yeah, she does. But this is only day three of the cruise. A lot can happen."

"True," Mac agreed. "But I haven't seen Jerry this relaxed in ... well, maybe ever."

"You know what this means, right?" Mac said, a mischievous glint in his eye.

"That we're going to be stuck as third and fourth wheels for the rest of this cruise?"

"Worse," Mac replied solemnly. "We're the comedic side characters in their romantic comedy. You know, the sassy best friend and the goofy sidekick who exist solely to push the main characters together while offering witty commentary."

Cami snorted despite herself. "Oh God, you're right. Quick, we need a subplot of our own before we're reduced to nothing but one-liners and knowing glances."

"Too late," Mac grinned, gesturing ahead where Scarlet and Jerry had paused, silhouetted against the setting sun. "Look at that framing. Pure rom-com gold. I bet there's even inspirational music playing somewhere."

"Kill me now," Cami said under her breath, but she didn't look away.

There was something about the way Scarlet leaned into Jerry, looking at peace, like she'd landed in the right place.

Cami wasn't one for sentiment, but this? This she could admire.

# Ten

The Blissful Harvest bustled with morning energy as Tortola's lush green hills rose dramatically through floor-to-ceiling windows, the ship having docked before dawn. At a corner table, Maude sipped her tea while Cami demolished a plate of tropical fruit. Scarlet stared at her untouched guava juice, lost in thought.

"Earth to Scarlet," Cami said, waving a piece of pineapple. "You've been staring at that same spot for five minutes. Either you've discovered the meaning of life in your juice glass, or something's up."

Scarlet blinked. "Sorry. Just thinking."

"Even the calmest waters can hide powerful currents beneath," Maude observed, silver-streaked hair catching the morning light. Her eyes held that knowing look that always made Scarlet feel transparent.

"Jerry has kids," Scarlet said finally, the words falling between them like stones in still water.

Cami paused mid-bite. "So? Most guys his age have a baby momma somewhere. Weekend visits and child support payments are pretty much the standard divorced dad package."

"No," Scarlet leaned forward, voice lowering. "He's an actual father. Two boys with special needs. Marty has cerebral palsy and Emmett has autism. He's raising them alone."

Cami set down her fork, truly attentive now. "Wait ... full-time single dad? Special needs children?"

"Yes." Scarlet traced the condensation on her juice glass. "He has this tattoo with both symbols intertwined. The mother's not in the picture. The boys are staying with his mom while he's here. It's his first real break in years."

Maude's eyes softened. "And this revelation troubles you?"

"That's what's strange," Scarlet admitted. "It doesn't. I've always bolted at the first mention of children. But with Jerry ..." She shook her head. "I wanted to know more. I asked questions. I'm still ... interested."

"Trust the current that pulls you toward open waters, not the one that keeps you circling the same shore," Maude said, touching Scarlet's hand briefly. The warmth of her fingers was steadying.

"What kind of father is he?" Maude asked.

Scarlet hesitated. "There's such love when he talks about them. But beyond that ..." She shrugged. "It was just one conversation. I know the older one can't speak verbally but is apparently the happiest kid ever. The younger one loves cooking shows and they spend time in the kitchen together." She looked up. "But who is he day to day? I have no idea."

Cami reached across the table, squeezing Scarlet's wrist. "Are we panicking because you might actually like someone real? Someone with a life that can't be neatly scheduled into your color-coded calendar?"

The directness of the question, combined with the genuine care behind it, made Scarlet's throat tighten unexpectedly.

"Maybe," she whispered.

"Some men are like shallow waters," Maude said, her eyes kind but penetrating. "Easy to navigate but offering little depth. Others are like deep harbors. They require more careful navigation, but they give you somewhere true to anchor."

"Or maybe I'm overthinking a vacation fling," Scarlet countered, straightening her spine. "It's been three days."

"Three days that already matter more than three months with anyone else I've seen you date," Cami said softly.

The vulnerable moment hung between them, neither comfort nor challenge, just truth. Scarlet felt exposed in a way that only these two women could achieve, completely seen in her fears, her desires, her contradictions.

"I should get going," Scarlet said, checking her watch and jumping up. "It's already 10:15!"

"The ferry doesn't leave until eleven," Cami pointed out.

"Yes, but I need to grab my bag and get to the dock by 10:30," Scarlet said, already backing away. "The purser said they're strict about boarding times."

"Running from this conversation won't make it disappear," Cami called after her.

Scarlet paused at the restaurant entrance to respond. "I know. But maybe I need a few hours in paradise to figure out what to do with it."

"Don't let fear be the anchor that keeps you from sailing," Maude called softly.

Scarlet nodded once, acknowledgment and promise in the gesture, before turning and hurrying toward the elevators.

The morning sun beat down on the dock as Scarlet scanned the line of passengers waiting for the Virgin Gorda ferry, her gaze darting hopefully toward the gangway with each new arrival.

"Looking for someone, Red?"

Scarlet turned to find Mac approaching, aviators glinting in the sunlight, a worn baseball cap pulled low over his eyes.

"Is Jerry coming?" she asked, still glancing past Mac.

"Sorry, Red. You only get me today," Mac said, adjusting his backpack. "The miniature sidekick to his love story."

Scarlet's shoulders fell slightly before she caught herself. "Oh."

"He wanted some alone time," Mac explained. "Said something about enjoying the empty ship while everyone's ashore."

"Smart," Scarlet nodded. "I think Cami's doing the same. Something about having the pool deck to herself."

"Want to buddy up?" Mac asked. "Safety in numbers and all that."

"Is this you being a gentleman, or just avoiding the solo travelers looking to mingle?"

Mac clutched his chest dramatically. "You wound me, Red. Can't a guy just enjoy intelligent company?"

Scarlet laughed despite herself. "Fine. But I draw the line at couple photos."

"Deal," he said. "Though we'd make an exceptionally attractive fake couple."

The ferry crossing was both quick and stunning. Azure waters stretched before them, dotted with smaller islands that rose like emerald jewels against the sea. After docking, they boarded a shuttle bus that wound uphill through lush vegetation.

Stepping onto the trail leading to The Baths, Scarlet's first glimpse stole her breath away. Massive granite boulders rose from pristine white sand like prehistoric monuments, stacked improbably atop one another, creating a landscape that seemed crafted by giants. Between these colossal stones, glimpses of turquoise water beckoned.

"This can't be real," Scarlet murmured.

Their guide gathered them near an opening between two towering boulders. "This is the entrance to the grotto trail. You'll need to duck in places, and there's a rope for the steeper sections. Take your time."

Scarlet eyed the dark gap skeptically. "You're sure this is worth it?"

"No idea," Mac said cheerfully, offering his hand. "Shall we, Red?"

The first steps inside plunged them into semi-darkness, Scarlet's fingers tracing the smooth, cool surface of granite walls worn silky by centuries of water and touch. Then the passage opened, and Scarlet froze in wonder.

They stood in a cathedral of stone, its ceiling a jigsaw puzzle of boulders with slender gaps between. Sunlight poured through these natural skylights in defined beams, illuminating pools of water so crystalline that the sand below appeared magnified rather than submerged.

"Oh, my God," Scarlet whispered, her voice carrying a gentle echo.

"Yeah," Mac breathed. "Room steward undersold it."

Each new chamber revealed its own wonder: a boulder suspended impossibly between two others; a pool so still it mirrored the stone above; a narrow passage that opened suddenly to frame the Caribbean in a perfect blue rectangle.

At a particularly steep section, Mac went ahead, then reached back to offer Scarlet his hand. "Thanks," she said as he helped her up.

"What are sidekicks for?" he replied with a grin.

They emerged onto Devil's Bay and found themselves on a perfect crescent of beach protected by the same massive boulders. They found a relatively secluded spot near a cluster of smaller rocks that provided patches of shade.

"Ready to dive in?" Mac asked, gesturing toward the inviting water.

Scarlet nodded, already shedding her cover-up to reveal a sleek black bikini. It was nothing like yesterday's modest tropical tankini. She'd chosen it this morning with a flutter of anticipation, hopeful that maybe Jerry would join the excursion. The realization that she'd dressed for someone who wasn't even there made her cheeks warm with a mixture of embarrassment and disappointment.

They waded into water so clear it barely seemed present at all. It looked more like suspended crystal than liquid. Below the surface, Scarlet could see every detail: colorful fish, rippled sand patterns, even the shadow of her own body moving across the seafloor.

They bobbed in the warm Caribbean water, standing chest-deep as gentle waves rocked them rhythmically. Schools of tiny silver fish darted around their legs, catching sunlight on their scales like scattered diamonds.

"So," Scarlet said, her voice casual as she brushed wet hair from her face, "how long have you known Jerry?"

Mac adjusted his position, hopping slightly as a larger wave passed. "About four years now. We met during my first Iraq deployment after he transferred into our unit a couple months in."

"And you live with him now?"

"Yeah. Funny how that happened." Mac grinned. "He locked the doors and wouldn't let me leave."

Scarlet laughed, splashing water in his direction.

"Kidding, kidding," Mac chuckled. "After we got back stateside, I needed a place to crash for a bit. Was only supposed to be temporary."

"What changed?"

"Jerry had just gotten custody of the boys right before that deployment. His mom kept them the whole year we were gone." He ducked under an incoming wave, emerging with hair plastered to his forehead. "When we got back, he was suddenly full-time dad mode."

"That must have been hard, to get custody and then immediately have to deploy," Scarlet said, wobbling as a wave hit her from behind.

"Whoa, careful there," Mac steadied her with a quick hand to her elbow. "Yeah, rough timing. But he made it work. Always does."

A particularly large wave crashed around them, and they both jumped to keep their heads above water, laughing as they regained their footing.

"What's he like as a dad?" Scarlet asked, watching a hermit crab scuttle along the sandy bottom.

Mac's expression softened. "He's trying to be the best dad in the world, and honestly, it's to a fault. Guy will never ask for help, even when he's drowning. Never wants anyone to think he can't handle it or, God forbid, feel sorry for him."

"Sounds familiar," Scarlet murmured.

"It wears on him, though. All that responsibility, all that pressure." Mac flicked water from his face. "There are a lot of people who love him and those boys, but he won't let the village help. Always has to be the hero."

"What about their mom?" Scarlet asked carefully.

Mac's playful demeanor dimmed. "That's Jerry's story to tell. Not mine." He scooped up a handful of water and let it trickle through his fingers. "Some details are his to share, you know?"

Scarlet nodded, respecting the boundary.

Mac shook water from his ears. "Getting pruney. Should probably dry off for a bit?"

Scarlet nodded, and they waded back to shore, water streaming from their bodies as they settled onto their towels in a patch of dappled shade.

Several minutes passed in comfortable silence, the only sounds being gentle waves and distant laughter from other beachgoers.

"Can I ask you something?" Scarlet finally said, turning her head toward Mac.

"Shoot," he replied, adjusting his cap over his face.

Scarlet took a deep breath. "So, be honest with me, does he have any space for anyone else?"

Mac pushed his cap back, looking out toward the horizon. He breathed in deeply, seeming to search for just the right words. After a long moment, he spoke softly.

"Oh, man ... God, I sure hope so ..." The sincerity in his voice was unmistakable. "The two of us have been in the same unit long enough that undoubtedly the Army's gonna come calling with new assignments before too long. I won't always be able to be that helpful roommate."

Scarlet nodded, absorbing his words.

"Ultimately, it's up to Jerry to decide to let someone in," Mac continued, his tone lighter. "But between you and me, I think he's more ready than he realizes." He gave her a pointed look. "If it matters."

"I'm just curious," Scarlet said, too quickly.

Mac's mouth quirked in a half-smile. "Sure, Red. Just curious."

They fell into easy conversation as the afternoon stretched on, discussing everything from favorite movies to the weirdest places they'd traveled. Mac had a gift for storytelling, painting vivid pictures of misadventures both in and out of uniform.

The tour guide eventually called for everyone to begin packing up, reminding them of the ferry's departure time. As they gathered their belongings, brushing sand from towels and water bottles, Mac glanced at Scarlet with feigned nonchalance.

"So ..." he said, slinging his backpack over one shoulder. "What's the deal with Cami?"

Scarlet nearly fumbled her sandal. "What do you mean?"

"Come on, Red. I answered your interrogation." Mac grinned. "Fair is fair."

"There's no 'deal' with Cami," Scarlet said, carefully folding her cover-up. "She's my best friend. Known her since college."

"That's not what I asked."

Scarlet raised an eyebrow. "Let me get this straight. You want to know if my best friend is single? The same best friend who could absolutely destroy you, by the way?"

"I didn't say that," Mac protested, though his expression said otherwise. "Just wondering if she's always that ... intense."

"Yes," Scarlet laughed. "That's her factory setting. Why? Scared?"

"Terrified," Mac admitted cheerfully. "But in an intriguing way."

They joined the line of tourists heading back up the trail, the afternoon sun casting long shadows through the boulders. The hike up was more strenuous than the descent had been, and conversation lapsed into comfortable silence as they focused on navigating the steep path.

At the top, before boarding the shuttle, Scarlet paused to look back at the breathtaking view. The massive boulders, crystalline water, and perfect curve of white sand all looked like something from a dream.

"Thank you," she said suddenly.

Mac turned. "For what?"

"For today. For ..." She gestured vaguely. "Being honest about Jerry."

Mac's usual smirk softened into something more genuine. "He's my brother. Not by blood, but in all the ways that matter." He shrugged. "I want him to be happy. It's been a long time since I've seen him like this."

"Like what?"

"Like someone who remembers he's not just Staff Sergeant Duncan or Marty and Emmett's dad." Mac stepped back as other passengers began boarding the shuttle. "Like someone who remembers he's Jerry, too."

On the ferry back, they sat side by side watching the sun begin its slow descent toward the horizon. Scarlet found her thoughts drifting not to the spectacular beauty they'd witnessed, but to a man who might be sitting alone on his balcony right now, quietly making space in his carefully ordered life for something new. Someone new, maybe.

# Eleven

T he Bubbly Bar's entrance was a cascade of soft light filtering through champagne-colored drapes. Scarlet and Cami paused at the doorway, taking in the elegant space with its rose gold accents and crystal chandeliers.

"Find us a spot?" Cami gestured toward the bar. "I'll grab drinks. What do you want?"

Scarlet shrugged, suddenly tired after the long day exploring Tortola's caves. "Surprise me. I trust your judgment."

"Dangerous words." Cami grinned and headed for the bar.

Scarlet wandered toward the far side of the lounge, drawn to a curved window that offered a panoramic view of the ocean. The Elysian Serenade was just pulling away from Tortola, the island's lush green mountains growing smaller against the horizon as twilight approached. She claimed a small table right against the glass, settling into a plush velvet chair that felt like sinking into a cloud.

A few minutes later, Cami returned, carefully balancing two vibrant red cocktails that sparkled in the soft light.

"Apparently," she announced, setting the drinks down, "this is their signature cocktail. The bartender described it as 'basically a grown-up bubbly strawberry lemonade martini,' but it's actually called a Scarlet Surrender." She pushed one toward Scarlet with a raised eyebrow. "Seemed fitting."

Scarlet rolled her eyes but accepted the drink. "Subtle."

"Read the description." Cami tapped the cocktail menu she'd brought back. "It's practically a sign."

Scarlet glanced down at the menu: *Scarlet Surrender – Surrender to the siren's call and let desire take the helm. This provocative blend of Cîroc Citrus Vodka, Red Curaçao, fresh lemon juice, and house-made strawberry syrup teases the senses, while a seductive splash of Prosecco ignites the spark as this shimmering temptress dares you to take just one more sip.*

"Well, that's not heavy-handed at all," Scarlet said, but took a sip anyway. The drink was perfectly balanced, sweet, tart, with just enough bite from the vodka and the effervescent finish of the Prosecco tickling her tongue.

Cami raised her glass. "To whatever happens next."

Scarlet clinked glasses, feeling the day's tension begin to melt away. Outside the window, the last glimpse of Tortola disappeared into the distance as the ship sailed toward open water.

"So," Cami said, setting down her glass with deliberate care. "Are we going to talk about the Jerry situation or pretend it's still just a cruise fling?"

Heat crept up Scarlet's neck. "There's nothing to talk about."

"Right. That's why you keep looking toward the door every time it opens."

Scarlet took another sip, avoiding Cami's eyes. "He's not like the guys I usually fall for."

"Babe, it's been five years since Alex and you haven't fallen for anyone else since." Cami's tone was gentle but matter-of-fact.

"That's not fair, I've dated." Scarlet's protest sounded weak even to her own ears.

There had been a stretch, after Alex, when even looking at a stroller in passing felt like being hollowed out. She'd buried that version of herself in spreadsheets and late nights, hoping the ache would go numb with time. Maybe it had. Maybe it hadn't.

"Sitting across a dinner table and grinding your teeth over bland small talk is not dating, and it's damn sure not falling for someone." Cami leaned forward. "When you say that Jerry isn't like the other guys that you've fallen for, that leaves all of ONE other guy in your life, Alex."

"Yeah, but—"

"But nothing! What you're saying is that Jerry is not like Alex. Excellent!" Cami threw up her hands. "Alex was a bum, and still is a bum. Jerry is great and you're trying to convince yourself that there must be something wrong with being great."

Scarlet fell silent, tracing the rim of her glass with her fingertip.

Cami's expression softened. "Look, is Jerry supposed to be your happily ever after? Fuck if I know. But, he's a great guy and he admitted to me earlier today that he is into you."

Scarlet's head snapped up. "Really?!"

"Yes!" Cami's smile was triumphant. "I think it actually caught him off guard when he admitted it to me, but that man is smitten for you and you shouldn't discount that." She took another sip of her drink.

"We have, what, three days left on this ship? It's time to make the most of it, babe ..." She wiggled her eyebrows suggestively. "At least take the soldier for a ride if nothing else."

"Cami!" Scarlet laughed despite herself, a flush spreading across her cheeks.

"What? He's hot, you're hot. Life's short." Cami shrugged, but her eyes were serious. "But honestly, Scarlet, I think it's okay to let yourself feel something. It's okay to let someone in."

Scarlet looked out the window at the darkening sea. "What if it doesn't work out?"

"What if it does?" Cami countered. "What if this is just the beginning of something good? Don't you want to find out?"

The truth of it hit Scarlet like a wave. She did want to find out. She wanted to know Jerry on every level: his body, yes, but also his mind, his heart, what made him laugh, what kept him up at night.

"Speaking of which ..." Cami tapped her watch. "Karaoke time. Mac promised us seats, but they'll disappear fast. Let's go."

"Right." Scarlet finished her drink in one smooth motion, the warmth curling outward like a slow exhale.

Just this once, she could let go.

She walked in step behind Cami, but her thoughts drifted.

*Had Jerry really said something to her?*

The Captain's Haven had transformed since they'd glimpsed it during the ship tour. By day, it was a nautical-themed lounge with brass fixtures and vintage maps. Tonight, it pulsed with energy as stage lights cast blue and amber patterns across the room, a sound system had appeared where bookshelves had been, and a digital screen displaying lyrics now dominated one wall. The crowd was already substantial, an eclectic mix of cruise guests clutching songbooks and liquid courage.

"There they are," Cami nudged her, nodding toward a corner booth.

Mac spotted them first, raising his hand in an exaggerated wave that made Scarlet smile despite herself. As they approached, she noticed Jerry was wearing a different shirt from earlier. The simple navy button-down brought out the blue in his eyes. His hair was slightly damp, like he'd recently showered, and the thought of him making an effort sent an unexpected warmth through her.

"Well, look who finally made it," Mac called out as they approached the booth.

"Sorry we're late," Cami said, sliding in. "Someone had to try on three different outfits."

Scarlet rolled her eyes. "It was two, not three."

"Ladies, your timing couldn't be better," Mac grinned as a waitress arrived with a tray laden with drinks. Four salt-rimmed margarita glasses glowed a vibrant lime green under the lounge lights, chunks of ice floating among slivers of fresh fruit. Beside them sat four shot glasses filled to the brim with clear tequila, lime wedges balanced carefully on the rims.

"You ordered already?" Scarlet asked, settling into the booth next to Jerry, their shoulders nearly touching in the small space.

Mac distributed glasses around the table. "First round of liquid courage, coming right up."

"Nice," Cami grabbed her margarita. "I was gonna need at least two drinks before I got up there anyway."

Jerry leaned closer to Scarlet. "Sorry about the head start. Mac was getting antsy."

"Yeah, they almost dragged me into hosting this thing," Mac said, passing shot glasses around. "Which I would've killed at, by the way."

"But Maude wasn't having it?" Cami guessed.

"Nope. Said something about 'maintaining the delicate ambiance' or whatever."

Scarlet sipped her margarita. "So that's why you ordered tequila? Drowning your disappointment?"

"More like preparing for disaster," Jerry said with a half-smile. "Some of us need it more than others."

"Wait," Scarlet turned to him, eyebrows raised. "You're not telling me Mr. Army Strong is scared of a little karaoke?"

"Petrified," Jerry admitted with a laugh. "Give me a combat zone over a microphone any day."

"Then why'd you come?" she asked, genuinely curious.

Jerry's eyes met hers. "Mac said it'd be fun." He shrugged, voice softening. "And it seemed like a good way to spend the night."

The way he looked at her made it clear: *with you.*

"Alright, enough flirting," Mac interrupted, raising his shot glass. "A toast!"

"To new friends," Cami joined in.

"And unexpected adventures," Mac finished.

"And totally embarrassing ourselves," Cami added with a wink.

They clinked glasses and threw back their shots, the tequila burning a warm path down Scarlet's throat. When she looked up, Jerry was still watching her, something new and unguarded in his eyes.

On stage, Maude had taken command of the mic, resplendent in an over-the-top bedazzled blazer that caught every beam of light in the room. She'd transformed from elegant cruise host to her version of a rock star, complete with dramatic hand gestures and an exaggerated swagger.

"Welcome, darlings, to our Mingle at Sea karaoke extravaganza!" Maude's voice carried through the room. "Remember, what happens on the Elysian Serenade stays on the Elysian Serenade ... unless someone catches it on Instagram, in which case, make sure you tag us!"

"She's something else," Jerry murmured, a hint of amusement in his voice.

"So," Scarlet asked, turning toward Jerry, "what's your go-to karaoke song? Everyone has one, even if they deny it."

"I plead the Fifth," he replied, but his eyes crinkled at the corners, inviting her to press further.

"Oh no, that's not how this works," she insisted, leaning slightly closer. "Mac, help me out here."

"Let it Go," Mac announced without a hint of apology. "From Frozen. It's Marty's favorite song."

Jerry groaned, covering his face with his hand. "Jesus, Mac. Really?" He shot his friend a look that promised retribution later.

She pictured Jerry belting out "Let It Go," the same Jerry who was always so serious and controlled with his perfect posture and measured words. The image struck Scarlet as absurdly endearing. A laugh escaped her, genuine and uninhibited. This wasn't the Staff Sergeant who calculated risk and maintained discipline; this was a father who sang Disney princess songs to make his son happy. The contradiction was utterly delightful.

"Marty lights up whenever he hears that song," Jerry admitted reluctantly, torn between mortification and the instinctive pride that always surfaced when he talked about his sons. "Bounces in his seat, bobs his head. Gets so excited he can barely contain himself at Elsa's high notes."

"And Jerry knows every word by heart," Mac added with a mischievous grin. "Complete with hand gestures. The boys and I have a whole rating system for his performances."

"I'm going to kill you in your sleep," Jerry muttered through a forced smile.

Scarlet watched the interplay, finding herself charmed by Jerry's embarrassment. Even the rigid military man had cracks in his armor. Beautiful, human cracks that let warmth shine through. Most men would treat childcare like a chore, but Jerry wore fatherhood like a second skin. Even in his mortification, pride for his son radiated through. The song itself didn't matter. What mattered was that he cared enough to make it special every time.

As if on cue, Maude's voice rang out over the speakers. "Next up, we have ... Jerry! Come on up, Soldier Boy!"

Jerry's head snapped toward Mac, who was failing miserably at looking innocent. "You didn't."

"I absolutely did," Mac confirmed, raising his glass in salute. "Consider it payback for the time you signed me up for that talent show in Kandahar."

"That was four years ago!" Jerry protested, but Maude was already scanning the crowd.

"Jerry? Where's my Jerry? Don't be shy, darling!"

Scarlet felt a moment of sympathy for Jerry, whose face had gone slightly pale. "You don't have to."

"No backing out now," Mac interrupted, nudging Jerry's shoulder. "The princess awaits."

Jerry shot Scarlet a look that was equal parts resignation and determination, then grabbed his margarita and downed the rest in one swift motion. "If I don't make it back, tell my boys I died with dignity."

"Not likely," Cami quipped, but there was a warmth in her voice.

Jerry squared his shoulders and made his way to the stage, accepting the microphone from Maude with a stiff nod that made Scarlet suspect he was drawing on every ounce of military discipline to keep from bolting.

The unmistakable piano intro of the snow queen's anthem filled the room, triggering excited murmurs throughout the crowd. Jerry stood paralyzed, his gaze finding their table, finding her, before the lyrics prompt appeared on screen.

What happened next defied all expectations.

Jerry dismissed the screen entirely, launching into the song with the practiced ease of someone who'd performed it a thousand bedtimes. His singing was spectacularly dreadful, consistently off-key and breaking hilariously on the high notes. But what he lacked in musical talent, he compensated for with extraordinary conviction.

Scarlet watched, entranced and amused. The incongruity was perfect: a military man who probably could bounce quarters off his bed transforming into an ice-empowered royal before a roomful of increasingly delighted singles.

The juxtaposition was delicious: the man who had seriously discussed tactical formations over breakfast was now dramatically flinging his arms wide, proclaiming his freedom with theatrical hand gestures. With each verse, his movements became less self-conscious, his expressions more animated.

Jerry was doing more than singing. He was performing, complete with power stances and dramatic finger pointing that had the entire room howling with delight.

As the chorus rang out, Scarlet's amusement gave way to something deeper.

It wasn't just the performance; it was the intention behind it.

Jerry wasn't just entertaining the room; he was showing, without realizing it, exactly who he was as a father.

The kind who would willingly become ridiculous, repeatedly, just to earn his child's smile.

The kind who had committed every word of a princess anthem to memory because someone small he loved requested it night after night.

The kind who, despite his careful control in every other arena, knew exactly when letting go mattered most.

As he delivered the final dismissive line with a dramatic hair-flip gesture so utterly contradictory to the reserved man she'd come to know, Scarlet couldn't contain her delighted laughter.

The audience exploded with cheers as Jerry executed an exaggerated, theatrical bow before practically racing back to their table.

"That," Cami declared as he slid back into the booth, face flushed and eyes bright, "was the best thing I've seen all cruise."

"I hate you," Jerry told Mac, but there was no heat in it.

"You crushed it," Mac replied, offering a high five that Jerry reluctantly returned.

Scarlet turned to Jerry, aware that she was grinning like an idiot but unable to stop. "That was …"

"Humiliating?" Jerry suggested.

"Amazing," she corrected, still smiling. "I didn't know you had that in you."

Something shifted in Jerry's expression, a quiet vulnerability beneath the post-performance adrenaline. "There's a lot you don't know about me yet."

"Yet?" she asked quietly. The word hung between them, filled with possibility.

Jerry's lips quirked into a small smile, as if he held other secrets he might share eventually. But not tonight.

From across the room, Scarlet became aware of someone watching them. At the bar sat Stacy, the brunette who'd been hovering around Jerry since the first mingle event. Her gaze was fixed unmistakably on their table. More specifically, on Jerry. Her expression was a carefully composed mix of interest and calculation that Scarlet recognized all too well.

Cami followed Scarlet's gaze and subtly nudged her under the table. "Don't look now, but Stacy is giving you the death stare."

"I noticed," Scarlet muttered, taking another sip of her drink. "She's been watching Jerry since we walked in."

"Give me two minutes," Cami said, sliding out of the booth with determined grace. "Need to use the ladies' room."

Scarlet raised an eyebrow. "The bathroom's the other direction."

Cami just winked and disappeared into the crowd, making a beeline toward Stacy.

Mac leaned forward. "My turn!" he announced, snatching the songbook. "Prepare to be blown away, amateurs."

As Mac discussed song options with Jerry, Scarlet kept one eye on Cami, who was now engaged in what appeared to be a tense but polite conversation with Stacy. Whatever Cami said must have been effective. Stacy downed her drink thirty seconds later, gathered her purse, and left without a backward glance.

Cami returned, sliding back into the booth with a self-satisfied smile.

"What did you do?" Scarlet whispered.

"Just a little girl chat," Cami replied innocently. "Nothing major."

Before Scarlet could press further, Mac launched into an absolutely over-the-top rendition of "Sweet Caroline," complete with dramatic air guitar and hip thrusts that had the entire lounge howling with laughter. Jerry's shoulders shook with genuine mirth beside her, his arm brushing against hers in the cramped booth.

Three songs and two drinks later, Cami checked her phone and abruptly stood. "Mac, didn't you say you wanted to check out that late-night jazz thing in the Celestial View?"

"Not really, I was having a good time here." Mac blinked in confusion but then jolted in his seat almost as if something, or someone, had kicked him in his shin under the table. "Oh!" Mac's face lit with sudden understanding. "Right. That thing. At that place. We should definitely go now."

Jerry frowned. "I thought you wanted to sing—"

"Next time," Mac cut him off, already sliding out of the booth. "You two stay, though. Have fun. Don't wait up."

Cami leaned down to hug Scarlet, whispering in her ear, "You can thank me later."

And just like that, they were gone, leaving Scarlet and Jerry alone at the table that suddenly felt much more intimate.

"That wasn't subtle," Jerry said, the corner of his mouth quirking up.

"Cami doesn't do subtle," Scarlet replied, feeling warmth creep up her neck.

They sat in an easy hush, watching a young couple stumble through "Islands in the Stream." Jerry's shoulder pressed lightly against hers, steady and sure.

"So," he murmured, almost blending into the music, "what's your karaoke song?"

Scarlet smiled without looking at him. "You've covered it for both of us tonight."

He chuckled, low and rough. "Thanks for not recording it. Some things are better left at sea."

"Some things," she agreed. Their gazes caught and held, the pull between them undeniable now.

Under the table, his hand found hers, slow and certain. Fingers slid together like pieces of something half-remembered.

Around them, the room blurred into noise. A group of students howled through "Don't Stop Believin'," off-key and fearless. Jerry grimaced, thumb brushing lazy circles against her skin.

"Another drink?" he asked.

She nodded, too wrapped up in the warmth blooming between them to find words.

He flagged a server, never letting go.

Their joined hands stayed hidden, secret and unhurried, as the night spun on around them. Songs rose and fell, laughter spilled, the world shrank to the slow weight of his thigh against hers, the cedar-salt scent of him clinging to the humid air.

When Scarlet shifted, Jerry didn't pull back. His eyes stayed on her longer than the moment needed, a silent tether.

The lights dimmed for a slow song and his arm drifted up behind her on the booth's backrest. He wasn't touching her yet, but he was close enough that she could feel the invitation in the air between them.

Without thinking, she leaned in. Not far. Just enough.

When Maude called for the final round of performances, Scarlet blinked, disoriented. Throughout the night she hadn't once thought of work, or time, or fear.

Only this. Only him.

# Twelve

Scarlet's hands were already in the air, body swaying to the reggae beat that pulsed through Da Party Bus when she spotted Jerry and Mac approaching. Her second rum punch had chased away any lingering self-consciousness, leaving behind a warm, fizzy feeling that had her whistling and waving wildly when she caught Jerry's eye.

"They're here!" she shouted to Cami over the music, already feeling lighter than she had in years. The rum punch was deceptively strong, tasting more of fruit than alcohol, but delivering a Caribbean kick that had melted her usual reserve within minutes of boarding.

Captain Coconut bounded down to greet the newcomers. Scarlet watched through the open windows as the guide draped plastic leis around their necks and pressed drinks into their hands, his sun-bleached dreadlocks swaying and his massive gold medallion bouncing against his tie-dyed tank top.

When Jerry slid into the seat beside her, Scarlet didn't hesitate. She grabbed his face and planted a rum-flavored kiss on his cheek, close enough to the corner of his mouth to feel the slight intake of his breath.

"You're late!" she shouted over the music, her fingertips lingering against his jaw. "We're already on drink number two!"

"Guess I'd better catch up," he replied, tipping back his cup.

Her gaze traced the line of his neck as he swallowed, then drifted to his shoulders, which held no tension, no guarded stance.

He looked … at ease.

And when he smiled, it wasn't the polite kind. It was open, genuine. It caught her off guard in the best way.

The bus lurched into motion with a horn playing the first notes of "Hot Hot Hot." Captain Coconut cranked the music impossibly louder as they pulled away from the pier, passing out more drinks with a flourish.

"Road drinks, beautiful people!" he proclaimed, refilling Scarlet's cup with significantly more rum than mixer.

Wind rushed through the open windows, whipping Scarlet's hair across her face and Jerry's. She laughed as he sputtered, her head tipping back with a joy that felt unfamiliar but perfect. Across the aisle, she spotted Stacy grinding playfully against a tall guy in board shorts. Their eyes met briefly, and Stacy raised her cup in a friendly toast before turning her full attention back to her new companion.

*Problem solved*, Scarlet thought with a mental shrug, the usual calculating part of her brain quieted by sun and rum.

Twenty minutes and two more potent rum punches later, Captain Coconut pulled the bus over at a roadside shack painted in Jamaican flag colors.

"Quick rum restock, my friends!" he announced, jumping off the bus. "Not that we running low, but Captain Coconut never lets the party run dry!"

With their guide momentarily absent, the party somehow intensified. Someone started a limbo competition using a beach towel as the bar, while others drummed on the bus seats. The coolers at the back were still well-stocked, and Cami was already mixing fresh drinks for anyone who held out an empty cup.

Scarlet felt a fierce current crackle to life inside her, snapping the cords of caution she normally held tight.

Without stopping to weigh it, she grabbed Jerry and yanked him upright.

"Dance with me!" she demanded, placing his hands on her hips and beginning to sway to the reggaeton beat.

Scarlet let her body move however it wanted, without thinking about how she looked or who might be watching. She spun, feeling her hair whip around like a flame, feeling Jerry's eyes follow the movement.

"You're different today," he said into her ear, his breath warm against her skin.

"So are you," she responded, her eyes catching his. "I like it."

Captain Coconut returned with a crate of additional bottles, setting off a fresh round of cheers. "Next stop—Orient Beach! Where the only rule is there are no rules!"

Scarlet perched comfortably in Jerry's lap, feeding him mango from the stash Cami had triumphantly produced.

Her fingers gleamed with juice, and she licked them clean with the kind of casual ease that turned electric under his steady gaze.

Thanks to Captain Coconut's enthusiastic top-ups, the rum was no longer disguised beneath fruit juice, turning their drinks into something that was essentially rum with a hint of color. But Scarlet couldn't remember the last time she'd felt this light, this present, this alive.

Orient Beach appeared around a bend like a postcard manifested into reality. The sand was blinding white, the water a gradient of turquoise that seemed impossible in its perfection. Palm trees swayed in the breeze, casting dappled shadows on the shoreline that danced with each gust of wind.

The group tumbled out of the bus in a cheerful tangle. While Captain Coconut led most of them to a spot on the main beach, Cami caught Scarlet's eye and nodded toward a more secluded area beneath a cluster of palm trees. Scarlet tugged Jerry's hand, and the four of them broke away from the main group.

They claimed a perfect patch of sand with just the right balance of sun and shade. Jerry spread out towels while Cami produced a portable speaker from her bag, instantly creating their own private sound bubble. Mac was already stripping down to his swim trunks, spinning Cami around in an impromptu dance that nearly sent them both tumbling.

Scarlet sat cross-legged on a towel, enjoying the way the sun warmed her shoulders as she slipped off her cover-up to reveal her emerald bikini. The fabric felt suddenly confining against her skin, too structured for this day of abandon. She watched Cami watching Mac, saw something mischievous flicker in her friend's eyes.

Without warning, Cami hooked her thumbs into her bikini bottoms and dropped them right there on the beach.

"Last one in the water buys drinks tonight!" she shouted, looking directly at Mac as she untied her bikini top while already sprinting toward the waves. The top fell abandoned on the sand as she ran.

Scarlet's mouth dropped open in shock and delight. Cami was always bold and confident, but in all their years of friendship, she'd never seen her do something quite this uninhibited.

Mac's eyes bulged comically. "Challenge accepted!" He lunged after her, attempting to run and remove his swim trunks at the same time. The coordination challenge proved impossible, ending with him face-planting spectacularly into the sand when his feet tangled in the fabric.

"Ten out of ten on the dismount!" Jerry called out, doubled over with laughter.

Mac recovered quickly, kicking free of his trunks and charging naked into the water with a rebel yell that turned heads all down the beach.

Scarlet laughed harder than she had in years, eyes stinging with tears.

But the laughter hit a wall as Jerry, still grinning, casually hooked his thumbs into his swim trunks and dropped them in one smooth motion, stepping free.

The sun caught on his skin, turning him golden as he ran toward the waves without hesitation, letting out a whoop of joy. The sight of such pure freedom, such complete absence of self-consciousness, shifted something inside Scarlet. He dove under a wave and emerged shaking water from his hair like a happy retriever.

Scarlet stood, suddenly certain. She turned her back to the water, to the three people who had somehow become the closest thing to real friends she'd had in years. Her fingers reached behind her back, untying her bikini top with practiced ease. She let it fall to the sand, feeling the sun warm her bare skin.

For a brief moment, she hesitated. The professional, polished Scarlet who maintained immaculate control and never let a hair fall out of place whispered caution. But that voice was drowned out by the reggae beat, the laughter from the water, and something deeper. A hunger to exist without constraints, even if just for a day.

With deliberate grace, she bent forward and slid her bikini bottoms down her legs. As she straightened, she flipped her hair back, feeling the strands capture the sunlight. She gathered the unruly red mass into a high ponytail with the hair tie from her wrist, a small concession to control in this moment of abandon.

When she turned toward the water, Jerry was watching her.

He stood waist-deep in the crystal sea, motionless save for the rhythm of his breath.

Their eyes met, and Scarlet smiled with genuine openness, free of the filters she usually wore.

She began jogging toward the water, feeling a strange combination of vulnerability and power in her nakedness. When she reached Jerry, she didn't slow down. Instead, she launched herself at him, wrapping her arms around his neck and legs around his waist with enough momentum to send them both underwater.

They burst upward together, coughing and laughing as the sea slid off their skin.

His smile was all brightness, with water dripping from his lashes and not a trace of pretense.

For all the drink and chaos, the moment snapped into undeniably real focus.

He kissed her, and she didn't pause to edit or interpret.

She moved with him, a seamless match of intent and need.

His mouth tasted of ocean and liquor, edged with promise.

As they met, skin against skin beneath the waves, she surrendered to the closeness without hesitation.

When they broke apart, she felt wonderfully disoriented, like waking up in a strange place but knowing you're exactly where you need to be.

"What was that for?" she whispered, hands still linked behind his neck.

"Being you," he answered simply. "Being here."

His unvarnished truth sank in like a balm, softening corners she hadn't realized were tense.

No measuring. No masks. Just this. Real and steady.

Before she could respond, Mac's voice shattered the moment. "Hey, Red! Jerry! Get a room already!" He sent a splash their way that caught Scarlet directly in the face.

Jerry retaliated with a massive wave in Mac's direction, and suddenly they were engaged in a chaotic water battle. Scarlet shrieked as cold water crashed over her head, launching her own counterattack on Cami.

She couldn't remember the last time she'd simply played without purpose or outcome. Even her occasional tennis matches were about networking or fitness goals. This was pure, purposeless joy, and it felt revolutionary.

"Wait, wait!" Mac shouted suddenly. "I have an idea. Water jousting!"

"What are you talking about?" Cami asked, already grinning.

"I'll get on your shoulders," Mac declared, moving toward her.

Cami burst out laughing. "You're kidding, right?"

"Dead serious," Mac said. "Me and you against Jerry and Red."

A competitive fire ignited in Scarlet's belly. She'd always been driven to win, even if she disguised it beneath professional courtesy. She looked at Jerry, the challenge clear in her eyes. "You game?"

"Oh, I'm going to destroy them," she said, wading closer.

Jerry ducked underwater, positioning himself between her legs. Scarlet felt his shoulders beneath her thighs as he stood, lifting her clear of the water. A startled squeal escaped her, something she'd never have permitted herself a week ago.

"Oh my God!" she yelped, barely staying upright as Jerry's short hair grazed over the most sensitive, yet criminally neglected parts of her. Five years. It had been over five years since anyone had been this close, unless she counted her gynecologist and lonely nights with her vibrator. Suddenly her body remembered exactly what she'd been missing and she was already halfway to losing her mind. She shifted higher, half for balance, half because *holy hell,* she might actually combust if she didn't. "This is insane!"

Across from them, Cami was trying to balance Mac on her shoulders, an absurd reversal given their height difference. Mac flailed wildly, nearly toppling sideways before somehow finding equilibrium.

Scarlet doubled over with laughter, her stomach sore from it. The image of four naked adults playing chicken in tropical waters was pure comedy gold.

Somewhere in another universe, the Scarlet Bellari who never took a sick day was gasping in disbelief.

Here, she was bare-skinned, balanced atop Jerry's shoulders, and ready for war.

"Tremble before us!" Mac shouted, pointing dramatically. "The water warriors have arrived!"

"Shut up and hold on, short stack," Cami growled, gripping his ankles. "Or I'm dunking you."

Scarlet leaned into the chaos, thighs firm around Jerry, hands braced to shove Mac.

It should've felt ridiculous ... and yet, here, it was electric.

"You're going down, Red!" Mac shouted, grabbing for her arms.

"In your dreams, pipsqueak!" she shot back, channeling her inner Cami as she shoved hard against Mac's chest.

Mac windmilled his arms dramatically, toppling with Cami in a spectacular splash.

"Victory!" Scarlet crowed, arms raised triumphantly. Power surged through her as she sat naked under the Caribbean sun, perched atop Jerry's shoulders, victorious and free. The professional restraint she wore like armor had been stripped away with her bikini, revealing something wilder and more alive beneath.

"Oh no, we're going down too!" Jerry called out unexpectedly. He twisted and fell backward, sending them both crashing into the water.

Scarlet came up sputtering, hair plastered to her face. "Traitor!" she accused, launching herself at him.

Jerry caught her easily, spinning her around in the water. "Couldn't let you get too cocky," he murmured against her ear, the vibration of his voice sending shivers down her spine despite the warm water.

The day dissolved into water fights, swimming races, and ridiculous challenges, each more frivolous than the last. Captain Coconut appeared with floating cooler of rum that Scarlet would have described as irresponsibly strong if she'd been in any state to make responsible judgments. They passed plastic cups back and forth, the alcohol and sun creating a bubble where deadlines and performance reviews couldn't reach her.

When they finally decided to return to shore, Mac made a startling discovery.

"Guys?" he called out, scanning the beach with increasing panic. "Where are my shorts?"

Despite a thorough search, Mac's swim trunks were nowhere to be found.

"Well, this is awkward," Mac said, hands on his hips, making no attempt to cover himself.

Cami rolled her eyes. "Oh, for God's sake." She rummaged through her bag and pulled out her bikini bottoms. "Here. These should fit your tiny ass."

"My ass is perfectly proportional to my body, thank you very much," Mac protested, but took the offered bikini bottoms.

"My cover-up is long enough," Cami shrugged, wrapping herself in a flowing beach dress. "Just don't bend over too much on the bus."

She bit her knuckle to keep from howling as Mac wriggled into the teal bikini bottoms.

The spandex clung to him like cheap drag, squeezing his anatomy as if the fabric had given up halfway through the job, with none of the charm.

"I think you've started a new fashion trend," she managed through her giggles, slipping back into her own bikini with a twinge of regret. The freedom of bare skin had felt revelatory, like discovering a version of herself that existed outside client meetings and careful planning.

"I make these look good," Mac insisted, doing an exaggerated catwalk strut. "I should've been wearing women's swimwear all along."

The rum flowed with even greater abandon on the return journey. Scarlet curled against Jerry's side, her head resting in the crook of his neck. Her ponytail had mostly escaped its confines, damp tendrils clinging to her neck and shoulders. Normally, she would have been irritated by the dishevelment, but today she couldn't find it in herself to care.

Mac held court across the aisle, narrating increasingly outrageous military stories. He'd wrapped a beach towel around his waist in a token gesture toward modesty over Cami's borrowed bikini bottoms.

"So there we were, surrounded by camels," he proclaimed, gesturing so wildly he sloshed rum punch onto his chest, "and the biggest one, I swear he was the size of a Humvee, locks eyes with the colonel and just ..." Mac paused dramatically, "... PFFT! Right in his face! Full camel spit! Like a Super Soaker filled with camel loogies!"

The bus erupted in laughter. Scarlet glanced at Jerry, who was shaking his head with a wry smile.

"You're completely full of shit," he called out.

"I swear on the sacred stripper pole!" Mac declared, swaying to his feet and grabbing the center pole. "Hey, Captain! This thing is sturdy, right?"

The glint in Mac's eye looked familiar to Scarlet. It was the same spark Cami got right before launching into something spectacularly unwise.

Normally, Scarlet played the role of buffer, voice of reason, keeper of calm.

Today, she was cheering it on.

"Do it!" she called out, shocking herself with her enthusiasm for potential disaster.

Captain Coconut glanced back from the driver's seat. "Built to withstand professionals, my friend, but I wouldn't recommend ..."

But Mac was already attempting to swing around the pole. "Ladies and gentlemen, for your viewing pleasure ... Magic Mac: The Uncensored Edition!"

Mac's pole dance was a beautiful disaster.

Scarlet watched, half-horrified, half-hysterical, as he attacked the pole with reckless glee and zero coordination.

A toddler on caffeine might've had more control.

The flip sent his towel flying while the bikini bottoms barely managed to stay put.

Scarlet caught a glimpse she would've paid to unsee.

She collapsed into Jerry, laughing so hard she couldn't breathe, her brain desperately trying to erase what her eyes had just endured.

"Work it, Mac!" someone shouted from the back.

"The teal really brings out your eyes!" called another.

Mac took a dramatic bow as he finished his routine. "And that, ladies and gentlemen, is how you rock beachwear."

He staggered back toward his seat. Instead of sitting down, however, he paused in front of Cami, who was wiping tears of laughter from her eyes.

Without warning, Mac grabbed her face in both hands and planted a kiss directly on her lips. The bus erupted in wolf whistles and applause.

Scarlet's eyebrows shot up. She exchanged a look with Jerry, silently communicating mutual surprise. When Mac finally pulled away, Cami looked momentarily stunned before a slow, wicked smile spread across her face.

"I'd give the dance a three," she said, voice carrying over the music, "but the kiss was at least an eight."

"I'll take it!" Mac crowed, flopping down beside her.

Captain Coconut stood at the front of the bus as they pulled to a stop. "Beautiful people! I hope you enjoyed the real St. Maarten experience! Remember, what happens on Da Party Bus ..."

"Stays on Instagram forever!" someone called out.

When they stumbled off the bus, Maude pulled Scarlet into a gentle hug, surrounding her with the comforting aroma of vanilla mixed with ocean breeze.

"I've guided many voyages, my dear," Maude whispered in her ear, "but nothing delights me more than watching someone finally discover their own golden shores."

The words settled into Scarlet's heart with unexpected profundity, whether despite or because of her rum-soaked state. She started to ask what Maude meant, but the older woman was already moving on to welcome other passengers.

Scarlet turned to look for Jerry, catching sight of him laughing as Mac nearly tackled him from behind. The scene radiated pure, unfiltered joy. There was Mac, still in his borrowed teal bikini bottoms, and Jerry pushing him away with mock disgust, both of them laughing like they had no history of pain between them.

"Come on," Cami said, linking arms with Scarlet. "Let's get back before security decides we need a breathalyzer test."

They started up the gangway together, heads close as they whispered.

"So," Cami murmured, "you and Army Boy, huh? Looking pretty cozy."

"Shut up," Scarlet replied without heat. "Also, what was that kiss with Mac all about?"

Cami's smile was enigmatic. "Who knows? The sun, the rum, the ridiculous bikini bottoms. It was a moment."

At the top of the gangway, Scarlet paused and glanced back.

Jerry stood below, eyes locked on her.

When their gazes met, a quiet, steady, unmistakable current passed between them.

She smiled, wide and open, like shedding one more layer of hesitation.

# Thirteen

"I still can't believe you packed this," Cami said, zipping Scarlet into the scarlet red satin gown. "It's like you knew you'd need something to knock some soldier boy off his feet."

Scarlet smoothed her hands down the structured corset bodice, appreciating how the beaded embellishments caught the light. "Every cruise has a formal night. And besides, this is actually the least stuffy of my formal dresses. Everything else screams 'tax season gala' or 'client appreciation dinner.'"

Last year, Jade had insisted during a rare shopping trip that Scarlet needed at least one dress that wasn't "aggressively professional." The strapless design with its subtle beading and delicate center cutout had been her impulse buy. Now, as Scarlet felt the cool satin against her skin, she was grateful for the indulgence.

She studied her reflection in the mirror as heat coursed through her, remembering the beach earlier today. Jerry lifting her out of the water, the surprisingly soft hair at the nape of his neck grazing her sensitive lips as her thighs had momentarily wrapped around his shoulders. The memory sent a pleasant shiver down her spine. If tonight presented another opportunity for closeness ... well, she was more than ready to jump his bones.

"Well, it's working," Cami said, stepping back to admire her handiwork. Her own royal blue dress with its square neckline and trumpet hem created a striking contrast to Scarlet's more dramatic silhouette, the deep blue complementing her warm complexion and elegantly styled braids. "Between my architectural masterpiece and your Jessica Rabbit situation, we're going to stop traffic."

"Jessica Rabbit?" Scarlet laughed, smoothing a stray red curl that had escaped her carefully arranged waves. "Great, so Jerry's going to have the full Roger Rabbit reaction: eyes bulging, tongue rolling out, steam coming out of his ears."

"You say that like it's a bad thing," Cami replied, adjusting one of her gold earrings.

Scarlet turned back to the mirror, applying a final coat of her favorite MAC Russian Red lipstick. The color wasn't quite an exact match to her dress, but the blue undertones made her teeth look whiter and complemented the light flush the St. Maarten excursion had left across her cheekbones and shoulders. She'd kept her eye makeup deceptively simple, using just enough liquid liner to elongate her eyes and a precisely blended neutral shadow to create depth.

"You think Jerry will like it?" she asked, then immediately regretted the question. It sounded juvenile, desperate for approval.

But Cami just smiled knowingly. "Honey, that man has been looking at you like you hung the moon since day one. In this?" She gestured to the dress with its high slit and liquid satin flow. "He's not going to know what hit him."

The ship rocked gently as Scarlet made her final preparations. Chanel perfume at pulse points, a simple diamond pendant at her throat, and a quick spritz of finishing spray to lock her waves in place despite the humid Caribbean air. She couldn't remember the last time she'd put this much effort into her appearance for a man. Maybe never. Her usual dates were scheduled around business meetings and networking events, where looking polished was about projecting competence, not inviting desire.

But tonight was different. She wanted Jerry to see her. Really see her.

"Shall we?" Cami asked, gathering her small clutch.

The corridor was filled with passengers in formal attire, a parade of tuxedos and gowns gliding toward the evening's festivities. An elderly couple posed by a decorative floral arrangement while their companion snapped photos. Nearby, a young couple held hands, stealing glances at each other as they navigated the narrow hallway. The ship's captain made his rounds in full ceremonial dress uniform, his crisp white tuxedo adorned with gold braid epaulets and a row of gleaming medals, smiling and nodding politely to passengers.

On the way to the Topaz Lounge, Scarlet scanned the faces around them, hoping to spot the one she couldn't stop thinking about.

The lounge was transformed for the evening. Soft lighting from crystal chandeliers cast a golden glow over everything, while waitstaff in crisp uniforms circulated with trays of champagne. Maude held court near the center of the room, resplendent in a flowing burgundy maxi dress with an intricate paisley pattern, her silver-streaked hair adorned with tiny wooden beads woven into loose braids.

"Well, don't you two look ready to cause trouble," Maude greeted them, her eyes twinkling as she took in their dresses. "The sea spirits will be restless tonight, I think."

Scarlet accepted a glass of champagne from a passing server, the bubbles tickling her nose as she took a sip. "Is that a good thing or a bad thing?"

"That depends entirely on what you're looking for," Maude replied with an enigmatic smile. "Sometimes a little restlessness leads us exactly where we need to be."

Scarlet was about to ask what she meant when she spotted Mac entering the lounge alone. He cut a surprisingly elegant figure in his light beige linen suit, the crisp white shirt unbuttoned at the collar in deliberate, casual contrast to the formal atmosphere. But it was the absence beside him that caught her attention like a hook.

No Jerry.

Mac approached their small group, greeting them with his usual easy charm, though Scarlet detected something strained behind his smile.

"Ladies, you all look incredible," he said, raising his champagne in a small toast. His eyes lingered appreciatively on Cami's blue dress before sweeping back to include them all. "Seriously, I'm going to have to up my game if I want to keep up."

"Where's Jerry?" Scarlet asked, unable to disguise the concern in her voice.

A flash of something that might have been guardedness crossed Mac's features before he defaulted to his easy grin. "He's ... he's just ... everything today was a little much for him. You know, the crowds, the noise." He gestured vaguely with his champagne glass. "Sometimes he needs to decompress."

It was plausible enough. The beach excursion had been wild, fueled by rum and sunshine and the kind of reckless abandon that left everyone drained. But something in Mac's careful tone told Scarlet there was more to it. On the beach, Jerry had seemed fine. Actually, more than fine. He'd looked at her with a warmth that had nothing to do with the Caribbean sun.

"Is he okay?" she pressed, setting down her champagne flute with deliberate care.

"Yeah, he's fine," Mac said, a touch too quickly. "Just not big on crowds sometimes. Military thing, you know?"

Scarlet didn't know, not really. But she recognized a protective dodge when she heard one. Mac was covering for Jerry, offering just enough explanation to satisfy politeness without revealing whatever was really going on.

The Topaz Lounge suddenly felt vast and empty despite the crowd. Without Jerry's steady presence beside her, nothing held any appeal: not the string quartet tuning up in the corner, not the elegant couples swaying to imagined music, not the champagne bubbles rising in perfect crystal flutes. The space that had seemed so magical moments ago now felt hollow, like a beautifully decorated stage without its lead actor.

"I need to go check on him," she said abruptly.

As she turned to leave, Mac caught her arm, his expression unusually serious. "Scarlet, wait." His voice dropped lower, the casual charm replaced by genuine concern. "Look, he's ... he just needs a little space right now. To reset. It's not you, I promise. Sometimes he just needs to..." He paused, seeming to search for the right words. "Sometimes he needs to remember where he is. Do you understand?"

Something in his tone made her realize there was much more beneath the surface than she knew. This wasn't just about Jerry needing alone time or avoiding social obligations.

"I understand," she said, though she wasn't sure she did, not completely.

Cami raised an eyebrow. "You sure you don't want to stay?"

Scarlet nodded, already backing away. "I'm sure. Don't wait up."

She moved through the crowds of formally dressed passengers, her mind racing. Halfway to Jerry's cabin, she slowed her steps, doubt creeping in. What was she doing? Mac had practically asked her to give Jerry space. Maybe Jerry genuinely wanted to be alone. Maybe her checking on him would only make things worse.

She stopped in the middle of the corridor, then began to pace back and forth, heels clicking softly on the carpeted floor. A few passing couples gave her curious glances, but she barely noticed them, lost in thought. She didn't want to push herself into Jerry's space if he truly needed solitude. But something in her gut told her that what he actually needed wasn't isolation, but a different kind of connection. Something quieter than what came with formal nights and social expectations.

She halted mid-stride, suddenly certain of her next move. She turned around, heading back toward her own cabin.

Inside, she quickly shed the elegant red gown, leaving it sprawled across her bed. She could hang it up later, assuming she even came back tonight. She plucked the red tankini hanging beside the bathroom door, still slightly damp from their paddleboarding adventure. The tropical print with its teal leaves and white flowers seemed to hold the memory of their earlier connection: easy, natural, without pretense.

She slipped it on, then wrapped herself in the standard-issue white terry robe provided by the cruise line.

As she made her way to Jerry's cabin, her heartbeat quickened. This was either going to be brilliantly intuitive or embarrassingly presumptuous. Either way, she couldn't turn back now.

She knocked firmly, holding her breath.

"No room service tonight, thanks," Jerry's voice called from inside, rough around the edges. "Just forgot to put up the sign."

"It's me," she replied.

There was a pause, then the sound of movement inside. When the door opened, the sight of him hit her like a physical force. He stood in partially undone formal wear: blue and white gingham shirt unbuttoned halfway down his chest, black tie hanging loosened around his neck, one polished dress shoe on and one off. His military-short hair was slightly mussed, as if he'd been running his hands through it.

He looked ... undone. And somehow more appealing for it.

"Mac said you weren't feeling well," she said carefully, taking in the details without judgment. His eyes were clear but shadowed, holding something she couldn't quite name.

"I'm just ..." he started, then stopped.

"Not feeling the formal night vibe?" she supplied, offering him an easy out. "Me neither, as it turns out."

His features softened with unmistakable relief, and the tension she'd been holding quietly slipped away. She hadn't imagined it.

"I was thinking the hot tubs on the aft deck are usually empty during formal night. Everyone's too busy showing off their fancy clothes." She tilted her head. "Care to join me for something a little less … formal?"

The invitation hung between them, and she watched as something tight in his expression began to unravel. Not gratitude, exactly, but recognition. He saw what she was offering: escape rather than rescue, partnership rather than pity.

"Give me two minutes," he said.

He invited her in while he changed, and Scarlet tried not to stare at the disheveled bed or the abandoned dress shoe lying haphazardly on the carpet. She was seeing behind the facade now, past the military precision and quiet control Jerry presented to the world.

Her eyes landed on a framed photograph on the nightstand, and she moved toward it without thinking. The image showed two young boys on a sidewalk, captured from behind as one pushed the other's wheelchair. A blue backpack looked enormous on the small boy's frame. Something about the scene caught at her heart, and it wasn't just the obvious care between the brothers. It was the quiet ordinariness of the moment. This wasn't a posed holiday photo or a milestone celebration. It was just life, simple and true.

She picked it up carefully, studying the details. Jerry's sons. She connected the dots, remembering the green wheelchair tattooed on his arm. The boys he'd mentioned but rarely elaborated on. The pieces of his heart he carried with him even on a singles cruise.

The bathroom door opened, and Scarlet gently replaced the frame, turning to find Jerry in swim trunks and a white robe identical to hers. His eyes flicked to the photo, then back to her face, a question in them that he didn't voice.

"Ready?" she asked, standing and adjusting her robe.

"Yeah," he said.

The ship corridors felt different now. Around them, elegantly dressed passengers headed to dinner, a reminder of the formal world they were momentarily stepping away from. Jerry walked beside her, close but not touching, as they made their way to the aft deck.

The night air was warm and salt-tinged, the sky above them a blanket of stars. The hot tubs steamed invitingly, empty just as she'd predicted.

"Why don't you get comfortable?" she suggested. "I'll grab us something to drink."

Scarlet approached the poolside bar and scanned the laminated menu. Champagne felt too formal, beer too casual, and wine wouldn't taste right in the hot tub. But the frozen drink section caught her eye, colorful and fun and perfect for their impromptu escape. After deliberating between margaritas, daiquiris, and coladas, she settled on piña coladas: tropical, sweet, and festive.

"Two frozen piña coladas, please," she told the bartender.

She returned a few minutes later with the drinks, their paper umbrellas bobbing cheerfully in the frozen concoction. Setting them at the edge of the tub, she untied her robe and draped it over a nearby chair. She felt Jerry's gaze on her as she lowered herself into the warm, bubbling water, the steam rising around her in wispy tendrils.

"That's from our paddleboarding date," he said, then froze, as if realizing what he'd called it.

A slow smile spread across her face. "So it was a date?" she asked, handing him his drink before settling against his side.

His answering smile was small but real. "I guess it was."

The warm water enveloped her legs as she nestled against him, the bubbles creating a pleasant massage against her skin. When his arm came around her shoulders, she leaned into the touch, her hand finding his thigh beneath the water.

"How'd you know this was exactly what I needed?" he asked after a moment.

She shrugged, not wanting to admit how carefully she'd been watching him, how attuned she'd become to his moods. "Just a hunch that you might prefer this to champagne and small talk."

The truth was more complicated. She'd recognized something familiar in him, maybe a kindred wariness or a shared discomfort with performances and pretense. She'd spent so many years perfecting the art of appearing fine that she could spot the same skill in others. The difference was that tonight, she didn't want either of them to have to pretend.

The jets hummed, the ship's distant rhythm filling the quiet.

Scarlet sipped her drink, the creamy sweetness cutting through the ocean air.

She hadn't felt this calm in ages.

And she didn't ask about earlier.

Some things deserved patience, not pressure.

A couple approached the tub and paused at the edge. She wore a classic black one-piece, he wore navy swim trunks.

Jerry went still beside her, tension flickering beneath the surface.

But he stayed put, and Scarlet, with a reassuring smile, gestured for them to join.

"We couldn't face another minute in formal wear," the woman, Lynn, explained as they settled into the water.

Scarlet smiled. "Great minds think alike."

Introductions faded into casual chatter of travel stories, excursion tips, shared laughs.

Jerry, once stiff beside her, eased into the moment, his voice gaining confidence with each exchange.

And then Lynn asked how long they'd been together.

The question caught Scarlet off guard ... but not unpleasantly.

"We're still counting in days, not years," she replied with a laugh.

"Newly-weds?" Dave asked, raising his eyebrows.

"No, no ... just ... new," Jerry said.

"We actually just met on this cruise, a couple days ago," Scarlet added, then couldn't resist a touch of mischief. "But you know, we had just hit it off so well since Sunday, we had the captain read us our vows yesterday after dinner."

She felt Jerry's silent laugh vibrate through his chest where she leaned against him, and Lynn's momentary confusion before catching the joke felt like a small shared victory.

"You really had me going there!" Lynn laughed. "I would have believed it. You two seem like you've known each other forever."

As they chatted about cruise destinations and shore excursions, Scarlet became increasingly aware of Jerry's solid presence beside her. The easy way his arm draped across her shoulders. The steady rise and fall of his chest against her cheek. The firm muscle of his thigh beneath her palm.

A bold idea began to form, fueled by the heat of the water and the lingering effects of Caribbean rum from earlier. Her hand on his thigh began to move, first in small, idle circles, then with more deliberate intent. She kept her expression neutral, contributing to the conversation about island hopping even as her fingers inched higher beneath the hem of his swim trunks.

"We absolutely loved Megan's Bay in St. Thomas," Lynn was saying, her voice floating across the steam rising from the hot tub. "The water is this incredible shade of turquoise."

"I've heard it can get crowded though," Scarlet replied, her voice remarkably steady as her fingertips ventured into forbidden territory. The accountant who calculated risk for a living, who never so much as jaywalked back home, was now engaged in the most reckless public intimacy she could imagine. The thought alone sent a delicious shiver through her that had nothing to do with the water temperature.

"Oh, if you go early enough, it's not so bad," Lynn continued, completely oblivious to Scarlet's wandering hand beneath the churning water.

Scarlet nodded thoughtfully, as though her full attention were on beach recommendations and not on the hardening length she was now discovering beneath the water. With each subtle stroke, she felt him responding, growing firmer against her palm. The silky-smooth head became more defined as it filled with blood. Her exploring touch discovered a fascinating contrast of textures, from velvet softness to rigid heat.

"Dave, honey, tell them about that little café we found near the port," Lynn prompted, while beneath the surface, Scarlet's fingers wrapped more boldly around Jerry's shaft, feeling it pulse with each heartbeat.

"Best conch fritters on the island," Dave enthused, gesturing with his drink, while Jerry's thigh muscles tensed beneath Scarlet's touch. Above the water, mundane conversation flowed. Below, something far more primal unfolded, hidden only by concealing bubbles and the thin fabric of Jerry's swim trunks.

"That sounds lovely," Scarlet managed, her Miami corporate voice perfectly composed even as her fingers traced the pronounced ridge where the head met the shaft, memorizing every detail through touch alone. The professional who held her emotions in check during brutal client meetings was now reveling in making this stoic military man come undone in public. She barely recognized herself. Maybe this was who she'd always been beneath the Miami facade: a bold, sensual woman who took what she wanted without apology.

When she finally reached his full length, she felt Jerry's muscles tense beneath her touch. Through her peripheral vision, she caught his sudden movement, a splash that must have been his drink spilling, but kept her own expression perfectly composed, even as a flutter of satisfaction rippled through her at this evidence of her effect on him.

"You okay there, buddy?" Dave asked.

"Fine," Jerry managed, his voice noticeably strained. Scarlet met his sidelong glance with an innocent look, though it took considerable effort not to smirk as she felt the heavy throb of his pulse quicken beneath her exploring fingers. "Just went down the wrong pipe."

"As I was saying about the markets in Charlotte Amalie," she continued smoothly, not missing a beat in the above-water conversation while her underwater exploration became more targeted, more deliberate. Two Scarlets existed simultaneously in this moment. Above water, the polished conversationalist. Below, the brazen seductress. Each feeding off the other's performance.

The thrill of this secret connection was intoxicating. Risk had never been Scarlet's territory; her entire career was built on minimizing it for others. Yet here she was, creating a hidden storm beneath calm waters. She felt Jerry's body responding to her every motion like an instrument perfectly tuned to her touch, while maintaining a conversation about duty-free shopping as if nothing extraordinary was happening. The accountant who scheduled her intimacy behind closed doors was now conducting a symphony of desire in plain sight. She felt powerful, desired, and deliciously reckless, discovering a version of herself she'd never known existed until this cruise, until this man.

Eventually, Jerry set his glass on the deck with deliberate care.

"You know," he said, interrupting a discussion about Caribbean cuisine, "I ... I think we might call it a night. It's been a long day of excursions."

"So nice meeting you both," Scarlet added, withdrawing her hand with one final, deliberate stroke that made his breath catch in a way only she could hear.

"Enjoy the rest of your cruise," Lynn called as they climbed out.

Scarlet pulled her robe around her body, the cool night air raising goosebumps on her wet skin despite the warmth that pooled low in her belly. As they walked toward the door leading inside, Jerry's hand found the small of her back, guiding her with a sureness that sent a shiver up her spine despite the warm night air.

"Your room or mine?" he asked quietly.

Scarlet's smile was slow and certain in the dim light. "Yours is closer."

# Fourteen

erry's hand trembled slightly as he patted his pockets, the panic building in his eyes with each empty pocket he discovered. Scarlet watched his growing distress with a mixture of amusement and frustration, their previous momentum temporarily stalled outside his cabin door.

"I don't believe this," he muttered, checking his swim trunks pocket for the third time. "I must have ... when I changed earlier ..."

"Locked yourself out?" Scarlet finished for him, a smile tugging at her lips despite the interruption.

Jerry ran a hand through his damp hair, frustration evident in the tense line of his shoulders. "I'm sorry. I was rushing to get changed and must have left the key inside. I can go to guest services, but it might take—"

Scarlet stepped closer, eliminating the space between them. She rose on her tiptoes, her lips brushing against the shell of his ear as she whispered, "Don't worry, Soldier, you're still getting laid tonight." She followed the promise with a gentle nibble on his earlobe, then trailed her lips down to place a lingering kiss just behind his ear, at that sensitive junction where neck met jaw.

She felt rather than heard his sharp intake of breath, his hands instinctively finding her waist through the terry cloth robe.

"Your place?" he asked, his voice dropping to a rough whisper that sent a shiver down her spine.

"Follow me," she replied, taking his hand and leading him down the corridor.

The walk to her cabin seemed both eternal and instantaneous, the anticipation building with each step. Their hands remained intertwined, thumbs occasionally brushing across knuckles in silent acknowledgment of what awaited them.

When the door finally closed behind them, Scarlet was struck by the sudden intimacy of the space. Her formal red dress lay sprawled across the bed where she'd discarded it earlier, a vibrant splash of color against the white linens.

"Sorry about the mess," she said, grabbing the expensive satin gown and tossing it carelessly onto the sofa. She was treating five hundred dollars worth of designer fabric like a beach towel, completely unlike her usual meticulous care of her wardrobe. But right now, nothing mattered except the man standing before her, his eyes never leaving hers.

Jerry fidgeted with the belt of his robe. "Is it okay if I hang my trunks in the shower to dry?" he called through the bathroom door a moment later.

"Of course," she replied, her heart rate accelerating both at the casual domesticity of the question and at the realization that beneath his robe, he was now completely naked.

While Jerry was in the bathroom, Scarlet moved quickly. She hung her damp tankini on a hook by the closet, then opened her suitcase and extracted the red lace teddy that Cami had insisted she pack "just in case." At the time, Scarlet had rolled her eyes at her friend's optimism. Now, she sent a silent thank you as she slipped into the delicate garment.

The lace felt cool and slightly scratchy against her skin as she adjusted the thin straps behind her neck. The plunging neckline dipped nearly to her navel, the sheer floral pattern offering tantalizing glimpses of skin beneath. The high-cut sides accentuated her hips while the scalloped edges framed her rear perfectly. When she checked her reflection in the mirror on the closet door, she saw how the vibrant red matched her bright red hair perfectly, creating a striking visual harmony that made her skin appear even more luminous.

She wrapped the robe around herself again, tying the belt loosely at her waist, just as Jerry emerged from the bathroom. His robe hung open at the neck, revealing his toned chest and the light dusting of hair that narrowed into a trail disappearing beneath the terrycloth belt.

"Hi," he said, suddenly shy, as if they hadn't just been groping each other in a hot tub.

"Hi yourself," she replied, charmed by his nervousness.

He approached her slowly, hands slightly uncertain as they found her waist. Their lips met in a soft, exploratory kiss that quickly deepened, the days of building attraction concentrated into this single point of contact. His tongue traced the seam of her lips, seeking entry that she gladly granted. She pressed herself closer, feeling the solid wall of his chest through the layers of terry cloth.

"I've been thinking about this all day," she confessed between kisses, her hands sliding inside his robe to feel the warm skin beneath.

"Me too," he admitted, his fingers tangling in her vibrant red waves. "Oh my God, I want you so bad."

It was the raw honesty in his voice that decided her. Scarlet stepped back, holding his gaze as her fingers found the loose knot of her belt. With deliberate slowness, she untied it, letting the robe fall open. Then, with a slight shrug of her shoulders, she let the white terry cloth cascade to the floor around her feet.

"Fuck." The word escaped Jerry's lips on an exhale as he took in the sight of her. He literally stumbled backward until his legs hit the edge of the bed, forcing him to sit down hard on the mattress.

The look in his eyes ignited something fierce in her.

He lingered on the plunging neckline, the way the lace skimmed her skin, the unapologetic rise of the fabric along her thighs.

It wasn't just desire she saw. It was reverence. And that hit harder than any business deal ever had.

Her stride was measured, confident, and he didn't look away.

With a single, fluid movement, she settled onto his lap, knees bracketing his hips, bringing them eye to eye.

The thin lace amplified every shift, every movement, as her hips met the rigid heat beneath her.

Her breath stuttered, lips parting as sensation swept through her, deep and insistent.

"You're so beautiful," he whispered, reverence in his voice as his hands came to rest lightly on her hips. "I can't believe this is happening."

Scarlet's smile curved, slow and knowing, as her tongue pressed lightly behind her teeth in the gesture that had become her signature when satisfaction simmered beneath the surface.

She took hold of his collar, easing the robe from his shoulders with deliberate care until it gathered at his waist, his arms briefly caught in the folds.

"Believe it," she told him, before capturing his mouth in another kiss.

Their kisses grew more heated, more desperate. Jerry managed to free his arms from the robe, his hands exploring the expanse of her back, tracing the thin straps that criss-crossed her skin. Each touch ignited a new spark of sensation, goosebumps rising in the wake of his fingertips. The feeling of his calloused hands against her smooth skin created a delicious friction that had her arching into his touch.

She moved against him, slow and deliberate, letting the pressure build where their bodies aligned.

No fabric could dull the message: he was hard, responsive, completely with her.

Heat gathered low and steady, dampening the lace at her center.

Each subtle grind drew breathy sounds from them both, a quiet dialogue made of motion.

He traced her side with deliberate patience, fingertips grazing skin until they met lace.

With one slow motion, he was beneath it, cupping her breast with a warmth that made her head tip back.

She surged forward, needing the contact, the weight, the wordless way he was learning her by hand.

Jerry's eyes met hers, seeking permission as he slowly began to ease her breast free from the confines of the lace. Scarlet nodded, breath catching as the cool air of the cabin met her newly exposed skin. His mouth descended, replacing his hand with his lips, and the wet heat of his tongue against her sensitive nipple sent a jolt of pleasure straight through her core.

While his mouth explored her exposed breast, Scarlet reached for the tie at the back of her neck. With nimble fingers, she loosened the delicate bow, allowing the top of the teddy to fall forward to her waist. Her breasts now fully bared to his gaze, she watched his pupils dilate further, his breath becoming more ragged.

"God, you're perfect," he murmured, his attention shifting to her other breast, giving it the same thorough appreciation.

His lips trailed from her mouth to her jaw, then down the column of her throat, eventually reaching her now fully exposed breasts. Each kiss, each gentle scrape of teeth, each flick of his tongue against her sensitive peaks sent currents of pleasure radiating through her body, centering in the throbbing heat between her thighs.

He took his time with her, warming her with reverent lips and gentle hands.

When his palms slipped down to cup her rear, the pressure was teasing, confident.

Then he stood, lifting her in one seamless move.

She hooked her legs around his waist, caught between laughter and shock at the ease of it.

The few steps to the head of the bed were a sensory blur. She felt the security of his arms holding her, the hardness of him pressed against her most sensitive place, the slight bounce as he lowered her onto the mattress. He followed her down, his weight settling over her, not crushing but substantial enough to make her feel deliciously trapped beneath him.

Their bodies aligned perfectly, his hips nestled between her thighs, as if they'd been designed as matching puzzle pieces. The pressure of him against her sent waves of anticipation coursing through her veins, her body already preparing for what was to come. Between her legs, she felt herself growing slicker, readier, her body responding to his proximity with primal enthusiasm.

The robe had fallen completely from Jerry's shoulders now, revealing the full expanse of his toned chest and arms. Scarlet ran her hands over his skin, exploring the defined muscles of his shoulders, the slight roughness of the sparse hair on his chest, the smoothness of his back. He was warm to the touch, almost feverishly so, and she could feel the rapid thudding of his heart beneath her palm.

They lost themselves in each other. Kisses deepened, touches grew bolder with every heartbeat.

Jerry trailed kisses down her throat, lingering as he found her bare curves and explored them with fervent devotion.

The drag of his stubble added a sharp, tingling heat that made her arch into him, wordless and wanting. His hand skimmed down her side, following the curve of her waist to her hip, then inward toward the junction of her thighs. The anticipation of his touch had her breath catching in her throat, her legs parting further in silent invitation.

His fingers dipped under the lace, finding her with a touch that made her gasp.

It had been five years.

Five years of her own hands, familiar and efficient.

This was different. Curious, alive, *his*.

Her hips surged upward, need overriding thought, every nerve demanding more.

"You're so wet," he murmured against her breast, his voice tinged with wonder and masculine pride.

"Just for you," she replied, her voice breathy and strained as her body responded to his skillful touch.

His fingers explored her slick folds with careful attention, discovering all the places that made her breath catch and her back arch. He circled the sensitive bundle of nerves at her apex, applying just enough pressure to build her pleasure without tipping her over the edge. Then his fingers slid lower, tracing her entrance before one slipped inside, curling forward to find that spot that had her seeing stars.

"There," she gasped, her nails digging into his shoulders, leaving little crescent marks in his skin. "Right there."

Jerry was a quick study, repeating the movements that drew the strongest reactions from her. He added a second finger, stretching her deliciously, while his thumb continued its maddening circles against her most sensitive spot. The dual sensations had her climbing rapidly toward release, her inner muscles clenching around his fingers.

"Wait," she gasped after a few minutes of his ministrations had brought her dangerously close to the edge. "I want you inside me when I come."

Jerry nodded, his pupils blown wide with desire, a thin ring of blue surrounding the darkness. "Do you have ... ?"

"Condom," she finished for him, then gestured toward the other bed. "Nightstand. Cami's side."

He raised an eyebrow.

"Thank God she's always prepared," Scarlet added with a breathless laugh.

Jerry retrieved the small foil packet from the drawer and returned to her, shedding his robe completely on the way. Scarlet took a moment to appreciate him: lean muscle and tanned skin, his arousal standing proud and ready. The sight sent another pulse of desire through her body, her inner muscles clenching in anticipation.

She reached for the condom, but he pulled back slightly. "Let me," he said, his fingers trembling slightly as he tore open the packet. The small sign of nervousness endeared him to her even more.

While he rolled on the protection, Scarlet slipped the teddy the rest of the way off, suddenly wanting nothing between them. The cool air of the cabin pebbled her skin, raising goosebumps across her breasts and stomach. She lay back, opening her arms to welcome him, her vibrant red hair spread across the white pillowcase like flames.

Jerry positioned himself between her thighs, his weight supported on his forearms. The blunt head of his shaft pressed against her entrance, seeking but not yet entering. Instead, it slid upward, gliding between her slick folds as if her body was welcoming him into a warm embrace. The sensation of his hardness sliding against her most sensitive flesh drew a shuddering gasp from her lips, her hips instinctively rising to increase the pressure.

"Please," she whispered, lifting her hips in silent invitation.

He entered her with a slow, careful thrust that had them both gasping. The initial stretch was intense after five years without anyone but herself, but her body was more than ready, slick and eager to accept him. He paused when he was fully seated within her, forehead pressed against hers, their breaths mingling in the small space between them.

"You feel amazing," he murmured, the strain of holding still evident in the tension of his muscles.

Scarlet wrapped her legs around his waist, changing the angle and drawing a groan from deep in his chest. "Move," she urged, her hands sliding down his back to grip his rear, encouraging him.

He began with slow, measured thrusts, allowing her body to adjust to his size and presence. Each withdrawal and return sent waves of pleasure radiating through her, building upon each other like ripples in a pond. The drag of his flesh against her inner walls created a delicious friction that had her moaning with each thrust.

Gradually, the pace increased, their bodies finding a rhythm that suited them both. The sound of skin against skin, of labored breathing and soft moans, filled the cabin. Scarlet let herself be carried away by the sensations, her mind emptying of everything but the feel of him moving within her, the weight of him above her, the scent of their mingled desire.

Jerry shifted his weight onto one arm, his other hand sliding between them to find that sensitive bundle of nerves. His fingers circled in time with his thrusts, adding another layer of sensation that had Scarlet gasping. Her inner muscles began to clench around him, the tension building to an almost unbearable level.

"I'm close," she warned, feeling the familiar tightening low in her belly, the tingling spreading through her limbs.

"Me too," he admitted, his rhythm faltering slightly as his own control began to slip.

"Don't stop," she urged, her nails raking down his back, leaving faint red lines in their wake.

When her climax hit, it was like a tidal wave crashing over her, starting at her core and radiating outward until even her fingertips tingled with sensation. She cried out, her inner walls clenching rhythmically around him, pulling him deeper. Waves of pleasure washed over her, each one slightly less intense than the last but no less overwhelming.

Jerry followed soon after, his body tensing above her, a strangled version of her name escaping his lips as he reached his own peak. She could feel him pulsing within her, his hips jerking with each wave of his release.

They collapsed together, limbs intertwined, bodies slick with sweat despite the cabin's air conditioning. For several long minutes, neither moved, simply breathing together in the quiet aftermath.

Eventually, Jerry rolled to the side, careful not to crush her beneath his weight. He disposed of the condom in the small trash bin beside the bed, then gathered her against his chest, her head finding a natural resting place in the crook of his shoulder.

"That was ..." he began, then seemed to run out of words.

"Yeah," she agreed, understanding exactly what he meant.

They lay in peaceful stillness for a while, her fingers tracing idle patterns on his chest, occasionally venturing to the tattoo on his bicep.

"Tell me more about them," she said softly, her finger outlining the infinity symbol. "What are they like as people, not just diagnoses?"

Jerry's smile was immediate and genuine. "Emmett talks enough for both of them. He's endlessly curious, always asking questions I don't know how to answer. 'Why is the sky sometimes pink?' 'How do planes stay up?' 'Do fish get thirsty?'"

Scarlet laughed. "Smart kid."

"Too smart sometimes. And Marty ..." His expression softened further. "Marty feels everything so deeply. He can't speak, but he communicates more with his eyes than most people do with a thousand words. He has this laugh that just ... it's like sunshine breaking through clouds."

The love in his voice stirred something in Scarlet's chest that felt dangerously close to longing. Listening to him talk about his sons, she could envision him as a father, patient, dedicated, finding joy in their smallest achievements. The image was surprisingly appealing.

"Before the cruise ..." Jerry began, but his voice trailed off, his words slowing as exhaustion finally claimed him.

She glanced over at him. His eyes were shut, his breath even, his body utterly still.

That quiet smile remained, subtle and unforced.

It caught her off guard, how deeply it moved her to see him finally at peace.

"This doesn't have to be just a cruise thing, you know," she whispered, though she knew he couldn't hear her.

She propped herself up on one elbow, studying his sleeping face. The worry lines that usually creased his forehead had smoothed out, making him look younger, more carefree. The vulnerability of him in sleep, entrusting himself to her presence, wasn't lost on her.

"Geography is just geography," she murmured, surprising herself with how much she meant it. "Maybe I'm tired of my life in Miami."

They hadn't figured anything out, of course. But something hung in the air between them, tangible as a promise. The possibility that what had begun as a cruise fling might survive the return to shore.

Scarlet remained awake a little longer, watching the gentle rise and fall of his chest, listening to his steady breathing. When had this vacation hookup transformed into something worth fighting for? She wasn't sure, but as she finally drifted toward sleep herself, nestled against his warmth, she was increasingly certain that she wanted to find out what that something could be.

# Fifteen

The bathroom mirror didn't lie.

Scarlet dabbed her face with the plush towel, studying her reflection. The woman staring back looked subtly different, perhaps something in the eyes. A softness that hadn't been there yesterday morning. Her hair was a disaster, curls twisting in every wrong direction. Her lips looked fuller, slightly swollen. And she couldn't stop smiling.

She brushed her teeth, hyperaware of the man still in her bed. This morning when she'd first woken, the sheets had carried his scent. Clean sweat and something deeper, masculine. Her body ached pleasantly in places she'd forgotten could ache.

"Hey." Jerry's voice floated from behind the partially closed door, sleep-rough and warm. "What do you think about ordering room service instead of fighting the breakfast crowd?"

Scarlet tucked a wild curl behind her ear. "Yes," she called back without hesitation. The idea of navigating the bustling breakfast buffet with its forced small talk and judgment-laden glances felt impossible. Not when they could stay here, private and uninterrupted.

"God, yes."

She heard his low chuckle, followed by the rustle of sheets and the soft beep of the room phone. She listened to him order breakfast. Pancakes for himself, a veggie omelet for her, coffee for both, a fruit plate to share. The easy confidence in his voice as he added orange juice, specified extra syrup. The fact that he remembered exactly how she took her coffee without asking.

When she emerged from the bathroom, Jerry had propped himself against the headboard, sheet draped strategically across his hips. His chest was bare, tanned and solid against the white linens. He looked relaxed, waiting for her, and the sight sent an unexpected flutter through her stomach.

"Hi," she said, suddenly shy.

His eyes crinkled at the corners. "Hi yourself."

She crossed to the bed, letting the towel drop from her hair. Standing naked before him felt strangely comfortable, devoid of the self-consciousness she usually carried in these moments. When she slipped back under the covers, his arm curved naturally around her shoulders.

"We should probably get dressed before room service arrives," she murmured, making no move to do so.

"Probably," he agreed, pressing a kiss to her temple. His fingers traced lazy patterns across her shoulder. "But I'm not sure I can. Pretty sure you broke something essential last night."

She laughed, the sound muffled against his skin. "Funny. I was about to say the same thing."

The quiet that followed wasn't awkward or loaded. It simply existed, comfortable and calm, punctuated only by the distant sound of waves against the ship's hull and their synchronized breathing. Scarlet couldn't remember the last time silence with someone had felt this easy.

Jerry's fingers wandered to her collarbone, tracing the line of it with gentle precision. His touch wasn't demanding, just appreciative. Present.

"I like this," she admitted softly, the words slipping out before she could censor them.

"This?" His voice rumbled pleasantly against her ear.

"This," she confirmed, gesturing vaguely to encompass them, the bed, the quiet bubble they'd created. "Not rushing. Not ... performing."

His hand stilled for a moment before resuming its path. "Yeah," he said simply. "Me too."

The peaceful moment shattered when the door flew open without warning.

Cami burst in, wearing what were unmistakably men's PT shorts and an oversized Army t-shirt, her hair a wild tangle. She clutched her blue dress and heels in one hand, aviator sunglasses pushed up into her curls despite the indoor lighting.

"Well, good morning, lovebirds!" she announced, kicking the door shut behind her.

Scarlet froze. Jerry tensed beside her.

Without missing a beat, Cami strode across the room and flopped down on the foot of the bed, grinning like she'd won something. Her eyes landed on a scrap of red lace peeking out from under the desk chair. "Well, well, well. That lingerie was worth every penny, wasn't it?" She waggled her eyebrows suggestively.

"Cami!" Scarlet hissed, clutching the sheet higher. "We're still naked under here!"

Cami waved this off, unconcerned. "Oh please, after yesterday's beach adventure, we've all seen everyone's everything. Nothing to be shy about now."

Jerry choked on what might have been a laugh, his ears turning pink.

"Oh my God," Scarlet groaned, pressing her face into Jerry's shoulder in mortification.

Cami rose from the bed, stretching casually. "Relax. I just need to grab some clean clothes." She sauntered toward the bathroom, pulling Mac's t-shirt over her head mid-stride and tossing it to the floor without a second thought. From Scarlet's angle, they could only see her bare back silhouetted briefly before she disappeared into the bathroom.

"I'm so sorry," Scarlet whispered, looking up at Jerry.

He shook with silent laughter. "No, no. This is ... educational."

"Is that what we're calling it?"

The bathroom door opened again. Cami emerged in black shorts and a teal tank top, looking refreshed and completely un-repentant.

"So," she said, applying lip gloss in the mirror by the door, "did you make her squeal? It's been forever for her."

"Oh my God, Cami!" Scarlet threw a pillow, which Cami dodged effortlessly.

Jerry cleared his throat, a sudden glint in his eye. "Actually, I think the whole floor knows the answer to that. The neighbors sent a thank you note."

Cami's mouth dropped open for a split second before she cackled with delight. "I knew I liked this one." She pointed her lip gloss tube at Scarlet. "This one's a keeper, babe."

Scarlet couldn't decide whether to die of embarrassment or high five Jerry for the perfect comeback.

Cami checked her phone, sliding it into her pocket. "I'm heading to the casino. Are you guys gonna join the living by lunchtime?"

"Yes, fine, please leave now," Scarlet begged, torn between laughter and mortification.

"Later, lovers!" Cami called, blowing a kiss before closing the door behind her.

The silence that followed felt deafening. Scarlet glanced at Jerry, afraid to see judgment or discomfort on his face. Instead, she found him grinning, shoulders shaking with suppressed laughter.

"She's something else," he said finally.

A startled laugh burst from her. "That's putting it mildly."

"I can see why you keep her around, though."

"When I'm not plotting her murder, you mean."

A knock at the door signaled the arrival of room service. Jerry quickly scooped a discarded robe from the floor, wrapping it around himself while Scarlet grabbed the second robe hanging in the bathroom. The server wheeled in their breakfast with professional discretion, barely glancing at their state of undress or the obviously slept-in bed.

When they were alone again, Scarlet lifted the silver domes covering their plates. Steam rose from perfectly golden pancakes and her veggie omelet, the scent of coffee rich and promising.

"Balcony?" Jerry suggested, already lifting the tray.

Scarlet nodded, grabbing the carafe of coffee and following him through the sliding glass door. The morning air was warm but fresh, carrying the clean scent of salt and endless horizon. They settled into the chairs, the small table between them laden with breakfast.

For several minutes, they ate in contented silence. Scarlet sipped her coffee, perfectly strong and sweet just as she preferred, and watched the sunlight dance across the waves. The world felt vast and intimate all at once.

"This is nice," she said finally.

Jerry looked up from his pancakes, a question in his eyes.

"This," she clarified, gesturing between them with her fork. "Breakfast. Not having to ..." She paused, searching for the right words. "Not having to be fascinating or impressive or professionally polished. Just eating eggs and watching the ocean."

He smiled with something deeper and more genuine than the quick, guarded expression she'd first seen at the welcome mixer. "Yeah," he agreed softly. "It is."

They shared the fruit plate, Jerry automatically sliding the extra pineapple to her side after noticing her preference. Such a small thing, but it lodged somewhere beneath her ribs, warm and unexpected.

"I should probably head back to my cabin after this," he said eventually. "Get some actual clothes on for the day."

Disappointment flickered, but Scarlet nodded. "I don't know, I'm not complaining about the current view." She wiggled her eyebrows suggestively.

Jerry glanced down and suddenly froze. The sea breeze had loosened his hastily-tied robe, leaving him completely exposed beneath the table. His eyes widened in horror. "How long has that been happening?"

Scarlet snickered into her coffee. "The whole time."

"And you weren't going to say anything?" His face flushed crimson as he frantically readjusted his robe, glancing around as if suddenly realizing they were on a balcony overlooking the open ocean.

"Like I said ..." She took another slow sip, eyes dancing with mischief. "Not complaining."

"Oh God." He sank lower in his chair, mortification washing over his features. "I just flashed half the Atlantic. There's probably a dolphin out there right now telling all his friends about the free show."

Scarlet burst out laughing. "If it helps, I think we're too high up for dolphins to see."

"Yeah, just the entire ship below us and possibly a passing cruise liner." He shook his head, but a reluctant smile tugged at his lips. "So we're still on for lunch with the chaos twins?"

"I guess we probably should," she replied, echoing his earlier nonchalance.

"Very funny." He reached across the table, his fingers lightly brushing hers. The touch, so casual and yet so deliberate, sent warmth curling through her.

After breakfast, Jerry reluctantly dressed in last night's clothes. They lingered at the door, neither quite ready to break the spell.

"See you at lunch," he said finally, pressing a kiss to her temple.

"See you then."

After he left, Scarlet tidied the room, gathering the breakfast dishes and straightening the rumpled sheets. She rescued her red lace lingerie from under the chair, remembering Cami's teasing. Worth every penny indeed.

She folded her red dress from last night with deliberate care, smoothing the fabric while memories flooded back. The weight of his hands at her waist, the heat of his mouth on her neck, the way the world had narrowed to just the two of them.

While organizing the nightstand, her fingers brushed cool metal. Jerry's dog tags. She lifted them, reading the stamped text: DUNCAN, GILMORE P. So Jerry was a nickname. She hadn't known that.

She turned the tags over in her palm, feeling their weight. These small metal identifiers had been with him through ... what, exactly? Desert heat and gunfire? Lonely nights in foreign lands? The birth of his sons? She traced the stamped letters with her fingertip, imagining these same tags pressed against his chest during moments she'd never see, never fully understand.

How many countries had these tags visited? How many times had he reached for them in fear or uncertainty? What had they witnessed that made the lines around his eyes deepen when he thought no one was looking?

The cool metal warmed in her hand, and for a moment, the distance between their lives felt both vast and bridgeable. He remained partly a mystery to her, full of layers she had only begun to unfold. The realization should have been daunting. Instead, it felt like promise.

She set the dog tags aside carefully. She'd return them at lunch.

The systematic process of packing forced her to acknowledge reality's imminent return. Tomorrow they'd dock in Miami. Real life waited with her job, her apartment, her carefully constructed routine. All the things that had felt suffocating a week ago now seemed distant and faded, like clothes that no longer quite fit.

And Jerry would return to Texas, to his sons and his responsibilities. To a life she'd only glimpsed through his stories. The miles between Miami and Killeen stretched in her mind, vast and daunting.

She zipped her suitcase with more force than necessary. One more day. One more night. That's what they had guaranteed. Anything beyond was uncharted territory.

The afternoon unfurled with silken ease. Smooth, sunlit, and just a little too fleeting.

Cami engineered a rainbow of frozen cocktails, and Mac's storytelling spun everyone into fits of laughter.

Jerry reached for her hand without a word, their fingers laced together while his thumb moved in lazy loops across her skin.

Scarlet didn't reach for the clock.

She was busy collecting fragments: the rise of Jerry's laughter, the crease at the edge of his smile, the way his attention tuned only to her when the rest of the world faded.

They were living on borrowed hours, but she refused to tally the cost.

The Topaz Lounge glowed with golden light as sunset painted the horizon. Light caught every surface and made it gleam. Polished wood, crystal glassware, the ocean itself burnished copper through the panoramic windows. Scarlet had dressed simply in a pale blue sundress, her hair loose around her shoulders.

Jerry stood at their usual table, easy to find in his rolled-sleeve navy shirt and sun-washed shorts.

His hair was damp, freshly combed, and something in her stilled at the sight.

He looked up, catching her gaze across the room. The smile that spread across his face hit her like a physical force.

"Hey, you," he said when she reached him.

"Hey, yourself." She leaned in as his hand found the small of her back, the gesture now familiar, welcome.

Mac and Cami arrived together, still bickering good-naturedly about something that had happened in the casino. They claimed their seats, Cami immediately signaling the server for drinks.

"Last night, people!" she announced. "Let's make it count."

The farewell toast was Maude's domain. She took the small stage as she had on their first night, elegant in flowing turquoise, her silver-streaked hair swept up. But where her welcome speech had been bright and buoyant, tonight she carried a quieter energy.

"My dear voyagers," she began, voice carrying effortlessly across the hushed lounge. "Our journey together reaches its final evening. Tomorrow, we return to the lives we temporarily left behind."

Scarlet felt Jerry's hand find hers beneath the table, warm and solid.

"But remember," Maude continued, "endings are often disguised beginnings. The sea has a way of revealing truths we carry back to shore ... if we're brave enough to honor them."

She raised her glass. "To discoveries made. To connections forged. To the courage that awaits us beyond the horizon."

"To courage," Scarlet echoed softly, turning to meet Jerry's gaze as they sipped their champagne.

Through the lounge windows, the distant lights of the Miami coastline flickered like stars fallen to earth. Reality waited there, full of all the complications and logistics they'd temporarily escaped.

Yet sitting here with Jerry's thumb tracing circles against her palm, Scarlet realized she wasn't dreading tomorrow the way she should be. This wasn't an ending. Terrifying, yes. Uncharted and exhilarating. But not an ending.

She leaned into Jerry's side, making a silent promise to herself: She would find a way to see what could exist beyond the ship, beyond the bubble, in the messy, complicated real world. Some things were worth the risk.

# Sixteen

The El Corazón lounge had been transformed from last night's salsa hub to a holding pen for the disembarking. Scarlet sat with her carry-on between her knees, scrolling through a week's worth of emails. The space still smelled faintly of lime and tequila, but the energy had changed. No more vacation magic. Just passengers with suitcases and dark circles under their eyes.

"You've got to be kidding me," she muttered, tapping an email from Eric.

Cami leaned over. "Work drama already?"

"Eric's pulling Maya off the Henderson acquisition to focus on some new client. Guess who gets all her overflow?" Scarlet locked her phone with a snap. "So much for easing back in after the holiday weekend."

Across from her, Jerry and Mac were huddled over Jerry's phone, both grinning.

"What's so funny over there?" she asked.

Jerry held out his phone. "Emmett built a fort in the living room and apparently convinced my mom it needed to stay up all week as a 'welcome home surprise.'"

The photo showed a blanket construction of impressive engineering, with a small face peeking from behind a pillow barricade. Something warm and unexpected bloomed in Scarlet's chest at the sight of Jerry's son. Those same warm eyes, that same thoughtful expression.

"He's got your serious face," she said before she could stop herself.

Jerry's smile softened. "Yeah, he does. Too much sometimes."

The overhead speaker crackled: "Now calling group seven for disembarkation. Group seven passengers, please proceed to Deck 4."

"That's us," Cami said, standing and stretching. "Back to reality."

Scarlet gathered her bag, then hesitated. "What time is your flight again?"

"Not until 9:15," Jerry said, pocketing his phone.

"So, my parents are hosting a Memorial Day barbecue today." She bit her lower lip. "You guys should come by before your flight. If you want."

She watched Jerry's face, her heartbeat suddenly loud in her ears.

"Yeah?" A slow smile spread across his face. "I'd like that."

"Free food? I'm in," Mac declared.

Scarlet couldn't hold back a smile, her tongue pressing briefly against the small gap in her front teeth when Jerry accepted. "I'll text you the address."

"Come on, Romeo," Mac said, tugging at Jerry's arm. "Let the ladies escape before they miss their exit call."

Their eyes held for a moment longer than necessary. One week ago, he'd been a stranger. Now, she wasn't ready for him to be nothing.

The terminal buzzed with the chaos of a thousand passengers reuniting with real life. After clearing customs, Scarlet and Cami emerged into the bright Miami sunlight. The humidity hit like a wall after a week of sea breezes.

"There she is!" Cami pointed.

Jade leaned against a canary-yellow convertible with the top down, oversized sunglasses perched on her nose.

"Let the re-entry trauma begin," Scarlet muttered.

"Drama queen," Cami laughed, bumping her shoulder.

Jade squealed when she spotted them, rushing forward for hugs. "My mermaids return to shore! How was it? Better or worse than the Bahamas trip?"

"Better food, worse karaoke," Cami said, tossing her bag in the trunk. "Shotgun!" she called, sliding into the front seat while Scarlet loaded the rest of their luggage.

"So?" Jade asked as Scarlet climbed into the back. "Did Maude work her usual magic? Any notable Mingle successes?"

"You know Maude," Cami laughed. "Still dispensing wisdom wrapped in innuendo."

"Drop me at my place first?" Cami added. "I've got a mountain of stuff to handle today."

"Oh no," Jade frowned, pulling into traffic. "You're not coming to Dad's barbecue?"

"Unfortunately, I won't be choking on Leo's criminally dry burgers today," Cami sighed dramatically. "I've got deadlines breathing down my neck."

"You're abandoning me?" Scarlet leaned forward between the seats.

"Speaking of the barbecue," Cami twisted to face Scarlet with a devilish grin, "shouldn't you warn your sister about your special guests?"

"Special guests?" Jade's eyes found Scarlet's in the rearview mirror.

"It's not a big deal," Scarlet said, shooting Cami a warning look. "Just a couple guys from the cruise who need somewhere to hang out before their flight."

"A couple guys?" Jade's perfectly shaped eyebrow arched. "Or one specific guy who kicked your roommate out of your cabin for the last two nights?"

Scarlet's cheeks burned. "Cami, you promised."

"I promised nothing," Cami laughed. "You owe me for making me bunk with Mac. He snores."

"Wait," Jade's voice rose an octave. "You're bringing a hookup to meet Mom and Dad? Today?"

"He's not a hookup," Scarlet said, then winced. "I mean—"

"You shared a bed with him for two nights, honey," Cami smirked. "And those walls were thin."

"Jesus, Cami!" Scarlet covered her face.

"I cannot believe this," Jade said, drumming manicured nails against the steering wheel. "You, Scarlet Bellari, queen of the five-year dry spell, not only got laid on a cruise, but now you're bringing him home?"

"Sorry, should I have hid him for eighteen months like you did with Lucas?" Scarlet quipped back.

"Not the point," Jade waved dismissively. "This is huge. Who are you and what have you done with my sister?"

"It's really not that dramatic," Scarlet insisted, though her racing heart suggested otherwise. "It's just a barbecue. They need somewhere to go before their flight. End of story."

"So what's his name?" Jade pressed. "What does he do? Is he cute? Do I need to run interference with Mom's third-degree questioning?"

"His name is Jerry," Scarlet conceded. "He's a soldier. That's it. End of biography."

"That's not nothing," Jade said, her voice gentler. "Military guy, huh?"

"It's been a week," Scarlet said firmly. "Seven days. Let's not make this into something it's not."

"Seven days is all it took for me to know about Lucas," Jade pointed out.

"And yet it took eighteen months to introduce him to anyone," Scarlet countered.

"Fair," Jade grinned. "But you can't blame me for being shocked. This is the most spontaneous thing you've done since ... ever?"

"I think it's sweet," Cami added, her teasing tone giving way to sincerity. "Jerry's a good guy. Even if he did displace me from my rightful bed."

They pulled up to Cami's apartment building, sunshine gleaming off the glass-fronted tower. Miami's heat enveloped them as they stepped out, the asphalt radiating warmth through their sandals.

"Thanks for surviving the cruise with me," Scarlet said, pulling her friend into a hug.

"Are you kidding? This is the most excitement you've had in years," Cami squeezed her back, then pulled away with a grin. "Text me how it goes? I want to know if Sergeant Hottie passes the Bellari family gauntlet."

"You're the worst," Scarlet said, but there was no heat in it.

"Love you too!" Cami blew kisses as she sauntered toward her building.

Scarlet slid into the now-vacant front seat beside Jade, who immediately turned to her with gleaming eyes.

"Okay. It's just us now. I need details … and I mean everything. Start with how he looks in swim trunks."

Scarlet groaned, but secretly, she was almost relieved. If she was going to panic about bringing Jerry home, at least she wouldn't have to do it alone.

The Bellari family home welcomed Scarlet back with its familiar wind chimes and the scent of charcoal from the backyard. It was a constant in her shifting life, which made what she was about to do feel even more disruptive.

"Mom! Dad! We're here!" Jade called as they entered, the screen door slapping shut behind them.

Elisa emerged from the kitchen, drying her hands on a dishcloth. She smiled warmly, enveloping Scarlet in a hug that smelled of cilantro and lime.

"Welcome home, sweetheart. How was the cruise? You look … rested." Her eyes traveled over Scarlet's rumpled sundress.

"It was good," Scarlet said, feeling suddenly self-conscious. "Listen, Mom—"

"Scarlet's bringing a boy home!" Jade announced, dropping onto the couch with theatrical flair.

"Thanks, Jade," Scarlet muttered.

Elisa's eyebrows rose, but her smile never faltered. "Is that so?"

"They're just friends from the cruise," Scarlet explained, setting down her bag. "Their flight doesn't leave until tonight, so I invited them to stop by. No big deal."

"Them?" Elisa asked.

"Jerry and his friend Mac," Scarlet said, trying to sound casual. "They're both in the Army."

"Military men," Elisa nodded sagely. "Your father will be pleased."

"Mom, please don't make this into a thing," Scarlet pleaded. "No third-degree, no embarrassing childhood stories, no comments about how I haven't brought anyone around since—"

"Since Alex," Jade supplied helpfully.

"Thank you, Jade," Scarlet glared.

"Of course not, dear," Elisa said, patting Scarlet's cheek. "We'll be on our best behavior."

Somehow, that was exactly what Scarlet was afraid of.

Through the sliding glass doors, she could see her father by the pool, methodically arranging charcoal in the grill. She slipped outside, crossing the sun-warmed tiles to give him a kiss on the cheek.

"Hola, Papi," she said.

Leo looked up with a smile that crinkled the corners of his eyes. "There's my girl. How was the boat?"

"Ship," she corrected automatically. "It was good."

His hands never stopped working, arranging the coals with practiced precision. "Meet anyone interesting?"

Scarlet tensed. "Just some friends. Two of them need somewhere to hang out before their flight tonight, so I invited them over."

Leo nodded, reaching for the lighter fluid. "The more the merrier. Your mother made enough food for the entire neighborhood anyway."

"She always does," Scarlet laughed, relieved he wasn't pushing for details.

"Tell her to double the garlic in the chimichurri this time," Leo said, eyes twinkling. "Last batch wasn't strong enough."

"I heard that!" Elisa called from inside. "The garlic was perfect!"

"See?" Leo winked at Scarlet. "Thirty-four years of marriage and we still can't agree on garlic."

Scarlet smiled as she headed back to the house. Her father, at least, wasn't going to make this awkward.

Jade, on the other hand, was waiting by the door with a devilish grin. "So when does Soldier Boy arrive? I need time to prepare my interrogation strategy."

"I don't know, probably any minute," Scarlet said, brushing past her to the guest bathroom to quickly fix her hair. "And they're just friends, Jade. Please don't make this weird."

"Too late," Jade sing-songed. "You've already made it weird by bringing him home. I'm just embracing the weirdness."

The sound of a car door closing out front made Scarlet jump. Through the window, she watched a yellow cab pull away, leaving Jerry and Mac standing in the driveway with their cruise luggage.

"They're here," she announced, her voice higher than intended.

Jade materialized beside her with supernatural speed. "Oh, he's cute. You weren't exaggerating."

"Stop it," Scarlet hissed, elbowing her.

"What? I'm being supportive."

Taking a deep breath, Scarlet opened the front door before Jerry could knock. "Hey. You made it."

"Yeah," he said, shifting his weight, looking slightly out of place with his carry-on still slung over his shoulder. He cleared his throat. "Thanks for inviting us."

Mac appeared beside him with their larger bags. "Nice neighborhood. Very ... palm tree-y."

Scarlet blinked. "Palm tree-y?"

"You know, Fresh Prince ... Welcome to Miami ... lots of palm trees."

She inhaled deeply, forcing a smile. "Come in," she stepped back, gesturing toward the living room. "This is my sister Jade. My mom's in the kitchen." she pointed toward the back of the house where sounds of chopping and the scent of cilantro wafted out. "And that's my dad, Leo, coming in from the back."

Leo had stepped in from the patio, wiping his hands on a dish towel. Jerry straightened slightly. "Nice to meet you all," he said, extending his hand to Leo first. "Jerry. Thank you for having us."

His voice sounded different here ... lower, more careful. He was blinking more rapidly than usual, a tell Scarlet had noticed when he was nervous on the ship.

"And I'm Mac," his friend said, offering his most charming grin. "Thanks for having us on such short notice."

"Any friend of Scarlet's," Leo said with a nod. He looked between the two men. "You boys want a beer? Got some cold ones in the fridge out back. Peroni, Corona, take your pick."

"Water would be fine, thank you," Jerry answered, his fingers fidgeting slightly.

Scarlet leaned close to his ear, whispering, "You might want that beer. Trust me."

Jerry glanced at her, surprised, then back to Leo. "Actually, a beer sounds great. Thank you."

"Absolutely!" Mac chimed in. "Hell, I'm not drivin'!"

The corner of Jerry's mouth lifted slightly when he caught Scarlet's eye. Just enough to let her know they were in this together, but she could see the tension in his jaw, the careful way he was holding himself.

Scarlet gave a small shrug that she hoped conveyed both apology and solidarity. She'd thrown him into the deep end, and now all she could do was hope he could swim.

The scent of grilled meat mingled with warm citrus as the Bellari backyard filled with the familiar sounds of a Sunday barbecue: a sizzle from the coals, the clink of glassware, laughter carried on the breeze. Scarlet stood by the patio table arranging napkins, stealing glances at Jerry as he took in his surroundings.

He looked good, if a little nervous. The awkward stiffness in his shoulders was subtle, but she noticed it immediately. Mac, naturally, was already charming Elisa, gesturing animatedly about a plant in her herb garden like he'd grown up alongside it.

Jerry hovered with a beer in hand, trying not to look like he needed a map.

Leo clapped him on the shoulder. "You a steak guy or more of a burger man?"

"Burgers, usually," Jerry said, straightening.

"Good. You're on flipping duty. Come keep me company."

Scarlet held her breath, watching as Jerry followed her dad to the grill. She'd seen this dance before when Alex had never made it past polite conversation with Leo. But Jerry was already asking questions about the cut of meat and the wood chips Leo used for smoke. It wasn't smooth, but it was real.

Jade sidled up to Scarlet, sipping from a sweating glass of sangria. "He hasn't bolted yet. That's promising."

"Jade," Scarlet warned.

"I'm just saying, Papi doesn't hand over grill tongs to just anyone. Remember that guy I dated in college who tried to flip a steak with a salad fork?"

Scarlet winced. "Please don't bring that up."

As she arranged napkins on the patio table, Scarlet kept stealing glances toward the grill. The conversation between her father and Jerry seemed to shift suddenly. Something in their posture changing. Jerry's shoulders tensed, his movements becoming more mechanical as he turned the meat with too-careful precision. Her father's expression had grown solemn, his usual animated gestures stilled.

She watched as they clinked bottles in what appeared to be a toast, Jerry's face partially turned away but his profile rigid with emotion. The exchange felt private, weighted with something she couldn't quite identify from this distance.

Whatever they were discussing, it wasn't casual small talk about meat temperatures anymore.

When Mac joined them moments later, the tension visibly dissolved. The grill area erupted in laughter. Mac was doing an impression of a drill sergeant while Jerry cracked up. Even Leo smiled, shaking his head.

Scarlet exhaled. Maybe this would be okay.

Over lunch, the group spread out across the backyard with plates balanced on laps and folding chairs arranged under the shade of a flowering jacaranda. The conversation bounced between childhood stories, wedding plans, and neighborhood gossip. When Lucas arrived halfway through the meal, he offered hugs all around and plopped beside Jade with a practiced ease.

"So, Jerry," Lucas said, spearing a grilled pepper, "What do you do when you're not cruising the Caribbean with my future sister-in-law?"

Jerry hesitated, then smiled. "I'm active duty Army. Based in Texas. I work in public affairs ... media coordination, documentation, that sort of thing."

Leo nodded from across the yard. "Good skill set. Not just muscle."

"Sometimes I get to use both," Jerry replied. His smile grew more confident as the laughter rolled around him.

Jade raised an eyebrow. "Any scandalous press conferences in your past? Should we be worried you'll end up on TMZ?"

Jerry chuckled. "Not unless they start covering military base openings."

Scarlet watched him ease into the rhythm of the afternoon as he responded with dry wit to Jade's ribbing, laughed at Mac's exaggerated tales, and offered to grab extra drinks before anyone asked. It was like watching someone figure out a dance just by hearing the music.

Her heart squeezed.

After a refill run to the kitchen, Scarlet returned to find Jade cornering Jerry near the rose bushes. She couldn't hear what was being said, but Jade had adopted that casually dangerous stance Scarlet knew so well: hip cocked, one finger gesturing, head tilted. Inquisition mode.

Scarlet moved closer, pretending to rearrange a bowl of chips.

"... just curious about your intentions with my sister," Jade was saying. "She doesn't do this, you know. Not since Alex. Five years."

Jerry didn't flinch. "I know it's a lot to bring someone home."

"It's monumental. So either you're just a casual fling she's feeling reckless about, or—"

"A friend," Jerry said quietly. "She invited me over as a friend. We're not dating, engaged or having a baby together ... just friends."

Scarlet nearly dropped the chip bowl.

"Hmm," Jade studied him. "And do you always move this fast? Or just on cruise ships?"

Jerry's smile was patient. "I don't really know what all is going to happen between your sister and I, and I'm not trying to push anything. But in general I don't tend to move fast in anything."

"Because of the military?"

"Because of a lot of things."

Scarlet retreated to the kitchen, needing a moment to compose herself. The sound of dishes clinking and her parents' synchronized movements greeted her as she slipped through the door. They moved in perfect choreography. Leo rinsed plates while Elisa dried and arranged dessert, a dance perfected over decades of marriage.

"Need any help?" she asked, grateful for the distraction.

Elisa looked up. "You could take these out to the table."

Scarlet nodded, reaching for the platter of sliced mango and coconut.

"He seems nice," Elisa said casually. Too casually.

"He is," Scarlet agreed, suddenly fascinated by the fruit arrangement.

"Good head on his shoulders," Leo added, not looking up from the dish he was scrubbing. "Carries himself well."

Scarlet glanced between her parents, sensing a tag-team approach forming. "What does that mean?"

"It means he has substance," Leo replied, handing a clean plate to Elisa. "Not like that other one ... what was his name?"

"Alex," Scarlet and Elisa supplied in unison.

"Right. Alex." Leo nodded. "This one's different."

Elisa cast an approving glance at her husband before turning back to Scarlet. "Handsome, too."

"Mom."

"What? I have eyes." Elisa's smile was knowing. "And so do you, apparently. You haven't stopped looking at him all afternoon."

Scarlet's face heated. "I'm just making sure he's comfortable."

"Mmhmm." Elisa exchanged a look with Leo, the kind of wordless communication that had always fascinated and frustrated Scarlet in equal measure.

"Did you know he lost someone?" Leo asked, his tone shifting subtly. "In Afghanistan. A friend named Hunter."

The information caught Scarlet off guard. Jerry hadn't mentioned anyone named Hunter to her. "How do you know that?"

"We talked," Leo shrugged, as if it were the most natural thing. "It's Memorial Day weekend. Means something different to people who've served."

Elisa's expression softened. "That poor boy. No wonder he seemed so solemn when he first arrived."

"He wasn't being solemn," Leo corrected gently. "He was being respectful. There's a difference."

Scarlet absorbed this new information, piecing it together with the quiet gravity she sometimes glimpsed behind Jerry's smile. "What exactly did he say about his friend?"

"Not much," Leo replied. "Just that he was a great photographer, better soldier. Best friend." He paused, his hands stilling in the soapy water. "Anniversary's coming up next month. You can see it in his eyes—the way he carries it."

Elisa moved to her husband's side and touched his arm briefly. It was an old gesture of support. Scarlet had forgotten that her father had lost friends too, in his youth.

"And does he make you comfortable?" Elisa asked Scarlet, shifting the conversation with the grace of someone who knew when to press and when to ease back.

The unexpected question made Scarlet consider it carefully, thinking of Jerry's steady gaze, his quiet laugh, the way he listened like every word mattered.

"Yeah," she said softly. "He does."

Elisa's face softened further. "Oh my God, you are smitten, my dear."

"Mom!"

"What? I'm observant. A mother knows." She reached out to brush a strand of hair from Scarlet's face. "It's been a long time since I've seen you look at someone like that."

"Like what?"

"Like you're afraid to hope."

Leo turned from the sink, drying his hands. "Your mother's right," he said, the words clearly significant coming from a man who rarely admitted such things. "And if it means anything, I think he looks at you the same way."

Scarlet swallowed hard, caught between wanting to dismiss their observations and desperately wanting them to be true. "It's only been a week."

"So?" Elisa shrugged. "I knew about your father in three days."

"That was different. You were both in the same place, with the same life—"

"Life adjusts, mija. If it matters enough." Elisa patted Scarlet's cheek while Leo nodded in agreement. "Just don't overthink it to death. That's always been your way."

Scarlet opened her mouth to argue, then closed it. She couldn't deny it, not when her mind was already spinning through logistics, obstacles, reasons to guard her heart.

"A good man who's faced loss like that," Leo added quietly, "knows what matters. Don't discount that."

Elisa smiled triumphantly at her husband's support. "Exactly. Now take this out and stop hiding in the kitchen."

Scarlet stepped back into the sunshine with the platter in hand, seeing Jerry differently now. Not just as the quiet, steady man who'd captivated her on the cruise, but as someone who carried invisible weights with grace, who honored absent friends while still opening himself to new connections.

As the afternoon wound down, Scarlet noticed Jerry slip away from the group. He wandered to the far end of the pool, setting his beer down before lowering himself to sit at the edge. The splash of his feet hitting the water was soft, private. Something about the quiet way he sought solitude tugged at her heart. She recognized that instinct in herself.

Scarlet grabbed two fresh beers from the cooler and made her way over, feeling a flutter of nervousness that seemed ridiculous after everything they'd shared on the ship. Yet somehow, this felt more vulnerable. Jerry was in her world, not the fantasy bubble of a cruise.

"Mind some company?" she asked, working to keep her voice casual.

Jerry looked up, his face softening immediately in a way that made her stomach flip. "I was hoping you'd find me."

She settled beside him, passing him a beer before slipping off her sandals. The water was cool against her ankles, a welcome relief from the late afternoon heat. Their shoulders brushed as she adjusted her position, and neither of them moved away. Somehow that small point of contact felt more intimate than the nights they'd shared on the ship.

"So," she said, "on a scale of interrogation to inquisition, how bad was it?"

Jerry laughed softly. "Somewhere between friendly questioning and enhanced interview technique."

"I'm sorry about Jade. She's in extreme protective sister mode."

"Don't be," he said, his voice warm. "She loves you. I get it." He paused, then added with a hint of amusement, "Though she did inform me your mother is allegedly already planning a double wedding."

Scarlet nearly choked on her beer, mortification and amusement fighting for dominance. "Oh my God. She's just trying to get under your skin. My parents got married after three months of dating, so they think everyone should follow suit."

"It worked," Jerry admitted. "For about ten seconds I considered jumping the fence and making a run for it."

The laughter they shared loosened something tight in Scarlet's chest. She watched the way the tension in his shoulders eased, the way the corners of his eyes crinkled when he smiled. This felt dangerously natural.

They sat in comfortable silence, watching light dance across the rippling water. A citrus tree nearby released its scent into the air, mixing with the chlorine from the pool. Scarlet was acutely aware of every point where their bodies almost touched, of the gentle rise and fall of his breathing beside her.

"Your family's nice," Jerry said finally. "I see where you get it from."

Scarlet snorted. "The cross-examination skills or the inability to stay out of each other's business?"

"The warmth," Jerry said, turning to face her. "The way you listen like you're collecting every word."

The words landed gently but unsettled her, like a forgotten melody stirred to life.

Most people admired her edge, her clarity, her precision.

They saw what she did, not who she was beneath the doing.

But Jerry's gaze found something quieter. Something she hadn't touched in a while.

Jerry seemed to hesitate before adding, "Though I did get a strange vibe from Lucas. Something felt ... off about how he talked about your family."

Scarlet tensed slightly. She'd only known Lucas for a couple of months herself, ever since Jade had surprised them all by announcing both the relationship and engagement simultaneously after apparently dating him in secret for over a year. Scarlet was still figuring him out too.

"Lucas?" she said, more dismissively than she felt. "He's still trying to fit in. We've all only known him for about two months, since Jade finally introduced him."

"Of course," Jerry nodded. "It just seemed—"

"Not everyone can waltz in and charm the Bellaris in one afternoon like the great Jerry Duncan," she teased, bumping his shoulder to lighten the moment. The last thing she wanted was to admit that she sometimes had her own questions about her sister's fiancé.

Jerry backed off immediately, his expression softening. "Fair enough. I've just had years of practice reading people. Occupational hazard."

"Well, save your people-reading skills for your own family," she said with a smile that felt slightly forced. "Trust me, Jade knows what she's doing." Even if the rest of them were still catching up.

She was surprised by her defensive response. Maybe it was because questioning Lucas meant questioning Jade's judgment, and that felt disloyal. Or maybe it was because Jerry had noticed something in an afternoon that she'd been trying to ignore for weeks.

"It's been nice seeing you here," Jerry added, his voice lower, changing the subject with a grace she appreciated. "Outside of vacation mode. In your real life."

Scarlet studied the way his eyelashes caught the late afternoon sun, the faint lines at the corners of his eyes. "And? Verdict?"

"I like Scarlet-in-her-element even more than Scarlet-on-vacation," he said simply.

Her breath caught. No clever comeback formed. "That's ... not what most people say after meeting my family."

"I'm not most people."

"No," she agreed. "You're definitely not."

The silence between them shifted, charged with something new. Scarlet watched as Jerry traced slow circles in the water with his toe, sensing he was gathering his thoughts. Her heart began to beat faster, anticipating and dreading whatever came next.

"So," he said finally. "What happens when I get on that plane tonight?"

The question hung between them, deceptively simple. Scarlet had been asking herself the same thing all day, cycling through practical scenarios, each more disappointing than the last.

She looked down at their reflection in the water, rippling and reconnecting. "Logically? You go back to your life in Texas. I stay here with mine. We text for a while until it fades."

Jerry nodded slowly, his shoulder still pressed against hers. "That's what logic says."

"But?"

"But I don't know if I want to put up walls just because there's distance," he said, his voice steady. "It feels like ... closing a door before we've even looked inside."

Something expanded in Scarlet's chest, a feeling that was terrifying and exhilarating: hope. She turned to face him fully. "I've spent so much time being practical. Always thinking ten steps ahead."

"And now?"

"Now I'm wondering what happens if I don't overthink it for once," she said, the corner of her mouth lifting. "If we just … see where it goes. No promises, no pressure."

He found her hand without a word, fingers fitting neatly between hers.

The warmth that followed moved through her in waves, anchoring her in a space that felt entirely safe.

That single, silent link held more than she could name.

"I'd like that," he said. "Not closing doors just because the path looks complicated."

"It's going to be complicated," she acknowledged, realism creeping back in. "Your boys, my job, the distance—"

"One day at a time," he suggested. "Phone calls. Maybe visits when we can manage it."

"One step at a time," she agreed, squeezing his hand and feeling strangely lighter for having no plan, no timeline, no guaranteed outcome.

"You know, for two people who just met a week ago, this is either very romantic or completely insane," Jerry said, a touch of humor returning to his voice.

Scarlet laughed softly, feeling the tension dissolve. "Let's go with romantic. It sounds better on paper."

He shifted closer, his free hand moving to gently brush a strand of hair from her face. The touch was feather-light but sent electricity dancing across her skin. Scarlet was hyperaware of every sensation … the cool water around her ankles, the warm evening air, the citrus scent intensifying as the breeze picked up.

"I'm really glad you invited us today," Jerry murmured, his eyes dropping briefly to her lips. "I wasn't ready to say goodbye."

"Me neither," she whispered, surprised by the honesty in her own voice.

The moment stretched between them, fragile and perfect. Then Jerry leaned forward, closing the distance between them. The kiss was gentle, more question than demand. His lips were warm against hers, tasting faintly of the beer they'd been drinking. Scarlet's hand came up to rest against his chest, feeling his heartbeat quicken beneath her palm, matching her own racing pulse.

Jerry lingered with his eyes shut, holding the silence like something precious.

Scarlet did the same, letting the moment imprint itself before the world could intrude.

Mac's voice called from the patio. "Yo, Duncan! Cab's on its way. T-minus ten!"

Jerry sighed, resting his forehead briefly against hers. "Timing was never my strong suit."

Scarlet laughed softly, reluctant to break the moment. "To be continued?"

"Definitely," he said, brushing his thumb across her knuckles. "That's a promise I can make."

They slipped their feet from the water and stood together, a shared reluctance in their movements. As they walked back toward the house, their hands remained loosely linked until the last possible moment, a silent agreement that whatever this was, it wasn't ending today.

By late afternoon, the food was gone and the sun had dipped low. Mac stood beside the taxi in the driveway, calling out the time.

"I swear," he said, climbing into the back seat. "If TSA confiscates my leftover chimichurri, I'm writing to Congress. This is cultural discrimination."

Elisa gave Jerry a tight hug. "You're welcome back anytime. Preferably with more notice so I can plan a proper meal."

Leo shook his hand. "Good man. Don't be a stranger."

"Thank you, sir. For everything."

Scarlet walked Jerry to the car. The driveway felt longer now, the breeze cooler.

"I'm glad you came," she said, tucking a piece of hair behind her ear.

"So am I," he said. "It meant more than I think I can explain. This whole week did."

They stood for a beat longer than necessary, both searching for the right words.

"I'll text you when we land," he said.

"I'd like that."

He bent to kiss her cheek with soft, careful tenderness, and then ... he was gone.

As the cab pulled away, Scarlet stood at the curb until the yellow blur disappeared.

She didn't go inside right away. Instead, she sat on the porch steps, arms wrapped around her knees, listening to the buzz of cicadas and the distant clink of dishes inside.

This hadn't been just a vacation fling. She knew it now, bone-deep. And she wasn't sure what came next.

But for the first time in a long time, she wanted to find out.

# Seventeen

Scarlet stared at the spreadsheet until the numbers blurred. Friday afternoon, and her desk looked like a war zone. Stacks of files Maya had cheerfully dumped in her inbox before skipping off to the Henderson acquisition project. The office hummed with the usual end-of-week energy, but Scarlet felt disconnected from it all, like she was still floating somewhere in the Caribbean.

Her phone buzzed. She flipped it over, disappointed to see it was just an email notification. Jerry hadn't texted since yesterday morning, a simple "Good morning" that had made her smile embarrassingly hard while waiting for coffee in the break room.

"Someone's distracted," Simon's voice broke her reverie.

Scarlet glanced up to find her colleague leaning against her doorframe, arms crossed, a knowing look on his face.

"Just trying to make sense of Maya's organization system," she said, tapping her pen against a particularly confusing file. "I think she deliberately made it incomprehensible before handing it off."

"Ah yes, the old 'file by chaos' method." Simon settled into the chair opposite her desk. "So, are we going to talk about it?"

"About what?"

"About whatever, or whoever, has you checking your phone every three minutes." He raised an eyebrow. "The cruise glow is strong with this one."

Heat crept up Scarlet's neck. "I don't have a cruise glow."

"You absolutely do. You walked into Tuesday's staff meeting wearing the same expression my sister had after she met her husband."

"It was just a good vacation," Scarlet muttered, shuffling papers.

"Oh, absolutely," Simon said, giving a dramatic eye roll worthy of a daytime soap. "Just the occasional casual dicking. Nothing too indulgent."

Despite herself, Scarlet laughed. Simon had been her office ally since day one, the only person who understood the particular hell of working under Eric's management style and alongside Maya's ruthless ambition.

"Alright, I met someone," she muttered. "It's messy."

"Messy like wedding ring messy, or messy like he's gay and you're hoping for a miracle?"

Scarlet rubbed her temples. "He lives in Texas. With his kids. So yeah ... messy."

"Well, shit!" Simon whistled low. "You don't do anything halfway, do you, Bellari?"

"Apparently not." She leaned back in her chair, the weight of the situation suddenly heavy. "And now I'm what ... going to have a long-distance relationship with a military dad I met on a cruise?"

"When you put it that way, it sounds like the plot of a Hallmark movie."

The phone on her desk lit up with Eric's extension. Scarlet groaned. "That's my third summons today."

"Go. I'll guard your phone." Simon winked. "In case your cowboy calls."

Scarlet grabbed her notepad and headed for Eric's corner office, mind drifting as she walked. The cruise already felt like another lifetime: the swaying deck beneath her feet, the salt-tinged breeze, the feeling of Jerry's hand at the small of her back as they leaned against the railing watching the sunset.

The memory of their last night together flashed through her mind: Jerry's fingers tracing patterns on her bare shoulder, his voice low in the darkness as he shared about his kids. She'd listened, curled against his chest, realizing that this man came with a world already built. It was a world she hadn't planned for.

"... the Henderson files ready by Wednesday," Eric was saying when Scarlet tuned back in.

She blinked. "I'm sorry, what about the Henderson files?"

Eric's forehead creased with annoyance. "The preliminary worksheets. Maya will need them for her first client meeting."

"Of course," Scarlet nodded, making a note. "I'll have them ready."

"Good." Eric shuffled through papers on his desk. "And I'll need you to cover the Mackenzie audit while Maya's focused on Henderson. Simon can assist."

Another project. Scarlet's pen paused on the page. "That wasn't on my schedule for this quarter."

"Plans change. Opportunities arise." Eric's gaze was challenging. "Unless you're not interested in advancement opportunities?"

The implied threat hung in the air. She knew this routine well. Additional work dangled like bait, with the suggestion of future rewards that never materialized.

Before the cruise, she would have nodded and accepted. Today, something inside her rebelled.

"I'd be happy to take on Mackenzie," she said carefully, "but I'll need to adjust my other deadlines. The Peterson account needs attention, and with Maya's regular work already on my plate."

"I'm sure you'll manage," Eric cut her off. "That's what makes you so valuable, Scarlet. You always find a way."

The familiar praise that wasn't really praise at all. Scarlet felt a flicker of resentment. Last week, she would have taken it as a compliment.

"Was there anything else?" she asked, standing.

Eric looked surprised at her abrupt conclusion to their meeting. "No, that's all for now."

Back at her desk, Scarlet found Simon spinning idly in her chair.

"How was Emperor Eric today?" he asked, relinquishing her seat.

"Imperious as ever." She slumped down. "Guess who just inherited the Mackenzie audit on top of everything else?"

"Ouch." Simon perched on the edge of her desk. "You could say no, you know."

Scarlet gave him a look. "And risk getting passed over again?"

"Would that be the worst thing in the world?" His voice was gentle. "You've been killing yourself for this place for years."

The comment hit closer to home than Simon could know. Before she could respond, Maya appeared in the doorway, stylish in a fitted blazer that probably cost more than Scarlet's entire outfit.

"Eric filled you in on Henderson?" Maya asked, hovering at the threshold rather than striding in as usual. There was something tentative in her posture that Scarlet might have noticed if she hadn't been so irritated.

"Yes." Scarlet kept her tone professional. "I'll have everything ready."

"Great. I've left notes on the shared drive." Maya's smile was all teeth, but her eyes flickered toward Scarlet's desk where a small tin of fancy tea sat, specifically the imported kind Scarlet had once mentioned liking. "They might need some ... interpretation. You know how my mind works."

"Chaotically?" Simon suggested.

Maya's confident facade cracked for just a second before she recovered. "I made some notes specifically for you, Scarlet. Thought it might help with the handoff," she said, ignoring Simon. "I'm heading out early. Big weekend plans." She wiggled her fingers in a wave and disappeared down the hallway.

"One day," Simon said, "I'm going to replace her shampoo with hair removal cream."

Scarlet laughed despite herself, though something about Maya's quick departure nagged at her. "You'd have to get past her security system. I'm convinced she has her condo booby-trapped."

The afternoon crawled by. Scarlet made progress on the Peterson account, fielded two client calls, and created a to-do list for the

Mackenzie audit that already looked impossible. Through it all, her phone remained stubbornly silent.

At 5:30, she gave up pretending to work and began packing her bag. Simon appeared with his blazer already on.

"Escape while you can," he advised. "It's Friday. The spreadsheets will still be depressing on Monday."

Scarlet didn't need to be told twice. She grabbed her purse and followed Simon to the elevator. As they waited, she opened Maya's shared notes on her phone and was surprised to find them actually thorough and clearly organized. Not what she'd expected at all.

"Got plans this weekend?" Simon asked as they descended.

"Happy hour with my sister and Cami. Beyond that, absolutely nothing, which sounds like heaven.""If I don't see you on Monday, I'll assume you ran away to Texas."

They said goodbye in the garage with vague plans to keep in touch about Mackenzie.

Scarlet didn't start the car right away. She just sat there, phone resting in her palm.

She read over their recent texts, all of them short, ordinary, easy.

And yet, each one lit up something warm and expectant inside her, as if she was waiting for more and pretending not to be.

She started to type a message, then deleted it. Too casual. Started again. Too forward. She dropped her phone into her purse with a groan. When had texting become so complicated?

The drive to Bayside Marketplace took longer than usual, Miami's Friday traffic at its peak. Scarlet used the time to mentally shift gears, pushing work stress and Jerry-induced butterflies to the background.

Tonight was about the girls and the kind of uncomplicated fun she badly needed.

The Market Terrace Bar overlooked the cruise port, where massive ships gleamed in the golden hour light, preparing for their evening departures. Scarlet found Jade and Cami already at a waterfront table, cocktails in hand, sunglasses perched on their heads despite the setting sun.

"There she is!" Jade called, standing up dramatically and waving as if Scarlet was half a mile away instead of ten feet. "The woman who went on a singles cruise and actually found someone!"

Cami made a show of slow-clapping. "What an overachiever. Some of us just wanted a tan and meaningless hookups."

"Don't start," Scarlet warned, dropping into a chair. "I've had a week from hell."

"Which is exactly why we ordered you this," Cami pushed a margarita toward her that was roughly the size of a small fishbowl. "Triple tequila, extra salt, and I told the bartender you'd been wronged by a man named Eric so he made it extra strong."

"Maya, Eric, spreadsheets that want to eat my soul." Scarlet took a long, grateful sip. "God, that's good."

"Uh-uh," Jade declared, snatching Scarlet's phone and dropping it into her own purse. "No work talk. The only acceptable topics tonight are trashy gossip, wedding drama, and of course," she wiggled her eyebrows suggestively, "... your Texas cowboy."

"First, he's not a cowboy. Second, he's not mine," Scarlet protested, reaching unsuccessfully for her phone. "And third, give that back!"

"Oh honey," Cami patted her hand condescendingly. "Your face lights up like the Vegas strip every time your phone buzzes. We're not blind."

"Or stupid," Jade added.

Behind them, a cruise ship's horn blasted with a deep, resonant sound that vibrated through the air. Hundreds of passengers lined the decks, waving to nobody in particular as the massive vessel began to inch away from port.

"To that!" Cami declared, holding up her glass toward the departing ship. "May Scarlet's vagina continue its own brave journey of exploration!"

"Cami!" Scarlet hissed, glancing at nearby tables while Jade practically snorted her drink.

"What? I'm being metaphorical," Cami grinned wickedly. "To boldly go where no—"

"If you finish that Star Trek reference, I'm leaving," Scarlet threatened, but couldn't suppress her smile.

"Fine," Jade raised her glass instead. "To Scarlet, who went on a cruise and came back with more than a sunburn!"

They clinked glasses, Scarlet shaking her head but joining in the toast.

"It was not a fling," she clarified as they settled back.

"Oh, I'm sorry, what's the proper term for sleeping with someone you met three days earlier?" Jade asked innocently.

"A triumph of efficiency," Cami suggested, and they all burst into laughter.

A waiter arrived with a platter of appetizers none of them remembered ordering.

"Compliments of the gentlemen at the bar," he explained.

They turned to see a group of suited men raising their glasses in their direction.

Jade waved politely while Cami muttered, "Amateurs. Don't they know we're celebrating our friend ditching all of you for a man who can actually find the clitoris?"

"Oh my God," Scarlet buried her face in her hands, shoulders shaking with laughter.

Despite her embarrassment, Scarlet felt the tension of the week melting away. She needed exactly this. Her sister's enthusiasm, Cami's outrageous honesty, the familiar rhythm of their friendship.

"Seriously though," Jade said, popping a fried calamari in her mouth, "Dad wouldn't stop talking about your guy after the BBQ. Apparently, he 'handles tongs with military precision.'"

"That sounds weirdly sexual," Cami observed.

"Leo Bellari, grill master, has given his approval," Jade continued, ignoring her. "That's practically a marriage proposal."

"It's more than Mom gave poor Lucas when they first met," Jade added. "Remember how she kept 'accidentally' calling him Luis?"

"To be fair, your dating history had a lot of L-names back in high school," Scarlet pointed out. "Luis, Lorenzo, Leo ..."

"Let's not forget Loser, Lame-o, and Li'l—" Cami began.

"Don't you dare finish that sentence!" Jade threw a lime wedge that hit Cami square in the forehead. "Like you're one to talk, Miss 'I Have a Man in Every Port.'"

"That's international businesswoman to you," Cami corrected, flicking the lime back. "And unlike some people at this table, I'm not hiding a secret marriage and three kids in Chicago." She shot a meaningful look at Jade.

"That was ONE Tinder date who lied about his status, and I never slept with him!" Jade protested.

They dissolved into laughter again, the conversation flowing into Cami's latest work disaster. A client who wanted to rebrand with a logo that looked suspiciously phallic.

"I swear to God," Cami said, using a breadstick as a prop, "it was THIS obvious. And my boss looks at it and goes, 'I don't see the problem.'" She lowered her voice to a gruff imitation. "'It's clearly a rocket ship!'"

"Maybe he was just saying that because he didn't want to admit he saw it," Scarlet suggested.

"Or maybe he has a tiny rocket ship himself and didn't recognize the resemblance," Jade added, causing another round of hysterics.

Another cruise ship sounded its departure horn. Scarlet watched it glide past, remembering how different the world had looked from that perspective just a week ago. How different she had felt.

"Earth to Scarlet," Jade snapped her fingers. "You're doing it again."

"Sorry, what?"

"I asked if you're coming to Lucas's gallery thing tomorrow," Jade repeated. "But clearly your brain is somewhere in Texas."

Cami leaned back in her chair. "You know, there are these magical flying machines called airplanes. They can transport you to Texas in just a few hours."

"I can't just fly to Texas," Scarlet protested.

"Why not?" Cami challenged. "It's called a weekend. Friday night flight, Sunday return. No vacation days required."

"Because I have responsibilities, and—"

"And nothing," Cami interrupted. "The only thing stopping you is you."

Scarlet stirred her drink, watching the ice swirl. "It's not that simple."

"It could be," Jade said quietly. "Look, I spent two years thinking Lucas and I needed the perfect timing before getting serious. If I hadn't taken a chance, we wouldn't be planning a wedding right now."

"And more importantly," Cami added, "you wouldn't have me as your maid of honor, planning the world's most epic bachelorette party. I've already been researching male strippers who dress as soldiers."

"Please tell me that's a joke," Scarlet groaned while Jade doubled over laughing.

"What, you don't think Jerry would find that funny?" Cami asked innocently.

"I think he'd find it grounds for a restraining order," Scarlet retorted.

The third cruise ship of the evening sounded its horn, the sound echoing across the water. Sunset painted the sky in shades of pink and gold, casting a warm glow over their table.

"Have you thought about what it means to date a guy with kids?" Jade asked, her tone gentler. "I mean, they haven't even met you yet."

Scarlet nodded, the question hitting a nerve. "I think about it all the time. The whole package deal. Him, two boys I've never met, a completely different life."

"But you're still thinking about it," Cami observed. "Which means something, doesn't it?"

"I need to use the bathroom," Scarlet said suddenly, grabbing her purse.

In the privacy of the bathroom stall, Scarlet pulled out her phone. Before she could overthink it, she typed:



Her thumb hovered over the send button. This was impulsive. Reckless, even. She should think it through, make a pro/con list, consider all the implications.

Instead, she pressed send.

When she returned to the table, Jade and Cami were plotting something that involved aggressive hand gestures and the words "floral disaster."

"So," Cami said, eyeing Scarlet's slightly flushed face. "Did you text him?"

Scarlet's jaw dropped. "How did you—"

"Please," Jade scoffed. "You had your 'I'm about to do something bold' face on."

"Plus, you took your purse to the bathroom," Cami added. "Classic 'I need privacy to send a risky text' move. We've all been there."

"I just asked if maybe ..."

Scarlet's phone buzzed in her hand. All three women froze, staring at it.

"Well?" Jade demanded, practically climbing over the table. "What does it say?"

Scarlet looked down at the screen, her heart pounding.

I'm already on my way to the airport to pick you up.

A smile spread across her face, impossible to contain. She looked up to find Jade and Cami watching her with matching grins.

"Ladies," Cami declared, raising her glass, "I believe our Scarlet is going to Texas."

"To Texas!" Jade echoed, nearly knocking over a water glass in her enthusiasm.

Scarlet lifted her drink. "I guess I am."

With a wink and zero warning, Cami leaned across the table desperate to inquire about Scarlet's underwear plans for next weekend. "So, are we talking crotchless or classy seduction? I need lingerie intel, woman!"

Scarlet nearly choked on her drink. The laughter hit so hard, it knocked the prior week's pressure right out of her.

Maya and Eric would still be there Monday. But in this moment, everything else faded. The loud friends, the loud drinks, Jerry quietly waiting in her texts. This was all that mattered.

# Eighteen

Unfamiliar shadows painted a ceiling she didn't know. For a breathless instant, her mind went completely untethered.

And then it came rushing in: Texas. Jerry's place. His bed.

She rolled over, hand stretching across sheets still warm from where he'd been. The digital clock on his nightstand read 7:36 a.m.. Memories from the night before came flooding back: her late arrival after a long Friday workday, Jerry's heart-skipping smile at baggage claim, the drive to his house with their hands clasped over the center console. Then closing his bedroom door and—

Heat rushed to her face. They'd barely made it three steps inside before clothes were being torn off, scattered across the floor in their desperation to touch, to reclaim what had been missing since Miami three weeks ago. No words, just gasping breaths and urgent hands. They'd fallen asleep tangled together, her head on his chest, his heartbeat a steady rhythm beneath her ear.

Now faint sounds filtered through the closed door. She could hear a child's voice, something clattering in the kitchen, the low rumble of Jerry's response. Reality crashed in. The boys were awake. She was about to meet Jerry's children.

Scarlet sat up, pushing vibrant red hair from her face, suddenly very aware of her complete nakedness. Her small weekend bag sat in the corner, still half-unpacked from their hasty entrance last night. She needed to get dressed before meeting Emmett and Marty, but what had she packed?

She slipped from the bed and padded to her bag. Unzipping it revealed a horrifying truth: she'd packed for romance, not family breakfast. The first items that greeted her were a black lace teddy and a sheer burgundy nightgown with matching panties. She dug deeper, growing increasingly frantic. Clothes for today, yes. Sundresses, sandals, even a casual t-shirt. But nothing appropriate for morning introductions to children.

"Oh my God," she whispered, panic rising. She couldn't exactly meet Jerry's sons wearing lingerie.

The solution stood across the room: Jerry's dresser. She crossed to it, hesitating only briefly before pulling open the top drawer. T-shirts, neatly folded. She selected a plain blue one that looked soft from washing. The second drawer yielded cotton gym shorts with a drawstring she could cinch tight enough to stay on her narrower hips.

The borrowed clothes smelled faintly of detergent and something unmistakably Jerry. That clean, grounding scent she'd come to associate with feeling safe. The shirt hung loose, the neckline dipping to reveal her collarbone. The shorts were comically large, requiring the drawstring pulled as tight as possible, but they'd stay up.

Taking a deep breath, Scarlet opened the bedroom door and followed the cacophony of morning sounds.

The hallway opened to an unexpectedly bright and airy space. The walls were lined with photos. The boys at various ages, moments at parks and beaches, formal portraits in Jerry's dress uniform. She paused at one showing a much younger Jerry in desert camo, arm slung around Mac, both sunburned and grinning despite the dusty backdrop.

The kitchen came into view, and with it, a scene of controlled chaos. Jerry stood at the stove, flipping pancakes with practiced efficiency, his back to her. A small boy was setting the table with colorful plastic plates, dropping a fork with a clatter. She guessed this was Emmett. In a specialized seat near the table sat a smaller child with Jerry's soft brown eyes, watching the proceedings with quiet intensity.

Mac spotted her first from where he leaned against the counter, coffee mug in hand. "The sleeping beauty arises!"

Jerry turned, spatula in hand, his expression softening at the sight of her. "Hey," he said simply, but the warmth in that single word wrapped around her like an embrace.

Emmett's head whipped around. "Is that her? Is that Scarlet?" Before anyone could answer, he bounded across the kitchen, skidding to a stop inches from her. His eyes were wide with curiosity as he stared up at her. "Your hair really is red! Dad said it was but sometimes he exaggerates. One time he said the spaghetti I made was the best in the whole universe but it couldn't be because we haven't tried all the spaghetti everywhere."

Scarlet blinked, momentarily overwhelmed by the torrent of words. "Yes, I'm Scarlet. You must be Emmett."

"That's me! I'm six but I'll be seven in forty-three days. That's Marty over there. He's my brother. He's eight but he doesn't talk like I do. He makes sounds though! And Dad says he understands everything, just like I do, only different."

Jerry approached, resting a hand on Emmett's shoulder. "Buddy, let's give Scarlet a chance to get some coffee before the interrogation, okay?"

"Is this an interrogation?" Emmett's eyes somehow grew wider. "Like the police shows Mac watches after I go to bed?"

"A figure of speech," Jerry clarified, shooting an amused look at Mac. "Why don't you finish setting the table while I get Scarlet some coffee?"

As Emmett zoomed back to his task, Jerry leaned in to kiss Scarlet's cheek. "Sorry," he murmured. "Morning volume control isn't his strong suit."

"It's fine," she whispered back, genuinely meaning it despite her nerves. "I like his energy."

Jerry moved to pour her coffee, adding cream and sugar exactly as she preferred without asking. The simple knowing gesture steadied her.

"I stole your clothes," she admitted. "I didn't exactly pack appropriate pajamas for meeting kids."

A hint of a smirk played at his lips. "I noticed. Looks better on you anyway."

Mac approached, lowering his voice conspiratorially. "Heads up: Emmett remembers everything and repeats it at the worst possible moments. And Marty notices everything, even when you think he's not paying attention."

"Great," Scarlet muttered, accepting the coffee mug Jerry offered. "No pressure."

"There's blueberry pancakes," Jerry said. "Emmett's specialty."

"I put in the blueberries!" Emmett confirmed from the table. "Dad says I'm the blueberry distribution expert."

Scarlet smiled, moving carefully toward the table. As she passed Marty's specialized seat, she slowed, meeting his intense gaze. "Good morning, Marty," she said gently.

The child's face transformed with a sudden, radiant smile. He made a soft sound and raised his hand in what might have been a wave.

"He likes you," Emmett announced with authority. "I can tell because his eyes got all crinkly. That means he's happy."

Something warm unfurled in Scarlet's chest as she settled into a chair. Jerry moved with practiced ease, transferring pancakes to plates, helping Marty with his specially adapted utensils, refilling Mac's coffee. The domesticity of it all felt alien yet somehow right.

"So," Emmett continued, seeming physically incapable of silence, "do you live in Miami? Dad said that's where he met you. On a boat."

"I do live in Miami," Scarlet confirmed, unable to resist smiling at his enthusiasm. "And it was a very big boat called a cruise ship."

Emmett nodded seriously, accepting this information as he drowned his pancakes in syrup. "Did you know Dad hasn't had a friend visit before? Just Grandma and Grandpa and Aunt Hannah, but they're family so they have to visit."

An awkward silence settled over the adults. Jerry cleared his throat. "Emmett—"

"It's true," Emmett insisted. "Not even a friend who's a girl. But Mac said—"

"Hey squirt," Mac interrupted swiftly, "tell Scarlet about your dinosaur collection."

The diversion worked spectacularly. Emmett launched into a detailed catalogue of his dinosaur figurines, ranking them by ferocity and historical accuracy. Scarlet caught Jerry's grateful glance toward Mac, filing away the revelation that she was apparently the first woman Jerry had brought home since ... well, since.

Scarlet observed as the morning settled into motion.

Jerry sliced pancakes into tidy squares, steadying Marty's hand with calm efficiency when it faltered.

Something tugged at her. Unexpected, quiet, but undeniable.

Mac picked up the threads of conversation with skill, looping Emmett into the moment without missing a beat.

"Do you have any pets?" Emmett asked suddenly, mouth still full of pancake.

"Chew first, then talk," Jerry reminded gently.

Emmett swallowed dramatically. "Sorry. Do you?"

"I have a cat," Scarlet answered. "A gray one named Storm."

Emmett gasped, dropping his fork with a clatter. "A real cat? I love cats! Dad says we can't have one because of Marty's allergies but I have Orange Cat!" He pointed to an obviously well-loved stuffed orange tabby propped in the empty chair beside him. "He sleeps with me every night and protects me from the vacuum."

Seeing a chance to engage, Scarlet reached over and picked up the stuffed animal. "He's very cute—"

"NO!" Emmett's sudden shout made everyone freeze. His face crumpled, hands reaching frantically for the toy. "You can't just TAKE him! You have to ASK first!"

Scarlet's stomach dropped, her face heating with embarrassment. "I'm so sorry, Emmett. You're absolutely right." She quickly handed Orange Cat back, feeling Jerry's gaze heavy on her.

The room fell painfully silent. Marty watched with wide eyes. Mac suddenly became very interested in his coffee.

Jerry cleared his throat. "Emmett, Scarlet didn't know. Remember how we talked about using our words calmly when someone doesn't know our rules?"

Emmett clutched Orange Cat to his chest, lower lip trembling slightly, but nodded. "I'm sorry I yelled," he said in a small voice. "But Orange Cat doesn't like strangers touching him without permission."

"That makes perfect sense," Scarlet said gently. "I should have asked first. I promise I'll always ask from now on."

Emmett studied her face, his own expression serious. Then, unexpectedly, he held out Orange Cat. "You can hold him now if you want. I give permission."

The simple gesture of forgiveness made Scarlet's throat tight. "Thank you. That's very kind."

As she carefully accepted the stuffed animal, she caught Jerry's eyes across the table. His small, reassuring smile told her everything was okay.

The rest of breakfast proceeded with the crisis averted. As Jerry cleared plates, he announced, "Bath time for Marty. Emmett, you're after."

By mid-morning, they had settled in the living room. Jerry was helping Marty with a colorful stacking toy while Emmett sprawled on the floor with paper and crayons, drawing what he claimed was a scientifically accurate Brachiosaurus. Scarlet sat on the couch, sipping fresh coffee, struck by how quickly chaos had given way to a comfortable rhythm.

Her attention was drawn to Jerry's hands as he gently guided Marty's movements. The same hands that had explored her body with such passion hours earlier. The contrast made her breath catch.

Marty suddenly abandoned his toy, crawling across the floor with surprising determination until he reached Scarlet's legs. Without hesitation, he pulled himself up, arms wrapping around her calves as he gazed up at her with a smile that crinkled his eyes.

"He wants up," Jerry translated, watching with a mixture of surprise and warmth.

Scarlet carefully lifted Marty onto the couch beside her. Instead of staying at arm's length, he scooted close, nestling into her side with a contented sigh.

"Oh," she breathed, uncertain where to place her hands.

"Around his middle is good," Jerry guided softly. "He likes the pressure."

She gently wrapped her arms around Marty's torso, feeling his body relax against her. Something powerful and unfamiliar welled inside her, a kind of protective tenderness she'd never experienced before.

"He doesn't usually take to new people this quickly," Jerry said, his voice hushed with wonder.

"Must be my natural charm," Scarlet quipped, though her own voice was thick with emotion.

She held him a little tighter, surprised by the ache blooming beneath her ribs. The warmth of Marty against her, his simple trust, stirred something she hadn't let herself feel in years. A flicker of the future she'd once let go, soft and almost too tender to look at directly.

"Must be," Jerry agreed, and the look in his eyes made her heart flip.

The moment was broken by Emmett, who scrambled up with his drawing. "Look! I made you into a dinosaur trainer! That's you with the red hair, and you're teaching the dinosaurs to do tricks!"

"That's amazing," Scarlet said, genuinely impressed by the colorful, if anatomically creative, artwork. "Is that Orange Cat in the corner?"

"Yes! He's the assistant trainer. He's very important."

Emmett beamed, then rushed off to create another masterpiece. Marty remained content in Scarlet's lap, occasionally reaching up to touch her hair with gentle curiosity.

Mac appeared from the kitchen, eyebrows rising at the sight of Marty curled up with Scarlet. He caught Jerry's eye, giving a subtle nod of approval before announcing, "Anyone up for backyard time? I set up the sprinkler."

Emmett's answering whoop of excitement was deafening. Even Marty perked up, making an eager sound.

As Jerry ushered the boys toward their rooms to change, Mac lingered, settling into the armchair across from Scarlet.

"So," he said, his usual joking tone replaced with something more serious. "Holding up okay?"

"Better than I expected," Scarlet admitted. "They're amazing kids."

"They're a handful," Mac corrected, though his affection was obvious. "But yeah, they're pretty great. Especially considering ..." He trailed off, seeming to catch himself.

"Considering what?"

Mac shook his head. "Not my story to tell. Just ... their mom wasn't exactly Mother of the Year."

Scarlet digested this, remembering the conspicuous absence of any maternal presence in the family photos lining the walls. "Jerry hasn't talked much about her."

"And he won't," Mac said firmly. "Just know that how quickly they're attaching to you means something. What you're seeing here isn't normal for them. Especially Marty. Kid's got an internal radar for good people."

"I'm not trying to replace anyone," Scarlet said quickly.

Mac's laugh held no humor. "Trust me, there's nothing to replace. Just ... be patient with Jerry. This is new territory for him."

"For me too," she confessed.

"You're doing fine," Mac assured her. "Want some unsolicited advice for surviving Duncan family chaos?"

"Absolutely."

"Emmett needs questions. Ask him about his interests, his opinions. Makes him feel heard. And with Marty ... he communicates through touch. That little head bump he does? That's his way of saying he likes you."

The afternoon danced by in spurts of water, sugary treats, and pure childhood joy.

Scarlet stepped into it naturally. She steadied Marty as the sprinkler tickled his feet, listened patiently to Emmett's dramatic narration, and traded quiet looks with Jerry that said more than words.

"Scarlet! Scarlet!" Emmett called, running toward her with water droplets flying from his hair. "Can you watch Orange Cat while I'm outside? He doesn't like water."

He thrust the stuffed animal into her hands, his expression earnest. "He likes to be held like a baby, and if he gets scared, you have to sing to him. His favorite song is about the wheels on the bus."

Scarlet blinked down at the worn plush cat now cradled in her arms. "I ... yes, of course I'll watch him."

Emmett's smile was blinding. "I knew you would! You're good at taking care of things."

As he ran back out toward the backyard, Scarlet sat frozen, Orange Cat clutched carefully in her arms. Something about that gesture felt monumental. The simple trust of Emmett entrusting his most precious possession to her care.

Jerry appeared with Marty, now dressed in swim trunks and a rash guard. He paused, taking in the sight of Scarlet holding Orange Cat.

"He gave you Orange Cat," he said, voice filled with quiet amazement.

"Is that significant?"

"Very." Jerry's eyes were soft. "Not even Grandma gets Orange Cat duty."

By early evening, both boys were exhausted, flopping onto the couch for what Jerry called "decompression time" before dinner. Emmett curled against one end, Orange Cat clutched to his chest. Marty sprawled on the other side, eyes heavy with approaching sleep.

Scarlet followed Jerry into the kitchen, where he began pulling ingredients for dinner from the refrigerator.

"Taco night?" he asked, and she nodded, reaching for a cutting board.

They worked side by side, falling into a comfortable rhythm. Scarlet chopped vegetables while Jerry browned meat, their movements coordinated despite never having cooked together before.

"Thank you," Jerry said suddenly, voice low.

"For what? Subpar dicing skills?"

"For this." He gestured vaguely. "For coming. For not running screaming after meeting the circus that is my life."

Scarlet set down her knife, turning to face him fully. "Did you think I would?"

"I wouldn't have blamed you." His honesty was stark. "This ..." he nodded toward the living room where both boys were now dozing, "... it's a lot. It's complicated and messy and demanding."

"And beautiful," Scarlet added softly. "Jerry, your boys are amazing. And watching you with them ..." She swallowed, emotion suddenly thick in her throat. "I've never seen anything like it."

Dinner was a lively affair, Emmett recounting the day's adventures as if Scarlet hadn't been present for all of them. Marty, refreshed from his nap, hummed contentedly through the meal, occasionally reaching for Scarlet's hand with sticky fingers.

Mac excused himself after helping clean up, mentioning plans with friends in town. The wink he gave Jerry wasn't remotely subtle.

Bath time and bedtime routines followed, with Scarlet finding small ways to assist without overstepping. When Emmett asked her to read his bedtime story, she felt a surprising flutter of pleasure at being included in this sacred ritual.

Tucking Orange Cat beside Emmett, she began reading about a dinosaur who was afraid of the dark, doing her best to provide different voices for each character. Emmett corrected her pronunciation of the dinosaur names but otherwise listened with rapt attention.

"Will you be here tomorrow?" he asked suddenly, voice small.

Scarlet's heart squeezed. "Yes. I'm here until tomorrow afternoon."

"Good." He yawned enormously. "I like you being here. Dad smiles more."

Scarlet froze for a second, caught off guard by the simple truth in his voice.

Rather than reply, she tucked the blanket a little tighter around him.

Marty's room was next. Jerry was already there, singing a soft lullaby as he tucked his son in. He glanced up at Scarlet standing in the doorway and mouthed, "Be right out."

She dipped her head in acknowledgment, backing away without disruption as Jerry persisted with the soft tune. The home's ambiance shifted to something unfamiliar. Gone were the animated show soundtracks, Emmett's relentless curiosity, the normal percussion of playthings and kitchenware. Just the murmur of Jerry's singing voice traveling down the corridor.

Only now, with calm settling over the house, did Scarlet begin to see what Jerry had built.

The day had pulled her in a hundred directions, each one louder than the last.

But in the hush of night, she drifted through the rooms, letting the quiet reveal a life shaped by care and intention.

The living room was modest and surprisingly sparse. It wasn't the impersonal bareness of someone who didn't care, but rather the intentional minimalism of someone who chose each item with purpose.

The walls held only a couple of art prints showing serene beach scenes with golden sand and turquoise water stretching to the horizon. Not what she'd expected in a military man's home, but somehow fitting for someone who seemed to crave peace amid chaos. She ran her fingers lightly over one frame, wondering if these places existed somewhere real or if they were just wishful thinking. Did Jerry dream of oceans when surrounded by desert deployments?

The entertainment center was clearly the heart of the home. This was where Jerry had chosen to display the things that mattered most. A collection of photographs in simple frames told fragments of their family story: Jerry with an infant Marty in hospital, looking both terrified and fiercely protective; a birthday party with cake smeared across Emmett's face; a Christmas morning with presents scattered around both boys.

A familiar photo caught her attention. She'd first noticed it in Jerry's cabin on the cruise. Now, seeing it here in its permanent place, she understood its significance differently. The frame showed signs of frequent handling. The edges were slightly worn, the glass faintly smudged with fingerprints. So different from the pristine frames surrounding it.

Emmett, perhaps four years old, stood behind his brother's wheelchair on a sunlit sidewalk. The blue backpack he wore seemed almost comically large on his small frame. Orange Cat's head poked deliberately out of the zippered top, as if the stuffed friend needed to see where they were going.

The metal frame looked more traveled than the others, as if this particular photo accompanied Jerry wherever he went on deployment, trips, even their cruise. This wasn't just a cute photograph; it was

Jerry's anchor, serving as a visual reminder of what waited for him during long absences.

Scarlet touched the frame lightly. She understood how this simple image of ordinary heroism might sustain someone through dark nights far from home. A little boy caring for his brother, taking on responsibility with joy, while a path stretched ahead of them into the distance.

The entertainment center held other treasures that spoke to the man himself, including a miniature 49ers helmet displayed on a small stand, a framed medal she didn't recognize, and a white University of Utah football covered in signatures, sitting on a custom wooden holder. The careful placement suggested these weren't just decorations but touchstones that connected him to memories, identity, and home.

"That's the 2008 squad," Jerry's voice came from behind her, warm with nostalgia. She turned to find him leaning against the doorframe, watching her with a soft expression that made her breath catch. "Best team Utah ever fielded. Went undefeated that year."

"You're from Utah?" she asked, realizing how little she knew about his roots.

"Born and raised," he nodded, pushing off from the doorway. "My dad and I never missed a game if we could help it. He took me to meet the team after their Sugar Bowl win. That's where all those signatures came from."

As he moved toward the kitchen, his eyes lingered on her for a moment longer than necessary, a hint of vulnerability in his expression. As if letting her explore his space was its own kind of intimacy.

"Feel like some wine?" he asked, voice casual in a way that didn't quite mask something deeper. "Fair warning: my wine expertise stops at 'red' and 'white,' but Mac left a bottle of Merlot he swears isn't terrible."

She laughed. "Coming from Mac, that's high praise. I'd love some."

As Jerry rummaged through a drawer for a corkscrew, Scarlet continued her exploration, fingers trailing along the DVD shelves. The collection told its own story. There were animated movies worn from repeated viewings, action films and comic book adaptations lined up in neat rows. But tucked in among them sat a surprisingly extensive collection of romantic comedies like "Fools Gold," "13 Going on 30," "Forgetting Sarah Marshall," "Love and Basketball," and "Just Friends."

Jerry approached with two glasses of deep red wine. "Before you comment ..." he started, nodding toward the romantic comedies as he handed her a glass, "... Mac claims those are his."

"And they're not?" she asked, accepting the wine, their fingers brushing.

"Not even close." His eyes crinkled with amusement. "Though I'll deny it if you tell him I said so."

"So which one's your favorite?" she asked, taking a sip and finding the wine surprisingly good.

Jerry considered for a moment. "'Fools Gold,' hands down. Treasure hunting, second chances, McConaughey being ridiculous ..." He shrugged, a bashful half-smile lighting his face. "I'm a sucker for a good laugh and love story every now and then, you know? Sometimes you need something lighter to balance out the heavier parts of life."

The moment was undemanding. No performance, no explanation.

He spoke plainly, and somehow, that simplicity made the room feel warmer, closer.

"No judgment here," she said, raising her glass in a mock toast. "I've seen 'The Proposal' at least twelve times."

His resulting laugh was warm and genuine, seeming to surprise even himself.

Scarlet's attention drifted to a small bronze sculpture sitting beside the DVDs. It depicted a rifle standing upright, dog tags hanging from the grip, with a helmet balanced on top and combat boots at the base. She reached toward it but stopped, instinctively sensing this wasn't a casual decoration.

Jerry's expression softened. "It's called a Battlefield Cross," he explained, moving beside her. "Traditional memorial when a soldier falls in combat."

She nodded, immediately understanding its significance. "Is it for someone specific?"

A shadow crossed his features, the easy warmth of moments before giving way to something more complex. "For all the brothers and sisters we've lost," he said quietly. "But particularly for Hunter." His voice caught slightly on the name.

The name sparked recognition. Scarlet remembered hearing it mentioned briefly at her family's Memorial Day barbecue a few weeks ago. She hadn't asked then, respecting the obvious weight of the moment.

"Hunter," she repeated softly, not pushing, just acknowledging.

She saw the pain flash in Jerry's eyes. Deep, personal grief that time had tempered but never erased. In that moment, she understood something fundamental about the man beside her. His life was built around honoring connections. To his children, to friends lost, to memories both painful and precious. He kept what mattered close, even when it hurt.

"The reverence in your voice tells me enough," she said softly, choosing not to pry further. "I understand the love behind it."

Jerry's eyes met hers with a mixture of gratitude and surprise, as if he hadn't expected to be read so easily. His hand found hers, squeezing gently. "Thanks," he murmured, the single word carrying more weight than a longer explanation could have.

They settled on the couch, the house quiet except for the soft hum of the air conditioner and the occasional creak of the settling home. Scarlet curled her legs beneath her, the borrowed t-shirt riding up to reveal more thigh than she'd intended.

Jerry's eyes tracked the movement, the shadow from earlier lifting as his gaze darkened slightly. "Been wanting to do this all day," he murmured, setting aside his wine to pull her closer.

His kiss was deeper than before, nothing like their frantic re-union the previous night. Scarlet felt her body respond instantly, arching into him as his hands slid beneath the borrowed t-shirt to trace the curve of her spine. She pulled back just long enough to whisper, "Bedroom?"

Heat bloomed in his expression as he nodded, entwining his fingers with hers as they moved down the shadowed hallway. Nothing broke the evening hush but the soft padding of their feet against the carpet. When the bedroom door sealed shut with a faint sound, they both felt the moment stretch between them. Time deliberately slowed. There was a wordless recognition that tonight marked something meaningful.

Scarlet stood in the center of the room, moonlight streaming through the blinds painting silver stripes across the bed. She reached for the hem of his borrowed shirt, pulling it over her head in one fluid motion. The cool air raised goosebumps across her skin, but Jerry's gaze was so heated she hardly noticed.

"Come here," she murmured, holding out her hand.

He moved to her like a man in a dream, fingers skimming her waist with reverence. There was something different in his touch tonight. Not the desperate hunger of last night, but something deeper, more intentional. She helped him remove his shirt, letting her palms explore the broad expanse of his chest, tracing the defined muscles and subtle scars that told stories she was only beginning to understand.

They sank onto the bed together, the mattress dipping beneath their combined weight. Jerry's mouth found the sensitive spot where her neck met her shoulder, drawing a soft gasp from her lips. His hands mapped her body with careful precision, as if memorizing every curve and plane. Scarlet surrendered to the sensation, letting her head fall back as he traced a path of kisses down her throat to the swell of her breast.

His breath brushed her skin. "You're incredible."

The words sank in slowly, stealing her breath more than his touch ever could.

She pulled him closer, wanting to give as much as she received. Her fingers tangled in his short hair, guiding him back to her mouth for a kiss that left them both breathless. Tonight wasn't about taking; it was about sharing, about showing him through touch what she wasn't ready to say in words.

He eased her onto her back, resting above her with arms planted on either side.

When he looked down, his expression held nothing hidden. Just raw, quiet truth.

She saw the change as it happened. A flicker in his eyes, not hesitation but clarity. A yes, fully formed.

"I'm falling for you, Scarlet," he said softly.

The words hung in the air between them. Scarlet felt her body tense involuntarily, panic flashing through her mind. It had only been three weeks. They barely knew each other. And yet, there was already so much at stake. Not just her heart, but those two innocent boys sleeping down the hall.

She opened her mouth, searching for words, but before she could respond, she saw something change in Jerry's expression. His body went rigid, eyes suddenly distant, jaw tightening as he pulled away from her. He sat up abruptly, back to her, shoulders hunched defensively.

"I'm sorry," he said, voice suddenly rough. "That was ... I didn't mean to push. Too soon. I know."

The transformation was so sudden it took her breath away. This wasn't just embarrassment or disappointment. This went deeper. A wound reopened. Scarlet recognized pain when she saw it; someone had hurt him badly for such simple vulnerability to trigger this response.

Without hesitation, she moved to sit beside him, deliberately not forcing him to face her. She placed her palm against his bare back, feeling the tension in his muscles.

"Jerry," she said softly. "Look at me."

When he turned, the guardedness in his eyes nearly broke her heart. She recognized this expression. She'd worn it herself years ago, staring into her bathroom mirror after Alex had left her for her colleague. That particular blend of shame and self-protection that came from having your heart handed back to you in pieces.

"Don't apologize," she said firmly, cupping his face in her palm. "I'm just ... processing. This is all so new, and there's so much at stake." She glanced briefly toward the door, thinking of Emmett and Marty sleeping peacefully, unaware of the emotional precipice their father stood on.

She could see him steadying himself, breathing returning to normal as her touch anchored him to the present moment.

"I know," he said. "We don't have to race to some finish line." He leaned his forehead against hers, the gesture both intimate and vulnerable. "I just wanted you to know."

"I'm here," she whispered, choosing her words carefully. She couldn't say "I love you too" because she wasn't ready for that. But not nothing. Something truthful, something real. "I'm not running. But I want to do this right."

She felt the tension gradually leaving his body, his shoulders relaxing beneath her touch. Scarlet drew him back down to the bed, her body curving against his deliberately, protectively. She kissed him with all the words she couldn't yet say. That she understood broken hearts. That she saw his strength in vulnerability. That she was choosing this complicated reality with open eyes.

Their bodies moved together in perfect harmony, tender and reverent where last night had been urgent and desperate. Scarlet gave herself to him completely, both physically and emotionally, holding nothing back. She wrapped herself around him, legs tangling with his, hands exploring and soothing in equal measure. When he trembled in her arms, she held him tighter, offering sanctuary in the storm of emotion.

Later, as sleep approached, Scarlet turned onto her side, pressing her back against Jerry's warm chest. She reached for his arm, pulling it around her and drawing his hand up to rest near her heart, their fingers naturally intertwining. The simple intimacy of their bodies fitting together perfectly, her curves nestled against his strength, felt like a wordless promise.

She'd come to Texas to see if reality matched the connection they'd forged on the cruise. What she'd found was something both more complicated and more precious than she'd imagined.

# Nineteen

"**Y**ou know what, that veil is giving serious nun-chic, and not in a good way," Cami whispered, leaning closer to Scarlet as they huddled on a plush cream settee in Elégance Bridal's VIP suite.

Scarlet bit her lip to keep from laughing. "Shh, she looks beautiful," she murmured, though she couldn't disagree about the veil, which somehow managed to simultaneously overwhelm Jade's petite frame while making her look like she was auditioning for a convent.

"Of course she looks beautiful," Cami shot back under her breath. "She could wear a garbage bag and look beautiful. That's not the point. The point is finding a dress worthy of her beauty, and that ..." she gestured with her champagne flute, "that, is not it."

They were three boutiques into their Saturday wedding shopping extravaganza, and Jade was emerging from behind heavy velvet curtains in wedding dress number seven of the day. Claudette, the consultant, was a rail-thin woman with an immaculate bob and French accent so exaggerated Scarlet was convinced it had to be fake. She circled Jade like a fashion predator, adjusting the massive skirt and nodding with practiced enthusiasm.

"Magnifique!" Claudette exclaimed. "The princess ball gown, it is so romantic, so traditional! The perfect silhouette for your frame."

Jade turned uncertainly before the three-way mirror, her expression clearly unconvinced despite the consultant's effusive praise. The dress was a confection of tulle and crystal beading, with a skirt so wide Jade would need to enter the church sideways. The bodice was elaborately beaded, the neckline stiff with embroidery that seemed to swallow her delicate collarbones.

"I don't know," Jade said, turning to face them. "What do you guys think? Honestly?"

The bridal consultant's smile tightened ever so slightly as she looked at Scarlet and Cami. "Your sister looks like a true princess, no? The sparkle, the volume ... it has such presence!"

Scarlet met Jade's eyes in the mirror and saw the silent plea there. Taking a slow sip of champagne to fortify herself, she set her glass down and stood.

"It's ... a lot of dress," she began diplomatically, moving to stand beside her sister. "And you look gorgeous, because you always do. But ..."

"But it's eating you alive," Cami finished bluntly. "You're drowning in tulle. I can barely see you in there."

"Cami!" Scarlet hissed, though she secretly agreed.

"What? We promised honesty." Cami raised her glass defiantly. "That dress is wearing her, not the other way around."

The consultant's smile had completely evaporated. "Perhaps mademoiselle would prefer something more ... simplistic? Though this is Marchesa, very exclusive, very sought-after."

Jade's shoulders relaxed visibly with her friends' assessment. "I think she's right. It's beautiful, but it doesn't feel like me." She turned to the consultant. "Could we try something less voluminous? Maybe more sheath or A-line?"

As Claudette helped Jade back to the dressing room, her professional enthusiasm notably dimmed, Cami leaned back on the settee and refilled her champagne.

"One more boutique after this?" she suggested. "My champagne buzz is just hitting its stride."

"We're shopping for Jade's wedding dress, not doing a vineyard tour," Scarlet reminded her, checking her phone briefly before returning it to her purse.

"Checking for Texas updates?" Cami asked, eyebrows waggling suggestively. "How is Sergeant Hottie and his tiny troops?"

Scarlet felt her cheeks warm. "They're fine. Just habit."

"Mmmhmm." Cami's knowing smile was infuriating. "Four months in and you've still got that glow. It's disgusting. I'm jealous."

"It's not that long," Scarlet protested weakly, though it both felt like they'd known each other forever and no time at all. The past few months had settled into a comfortable rhythm that included weekend visits every few weeks, daily texts, and late-night calls that left her smiling into her pillow like a teenager.

Cami stretched languidly, her bright yellow sundress riding up to reveal more thigh than was probably appropriate for a bridal salon.

"So, how's the insta-family treating you? Ready to trade your designer handbags for dinosaur backpacks and sippy cups?"

Scarlet opened her mouth to reply, then closed it again, surprised by how much she cared about the answer.

"Relax," Cami said with a sly grin. "The point is, you've gone from 'devoted career woman who occasionally feeds her cat' to 'helps with homework and knows snack preferences by brand' in record time."

Had she? Scarlet considered this. It was true that her last Amazon order had included both a professional reference book for work and a set of sensory-friendly markers for Marty that Jerry had mentioned were hard to find in Killeen. She'd started bookmarking recipes that aligned with Emmett's picky preferences. And yes, she did know their shoe sizes. Both in regular and adaptive footwear.

"I like them," she said simply. "They're great kids."

Cami's expression softened. "I know you do. That's what makes this whole thing so much more than a fling. You're not just falling for the hot dad; you're falling for the whole package."

Before Scarlet could respond, the curtains parted again. Jade emerged in a completely different style. A sleek, form-fitting sheath with delicate lace overlay and an elegant, open back.

"Better," Cami nodded approvingly. "Much better."

Scarlet moved to join her sister at the mirror. "This is gorgeous on you. The silhouette is perfect."

Jade turned, examining her profile. "I do like it better. The other one felt like I was being swallowed whole."

"This is also Marchesa," Claudette noted, clearly relieved they approved of something in her luxury price range. "Very elegant, very modern."

Jade smoothed her hands over the hips, frowning slightly. "But is it ... I don't know ... special enough? I want to feel like it's magic. Like it couldn't possibly be anyone else's dress."

The hunt continued through two more styles. First, a fit-and-flare that was "almost but not quite." Then a vintage-inspired gown that Jade loved until she realized the heavy beading would make dancing nearly impossible.

During the next change, Scarlet's phone buzzed with a text from her boss about a Monday client meeting. She sighed, typing a quick acknowledgment.

"Work?" Cami asked, topping off their champagne.

"Yeah. Eric needs me to cover a client presentation because Maya's 'not feeling well.'" She made air quotes around the excuse. "Which probably means she's nursing a hangover after another club night."

"The joys of being reliable," Cami commiserated. "Speaking of which, have you thought about the logistics of this whole long-distance thing?"

Scarlet tensed. "It's only been four months, Cami."

"Four months of more travel than most people do in a year. Your frequent flyer miles must be through the roof."

It was true. Between her visits to Texas and Jerry's trips to Miami when his mother could watch the boys, they'd established a rotation that kept them seeing each other every two to three weeks. It wasn't ideal, but it worked well enough for the time being.

"We're taking it one step at a time," Scarlet said carefully. "There are a lot of factors to consider."

"Like whether you're ready to be a mom to two special needs kids?" Cami's bluntness wasn't unkind, just characteristic.

"Among other things," Scarlet admitted, swirling the champagne in her glass. "I adore those boys. But stepping in as a permanent fixture in their lives … that's a huge responsibility. What if I mess it up?"

"You won't," Cami said with surprising confidence. "Those kids already worship you, from everything you've told me. Emmett calls you every other day to tell you about dinosaurs."

Scarlet smiled despite herself. With Jerry's supervision, Emmett had indeed taken to calling her to share his latest discoveries about prehistoric life or to report on how Orange Cat was enjoying the new blanket she'd sent him.

"And Marty lights up when you're around. Jerry told me he has a picture of you guys that he keeps by his bed."

"He does?" That detail was new, and it made something in Scarlet's chest tighten.

"Apparently so," Cami replied. "Look, I'm not saying it's simple. But from where I'm sitting, you're already halfway there. You're just overthinking the label, which is very on-brand for you, Ms. Spreadsheet-For-Everything."

Before Scarlet could defend her organizational methods, the curtains parted dramatically, and they both turned.

Jade stood framed in the doorway, and Scarlet's breath caught. The dress was absolutely perfect. Fluid, champagne-tinted silk seemed to float around her sister's form, while subtle vintage beading across the bodice and shoulders caught the light with every movement. The silhouette was classic but relaxed, elegant without being rigid.

"Oh," Scarlet said softly, standing.

Jade's eyes were bright with unshed tears. "This one feels different."

"It's stunning," Scarlet moved closer, taking in the details. "The color with your skin tone ... it's like it was made for you."

"Turn," Cami commanded, making a circular motion with her finger.

Jade complied, and the subtle train floated behind her like a whisper of silk. The back featured a delicate row of covered buttons from nape to waist, framed by sheer panels that revealed just enough skin to be alluring without crossing into inappropriate-for-a-church territory.

"Merde," Claudette whispered, clearly impressed despite herself. "It is perfection."

"This is it," Jade said, her voice wavering slightly. "I can see myself walking down the aisle in this. I can picture Lucas's face when he sees me."

Claudette, sensing a sale, swiftly produced a simple tulle veil and a pair of earrings that complemented the gown's vintage feel. With the accessories in place, even Cami looked momentarily speechless.

"Well?" Jade looked between them, seeking final confirmation.

"It's perfect," Scarlet said, blinking back unexpected tears. "Absolutely perfect."

"But then again," Cami piped up, her voice sly, "I don't know, do we really want to take the risk that there might not be a better dress at another store? Perhaps one that has even more free champagne?"

Scarlet smacked her arm, laughing despite herself. "Ignore her. You can get champagne at the grocery store! The dress is perfect, sis."

Jade beamed, turning back to the mirror. "I think so too."

The next hour dissolved into a flurry of measurements, deposit arrangements, and discussions of fitting schedules. By the time they emerged from the boutique, Scarlet felt simultaneously drained and elated.

"Lunch?" Jade suggested. "I'm starving after all that emotional labor."

"God, yes," Cami agreed. "All this wedding planning is exhausting, and I'm not even the bride."

They settled at a sidewalk café a few blocks from the boutique, Miami's September heat tempered by a pleasant breeze off the water. After ordering a round of cocktails and enough tapas to feed a small army, Jade pulled out her wedding planning binder.

"Okay, so dress is checked off," she said, making a satisfying mark in her spreadsheet. The habit was one Scarlet recognized as her own influence. "Next is bridesmaid dresses, which we can schedule for next month ..."

"One wedding task per day," Cami protested. "That was the agreement. No more bridal bootcamp after the main mission is accomplished."

Jade rolled her eyes but closed the binder. "Fine. But I was thinking ..." she turned to Scarlet, her expression suddenly hesitant. "Would it be weird to ask if Jerry's kids could be part of the wedding party? Since they're obviously going to be there anyway. Emmett could be a ring bearer, and Marty ..."

Scarlet blinked, caught off guard by the suggestion. "You want the boys in your wedding?"

"Why not? They're practically family at this point. And Lucas has his niece as a flower girl, so we need to balance the child cuteness quotient." Jade's casual tone couldn't quite hide the genuine sentiment behind the offer. "I already found the perfect matching mini-tuxes online. They'd be adorable."

Emotion welled up unexpectedly in Scarlet's throat. The simple inclusion of Jerry's children in such an important family event felt significant in ways she hadn't anticipated.

"That's ... really sweet," she managed. "But I'd have to ask Jerry. Marty can get overwhelmed in crowds, and a wedding is a lot of stimulation. And Emmett might be too excited to actually follow directions."

"We could make adjustments," Jade said immediately. "Whatever they need to be comfortable. I just thought ..." she hesitated, then added more softly, "They're important to you, which makes them important to us."

Cami made a gagging noise. "God, when did we all get so sappy? Next thing you know, I'll be cooing over baby pictures and knitting booties."

"Speaking of babies," Jade segued with all the subtlety of a freight train, "have you and Jerry talked about that whole aspect of things? I mean, he obviously has his hands full with two already, but do you think you might want ... you know ... one of your own someday?"

Scarlet nearly choked on her mojito. "Jade! We've only been together four months!"

"I'm just asking!" Jade held up her hands defensively. "You're turning thirty-two in December. These are practical considerations."

"Subtle, sis," Scarlet muttered, dabbing at her chin where she'd dribbled her drink.

"What? You've always said you wanted kids someday. And now you've got this readymade family, which is great, but ..." Jade trailed off, clearly uncertain whether she'd crossed a line.

"It's too soon to have that conversation with him," Scarlet said finally. "I'm still figuring out what my role is with the boys. Adding another baby to the mix ..." She shook her head. "Besides, we live in different states. That's a more pressing logistic issue than hypothetical future children."

"Have you thought about relocating?" Cami asked, surprisingly serious for once. "I know there are accounting firms in Texas. Or Jerry could potentially transfer to a base in Florida, right?"

"Maybe," Scarlet allowed. "But his support system for the boys is in Texas. His mom, his siblings ... it wouldn't be fair to ask him to leave that behind."

"So you'd be the one to move," Jade concluded, watching Scarlet carefully.

"I don't know," Scarlet admitted. "We haven't seriously discussed it. But ... I have been looking at firms with offices in both Miami and Texas. Just, you know, hypothetically."

"Hypothetically," Cami repeated with a knowing smirk. "Just like you're hypothetically researching school districts and pediatric specialists in the Austin area?"

Scarlet's cheeks burned. "How did you—"

"You left your browser open on my laptop when you were looking up that recipe during girls' night last week." Cami's expression softened. "It's okay to be planning ahead, you know. It doesn't mean you're U-Hauling after four months if you're just exploring options."

Their tapas arrived, temporarily halting the conversation as they distributed plates and refilled drinks. Scarlet welcomed the reprieve, unsettled by how transparent her private thoughts had apparently been to her friends.

"For what it's worth," Jade said after they'd eaten for a few minutes, "I think you'd be an amazing mom: step, biological, whatever. You've always been the one who takes care of everyone else. Remember when I had chicken pox in third grade and you read me an entire 'Baby-Sitters Club' book because I was too itchy to hold it myself?"

"Or when you stayed up all night helping me finish my portfolio for that job interview," Cami added. "You've got the nurturing thing down."

"That's different," Scarlet protested. "You're my sister and my best friend. Taking care of two kids with complex needs, permanently, as their primary female role model ..." She swallowed. "What if I mess them up?"

"Oh please," Cami rolled her eyes. "Have you met their biological mother? The bar is on the floor. You're already leagues ahead just by showing up consistently."

Scarlet tensed. Jerry rarely spoke about his ex-wife, but the few details she'd gleaned suggested a woman who had viewed her children's diagnoses as inconveniences rather than aspects of who they were. Most of what she knew had come from Mac during a particularly candid moment.

"That's not the point," Scarlet said. "They deserve the best, not just 'better than before.'"

"And you don't think you're their best option?" Jade asked gently. "Because from everything you've told us, those boys adore you. Especially Marty, who I gather doesn't warm up to just anyone."

She thought of Marty's gaze brightening when she walked through the door. That serious, searching look would transform as he folded into her side as if her presence was a place to rest.

And Emmett, wild with ideas, who insisted she was the only one who could do justice to his dinosaur sagas.

"I love them," she said, not as confession, but as fact. "But that doesn't make me ready, does it? I don't know what they'll need tomorrow, let alone years from now."

There was a time, years past, when she imagined a child of her own.

That hope had slipped away quietly, unannounced.

Not erased, just stored in the corners she didn't dust often.

But now and then, like this, it stirred. Not loudly. Just enough to be felt.

"So you learn," Cami shrugged. "Like any parent does. No one gets a manual, not even for neurotypical kids."

"I know you're overthinking this," Jade said, reaching across the table to squeeze Scarlet's hand. "But for what it's worth, seeing you interact with those kids even over the phone ... it's like watching you become more yourself, not less. I've never seen you happier."

Scarlet's phone buzzed on the table, Jerry's name lighting up the screen. All three women's eyes darted to it simultaneously.

"Speak of the handsome devil," Cami grinned, making a grab for the phone. "Let's see what Sergeant Sexy has to say."

"Don't you dare," Scarlet snatched the phone, but not before catching the simple message displayed on her lock screen.

Miss you. Any chance you're free next weekend? I need to see you.

She read his message twice, smiling by the second pass.
Her fingers moved before doubt could catch up.



Missing you too. Absolutely free. Just name the time.

"Oh my God, look at her face," Jade laughed, nudging Cami. "It's the same dopey expression every time he texts. Like someone just handed her a puppy and a winning lottery ticket simultaneously."

"I do not make a face," Scarlet protested, though she could feel the telltale heat in her cheeks.

"You absolutely do," Cami confirmed. "It's this whole ..." she demonstrated an exaggerated dreamy expression, complete with batting eyelashes and a hand pressed to her heart.

"I hate both of you," Scarlet muttered, though she couldn't suppress her smile.

"No you don't," Jade said confidently. "You love us. Almost as much as you love your sexy soldier and his adorable mini-mes."

While Cami launched into her signature dramatization of a truly unfortunate date, Scarlet's focus wandered to her phone.

Jerry's message still lingered in her mind: *I need to see you.*
Their tone felt heavier than their usual planning conversations.
Maybe it was nothing. Or maybe it was everything.
She drew a breath, tamping the thought down.
Four months didn't qualify as a forever conversation.

Still, something in her life had tilted since that cruise, reshaping the way forward without asking permission.

Her heart, inconveniently, was already walking the path.

"Scarlet!" Jade waved a dessert menu. "Key lime. You in?"

"Hmm? Oh, yes. Sounds perfect."

# Twenty

Scarlet woke to the sensation of Jerry's lips on her shoulder, the weight of his body pressing her into the mattress as morning light filtered through her bedroom blinds. His breath was warm against her neck, hands exploring with a confidence that hadn't been there during those first tentative nights on the cruise.

"Good morning to you too," she murmured, her voice still husky with sleep.

Jerry's response was to slide his hand up her ribcage to cup her breast, his thumb circling her nipple with deliberate pressure that made her gasp. Scarlet felt her body respond immediately, heat pooling between her thighs as his other hand slipped lower, tracing the curve of her hip before sliding between her legs.

"Already?" he murmured against her ear, finding her wet and ready for him.

"It's been three weeks," she breathed, reaching behind to thread her fingers through his hair.

She turned in his arms to face him, finding his eyes dark with desire. She trailed her hand down his chest, over the ridges of his abdomen, following the line of hair that disappeared beneath the sheet. When her fingers wrapped around him, Jerry's breath hitched, his eyes fluttering closed briefly.

"I missed you," she whispered, sliding her leg up over his hip, opening herself to him.

In answer, Jerry rolled them so she was beneath him, his weight supported on his forearms as he looked down at her. There was something almost worshipful in his gaze. Scarlet pulled him down, mouths meeting with a hunger that three weeks of separation had only intensified.

When he finally pushed into her, they both gasped at the exquisite sensation of being joined again. Jerry held still for a moment, his forehead pressed against hers, breathing ragged.

"God, I've missed you," he groaned, the words almost a prayer against her lips.

"Show me how much," she challenged, wrapping her legs around his waist to draw him deeper.

Jerry began to move with deliberate strokes that hit exactly where she needed. Scarlet met each thrust, her body remembering this dance, falling into sync with his. Unlike the frantic coupling of their first night together, this was something deeper, more intimate.

The pressure was building inside her as Jerry slipped a hand between them, his thumb finding her most sensitive spot with practiced ease. The dual sensations sent her spiraling toward the edge.

"Look at me," Jerry commanded softly, and she opened her eyes to find his gaze locked on hers.

The intimacy of eye contact while joined like this heightened everything, creating a connection that transcended the physical. She couldn't look away, even as she felt herself approaching climax.

"I'm close," she gasped, hands gripping his biceps.

"I know," he replied, his voice strained as he maintained the perfect rhythm. "Let go, Scarlet. I've got you."

She came apart with his name on her lips, pleasure crashing through her in waves. The sight of her release triggered Jerry's own; he buried his face in her neck, his rhythm faltering as he followed her over the edge with a deep groan.

For several moments they remained locked together, hearts racing in tandem. Scarlet ran her hands along the ridges of his back, savoring the way their bodies fit together so perfectly.

Eventually, Jerry rolled to his side, taking her with him so they remained face to face, legs still intertwined. He brushed a strand of vibrant red hair from her cheek, tucking it behind her ear with surprising tenderness.

"Now it's a good morning," she murmured, enjoying the way his eyes crinkled at the corners when he smiled.

"The best," he agreed, pressing a kiss to her forehead before pulling her closer.

Scarlet traced lazy patterns on his skin, following the lines of his tattoo with her fingertips. Four months into whatever this was becoming, and she still couldn't get enough of him.

"Coffee?" she offered, sitting up and completely comfortable in her nakedness.

Jerry folded his arms behind his head, making no effort to hide his appreciation as she stretched. "Please."

Scarlet stood, feeling his eyes follow her as she moved naked around the bed, pausing to pick up her robe before deciding against it. She felt liberated by this level of comfort with him, by being completely bare both physically and emotionally. She padded toward the kitchen, aware of his gaze tracking her every movement.

Warm, golden Miami morning light bathed her apartment, so different from the harsher Texas sun she was growing accustomed to during her visits. She moved through her space with easy familiarity, the cool tiles beneath her feet a pleasant contrast to the growing heat of the day outside.

The kitchen was small but efficient, designed with her preferences in mind. Sleek appliances, marble countertops, and everything within easy reach. She measured coffee grounds with practiced movements, her mind drifting to how strange yet right it felt to have Jerry in her space, in her bed, in her life. Just four months ago, she'd been a woman focused solely on her career, skeptical of the very idea of a singles cruise. Now here she was, brewing coffee for a military man with two special needs children, planning her weekends around flight schedules to Texas.

While the coffee brewed, she glanced back toward the bedroom doorway. Jerry had sat up, sheet pooled around his waist, watching her with open admiration. The vulnerability in his expression made something catch in her throat. This strong, capable man who commanded respect in his uniform and managed chaos with his children looked at her like she was something precious, something exceptional. It still took her breath away sometimes.

"See something you like?" she teased, turning to reach for mugs in the cabinet, deliberately stretching to give him a better view.

"Everything," he replied simply, the single word containing volumes.

Coffee ready, Scarlet returned to the bedroom with both mugs. She set his black coffee on the nightstand before slipping back under the sheets with her own. Jerry immediately adjusted to make room for her, his arm coming around her shoulders as she settled against him, their bodies fitting together as naturally as if they'd been doing this for years instead of months.

"I was talking with Jade last week about the wedding," she said after they'd sipped their coffee in comfortable silence. "She wants the boys to be part of it."

Jerry raised an eyebrow. "In the wedding party?"

"Mmhmm," Scarlet nodded, curling her feet beneath her. "She's already found matching mini-tuxes online. She thinks Emmett would be perfect as a ring bearer, and Marty could either join him or be an honorary usher with one of the groomsmen." She smiled, remembering her sister's enthusiasm. "She said, and I quote, 'We need to balance the child cuteness quotient since Lucas has his niece as flower girl.'"

Scarlet watched Jerry's face, expecting the smile that normally appeared when someone included his sons. Instead, she caught a tightening around his eyes, something flickering in his expression that she recognized as tension.

"That's really nice of her," he said carefully, setting his coffee aside. "But I'm not sure we'll be able to make it to the wedding."

Scarlet felt a sudden chill despite the warm morning. "What? Why not? It's not until spring, so we have plenty of—"

"I won't be around then," Jerry interrupted, the words dropping between them like stones.

The world seemed to stop spinning. Scarlet felt the coffee grow cold in her hands as his words registered, their meaning still hovering just out of reach. Her lungs forgot how to work properly as her mind frantically searched for an interpretation other than the obvious one.

"Not ... make it?" she repeated, her voice smaller than she intended. Her heart began to race, a sick feeling spreading through her stomach. "Is this ... are you ..."

The thought crystallized with horrifying clarity: he was ending things. He'd flown all the way to Miami to break up with her in person. The realization must have shown on her face because Jerry's eyes widened, and he quickly reached for her hand.

"No, Scarlet, I'm not breaking up with you," he said firmly, squeezing her fingers. "That's not what this is about at all."

Relief washed through her, quickly replaced by confusion. "Then what?!"

"I'm being deployed to Kuwait," he explained, his voice steady but tight. "The orders came down a week and a half ago. Nine months, starting right after Christmas."

"Nine months?" Scarlet set her mug down with unsteady hands. "But that's ... that's almost a year."

Jerry nodded, watching her closely. "I wanted to tell you in person. That's why I came down this weekend."

She tucked the sheet closer, though the chill she felt had nothing to do with the air.

Nine months.

A timeline that stretched in her mind, lined with absence. Missed voices, empty rooms, and love that had to live through screens and time zones.

"What does this mean for … us?" she asked, hating how uncertain she sounded.

Jerry shifted to face her more directly. "That depends on what you want it to mean."

"I don't understand."

"Scarlet," Jerry said gently, "military relationships are hard. When I'm deployed, communication will be limited. Sometimes there will be blackout periods where you can't reach me at all. I'll be seven time zones away, working long hours in a different world."

She nodded, trying to process. "And the boys?"

"They'll stay with my mom in Utah for the entire deployment. We have doctors and specialists already lined up from last time. They have a whole support system there. It's just a matter of getting them settled before I leave."

Scarlet stood abruptly, needing to move. She grabbed her robe from the back of the door, wrapping it around herself as her mind raced.

"We should get dressed," she said, gathering his clothes from where they'd been discarded the night before. "This feels like a conversation we should have with clothes on."

Jerry nodded, accepting the shift with typical understanding. While he dressed, Scarlet retreated to the bathroom, closing the door and leaning against it. She stared at her reflection, taking in the flushed cheeks from their lovemaking, her wild hair, and eyes now filled with confusion. Three days ago, she'd been planning weekend visits and looking forward to Christmas together. Now everything had changed.

When she emerged, Jerry was sitting on the edge of the bed, fully dressed, elbows resting on his knees. He looked up as she entered, and the careful neutrality in his expression made her heart ache. She recognized his soldier face, that careful expression he wore when emotions needed to be managed.

"Let's go sit in the living room," she suggested, reaching for his hand.

The gesture seemed to surprise him, but he took her hand and followed her to the couch. Sunlight streamed through the balcony doors, creating pools of gold on her hardwood floors. The normality of it felt surreal against the weight of their conversation.

"When did you find out?" she asked, tucking her feet beneath her on the couch.

"Last week. Thursday. Command called an unexpected meeting." Jerry sat beside her, leaving space between them. "Division confirmed the orders. The whole brigade is going."

"And Mac?"

"He'll be there too." Jerry's mouth quirked slightly. "Someone has to keep me out of trouble."

Despite everything, Scarlet found herself smiling. The brief lightening of the mood gave her a moment to collect her thoughts.

"So what happens now?" she asked, more directly this time.

Jerry studied her face. "For deployments? There's a preparation phase. Lots of paperwork, medical checks, training. I'll need to get the boys settled with my mom, prepare the house. There's usually a farewell ceremony just before we leave."

"No," Scarlet shook her head. "I mean with us. What happens with us, Jerry?"

He took a deep breath. "That's up to you. I would never ask you to put your life on hold for nine months, especially when we've only been together for four. I know that's a lot to ask of anyone."

"Don't do that," she said, more sharply than she intended.

"Do what?"

"Give me the easy out. Tell me what this is really like. What will it mean if we stay together?"

Jerry's expression softened slightly. "It means a lot of waiting. Letters that arrive late. Video calls at odd hours because of the time difference. Care packages that take weeks to arrive. It means I won't be there for birthdays or anniversaries or if something goes wrong. It means trusting that things will still be there when I get back."

Scarlet absorbed this, thinking about the past four months. They'd already been navigating the distance of weekends together interspersed with lengthy separations. But this was different. This wasn't a three-hour flight; it was seven time zones and a war zone.

"Have you done this before?" she asked. "The relationship-during-deployment thing?"

A shadow crossed Jerry's face. "Yes. It doesn't always work out."

She heard the unspoken history in his words, all those previous relationships that hadn't survived the strain of separation. The realization that she might be just another woman who couldn't handle military life stung.

"I'm not them," she said simply.

Jerry blinked, surprised. "What?"

"Whoever they were. The ones who couldn't wait. I'm not them." Scarlet moved closer, taking his hand between both of hers. "This isn't what I expected, and I won't pretend it doesn't scare me. But I'm not walking away just because it got complicated."

The relief that flooded his expression made her heart twist. Had he really expected her to end things? Had he been carrying that fear all week?

"It will be hard," he warned, though his fingers tightened around hers. "There will be days when you don't hear from me, when you have no idea what's happening. Days when the boys are struggling, and I can't help."

"Jerry," Scarlet said firmly, "I care about you. I care about your boys. That doesn't stop because there's distance between us."

He studied her face, as if searching for uncertainty. "We can figure out a communication schedule that works with the time difference. I'll have limited internet access, but enough for video calls most of the time, barring operations or blackouts."

Scarlet nodded, the practical details helping to ground her. "And I can write letters. Real ones, on paper. Emmett can send drawings for you to put up."

"You'd do that? Keep in touch with the boys too?"

The question held more than the words themselves. It revealed what Jerry was really asking. Would she maintain a connection not just with him, but with his children during his absence?

"Of course I would," she said softly. "They're part of you. And they're ..." she hesitated, then continued, "they're important to me too."

Jerry exhaled slowly, as if releasing a breath he'd been holding for days. "I've been terrified of having this conversation."

"Why?"

"Because I know what I'm asking. I know how selfish it sounds to say 'wait for me' when we're still figuring out what this is. Because deployment changes people. Because it's not fair to you to—"

"Fuck you!" Scarlet's voice cracked like a whip between them. She lunged forward, seizing his face between her palms. "You don't get to tell me what's fair. You don't get to decide what I can handle."

Her eyes blazed into his, daring him to argue. "I know exactly what I'm choosing, Jerry. Don't you dare try to protect me from my own decisions."

Their kiss was fierce, born of defiance and fear and love so loud it didn't know where to go. When Scarlet finally pulled back, her breathing was uneven, her lips parted as if a hundred more words waited inside her that she couldn't find a way to say.

She looked down at their joined hands for a long moment.

"I need to tell you something," she said softly, so softly he almost missed it. "And I don't know how."

Jerry stilled, his thumb still brushing over her knuckles. "Okay."

She swallowed, hard. "Eight years ago ... I was pregnant."

His eyes widened slightly, but he didn't interrupt.

"I didn't tell anyone. Not Jade. Not Cami. Not even him." Her voice broke on the last word, brittle and sharp.

She shook her head, blinking fast. "It ended before I ever really understood what it meant. Just a couple months in. I went to the ER alone. Bled alone. Went to work the next day like nothing had happened." Her voice cracked. "And I never talked about it. Not once. I buried it so deep I thought maybe I'd imagined it."

Jerry's grip tightened, but he stayed silent, listening with the complete, unwavering presence that only he could give.

Scarlet let out a shaky breath, the weight of the truth pressing into her chest like a fist. "But I didn't imagine it. I feel it every time I'm with your boys. Not in a way that replaces anything. Not like that. But there's a version of me that still wonders who they would've been. Who I would've been."

She met his gaze then, her eyes glassy and red-rimmed. "I didn't mean to keep this from you. I just ... didn't know where to put it until now."

Jerry cupped her face gently, his thumb brushing away a tear she hadn't realized had fallen. "Scarlet ..."

"I'm not broken," she said quickly, defensively. "This isn't me asking for your pity. I'm telling you because if I'm going to walk through this deployment with you ... if I'm going to love your boys like they're already becoming part of me ... you deserve all of me. Not just the shiny parts."

His hands slipped around her, pulling her against his chest as she let out a breath she hadn't realized she'd been holding. Instead of speaking, he held her tightly, as if he could fuse the broken pieces back together with the sheer strength of his arms.

When he finally spoke, it was a whisper against her hair. "Thank you for trusting me. And I'm so fucking sorry you went through that alone."

Scarlet closed her eyes, letting herself be held. For the first time in eight years, she didn't feel like she was carrying it by herself.

"Okay," she took a deep breath, some of the heat cooling as she settled back. "So tell me the plan. When exactly do you leave? Will you be somewhere safe? What can I send in packages?"

The tension in his shoulders eased slightly as she shifted to practical questions. This was the Jerry she knew, the man who navigated complex logistics as naturally as breathing.

Scarlet leaned into his chest, her cheek pressing against the soft cotton of his shirt, letting the steady rhythm of his heart tether her to the present.

Nine months. The number kept echoing in her mind, louder than the city noise outside, louder than the worry trying to claw its way back in. Nine months of not touching, not seeing, not knowing. Nine months of trusting that what they had would still be here on the other side of distance and silence.

Jerry had explained the logistics: deployment dates, base details, the lack of mid-tour leave. She'd nodded, asked practical questions, filed away names and timelines like they mattered more than the truth swelling in her chest: she was already grieving the time they were about to lose.

But even that wasn't the biggest shift.

She'd said it.

The words had just *come out*. They ripped through her like a current she hadn't planned to unleash. Eight years of silence cracked open in one breathless confession. Her miscarriage, the lonely hospital visit, the quiet grief no one ever saw.

She hadn't *meant* to tell him. But now that she had, she didn't regret it. Not one word.

God, she'd carried that weight for so long, it had fused to her bones. But something about his steadiness, the way he held space without needing to fill it, made the truth escape before she could stop it.

And he hadn't flinched. He hadn't looked at her like she was fragile or damaged or less than whole.

He'd just held her tighter.

It wasn't closure. Not yet. But it was the first time she hadn't felt completely alone inside that memory. That mattered. Maybe more than she could say.

Scarlet closed her eyes, listening to the world move on outside her apartment. Horns. Wind. Someone shouting down the block. Normal things that hadn't changed, even though everything *inside* her had.

Jerry was leaving. The countdown had already started.

But before that, there was still time. There were still mornings like this. Still laughter to have and Christmas to plan and a pair of boys who, somehow, had started carving out space inside her heart.

She didn't know what would come after the waiting. She didn't know how she'd feel when the silence stretched too long, or if grief might creep back in.

But for now, for this quiet breath of morning in his arms, she knew only this: she'd told the hardest truth she had. And he'd stayed.

And for the first time in a long time, Scarlet didn't feel like something was broken inside her.

She just felt *brave.*

# Twenty-One

Scarlet stood in Jerry's kitchen, watching Maggie expertly roll balls of gingery dough between her palms before placing them on the baking sheet. A spicy-sweet aroma filled the otherwise empty kitchen, its warm, homey scent defiantly cheerful against the backdrop of half-packed boxes and bare countertops.

"These smell amazing," Scarlet said, inhaling deeply. "No wonder Jerry insists on them every year."

A twinkle danced at the edge of Maggie's expression, carving faint creases near her eyes that looked so much like Jerry's it tugged at Scarlet's chest. "Thirty years old, and he still acts like a little boy around these cookies. Some things never change." She paused, glancing up with sudden warmth. "I could send you the recipe, if you'd like. So you can make them for him sometime."

let could sense the unmistakable significance in the simple offer. Maggie wasn't just sharing a family recipe; she was acknowledging Scarlet's place in Jerry's future. "I'd love that," Scarlet replied, touched by the gesture.

The kitchen embodied contradictions, with drawers emptied except for essential utensils and cabinets partially bare, yet Christmas music played from a portable speaker balanced on a stack of boxes labeled "STORAGE." Maggie had unpacked just enough baking equipment for this one tradition: her famous gingersnap cookies that Jerry had apparently requested every Christmas since he could speak.

From the living room came the sound of Emmett's excited chatter, punctuated by Mac's deep laugh. Marty's distinctive happy humming drifted down the hallway, where Jerry was helping him dress for dinner. The house felt simultaneously like a home and like a place people were leaving, which, Scarlet supposed, they were.

The past week had been a whirlwind of activity. She'd flown in seven days ago to help with the deployment preparations, spending her days assisting Jerry with packing, addressing the boys' questions about their upcoming stay with Grandma, and trying to create Christmas magic amid the chaos. Maggie had arrived two nights ago, bringing an extra pair of hands and a calming presence that seemed to soothe everyone's nerves.

"These are the last batch," Maggie said, sliding the cookie sheet into the oven. "We should have enough to get that son of mine through at least the first week of deployment. I'll send more in his first care package."

The words "care package" sent a small flutter of anxiety through Scarlet's chest. She'd been helping Emmett create artwork for Jerry's deployment wall, learning which items were allowed to be sent, memorizing the APO address. The practical details helped mask the emotional weight of what was coming.

"I've been researching what I can send," Scarlet said, wiping down the counter. "Emmett helped me make a list of Jerry's favorite snacks."

Maggie's eyes softened as she looked at Scarlet. "You're good for them, you know. All of them."

Before Scarlet could respond, thundering footsteps announced Emmett's arrival. He appeared in the kitchen doorway, his red Christmas sweater declaring his holiday spirit with a dinosaur sporting a Santa hat.

"Are the cookies ready? Dad says we're leaving for dinner in ten minutes, and I'm STARVING!" He punctuated this declaration by clutching his stomach dramatically.

"Almost done, sweetheart," Maggie replied, checking the timer. "But these are for after dinner and tomorrow morning."

"I smell cookies," Jerry said, appearing in the doorway with Marty balanced on his hip. Marty was dressed in a matching dinosaur sweater, his eyes bright with excitement.

Jerry crossed to the cooling rack where the first batch sat, reaching out with his free hand only to have Maggie swat it away with a dish towel.

"Gilmore Paul Duncan, don't you dare," she warned, though her tone held no real heat. "You'll spoil your dinner."

"Come on, Mom," Jerry pleaded, setting Marty down in his adaptive chair. "They're best when they're still warm and gooey. Just one."

Scarlet bit back a smile at the sight before her. Here was a staff sergeant, a father of two, a pillar of responsibility, reduced to a pleading child in his mother's kitchen.

"Better listen to your mom," Mac advised, appearing behind Jerry. "I hear she knows karate."

Maggie rolled her eyes. "I do not know karate, Jude MacIntyre, and you know it."

While Maggie was distracted by Mac, Jerry quickly snatched four cookies from the rack, passing one to Scarlet with a conspiratorial wink, another to Emmett who took it with wide-eyed delight, and carefully placing the fourth in Marty's hand. The cookies were perfectly soft throughout, just as Jerry had described them.

"I saw that!" Maggie called without turning around.

Jerry grinned unrepentantly, taking a bite and closing his eyes in apparent bliss. "Worth it," he murmured.

Scarlet bit into her stolen cookie and had to agree it was perfect. The texture was warm and chewy, with an ideal balance of ginger, cinnamon, and molasses that tasted like everything Christmas should be.

Amid the commotion of getting everyone ready, Scarlet witnessed Jerry's former life in small moments: the cookie theft traditions with his mother, his playful banter with Mac, all those daily routines with the boys. She felt simultaneously like a witness and a participant, standing at the intersection of their past and whatever came next.

"Everyone ready?" Jerry announced, helping Marty with his sweater. "It's a bit chilly tonight."

They sorted out the logistics quickly. Mac offered to drive Maggie in his car and meet them at the restaurant because Jerry's truck could only comfortably fit four with Marty's specialized seat.

"Three Duncan men, one Duncan lady in training," Mac said with a wink at Scarlet as they headed toward the vehicles. "See you there!"

he restaurant was decorated with twinkling lights and plastic garlands, busy but not packed. Their table near the center wasn't ideal for privacy, but Scarlet appreciated that it gave Marty's wheelchair plenty of room to roll right up to the edge.

While Jerry settled the boys, Scarlet found her attention drawn to a small stage set up near the bar area, where a man in a Santa hat was adjusting a microphone stand. A sign on an easel read "Christmas Eve Karaoke! 6-9 p.m."

"Oh no," Jerry muttered, following her gaze. "Is that—"

"Karaoke night?" Mac finished as he and Maggie joined them. "I believe it is. Christmas Eve special edition, from the looks of it."

Jerry's forehead creased with concern. "Maybe we should try somewhere else. The noise might be too much for Emmett."

Scarlet glanced at Emmett, who was watching the stage with curious interest. "What do you think, buddy? Will the singing bother you?"

Emmett considered this seriously. "Will it be very loud?"

"Probably," Jerry admitted. "And there might be some bad singers."

Emmett's face scrunched in thought. Then he looked at Scarlet. "I'll be okay if I can sit next to Mom. She can help if it gets too noisy."

The word hit Scarlet like a physical force. *Mom.*

Her breath caught, heart suddenly hammering against her ribs. The casual certainty in his voice stunned her. Not a slip, not a question, but a simple statement of fact that made her dizzy with unexpected emotion. A flicker of something old and buried twisted deep in her chest. Something raw and aching and unspeakably tender. She felt the ghost of another name linger in the silence that followed, a name that had never been spoken.

A title she had grieved once in secret, now spoken aloud by a boy who simply saw her. Chose her.

She glanced at Jerry, whose expression mirrored her own stunned quiet. Somewhere beneath his surprise, she saw the same realization forming: something had shifted.

"Um," she began, unsure how to respond. Her throat felt tight, her eyes suddenly warm.

"Sure thing, buddy," Jerry said smoothly, giving her a small nod. "Scarlet can sit right next to you."

They rearranged themselves, Scarlet still processing what had just happened. Emmett seemed completely unaware of the emotional earthquake he'd caused, happily examining his children's menu. A gentle squeeze from Maggie's hand on her arm communicated what words couldn't: silent acknowledgment and perhaps approval.

A server appeared to take their drink orders, and the moment passed, conversation shifting to safer topics. But Scarlet felt the word reverberating inside her, equal parts terrifying and exhilarating. *Mom.* Not a title she'd expected, certainly not this soon, probably not ever given the boys' situation. Yet here it was, casually bestowed by a seven-year-old who apparently saw her in that light.

Mac steered the conversation toward the impending deployment, cutting through the emotional undercurrent with his typical directness.

"Maggie, are your husband and daughter still coming for the deployment ceremony?" he asked, spreading butter on a warm roll.

Maggie shook her head. "Thomas and Hannah are staying in Utah to get the house ready for the boys. We decided it made more sense for them to prepare things there rather than flying down just to turn around and go back."

"Makes sense," Jerry nodded, helping Marty with his drink. "They'll have their hands full getting everything set up."

"What about your parents, Mac?" Maggie asked. "Will they make it this time?"

Mac nodded, stealing a cherry tomato from Jerry's salad. "Sarah and Bruno get in the day before. They're spending Christmas with my brother in Louisiana, but they'll drive over for the ceremony."

"Last deployment, his mom brought enough cookies to feed the entire battalion," Jerry told Scarlet. "Mac had to fight off sugar-crazed infantrymen."

"That sounds like Sarah MacIntyre," Maggie laughed. "Still trying to fatten you up after all these years."

"That's a mother's prerogative," Mac said with a grin. "Isn't that right, Scarlet?"

Scarlet blushed at the callback, her smile slipping in almost before she noticed. "I wouldn't know yet, but I'm learning fast."

As their appetizers arrived, Scarlet made a split-second decision. "I'll be right back," she told Jerry, rising from her seat. "Just need to visit the ladies' room."

Instead of turning toward the restrooms, however, she made a beeline for the karaoke setup. The DJ was scrolling through a tablet, barely looking up when she approached.

"Hi," Scarlet said, feeling suddenly nervous. "Can I sign up for a song?"

"Sure thing," he replied, offering her the tablet. "List is right there. What's your name?"

"Scarlet," she replied, scanning the song selection. When she found "Stacy's Mom" listed, she smiled. Perfect. "I'd like to do this one, but I'm going to change the lyrics a bit. Is that okay?"

The DJ shrugged. "Your show, darlin'. Just don't make it R-rated; we've got kids in here."

"It'll be family-friendly," she promised, adding her name to the list.

When she returned to the table, no one seemed to have noticed her detour. Their meal progressed amid laughter and storytelling, punctuated by occasional carols from the karaoke stage. Scarlet helped Marty with his chicken fingers, cutting them into manageable bites while listening to Mac recount a disastrous Christmas tree incident from Jerry's first year of fatherhood.

"So there he is," Mac continued, gesturing with a french fry, "covered in pine sap, ornaments scattered everywhere. And Emmett, this tiny little three-year-old, just looks up and says, 'I think we need a plastic one, Daddy.'"

"Which is exactly what we've had ever since," Jerry confirmed, smiling at the memory.

"Smart kid," Scarlet said, giving Emmett a wink that made him beam with pride.

The current singer wrapped up his butchered version of "Jingle Bell Rock," his reindeer sweater as unfortunate as his vocal performance. As they finished their main courses, Scarlet felt a flutter of nerves. She'd been mentally revising lyrics since signing up, and her moment was approaching faster than she'd anticipated.

"Next up," the DJ announced as Reindeer Sweater took a bow, "we've got Scarlet performing 'Stacy's Mom'! Come on up!"

Jerry's head whipped toward her, eyebrows raised in surprise. "You signed up?"

"Surprise?" Scarlet replied with a nervous laugh, already standing.

Emmett cheered so loudly that several nearby tables turned to look. Even Marty joined in, hands flapping with excitement.

"You don't have to," Jerry said, but his eyes were bright with anticipation.

"It's Christmas Eve," Scarlet said, squeezing his shoulder as she passed. "Might as well make it memorable."

She made her way to the stage, heart pounding. The emcee handed her a microphone, and the opening notes of the familiar rock song filled the restaurant. Scarlet took one look at her makeshift family. Jerry watched her with that intense focus that still made her stomach flip, Emmett bounced in his seat, Marty's face was alight with joy, Mac gave her an encouraging thumbs-up, and Maggie beamed with approval. She found her courage.

"This is for the Duncan men," she announced into the microphone, "who have made this the most unexpected Christmas ever. I'm improvising a bit, so bear with me!"

As the introduction played, Scarlet channeled every bit of confidence she could muster. When she began to sing, she locked eyes with Jerry, letting the playful lyrics she'd hastily composed wash away her nervousness.

*"Marty's dad has got it goin' on ..."* she began, watching Jerry's face shift from surprise to delight. She continued with the verse she'd been rehearsing in her head, something about juice boxes and sunscreen that made Mac burst out laughing.

By the chorus, Emmett had left his seat to stand at the edge of the stage, clapping along enthusiastically, if not entirely on beat. Other diners were smiling, some joining in when she encouraged them.

When she reached the bridge, she slowed the tempo, the playfulness giving way to genuine emotion. "*And soon you'll lace up boots again,*" she sang softly, "*chasing shadows with your steady hands ...*"

She saw Jerry's expression transform, the teasing light in his eyes replaced by something deeper. "*But I'll be here, a beat behind ... your girl, your crew, your peace of mind ...*"

Scarlet felt her voice waver slightly but pushed through, seeing tears glimmering in Maggie's eyes. "*No rings, no rush, just what is real, this slow and steady kind of feel ...*"

The final chorus allowed Scarlet to soak in every joyful detail: Emmett's enthusiastic dancing, Marty's excited rocking, the unmistakable pride in Jerry's eyes. Somehow this strange, beautiful patchwork family had become hers, temporary though it might be, deployment looming though it was.

She finished with a wink and a theatrical bow that made their table erupt in applause, with Jerry on his feet whistling between his fingers. Scarlet made her way back, cheeks flushed with exhilaration and embarrassment.

"That was AWESOME!" Emmett declared, throwing his arms around her waist. "You're the best mom EVER!"

He said it so easily, that word. Mom. It stole the air from her lungs.

A flood of warmth surged through her, tempered by a flicker of fear she couldn't quite name.

She glanced at Jerry, standing now, his features unguarded and achingly sincere.

"That was something else, Bellari," he said quietly when she reached him, pulling her into a hug that felt more intimate than appropriate for a family restaurant. "Thank you."

"I just wanted to give you something to remember," she murmured against his chest.

"Mission accomplished," he replied, his voice low enough that only she could hear. "That's going to get me through a lot of lonely nights."

The promise in his words sent a pleasant shiver down her spine.

# Twenty-Two

The rest of dinner passed in a blur of dessert, more carols from other performers, and Mac's increasingly ridiculous stories. Through it all, Scarlet felt Jerry's eyes on her. His gaze carried desire, yes, but something deeper and more complex lay beneath it.

By the time they headed out to the parking lot, Emmett was half asleep despite his sugar intake, and Marty was contentedly humming Christmas songs. They arranged the same driving configuration, with Mac and Maggie following behind Jerry's truck.

"You should go on America's Got Talent," Emmett mumbled sleepily against Scarlet's shoulder during the drive.

"I think I'll stick to once-a-year performances," she replied, smoothing his hair.

Back at the house, bedtime routines took over. Scarlet helped Emmett into his Christmas pajamas while Jerry got Marty ready. Christmas Eve excitement battled with exhaustion, resulting in Emmett bouncing between hyper chatter and heavy-lidded yawns.

"Will Santa still find me at Grandma's house?" he asked as Scarlet tucked him into bed.

The innocent question held heavier implications than Emmett realized. "Of course," she assured him. "Santa knows exactly where all children are, especially when they're staying with grandparents."

"And will he find Dad in the desert?"

Scarlet sat on the edge of the bed, choosing her words carefully. "Your dad will be very busy keeping everyone safe, but he should be home before next Christmas."

Emmett nodded, satisfied with this answer. Then, more hesitantly: "Is it okay that I called you Mom? Dad said I should have asked first."

The directness of the question caught Scarlet off guard. She opened her mouth, but for a heartbeat, no words came.

Months had passed since Miami, since that pivotal night when she first spoke aloud the secret she'd buried for nearly a decade. She hadn't planned to tell Jerry, hadn't rehearsed it. It had simply *escaped* her, torn loose by a moment too intimate to hide from. Since then, she still hadn't told a soul. Not Cami. Not Jade. Only Jerry knew.

She sat beside him, his wide eyes filled with wonder and belief, and for the first time in years, the sharp edge of her sorrow softened.

It was still there, that old hurt, but she no longer let it rule her.

"It's okay, buddy," she said softly, her voice catching only slightly. "It just surprised me because it's new."

"But you don't mind?"

Scarlet felt a lump form in her throat. "I don't mind at all. I'm honored, actually."

"Good," Emmett said decisively. "Because you act like a mom. You help with homework and cook dinner and sing karaoke."

The simplicity of his logic made Scarlet smile. "Those are very mom-like qualities."

"And you love us," Emmett added, matter-of-factly. "That's the most important mom thing."

"Absolutely. Now, Time for sleep, soldier. Santa won't come until you're dreaming."

Emmett accepted a kiss on the forehead before snuggling deeper under his dinosaur sheets.

With both boys settled, they joined Mac and Maggie in the living room, where whispered conversations about "Santa duties" immediately ceased.

"All tucked in?" Maggie asked.

Scarlet nodded, still processing the weight of Marty's gift and Emmett's simple declaration.

"Excellent," Mac said, raising his own spiked eggnog. "Operation Christmas Cheer continues at 0900 tomorrow. But first," he produced a small flask from his pocket, "a toast, to surviving karaoke night with our dignity mostly intact."

They each took a small sip, the warmth of whiskey spreading through Scarlet's chest. For the next hour, they shared quiet conversation, carefully avoiding any mention of the deployment just three days away. Eventually, Maggie announced she was turning in, followed shortly by Mac, who winked at them before disappearing down the hall.

"Subtle," Jerry muttered, though he was smiling.

Once they were alone, Jerry reached under the couch and pulled out a bag of wrapped presents. "Santa duty," he explained. "Care to help?"

Together, they arranged gifts under the already-crowded tree, working in comfortable silence. The house was quiet except for the gentle ticking of the clock and the occasional creak of floorboards. Despite the half-packed state of the living room, the tree lights cast a warm, magical glow that made everything feel right.

"So," Jerry said casually as they finished, "about that karaoke performance ..."

Scarlet felt heat rise to her cheeks. "I can't believe I actually did that."

"I can't believe you came up with those lyrics on the spot," Jerry said, moving closer. "You planned that, didn't you?"

"Maybe," she admitted. "I had about fifteen minutes between signing up and performing to figure out what I was going to sing. The bridge was the most important part to get right."

Jerry's expression softened. "It was perfect. All of it." He paused, then added, "Emmett called you 'Mom' again during bedtime. We talked about it while you were with Marty. I told him he should have asked first."

"He did," Scarlet confirmed. "Asked if it was okay, I mean. I told him I was honored."

"Are you? Really?" Jerry's question held genuine uncertainty. "It's a lot. Too much, maybe, too soon."

Scarlet considered this, reflecting on everything the past week had taught her about helping with homework, bandaging scraped knees, and learning each boy's unique needs and preferences. It had happened so gradually that she hadn't realized how maternal her role had become until Emmett named it.

"I think," she said slowly, "that titles matter less than actions. I care about them. I want to be part of their lives, however that looks. If 'Mom' works for Emmett right now, I'm okay with that."

Jerry's arms tightened around her. "You're remarkable, you know that?"

"I'm just doing what feels right," she replied. "One day at a time."

He kissed her then, soft and sweet, before pulling back with a smile. "Santa's work is done. Ready to turn in?"

"Almost," Scarlet said, a mischievous smile playing at her lips. "I've got one more gift for you that didn't make it under the tree."

"Oh?" Jerry raised an eyebrow. "And where might this mystery gift be?"

"Bedroom," Scarlet said, taking his hand and backing slowly toward the hallway. "Very private. Unwrapping required."

Jerry's eyes darkened with understanding. "Well, we shouldn't leave any presents undelivered on Christmas Eve. That would be irresponsible."

As she led him down the hallway, Scarlet glanced back at the glowing tree, the carefully arranged presents, the half-packed boxes that represented both endings and beginnings. Tomorrow would bring Christmas joy, deployment countdown, and this new role she was stepping into. But tonight was for creating memories that would sustain them through the separation ahead.

And as she pulled Jerry into the bedroom and closed the door behind them, she was determined to make this particular memory unforgettable.

As the bedroom door closed behind them, Scarlet felt a flutter of anticipation. Jerry pulled her close, his hands finding her waist as he backed her gently against the door. Their lips met in a kiss that started soft but quickly deepened, his body pressing against hers with unmistakable intent.

"Mmm, best Christmas Eve ever," he murmured against her neck, sending shivers down her spine.

Scarlet smiled, fingers tangling in his short hair. "It's not over yet."

They moved toward the bed, lips still connected, hands exploring with growing urgency. When the backs of her knees hit the mattress, she broke the kiss, both of them breathing heavily.

Jerry gazed down at her, eyes dark with desire. "This is the best gift you could give me, you know that? Just being here."

"Hold that thought for a second," Scarlet said, pressing a finger to his lips. "Don't move."

Jerry tilted his head in mild amusement, watching her retreat before settling onto the bed.

Behind the bathroom door, Scarlet exhaled and reached behind the towels for the bag she'd hidden days ago, waiting for tonight.

One final night before everything sped up: wrapping paper, good-byes, the weight of what came next.

She quickly changed, examining her reflection in the mirror. The outfit was undeniably festive, consisting of a bright red bra trimmed with soft white fur that emphasized her curves, matching barely-there bottoms with the same fur trim, and even a thin garter belt with dangling red ribbons. It was equal parts playful and seductive, perfect for a Christmas Eve surprise.

Taking a deep breath, Scarlet opened the bathroom door and leaned against the frame.

"Merry Christmas," she said softly.

Jerry's reaction was everything she'd hoped for. His eyes widened, lips parting slightly as he took in the sight of her. He seemed momentarily frozen, gaze traveling slowly from her face down the length of her body and back up again.

"Holy—" he swallowed a lump in his throat, unable to finish the thought.

Scarlet crossed the room slowly, enjoying the weight of his stare. When she reached him, Jerry's hands immediately found her hips, fingers tracing the edge where red fabric met white fur.

"Like your present?" she asked, standing between his knees.

In answer, Jerry pulled her closer, pressing his lips to her stomach just above the waistband. "You are ..." he murmured against her skin, "absolutely incredible."

His hands moved up her sides, thumbs brushing the undersides of her breasts as he explored the silky material. Scarlet closed her eyes, savoring his touch. When she opened them again, she found him looking up at her with an expression of wonder that made her heart swell.

She moved to straddle his lap, knees on either side of his hips. Jerry's hands slid down to cup her backside, squeezing gently as she settled against him.

"The lingerie isn't the actual gift, you know," she said, rocking slightly against him.

Jerry's thumbs traced circles on her hips, fingers splayed across the small of her back. "No, I get it," he replied with a playful smirk. "It's the sex that's about to follow shortly."

"No," Scarlet laughed, then reconsidered. "Well, yes, you are absolutely getting sex ... but, no, I actually have something for you."

Jerry looked intrigued as Scarlet reached into the fur-lined edge of her bra and pulled out a small item. His hands moved restlessly up her sides, then back down to her thighs as she revealed a simple bracelet. Gold thread with a small silver helm charm.

"Is that—" Jerry began, recognition dawning in his eyes.

"My Mingle at Sea bracelet," Scarlet confirmed, holding it out to him. "I want you to wear it while you're away. To always remember me."

Jerry took the bracelet, turning it carefully in his fingers. His expression had transformed from playful desire to something deeper, more vulnerable.

"You've kept this all this time?" he asked quietly.

Scarlet nodded. "Since the day we met. It seemed right that you should have it now."

Jerry examined the woven gold thread, running his thumb over the small helm charm. "It's not really standard uniform attire," he said with a small smile, "but I'll wear it anyway."

He slipped it onto his wrist, then cupped her face in his hands, bringing her down for a kiss that was achingly tender. His hands resumed their exploration, moving across her back, down to her thighs, fingertips tracing patterns that made her skin tingle.

"Thank you," he whispered against her lips. "For this. For tonight. For being here."

Scarlet could feel everything they weren't saying hanging in the air between them. The separation looming ahead, their uncertain future, this connection that had caught them both off guard. But tonight wasn't about what was coming. Tonight was about making memories that would sustain them both through whatever lay ahead.

"Now," she said, pushing him gently back onto the bed, "about that other gift I mentioned ..."

Jerry's hands slid up her thighs to her hips, holding her firmly as she leaned down to kiss him. "Merry Christmas to me," he murmured, and Scarlet laughed against his lips before settling into his embrace.

# Twenty-Three

The Fort Cavazos gymnasium smelled like floor wax and anxiety. Scarlet sat in the designated family section, Marty a solid weight in her lap while Emmett pressed against her side, his small fingers worrying the edge of his dinosaur-patterned sweater. Around them, a sea of families tried to maintain composure, including mothers with infants, elderly parents, and spouses with the thousand-yard stare of those who'd done this before.

Scarlet hadn't. Seven months ago, she'd been a woman with a spreadsheet for a soul and a cat for company. Now she held children who were not her own while watching their father prepare to leave for nine months.

"He looks different in uniform," she whispered to Maggie, who sat straight-backed beside her, experience etched in the lines around her eyes.

"But he's still Jerry," Maggie replied softly. "The uniform just reminds them who he belongs to for the next nine months."

Not to us, Scarlet thought but didn't say. Marty shifted in her arms, his gaze fixed on the formation of soldiers standing at perfect attention. Jerry was third from the left in the second row, his posture impeccable, face unreadable. She'd seen that same body soft with sleep in her bed just weeks ago. Now he looked hewn from stone.

Colonel Sharp approached the microphone, his voice booming through the gym with practiced authority. "Families of the 3rd Brigade Combat Team, on behalf of the United States Army, I want to thank you for your sacrifice ..."

Sacrifice. The word echoed in Scarlet's mind as she adjusted Marty on her lap. What did she know about sacrifice? She was the accountant who'd fallen for a single dad on a cruise ship. This wasn't supposed to be her life, navigating military farewells and special needs children, torn between Miami and Utah while Jerry was half a world away. But here she was, and somehow it felt exactly right.

She committed every detail to memory. The warm pressure of Emmett against her ribs, his steady inhale beside her, the way Jerry's uniform clung to shadows like something freshly pressed.

"... proud tradition of service," the Colonel intoned. "Behind every soldier stands a family whose courage often goes unrecognized ..."

Maggie's fingers curled around hers, steady as a metronome.

"Breathe," she whispered. "In for four. Out for four."

Scarlet obeyed, drawing air deep into lungs that had forgotten how.

With each breath, Marty moved in time with her.

Then, across the polished gym floor, Jerry met her gaze. It only lasted a second, but something skipped inside her anyway.

"Our mission in Kuwait will last approximately nine months," Colonel Sharp continued. "During this time, your soldiers will be serving as part of Operation Spartan Shield ..."

Nine months. The same amount of time it took to create a human life. Enough time for seasons to cycle from winter through summer, for Emmett to advance a grade level, for Marty to reach developmental milestones. For relationships to wither or strengthen.

The Colonel's voice faded to background noise as Scarlet focused on Jerry's face. What would those nine months do to him? Would he return the same man who'd sung along to her playlist in the car, who'd taught her how to help Marty with his exercises, who'd begun to show her parts of himself he kept hidden from others?

"... and now, families, you have fifteen minutes to say your goodbyes before the buses depart."

The gymnasium erupted into movement as soldiers broke formation and families surged forward. Emmett was instantly on his feet, pulling at Scarlet's hand.

"Come on! We have to hurry!" he urged, the anxiety in his voice betraying his understanding of what was happening.

Scarlet rose with Marty balanced on her hip, following Emmett's lead through the crowd. Jerry was moving toward them, his face softening from soldier to father with each step. When they met in the middle of the gym floor, he knelt to Emmett's height first.

"Remember what we talked about, soldier?" Jerry asked, voice gentle but firm.

Emmett nodded solemnly. "Take care of Marty and be brave."

"That's right. And I'll call whenever I can," Jerry promised, pulling Emmett into a tight hug. "I love you, buddy. To the moon ..."

"... and back and to the moon again," Emmett finished, their private ritual making Scarlet's throat tighten.

Jerry stood, reaching for Marty. Scarlet transferred him carefully, watching as Jerry held his son close, whispering words meant only for Marty's ears. Marty's small hands patted Jerry's cheeks, a gesture so pure it made Scarlet turn away, feeling like an intruder on their goodbye.

"I've got them," Maggie said, appearing at her side. "Take a moment."

With practiced efficiency, Maggie gathered both boys, leaving Scarlet and Jerry standing slightly apart from the crowd. The gymnasium continued to buzz with conversations, crying children, last-minute instructions, but in their small bubble, silence fell.

"So," Scarlet began, then stopped. Words seemed suddenly inadequate.

Jerry looked at her with an intensity that made her skin prickle. "Scarlet, I—"

"I love you," she blurted, the words rising from somewhere deeper than thought. What surprised her wasn't the feeling itself, which had been growing for months, but the timing of it, the sudden certainty that settled in her chest.

Jerry went still, his eyes widening slightly. Then his face transformed with a smile that started in his eyes and spread until it seemed to illuminate him from within.

"I love you too," he replied, the words falling easily, as if he'd been waiting to say them.

Relief washed through Scarlet, followed by a wave of something warmer. She stepped forward as Jerry's arms enfolded her, his uniform rough against her cheek. She memorized the sensation of his heartbeat against hers, the scent of his skin beneath military-issued soap, the strength in his hands as they pressed against her back.

"Nine months," she whispered against his chest.

"I'll be counting every day," he promised, his voice a low vibration she felt more than heard.

"Me too. I'll fly out to see the boys in Utah as often as I can," she added softly, both of them aware that tomorrow would scatter their makeshift family across the country.

There was so much more to say, but time was evaporating. Across the gym, soldiers were beginning to shoulder their duffels, families stepping back with brave faces.

"Duncan," Mac's voice broke through their bubble. "Time to move out, brother."

Jerry nodded without looking away from Scarlet. His hands framed her face, thumbs brushing her cheekbones with a gentleness that belied his strength. "Wait for me," he said softly.

"Always," she promised.

Their final kiss was brief but charged with everything unsaid. Then he was stepping back, the physical space between them expanding like a wound. Scarlet's arms felt suddenly empty, her body too light without his presence anchoring her.

Maggie appeared beside her, one arm sliding around Scarlet's waist as Jerry walked toward the buses. "The first goodbye is the hardest," she murmured. "It gets easier. Not better, just easier."

Emmett's hand slipped into Scarlet's, his small fingers curling with surprising strength. "Dad said you're going to visit us at Grandma's house," he said, his voice small but hopeful.

"As often as I can," Scarlet promised, squeezing his hand. "We're a team, even when we're apart."

Marty reached toward the retreating line of soldiers, understanding loss in his own way. Scarlet stroked his hair as he nestled against Maggie, watching as Jerry boarded the bus with one final glance back. She raised her hand in farewell, forcing a smile she didn't feel.

She watched the buses disappear, rooted beside Maggie and the boys, holding her composure while the quiet tried to unravel her.

Nine months to prove that what they'd said wasn't a fluke of parting breath.

Nine months to navigate the strange math of devotion divided by distance.

"Let's go home," Maggie said gently, the word 'home' carrying different meanings for each of them now.

Together, they walked into the bright December sun, four people bound by the man who'd just disappeared down the road, and by something else that was still taking shape between them.

# Twenty-Four

S carlet smoothed her pencil skirt as Storm wove between her ankles, meowing with increasing desperation.

"I know, I know. You'll die of starvation in the next five seconds," she muttered, bending to scratch behind the grey cat's ears before filling his bowl. Storm immediately abandoned her for breakfast, loyalty forgotten in the face of kibble.

"At least you're consistent," she said, watching him for a moment before grabbing her travel mug.

The kitchen counter gleamed in the morning sunlight. Pristine, ordered, exactly as she'd left it the night before. So different from Jerry's chaos of half-empty juice cups and dinosaur-shaped cereal bowls. Her gaze caught on the small T-Rex figurine perched near her coffee maker, its tiny arms outstretched in what she'd come to think of as a perpetual hug.

Scarlet brushed her finger across the plastic toy, remembering how she'd discovered it nestled between her sweaters when unpacking three weeks ago. Emmett must have tucked it into her suitcase before she left

Texas, his way of giving her a small piece of himself to carry with her. The gesture had nearly broken her when she'd found it. Now it served as a daily touchstone, a reminder of what waited beyond spreadsheets and tax codes.

"See you tonight," she told Storm, who ignored her in favor of methodically cleaning his whiskers. "Try not to destroy anything valuable while I'm gone."

She locked her apartment door behind her, already mentally calculating time zones as she checked her phone. Seven hours ahead in Kuwait meant Jerry was well into his afternoon. No new messages since their brief text exchange the previous evening.

Jerry

> Remember our call at noon your time. Miss your face.

The simple line had made her smile despite the exhaustion of another day gone. She'd adjusted surprisingly quickly to their new normal. Scheduled video calls became routine, sporadic texts brightened random moments, and she found herself replaying his occasional voice messages until she'd memorized every inflection.

Descending to the parking garage, Scarlet mentally reviewed her calendar. Client meeting at ten, lunch break at exactly noon for Jerry's call, then the Westwood presentation prep in the afternoon. She'd need to be focused, efficient, and present. All things that had come naturally before a military boyfriend and his two special-needs children had rearranged her emotional landscape.

The drive to the office passed in a blur of familiar landmarks and mindless radio chatter. By the time she parked, Scarlet had slipped back into her professional persona, that careful compartmentalization she'd perfected over the years. Today was Wednesday. Day twenty-four of deployment. Just another day.

"Morning, Superstar," Eric's voice carried across the open-concept office space as Scarlet settled at her desk. He approached with that particular smile that always preceded additional work. "Got a minute?"

"Of course," she replied, the practiced response automatic.

Eric dropped a thick folder beside her keyboard. "Need these reconciled for the Pritchard audit. And the Jackson numbers still look off, so can you go through them again?"

"I already sent you the revised Jackson file yesterday afternoon," Scarlet said, keeping her tone neutral despite the flicker of annoyance. "The discrepancy was in their Q3 reporting, not our analysis."

"Right, right," Eric nodded distractedly, clearly not having read her email. "Well, double-check it anyway. I want to get ahead of any questions from the partners."

Before she could respond, he was already walking away, phone pressed to his ear. Scarlet watched him go, a familiar irritation brewing. Six months ago, she'd have immediately opened the Jackson file again, desperate to prove her worth. Now she simply filed Eric's request under "unnecessary redundancies" and turned to the Pritchard materials instead.

"He's still doing that, huh?" Simon appeared beside her desk, two coffee cups in hand. He placed one near her keyboard, the aroma of cinnamon and nutmeg wafting upward.

"Thanks," Scarlet said, genuinely grateful. "And yes, still doing what?"

"The thing where he pretends he's never seen your work before," Simon replied, leaning against her desk. "As if the infamous Bellari spreadsheets could possibly have errors."

"If I were feeling generous, I'd call it selective memory loss," Scarlet said, taking a sip of coffee. "But really, it's just good old-fashioned incompetence wrapped in a Brooks Brothers suit."

Simon snorted, nearly choking on his coffee. "Remind me never to get on your bad side."

"Oh, this isn't my bad side. This is my Wednesday side. You should see my Monday morning side."

He grinned, about to respond when Maya approached, her expression a careful blend of professionalism and forced casualness. She carried a small paper bag from the artisanal bakery down the street that Scarlet had once mentioned liking.

"Morning, Scarlet," she said, balancing a tablet against her hip. "Got a second? I'm having trouble with the Stewart portfolio projections." She placed the bakery bag on Scarlet's desk. "Thought you might need these almond croissants. I remembered you mentioned they help you think. And I figured with everything going on ..." She let the sentence trail off, her eyes flickering briefly to the small framed photo of Jerry that had recently appeared on Scarlet's desk.

Scarlet bit back a sigh. The Stewart account should have been simple for Maya, especially considering she now sat in the corner office with the window view that once had Scarlet's name on the promotion short list. Yet here they were, with basic errors that should have been caught years ago. The gesture with the croissants felt calculated, though the timing was oddly considerate.

"What part?" Scarlet asked, maintaining a collegial tone while shooting Simon a look that conveyed volumes. She left the bakery bag untouched, though the smell was tempting.

"The tiered tax structure is giving me fits," Maya admitted with a practiced self-deprecating laugh. "I know you did that analysis for Zhang Industries last year …"

Simon raised an eyebrow behind Maya's back, his expression communicating clearly: Here we go again.

"I've got a meeting at ten," Scarlet replied, gesturing to her calendar. "But I can probably spare twenty minutes now to walk you through it." She added with the barest hint of sweetness, "It can be a bit complex if you haven't worked with progressive structures before."

Maya didn't seem to catch the subtle dig. "You're a lifesaver. This partnership track is so demanding."

As she pulled up the reference materials, Scarlet caught Maya watching her. The expression was curious, mixed with something harder to read. Concern, maybe. Or just nosiness.

"How are you doing with, you know, everything?" Maya asked, her voice lowered. She twisted her bracelet nervously. "The whole long-distance thing must be hard. My sister's husband was deployed last year, and it nearly broke her." Maya's voice trailed off as she realized what she was implying. "Not that I'm saying you can't handle it. I just meant, if you need to offload some work … I could talk to Eric."

Scarlet maintained her professional smile, the one that revealed nothing while appearing completely open. The offer was so unexpected it had to be calculated. Probably hoping Scarlet would decline and appear weak, or accept and seem incapable.

"It's an adjustment. But we're making it work."

"I could never do it," Maya shook her head. "Nine months is such a long time. And with the boys, too? That's like … almost playing stepmom from a distance." She hesitated, then added softly, "You must really love them."

Eight months and six days now, Scarlet thought but didn't say. Instead, she smiled thinly. "I suppose some of us are just better at commitment than others. Now, back to the Stewart tax structure. I assume you're familiar with the baseline calculations?"

It took thirty minutes instead of the promised twenty before Scarlet finally reclaimed her desk, the morning half gone. Maya had lingered afterward, awkwardly mentioning a book about long-distance relationships she'd seen at the bookstore. "Not that you need it. You're handling everything so well. I just thought … anyway, never mind." She'd retreated to her office, leaving the bakery bag still unopened on Scarlet's desk.

Scarlet checked her phone quickly. No new messages from Jerry, but a text from Maggie with a photo of Marty at his new physical therapy session. His smile was brilliant, even through the pixelated image.

He's adjusting well to Dr. Parker. Session went great!

Scarlet sent back a quick heart emoji before returning to the Pritchard audit, the familiar numbers and patterns creating a soothing rhythm that carried her through until her calendar alert chimed.

*Video call with Jerry - 12:00*

Gathering her phone and bag, Scarlet made her way to the elevator with measured steps that belied her internal countdown. Three minutes to get to her car. Another two to set up her phone. No time for actual lunch, but that hardly mattered.

The privacy of her car felt like a sanctuary after the fluorescent lighting and constant hum of the office. Scarlet positioned her phone against the dashboard, checking her appearance in the camera preview. She smoothed her hair, applied a quick touch of lip gloss, then waited as the call connected.

One ring. Two. Three.

Her heart stuttered when Jerry's face finally appeared, grainy but unmistakable. He looked tired. New lines around his eyes, a tension in his jaw that hadn't been there before. But his smile when he saw her was genuine, crinkling the corners of his eyes in the way that always made her breath catch.

"Hey, beautiful," he said, his voice slightly distorted by the connection.

"Hey yourself, soldier," she replied, drinking in the sight of him. The background behind him was nondescript. Beige walls, metal furniture, other soldiers moving in and out of frame. "How's your day been?"

"The usual. Hot as hell, sand in places I didn't know sand could go." His voice was deliberately light. "Better now, though."

Scarlet leaned closer to the screen, wishing the digital distance could dissolve. "Did you get my email with the pictures Maggie sent? Marty started with the new PT this week."

"Yeah, got 'em. He looks like he's doing great." Jerry glanced over his shoulder as someone called his name, then back to the screen. "I see you're car-calling again. Still no privacy in the office?"

"The conference rooms are always booked, and I refuse to conduct our calls with Maya eavesdropping from the break room," Scarlet replied. "Besides, I like having you all to myself."

His expression softened. "How's Storm? Still judging your life choices?"

"Constantly. He's appointed himself official bed guardian in your absence. Takes up your entire side."

"Smart cat." Jerry's smile turned wistful. "How's work?"

Scarlet considered glossing over the day's frustrations but decided against it. Their time was too precious for false cheer. "Eric's being Eric. Maya's trying to mine my brain for responsibilities she should already understand. The usual."

"And you're letting it roll off your back, right?" Jerry asked, knowing her too well.

"Trying to," she admitted. "It all seems so ... inconsequential now."

A voice called from offscreen again, more insistent this time. Jerry glanced away, his expression shifting back to the professional mask she'd seen during the deployment ceremony.

"I've gotta go, babe. Emergency squad meeting. Something about the communication systems.."

"Already?" Scarlet couldn't keep the disappointment from her voice. Eight minutes. That's all they'd had.

"I'm sorry. I'll try to call again tomorrow, same time?"

"I'll be here," she promised. "I love you."

"Love you too. More than you know." Jerry's expression was suddenly intense, like he was trying to memorize her face. Then the screen went dark.

Scarlet sat motionless in her car, the absence of his presence a physical ache. Eight minutes out of twenty-four hours. She allowed herself exactly thirty seconds of sharp longing before straightening her shoulders and checking her makeup in the rearview mirror.

Eight months and six days to go.

"So as you can see from our projections, the restructured approach would yield a twelve percent increase in tax efficiency while maintaining full compliance with current regulations."

Scarlet concluded her presentation, the numbers on the projector screen reflecting weeks of careful analysis. The clients nodded appreciatively. Both were middle-aged men in expensive suits, and Eric leaned forward with his trademark closing smile.

"What Scarlet has developed here is exactly the kind of innovative approach our firm prides itself on," he said smoothly, as if the strategy had been collaborative rather than entirely her work. "We're fortunate to have such dedicated professionals on our team."

The clients seemed suitably impressed, and Scarlet maintained her professional demeanor throughout the handshakes and small talk that followed. Only when they had left did she allow herself to acknowledge the familiar frustration bubbling beneath her calm exterior.

"Nice work, Bellari," Eric said, collecting his notes. "Really solid insights."

"Thank you," she replied automatically. "Though I'd appreciate if next time you'd acknowledge it was my analysis rather than presenting it as a group effort."

The words slipped out before she could censor them. Six months ago, she'd have swallowed the comment, grateful for any recognition at all. Now the carefully maintained peace of the office hierarchy seemed increasingly unimportant.

Eric blinked, clearly taken aback by her directness. "I ... of course. You're right. Excellent job on this one."

He left the conference room quickly, and Scarlet gathered her materials, surprised by her own assertiveness. She caught Simon watching her from the doorway, an amused expression on his face.

"Well, look who finally decided to claim her territory," he remarked. "I thought Eric was going to swallow his tie."

Scarlet felt a sudden, unexpected lightness. "Maybe it's time I stopped being the office doormat."

"Maybe it is," Simon agreed, falling into step beside her. "Though I'd avoid pissing off the management too much until after bonus season."

"Because that promotion worked out so well for me last time?" Scarlet replied with a sardonic lift of her eyebrow. "Please. I've officially entered my 'what's the worst they can do, fire me?' era."

Simon laughed. "Military boyfriend is clearly a bad influence. Next thing you know, you'll be demanding combat pay for sitting through budget meetings."

"Not a bad idea, actually."

Maya caught her eye from across the bullpen, curiosity evident in her expression. When their eyes met, Maya didn't look away but instead gave a small, almost encouraging nod. On Scarlet's desk, she noticed a conference room reservation confirmation for noon tomorrow had been printed and placed beside her keyboard. Someone had blocked it for "S. Bellari - Private Call" in the system. The handwriting on the sticky note was unmistakably Maya's: "Thought you might prefer this to your car. No one will bother you."

The gesture was so unexpected that Scarlet's first instinct was suspicion. No doubt Scarlet's small act of rebellion would feature prominently in the office gossip within the hour. Yet the conference room booking seemed strangely thoughtful.

Her phone vibrated with a message from Maggie, another photo of the boys at dinner. Emmett was making a face at the camera, while Marty beamed with pasta sauce on his chin. The simple text beneath it made her throat tighten: They asked to send this to you. Miss their Mom.

Mom. The word still sent a complicated mix of emotions through her every time. Fear, joy, inadequacy, fierce love.

Scarlet tucked the phone away, saving the image for later when she could properly absorb it without an audience. Eight hours until she could leave this building and return to her apartment, where Storm and takeout and maybe another message from Jerry awaited.

Eight months and six days until the real world came back into focus.

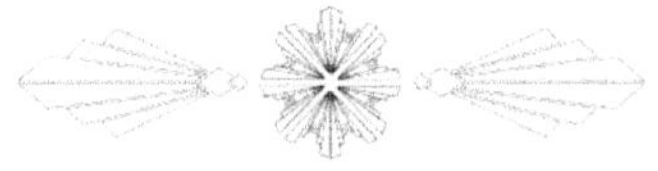

Storm greeted her with his typical blend of indifference and demanding attention, winding between her legs as she set down grocery bags on the kitchen counter. The apartment felt almost startlingly quiet after the constant background noise of the office.

"I bought the fancy food," Scarlet informed him, pulling out a small tin of gourmet cat food. "Consider yourself spoiled."

While Storm attacked his dinner, she unpacked the rest of her groceries and poured herself a glass of wine. The T-Rex figurine watched from its place near the coffee maker, plastic eyes somehow managing to look hopeful.

"Yeah, I miss them too," she told it, feeling only slightly ridiculous for talking to a toy.

Dinner was a practical affair. A microwave meal eaten standing at the counter while she sorted through mail. Bills, advertisements, a letter from her insurance company. Nothing from Kuwait, though she knew better than to expect frequent mail. Video calls and texts were their lifelines now, physical letters a slow-moving luxury.

With dinner finished, Scarlet moved to the living room and pulled out her deployment care package supplies. Her care package routine had become methodical, built around a detailed spreadsheet that tracked approved items, shipping restrictions, and estimated delivery times. Tonight she was finalizing a package that included jerky (the kind he liked from the local butcher shop), new socks (because he'd mentioned the sand destroyed them), and a flash drive loaded with photos and videos of the boys that Maggie had sent.

She also included a letter. An actual handwritten letter on stationery, something tangible he could hold. Scarlet had discovered a talent for letter-writing over the past few weeks, her thoughts flowing more honestly on paper than they sometimes did in their rushed video calls.

*I keep finding dinosaurs everywhere*, she wrote. *Emmett's influence has spread to my grocery list. Dinosaur chicken nuggets in my freezer, though I have no excuse since I'm the only one eating them. I told myself they were on sale, but the truth is they make me feel closer to him somehow.*

She paused, tapping her pen against the paper, trying to capture the strange dual existence she now inhabited.

*Work feels both exactly the same and completely different. Today I actually stood up to Eric about taking credit for my analysis. You would have been proud. Or maybe horrified, since office politics aren't exactly your style. But it felt good, like I'm finally shedding some skin that doesn't fit anymore.*

*I miss you in the strangest moments. Making coffee. Folding laundry. Sitting at stoplights. It's like my body still expects you to appear around corners or call from the other room. Storm has claimed your side of the bed completely, the traitorous beast.*

Scarlet continued writing, filling three pages with the ordinary details of her day interspersed with deeper reflections. She ended the letter not with platitudes about missing him, but with a promise that felt increasingly true with each passing day:

*Whatever shape our life takes after this, I know it will be better than what came before. The distance has taught me who I am when everything else falls away. And who I am is someone who loves you, loves the boys, and is starting to question everything else I thought mattered.*

*Always, Scarlet*

She sealed the envelope and added it to the care package, checking her list one final time before closing the box. Tomorrow she'd mail it, one small bridge across seven time zones.

Her phone chimed with an email notification from Maggie, containing Emmett's weekly video message. Scarlet settled onto the couch, Storm immediately claiming her lap, and pressed play.

"Hi Mom!" Emmett's face filled the screen, his gap-toothed smile so similar to Jerry's that it made her heart twist. "Guess what? I got to be line leader at school today, AND I remembered all the states in alphabetical order! Wanna hear?"

Scarlet watched as he launched into an impressively accurate recitation, stumbling only briefly between Minnesota and Mississippi. TThe background showed Maggie's kitchen in Utah, now adorned with crayon drawings and homework papers. Evidence of the boys' growing presence there.

"Marty wants to say hi too," Emmett continued, tilting the phone to include his brother, who was seated in his adaptive chair. Marty's face lit up at the sight of the camera, his hands flapping with joy. "He misses you too. Grandma says you're coming to visit soon. How many days? I'm counting!"

The video continued for a few more minutes with Emmett showing her a science project, promising to be good for Grandma, and asking when Dad would call next. When it ended, Scarlet replayed it immediately, the sound of his voice filling the quiet apartment.

She sent a reply message, knowing Maggie would share it with the boys in the morning.



Scarlet checked the calendar on her refrigerator, where she'd been X-ing off days. Sixteen until her first visit to Utah. One hundred and eighty-six until Jerry's expected return. She'd always found comfort in numbers because they were concrete, countable, reliable in ways that emotions never were.

By ten o'clock, she'd showered and changed into pajamas, Storm already curled at the foot of the bed. She was about to set her phone on the nightstand after one final check when she frowned at a new message from Jerry.

The timestamp showed 4:17 a.m. Kuwait time.

Jerry

Can't sleep. Thinking about your eyes when you laughed. The way your skin tasted like salt after swimming. The sound of your voice when you first said my name. Need those memories tonight.

Scarlet stared at the message, confusion furrowing her brow. Four in the morning? He should be sound asleep at that hour. The message itself was unusually personal compared to their typically practical texts about call schedules and care packages.

Technical delay, she decided. He must have sent it earlier, and it had only just come through. Kuwait's internet was notoriously spotty, according to Mac's warnings before deployment.

She considered replying, then decided against it. No need to disturb him if he'd finally managed to get some sleep. Instead, she set the phone down and reached for the small dinosaur figurine she'd moved to her nightstand, turning it over in her palm.

"Sixteen days," she whispered to it, a promise to Emmett and herself.

Storm stretched and repositioned himself, taking up an impressive amount of space for a medium-sized cat. Scarlet settled under the covers, her mind drifting between Jerry's strange late-night message and her unexpectedly assertive moment with Eric.

Priorities had begun to shift.

The job, the climb, the image of success she'd once protected. None of it felt quite as urgent anymore.

The promotion she'd lost?

Maybe it wasn't a loss at all.

Drifting toward sleep, Scarlet let her thoughts wander down un-explored paths, imagining roads not taken and choices she might still make.

Not dreams. Blueprints.

And just before surrendering to rest, she thought of Jerry's message.

Glitch or not, it had cracked something open.

And that opening mattered more than she could say.

# Twenty-Five

Wednesday evenings had settled into a predictable routine over the past seven weeks. Takeout eaten at the kitchen counter, spreadsheets updated with care package deliveries, occasional texts to Utah checking on the boys. This steady rhythm had become Scarlet's new normal. She'd even grown accustomed to the hollow space Jerry's absence had carved into her days, learning to navigate around it like furniture in a darkened room.

But nothing in her carefully structured deployment routine had prepared her for the sound that greeted her as she approached her apartment door: the unmistakable, gut-wrenching sobs of her sister.

Jade sat huddled against Scarlet's door, knees drawn to her chest, face buried in her hands. Her body shook with each ragged breath, designer purse spilled open beside her like she'd forgotten it existed. She didn't even look up at Scarlet's approach, lost in the gravity of her own breakdown.

"Jade?" Scarlet dropped her laptop bag, crouching immediately. "What happened? Are you hurt?"

When her sister finally looked up, mascara had streaked down her cheeks, her eyes were swollen, and her lips trembled so violently she could barely form words. "He … I … walked in … I can't …" Fresh sobs overtook whatever she was trying to say.

"Okay, let's get you inside," Scarlet said, fumbling with her keys. "Why didn't you use your spare key?"

"L-left it," Jade managed between gasping breaths. "When I … ran out …"

A cold dread settled in Scarlet's stomach as she helped her sister to her feet. This was Jade, who maintained perfect composure through flat tires and fashion emergencies, who laughed off disasters with reliable good humor. And something had reduced her to this shattered version of herself. Whatever had happened was catastrophic.

Storm appeared as they entered, weaving cautiously between their legs before retreating to observe from the safety of the couch. Scarlet guided Jade to sit, kneeling in front of her as her sister's body continued to convulse with sobs.

"Take a breath," Scarlet said, gripping Jade's trembling hands. "Just one breath, then tell me what's going on."

Her breath stuttered, collapsing halfway through.

"Lu-Lucas," she said, each syllable dragging grief with it.

"I f-found him … with … in our b-bed …"

The pieces clicked into terrible clarity. Scarlet's blood turned to ice, then fire. "He cheated on you?"

Jade nodded, a keening sound escaping her throat. "Walked in … Melissa from accounting … our sheets … wedding invitations on the … counter …"

Fury burned through Scarlet like wildfire. Lucas had played his part perfectly: the devoted fiancé with his two-carat ring and heartfelt promises after eighteen months of secretive dating, the charming future son-in-law who won over their parents with talk of family traditions during a year of wedding planning. He had worn the mask of devotion so convincingly, right up until he destroyed her sister in the most clichéd, unforgivable way possible.

"I'm calling Cami," Scarlet said, reaching for her phone. This was a level-five friendship emergency if ever there was one. She maintained physical contact with Jade as she dialed, watching her sister rock slightly, arms wrapped around herself as if trying to physically hold together the pieces of her shattered heart.

Cami answered on the second ring. "What's up, babe?"

"Emergency. My place. Jade caught Lucas cheating."

"That motherfucking piece of ..." Cami cut herself off. "I'm bringing wine. And ice cream. Lots of both. Don't move."

"She's not going anywhere," Scarlet replied, ending the call as Jade dissolved into another round of broken sobs.

She guided her sister to lie down, grabbing the throw blanket from the back of the couch to drape over her shaking form. Storm, sensing the distress, cautiously approached, settling near Jade's feet in a rare display of feline empathy.

"I don't understand," Jade whispered between sobs. "Everything was ... perfect. May wedding ... the flowers ... his vows ... he wrote them already ..."

Scarlet smoothed her sister's hair back from her tear-stained face. "I know. I know."

"Two and a half years," Jade continued, voice rising with sudden anger before crumbling again. "All that time and he ... with her ... they were laughing ..."

Scarlet winced at the thought of what Jade had witnessed. Not just the physical betrayal, but the emotional cruelty of it, the shared joke at her expense.

The vibration in her pocket broke her thoughts.

Jerry had texted.

Their agreed-upon check-in time. Without looking, she silenced it. Jerry would understand; Jade needed her now.

"I'm going to get you some water," Scarlet said, squeezing her sister's shoulder. "Then we'll figure this out. Cami's on her way."

In the kitchen, Scarlet let the fury consume her completely. Her fingers dug into the counter edge, jaw locked tight, eyes burning with unshed tears. How dare he. How fucking dare he destroy her bright, beautiful sister who had spent the past year comparing bridesmaid dresses and crafting handmade centerpieces for their perfect May wedding.

Her phone vibrated again. She silenced it once more, grabbing a glass and filling it with water, adding ice cubes because Jade had always insisted room-temperature water was "sad water."

When Scarlet returned, her sister had curled onto her side, staring blankly at nothing. "He said it wasn't ... wasn't serious," she whispered, not even reaching for the water. "Like that makes it better ..."

"It doesn't," Scarlet agreed, sitting beside her and gently urging her to drink. "Nothing makes this better."

"Everything is ruined," Jade continued, her words slurring slightly as exhaustion from emotional overload began to set in. "All those ... months hiding our relationship ... for what?"

"Don't worry about any of that right now," Scarlet soothed. "We'll figure it out."

The front door burst open without warning and Cami appeared, arms loaded with supplies. She clutched three bottles of wine in each hand while balancing a separate bag clearly filled with ice cream containers.

"Where is she?" Cami demanded, dropping everything unceremoniously on the counter and immediately zeroing in on the couch. Without pause, she crossed the room and dropped to her knees in front of Jade.

"Oh, sweetie," she said, voice uncharacteristically gentle. Without hesitation, she gathered Jade into a fierce hug.

Cami's fierce, protective embrace shattered Jade's remaining composure. She collapsed against her friend, raw, guttural sobs wracking her body.

"I've got you," Cami murmured, meeting Scarlet's eyes over Jade's shoulder with a look that communicated volumes. "Let it out. That's it."

Scarlet joined them, creating a protective circle around her sister. For several minutes, they simply held her through the storm of ugly, honest tears, no attempt at composure or restraint, just raw grief finally finding its voice.

Finally, Jade's sobs subsided into hiccupping breaths. Cami pulled back, her expression fierce. "I need details. Names. Addresses. Do you want his testicles vacuum-sealed or preserved in formaldehyde?"

Despite everything, a ghost of a smile flickered across Jade's tear-stained face.

"Wine first," Scarlet decided, moving to open one of the bottles Cami had brought. "Details second. Castration plans third."

While Scarlet poured three generous glasses, Cami transformed the living room into her version of "crisis headquarters," strategically placing blankets and tissues within reach and ensuring easy access to drinks. Scarlet's phone rang as she carried the wine glasses over. She checked the screen: Maggie.

"I need to take this quickly," she told them, stepping into the kitchen. "It's about the boys."

Maggie's voice was warm with her typical southwestern lilt. "Sorry to call so late. The boys wanted to show you Marty's new communication board before bedtime."

Scarlet's heart squeezed. Any other night, she would have treasured this call. "Maggie, I'm so sorry, but it's not a good night. My sister just had a major crisis, and I—"

"Say no more," Maggie interrupted gently. "Family comes first. We'll try again tomorrow?"

"Absolutely. Please give them both kisses from me. I'll explain everything tomorrow."

As she hung up, she found Jade watching her with red-rimmed eyes. "You didn't have to do that," she said hoarsely. "You could have talked to them."

Scarlet rejoined them on the couch, handing out wine glasses. "They'll understand. Tonight, you need me more."

Cami already had a pint of ice cream open, three spoons stuck haphazardly into rocky road. "To men being absolute trash," she said, raising her wine glass.

They drank deeply, the wine warming a path through Scarlet's chest. She sent Maggie a quick text explaining there was a family emergency, promising to call tomorrow with details.

"Okay," Cami said, setting down her glass with determination. "I need the play-by-play. Every sordid detail so we can properly destroy him."

Jade took another long swallow of wine, tears still flowing but her breathing more controlled. "I was ... supposed to be at my final dress fitting until six. B-but they finished early, so I thought I'd ... surprise him with takeout from that Thai place he likes."

The irony of Jade being the one to deliver the surprise made Scarlet's stomach turn.

"I heard them before I saw them," Jade continued, voice hollow. "Laughing. In our bedroom. Our bed where we ..." Her face crumpled. "I opened the door and they just ... stared at me. Then she grabbed her clothes and ran to the bathroom while Lucas kept saying it wasn't what it looked like."

"That lying sack of shit," Cami muttered darkly, digging her spoon aggressively into the ice cream.

"Except it was exactly what it looked like," Jade continued, anger flickering through her grief. "She left without even looking at me, and that's when he started making excuses. Said it was a mistake. Said it only happened twice." A bitter laugh escaped her. "Only twice. Like that's supposed to make me feel better."

"What did you do?" Scarlet asked softly.

"I grabbed my purse and ran. He followed me to the elevator, kept saying we could work through it. That the wedding wouldn't be affected." Jade's eyes flashed. "The wedding! Like I'd still marry him after …"

Scarlet's phone vibrated with a text. She ignored it, focusing entirely on her sister. "You're staying here tonight," she said. "However long you need."

Cami nodded firmly. "And I'm staying too. Girl army activated. No man is worth your tears, but if you're going to cry, we're damn well going to be here for it."

Something about the absolute certainty of female solidarity in those words brought fresh tears to Jade's eyes. "I don't understand," she whispered. "Everything was perfect. We were happy. At least, I thought …"

Her thought was interrupted by Scarlet's ringtone. She checked the display: their mother.

"How does she always know?" Jade asked, wiping her eyes.

"Mom radar," Scarlet replied, putting the call on speaker.

"Hello, my loves," their mother's voice came through, warm and knowing. "Why do I have this feeling I should be checking on my daughters?"

Jade's face crumpled. "Mom," she managed before fresh sobs overtook her.

"Jade? What's happened, mi corazón?"

Bit by bit, the story came out, shaped by fragments and Scarlet's quiet interjections.

Worry hardened into steel in their mother's voice.

"That boy," she said, with a venom that needed no embellishment.

"Jade, hear me now. You are not to blame. Not for one second of this."

"But maybe if I had been home more, or if I hadn't been so obsessed with wedding plans—"

"No," their mother cut in firmly. "No. A man who seeks comfort elsewhere instead of talking to his partner is a man who was always going to betray you. Today, next month, next year. Better now than after vows."

The practical wisdom in those words seemed to reach Jade in a way nothing else had. She nodded, clutching the phone like a lifeline.

"I'll come over tomorrow," their mother continued. "We'll start making calls. One step at a time. Tonight, you cry. Tomorrow, we fight."

After the call ended, Cami refilled their glasses while Scarlet distributed fresh pints of ice cream. "Your mom is badass," Cami said admiringly.

"She really is," Jade agreed, her voice steadier. "Do you think she's right? That he was always going to do this?"

Scarlet considered her answer carefully. "I think people who cheat make a series of choices. They choose themselves over their partner, over and over. It's not a mistake. It's a pattern of decisions."

"It's because he has a tiny dick," Cami declared, opening her second pint of mint chocolate chip. "Men with tiny dicks always cheat. It's science."

Jade choked on her wine, caught between a laugh and a sob. "It's not ... I mean, he's not ..."

"Oh my God, it IS tiny!" Cami crowed, pointing her spoon triumphantly. "I fucking knew it!"

"It's not tiny," Jade protested weakly. "It's … average."

"Average means tiny," Cami informed her. "No wonder he was compensating with Miss Fake Tits from accounting."

Three-quarters of a bottle later, Jade had progressed from devastated sobbing to righteous anger. The wine had loosened her grief, transforming it into articulate fury.

"Two and a half years down the drain," she said, gesturing broadly with her glass. "All that time sneaking around, keeping it secret from everyone, and for what? So he could fuck Melissa from accounting with her fake tits and her 'Lucas, you're so funny' laugh."

Cami snorted into her wine. "She has fake tits?"

"Spectacular ones," Jade confirmed darkly. "I bet that's what caught his wandering eye. Certainly wasn't her personality. She talks about her keto diet like it's a religion."

Scarlet couldn't help but smile at the glimpse of her sister's usual sharp wit emerging from the wreckage. "You're better off without both of them."

"Did I mention," Jade continued, fueled by wine and gathering steam, "that I found her underwear under our bed? Which means this wasn't the first time. They've been doing this in my home, on my Egyptian cotton sheets that I special ordered."

"Burn them," Cami advised sagely. "Burn everything he's ever touched. Including his car."

"I paid for half that car!"

"Burn your half."

They dissolved into semi-hysterical laughter, the kind that borders on tears. Scarlet felt lighter seeing her sister able to laugh, even in this broken way.

Cami twisted open the second bottle while Scarlet checked her phone with a flick of her thumb.

No new messages.

Just the two she'd let sit unread.

Jerry would usually follow up, especially when she didn't answer.

The silence sparked a sliver of unease. She waved it off with practiced logic.

He was giving her space.

But as the night wore on, she became increasingly aware of a slow drift.

What had once been spontaneous, consuming, had slipped into check-ins and calendar slots.

When was the last time he'd sent her a message just because he was thinking of her? When was the last time they'd had a call that wasn't interrupted by duty or cut short by fatigue?

"Men are trash," Cami declared, refilling glasses with practiced precision. "Sorry, Scarlet, I know you've got a good one, but as a species? Garbage."

"Not all men," Scarlet began automatically, the defense feeling hollow even as she voiced it.

"Yes, all men," Jade countered, wine loosening her restraint. "Some just hide it better. Or maybe some actually mean their promises." She gestured vaguely toward Scarlet. "But distance changes people. Makes them forget what they're missing."

The comment hit Scarlet like a physical blow. She tried to keep her expression neutral, but Cami's sharp eyes caught the flinch.

"Jerry is different," Cami said firmly, surprising Scarlet with her defense. "That man looks at you like you're the answer to a question he's been asking his whole life."

Jade nodded, waving her glass for emphasis. "You're right. I'm sorry. I'm just ... bitter and destroyed and wondering if love is even real anymore." Her voice cracked on the last word.

"It's real," Scarlet said softly. "Just rarer than we want to believe."

But even as she spoke the words, a small voice inside her whispered traitorously: How do you know? How can you be sure when he's seven time zones away, surrounded by people you've never met, living a life you're not part of?

Jade's phone buzzed for the twentieth time that evening. She glanced at it, then immediately threw it across the room where it landed with a thud on the armchair. "He won't stop calling. Texting. Begging for a chance to explain." Her voice rose in mocking imitation: "'It's not what you think, babe. Just a moment of weakness. I love you, not her.'"

Cami's expression darkened. "Block him. Tonight. Right now."

"I can't just—"

"You can," Scarlet interjected. "And you should. At least for now. Nothing he says tonight will make this better."

"But what about—"

"Fuck him," Cami interrupted, her voice heated. "Seriously. Fuck. Him. He lost all rights to your attention the minute his dick went wandering. Did I mention my roommate's brother is a hacker? We could ruin his credit score."

"That's illegal," Scarlet pointed out.

"Only if we get caught," Cami countered. "Oh! We could send glitter bombs to his office every day for a month."

Despite everything, Jade smiled weakly. "You're both terrible influences."

"The best kind," Cami agreed, raising her glass. "To terrible influences and best friends."

Glasses clinked again, and Scarlet poured herself another round.

Her mind slid helplessly between two men, two silences, unable to stop the comparison.

Lucas filled the void with noise.

Jerry offered none at all.

Somehow, that absence stung more.

She sipped, slow and thoughtful, the doubt creeping in:

Was he drifting?

Or just occupied?

There was no way to tell, and no reassurance to reach for.

"You know what hurts almost as much as finding them together?" Jade said after a moment. "Realizing that every perfect moment we've had for the past ... however long this has been going on ... was a lie. Every time he said 'I love you,' every future plan, every night he held me ... all while he was ..." Fresh tears spilled down her cheeks.

Rather than crashing over her, the truth settled quiet and final.

Scarlet's gaze drifted to her phone. Still blank.

Earlier messages now read like artifacts of something that had already started to change.

She saw Jerry again, barefoot by the pool, voicing his unease about Lucas with careful restraint.

She'd laughed.

*Not everyone charms the Bellaris like you.*

She hadn't listened.

Maybe she hadn't wanted to.

The clarity came too late. What Jerry had seen in hours, she'd been ignoring for weeks.

"Scarlet?" Cami's voice broke through her thoughts. "You okay, sweetie?"

"Fine," she said quickly, setting her phone aside. "Just checking the time."

But Jade, even through her own misery, caught the flicker of concern. "Has Jerry been different? Since he left?"

Scarlet hesitated. Tonight wasn't about her or her relationship. But with wine softening her usual careful filters, the truth slipped out. "A little. More distant in the last few weeks. Calls are shorter. Texts are ... I don't know, more like status updates than conversations."

"That's just deployment," Cami said confidently. "Mac warned you about communication blackout periods and all that military stuff."

"It's not a blackout," Scarlet corrected, the wine making her more frank than she'd intended. "He's communicating. Just ... differently. Sometimes I feel like I'm talking to his sergeant version, not the guy who held me all night after Marty had that meltdown, you know?"

Jade straightened, momentarily distracted from her own pain. "Different how?"

The dam finally gave way, and the words spilled out. Fears she'd kept under lock for weeks.

"It's little things. Video calls that used to last thirty minutes are done in ten. Texts are just logistics now. Nothing personal. And that strange late-night message ... it didn't even sound like him."

She swirled her wine, the deep red catching the overhead light.

"I don't know if it's just the deployment or if ..."

The rest caught in her throat, too heavy to say aloud.

"If he's pulling away," Jade supplied quietly.

"It's probably nothing," Scarlet backtracked, the reality of her voiced fears suddenly overwhelming. "He's tired. Busy. It's a war zone, not summer camp."

"Kuwait is hardly a war zone," Cami pointed out, then caught herself. "But yeah, still stressful and all that."

"I shouldn't have said anything," Scarlet added quickly, shame washing through her. "Seriously, it's normal adjustment. Nothing like ..." She gestured to Jade, unwilling to even draw a comparison between Jerry's deployment behavior and Lucas's betrayal.

Jade reached for her hand, squeezing with surprising strength. "I didn't mean to project my disaster onto you," she said, her eyes clearing slightly through the wine fog. "I've seen you two together. It's different. Real."

"I know," Scarlet agreed softly. "Just deployment blues."

The seed had been planted, and under the haze of wine and growing dread, it began to grow.

By the time the third bottle was uncorked, Scarlet was already tracing the pattern she'd been trying to ignore. Video calls tapering off, texts turning impersonal, and Jerry's quiet evasions whenever she asked about him, not just his schedule.

Jade's devastation had cracked something open. A fault line of insecurity Scarlet had been carefully avoiding. Because if Lucas could betray Jade after two and a half years, what guarantee did she have about a military man seven time zones away? A rational voice in her head argued that Jerry was nothing like Lucas, that deployment was nothing like normal separation. But wine and sisterly heartbreak had eroded her usual logical defenses.

By midnight, after four bottles between the three of them, Jade had finally cried herself into exhaustion, curled in Scarlet's bed with Storm keeping protective watch. Cami sprawled on the couch, scrolling through her phone with determined focus.

"I've got seventeen ways to make Lucas regret he was ever born," she announced as Scarlet emerged from checking on Jade. "Also, I may have signed him up for erectile dysfunction email newsletters. And furry dating sites."

Despite everything, Scarlet smiled. "You're a good friend, Cami."

"The best," she agreed without false modesty. "Now get some sleep. Tomorrow's going to be brutal for her."

Scarlet retreated to her bedroom, careful not to disturb her finally-sleeping sister. Before settling beside her, she checked her phone one last time. Jerry had finally sent a message an hour ago.

Jerry

> Everything okay? Haven't heard from you today. Call tomorrow?

So normal. So reasonable. Nothing like Lucas's desperate barrage of texts to Jade.

But something about it felt hollow, as if it were a required check-in rather than genuine concern. Or was she reading too much into it, poisoned by proximity to her sister's betrayal?

Scarlet typed a response, then paused, deleting it. The wine and the emotional evening had lowered her usual guards. She started again.

Scarlet

> Family emergency. Jade caught Lucas cheating. You were right about him. I'm sorry I dismissed your concerns that day by the pool. Will explain everything tomorrow. Love you.

Her thumb hovered over the send button, a moment of vulnerability in acknowledging that Jerry had seen something in Lucas she'd missed. That maybe she should have trusted his judgment more. She hit send before she could overthink it.

She stared at the screen, waiting for the three dots that would indicate Jerry was responding. Nothing came. She set the phone aside, trying to ignore the hollow feeling expanding beneath her ribs.

Scarlet settled beside her sister, eyes catching on the dinosaur figurine, arms perpetually reaching.

Tonight had shaken more than Jade's life.

It had exposed the very fractures in her long-distance love that she'd been refusing to acknowledge.

What if this was how it started? Not with dramatic betrayal but with the slow erosion of connection. Calls growing shorter, messages becoming perfunctory, emotional intimacy fading so gradually you barely noticed until it was gone? What if seven time zones and nine months was simply too much for any relationship to bear?

The difference, Scarlet decided as she finally drifted toward sleep, was her choice to stand firm despite the tremors. Seven more months. She could weather this distance, these subtle shifts. Unlike Lucas, Jerry's promises weren't empty.

She had to believe that. The alternative was too much to bear.

# Twenty-Six

The scent of guava paste and cinnamon filled Elisa Bellari's kitchen as Scarlet carefully removed the last batch of pastelitos from the oven. The golden pastries glistened under the morning light streaming through the window, their edges perfectly crisp, the filling still bubbling.

"These look better than mine," Elisa said, peering over her daughter's shoulder as Scarlet arranged them on a cooling rack. "You're getting too good, mi vida. I'll have nothing left to teach you."

"I had a good teacher," Scarlet replied, wiping her hands on a dish towel. "Besides, yours taste better. They always do."

From the other side of the kitchen island, Jade rolled her eyes affectionately as she dusted powdered sugar over a separate tray of pastries. "Can we skip the humility competition? You're both baking goddesses. Accept it, own it, and pass me another coffee."

Scarlet chuckled, sliding the coffee pot toward her sister. Jade had bounced back remarkably in the three months since the catastrophic end of her engagement. Gone was the hollow look, replaced by the familiar spark of playful confidence. Even her dark humor had returned, sharper and brighter.

"So," Elisa began, casually leaning against the counter, eyes sparkling with maternal mischief. "Any big plans for this afternoon, Jade?"

Scarlet recognized that tone immediately, glancing sideways at her sister. Jade remained surprisingly unruffled, sipping her coffee and meeting their mother's probing gaze without flinching.

"Actually, yes," Jade said smoothly. "I have a date."

Scarlet raised her eyebrows, intrigued. Elisa paused in surprise, clearly expecting her daughter's usual vague deflection.

"Oh?" Elisa asked carefully, clearly trying to hide her excitement. "With ... ?"

"Dave," Jade replied evenly, a faint smile playing at the corners of her lips.

Scarlet exchanged a quick glance with her mother. For as long as either of them could remember, Jade's casual dates had all been indistinctly labeled as "John." Hearing her use an actual name so openly felt monumental, a small but significant shift that hinted at deeper healing beneath the surface.

"Dave," Elisa echoed gently, clearly pleased but cautious. "Well, this is new. You never mention names unless it's serious."

"It's not serious. Yet," Jade corrected firmly. "But I figured after ... everything, maybe it's time I tried something different. You know ... actual honesty, no hiding, all that terrifying grown-up stuff you keep lecturing me about."

Scarlet nudged her sister gently with her elbow. "Look at you, breaking lifelong traditions."

Jade shot her an affectionate smirk. "Yeah, well. Lucas proved traditions aren't always worth keeping."

The air tightened briefly around them, but Jade shrugged it off with surprising ease, dusting her hands on a kitchen towel. Scarlet recognized the strength it took to treat her past heartbreak so casually; it wasn't denial, but genuine, hard-earned resilience.

"You know what they say," Scarlet teased gently, carefully shifting the conversation lighter. "Nothing says personal growth like pastries and first names."

Jade laughed, rolling her eyes again. "Speaking of growth, what about you and Mr. Soldier? Still navigating the thrills of satellite romance?"

Scarlet felt the brief stab of unease that had become routine lately, but masked it behind a practiced smile. "Still navigating," she said lightly. "You know, one scheduled call at a time."

Elisa saw right through the smile, as mothers often do.

She brushed a loose strand behind Scarlet's ear, her touch gentle and unhurried, carrying all the patience that only time and love can teach.

It was the kind of gesture passed down more often than spoken aloud.

And Scarlet let herself lean into it, just a little.

A text notification lit up her phone on the counter. Scarlet's hand moved toward it with reflexive quickness, but she forced herself to finish arranging the pastries first. Five months of deployment had taught her that most messages could wait, while the meaningful ones had grown increasingly scarce.

When she finally checked the screen, she saw Maggie's name.

Just checked into the hotel. Ready to meet at South Beach at 11? The boys are BEYOND excited to see you.

Scarlet smiled despite the flutter of anxiety in her stomach. "They're at their hotel," she told her mother and sister, typing a quick reply. "We're meeting at eleven."

Jade leaned over Scarlet's shoulder, reading the message. "Give those boys an extra squeeze for me, okay?"

Elisa glanced at the pastries cooling on the rack. "You think these will be enough? I could whip up another batch."

"Mom, there are already three dozen. Enough to feed an army, let alone four people."

"Five," Elisa corrected, nodding at Scarlet. "Unless you're planning to starve."

Scarlet smiled, tapping another message to Maggie to confirm the meeting spot. When she looked up, her mother was watching her with that familiar look of half concern, half careful assessment that she'd come to recognize.

"What?" Scarlet asked, though she already knew.

"You seem distracted. More than usual." Elisa leaned against the counter, her eyes never leaving Scarlet's face. "Is everything okay with Jerry?"

The question hung in the air, deceptively simple. Was everything okay? Scarlet had been asking herself the same thing for weeks now, trying to gauge whether the growing distance in their communication was normal deployment adjustment or something deeper.

"He's fine. Busy." The automatic response felt hollow even to her own ears.

Elisa raised an eyebrow, unimpressed. "I didn't ask if he was fine. I asked if everything was okay between you."

Scarlet sighed, setting her phone down. There was no point hiding concerns from her mother; Elisa had an uncanny ability to see through pretense.

Jade reached over, squeezing Scarlet's hand lightly, a silent reassurance that spoke volumes about her sister's newfound emotional insight. "It's okay, Scar. You don't have to pretend everything's perfect. Trust me."

Scarlet offered her a grateful glance, then took a steadying breath. "I don't know," she admitted, the words feeling like small betrayals. "The calls are shorter. His texts are ... perfunctory. Sometimes it feels like I'm talking to a stranger wearing Jerry's face." She shook her head. "That sounds dramatic, I know."

"It sounds honest," Elisa corrected gently. "Long distance is hard, even without a war zone involved."

"Kuwait's hardly a war zone," Scarlet said, echoing Cami's reassurance from weeks ago. "It's a support base. He's safer there than he'd be on a typical training exercise."

"The danger isn't what makes deployment hard, mi vida. It's the distance. The parallel lives you start to lead." Elisa placed a hand over Scarlet's. "All relationships have seasons. This is just a difficult season."

The well-meaning advice fell slightly flat. Her mother had never navigated military life, had never balanced love across seven time zones and against the backdrop of special needs parenting. But the tenderness in her touch was genuine, and Scarlet squeezed her hand gratefully.

"I know," she said, more to herself than to her mother. "It'll get better."

Jade met Scarlet's gaze evenly, her eyes filled with quiet strength forged from her own recent trials. "It will," she said firmly, surprising Scarlet. "And if it doesn't, we'll get you through it."

Scarlet's heart swelled with gratitude. Jade's certainty that was newly discovered and fiercely protective felt like a lifeline.

Elisa smiled warmly at her daughters, then glanced at the clock. "Are you sure your father and I can't join you today? We'd love to finally meet Thomas and Maggie in person."

"They'd love that too, but you've got that big spa appointment, remember? Dad would never forgive me if I ruined his Mother's Day surprise."

Elisa laughed. "That man. Thirty-five years together, and he still thinks I don't know exactly what he's planning." She glanced again at Jade, who was refilling her coffee with a casual ease Scarlet hadn't seen in months. "And you, Jade ... have fun with Dave. Be honest, be brave. You deserve it."

Jade raised her coffee mug, smiling warmly. "Brave and honest. Terrifying, but I'll give it a try."

As her mother disappeared upstairs, Jade leaned close to Scarlet, her voice lower, softer. "You okay, really?"

Scarlet squeezed her sister's arm, returning the warmth and concern. "I will be."

"Good. Because I owe you about five hundred hours of emotional support after the Lucas thing. I'm ready to start paying that back."

Scarlet chuckled softly. "Deal."

She finished packing the pastries, a new sense of calm settling around her. Whatever had shifted between her and Jerry, she had her family, and right now, that felt like enough.

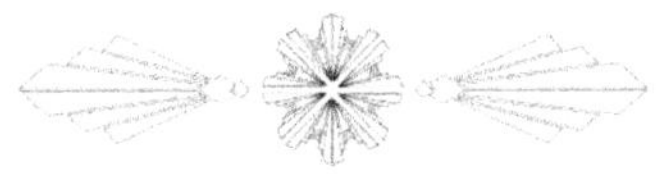

The May sun hung high over South Beach, transforming the ocean into a canvas of turquoise and sapphire. Scarlet walked across the warm sand, scanning the colorful umbrellas and beach towels. There they were: Maggie waving with enthusiastic vigor while Thomas arranged chairs, and the boys playing near the shoreline in matching green sun hats.

Emmett saw her first. His head snapped up mid-sandcastle construction, eyes widening with recognition before his whole face transformed with joy.

"MOM!" he shouted, abandoning his plastic shovel to sprint across the sand toward her. "MOM, YOU'RE HERE!"

The title still hit Scarlet with a mixture of warmth and disorientation, even after months of hearing it. Emmett launched himself into her arms, all skinny limbs and boundless energy, nearly knocking her backward with the force of his enthusiasm.

"Careful, buddy," she laughed, steadying herself while lifting him onto her hip. "I missed you too."

"Did you bring special Miami snacks?" he asked, already peering at the bag slung over her shoulder. "Grandma said you might."

"I definitely did," Scarlet confirmed, carrying him toward the rest of the family. "My mom made pastelitos. They're like pastries with sweet filling inside."

"Like Pop-Tarts?"

"Way better than Pop-Tarts, I promise."

As they approached, Marty's face lit up from where he sat in his beach chair. His hands began to flap with excitement, his entire body communicating joy even without words. The sight made Scarlet's chest tighten with an emotion she couldn't quite name.

"There she is," Maggie said warmly, stepping forward to envelop Scarlet in a hug. "We've been counting down the days to see you."

Thomas followed, his hug gentle but firm. "Good to see you on your home turf this time," he said, his smile so reminiscent of Jerry's that Scarlet felt a sharp pang of longing. "The boys haven't stopped talking about Miami since we told them we were coming."

Maggie glanced around, as if expecting more people. "No Elisa or Leo today? I was hoping to finally meet them."

"Mom had a big spa appointment," Scarlet explained, setting Emmett down. "Getting all dolled up for her Mother's Day brunch tomorrow. Dad always tries to treat her big every year ... massage, facial, the works." She approached Marty, crouching to his eye level. "Hey, sunshine. Look at you in that hat."

Marty hummed happily, reaching for her with both hands. She leaned in closer, and he pressed his forehead to hers in what had become their special greeting from the very beginning. The simple connection grounded her, reminding her why she was navigating this complex path.

"I brought something that might make Marty more comfortable," Scarlet said, straightening up. "A small beach tent so he doesn't overheat. It's in my car. Thomas, would you mind helping me grab it?"

"Smart thinking," Thomas nodded, immediately understanding. "He struggles with the heat sometimes. Let's go get it."

As they walked back toward the parking lot, Thomas fell into step beside her. "Jerry mentioned you're always thinking ahead like this. The boys' needs, I mean." His tone was conversational, but Scarlet heard what Thomas wasn't saying directly. Jerry still talked about her, still noticed the ways she cared for his sons.

"I try," she said simply. "Their comfort matters."

Together, they retrieved the compact beach tent from her trunk, Thomas carrying the lightweight frame while Scarlet gathered the remaining beach supplies. Back on the sand, they worked together to set it up in a sheltered spot that would provide maximum shade while still allowing Marty to see the ocean.

"Perfect," Maggie declared once it was secured. "Now, I believe someone mentioned pastries?"

The next hour passed in a comfortable rhythm. They shared Elisa's pastelitos, which earned enthusiastic approval from everyone, especially Emmett, who declared them "better than five Pop-Tarts stacked together." Conversation flowed naturally, covering updates on the boys' progress with their therapists in Utah, excitement about tomorrow's cruise departure, and careful avoidance of deployment details that might cast shadows over the bright day.

"So you board tomorrow morning?" Scarlet asked, helping Emmett build a sand fortress beside Marty's protected spot under the tent.

"We check in at eleven," Thomas confirmed. "Cruise leaves at five. Seven nights around the Caribbean."

"Grandma says we'll see pirates," Emmett informed her solemnly.

"No, I said we might see where pirates used to live," Maggie corrected with a laugh. "We're going to visit a pirate museum in Nassau."

"That's good. I'd be sad if my Emmosaur was attacked by pirates," Scarlet admitted. "But I bet you'll see some amazing fish and beaches."

"I wish you could come," Emmett said, digging a moat around their sand structure. "It would be more fun with you."

The simple declaration warmed Scarlet's heart. "I'd love that, buddy, but I've got a special Mother's Day brunch with my mom tomorrow. Plus, I have to work next week. But I'll come visit you in Utah again soon, I promise."

"Dad says you might come for longer next time," Emmett continued, focused on his digging. "Maybe for two whole weeks instead of just one."

Scarlet's hands stilled in the sand. "Did he? When did he say that?"

"On our video call last week. He said maybe you could stay longer next time because …" He scrunched his face in concentration, "because the distance is stupid. That's what he said. But don't tell Grandma I said stupid."

Before Scarlet could process this unexpected insight into Jerry's thinking, Thomas stood, holding out his hands to both boys. "Who wants to go play in the sand down by the water? Marty, want me to carry you down?"

Marty nodded enthusiastically, arms reaching up for his grandfather. Thomas lifted him with practiced ease, settling him against his hip.

"I want to splash in the waves!" Emmett declared, abandoning the sand fortress to grab Thomas's hand.

"We'll be right back," Thomas told Maggie and Scarlet with a knowing smile. "Take your time."

They moved toward the shoreline together, Thomas settling Marty on a smooth patch of sand while Emmett bounded ahead toward the gentle waves. As they walked, Scarlet felt a shift in the atmosphere. Thomas had created this moment of privacy with deliberate intent, and from Maggie's expression, she had something specific to say.

But before Maggie could speak, Emmett came racing back up the beach, eyes wide with excitement.

"Wait! I almost forgot! We have to give Mom her present before we go to the water!"

Scarlet blinked in surprise. "Present?"

Emmett looked to Maggie, who nodded encouragingly. He darted to their beach bag, digging through it with determined focus before emerging with a small gift bag.

"It's for Mother's Day," he announced proudly, holding it out to Scarlet. "From me and Marty."

The words hit Scarlet with unexpected force. Mother's Day. She'd been so focused on her mother's celebration tomorrow that it hadn't occurred to her that the boys might include her in the holiday.

"I ... um ... thank you," she managed, taking the bag with fingers that trembled slightly. "I wasn't expecting this."

"Open it!" Emmett urged, bouncing on his toes.

Inside the bag, Scarlet discovered two treasures. The first card featured Emmett's carefully drawn dinosaurs and detailed "Happy Mother's Day" lettering, while the second bore Marty's painted handprint with what was clearly Maggie's assisted writing. Beneath them lay a small jewelry box.

"The bracelet was my idea," Emmett informed her. "Grandma helped me pick the charms."

Scarlet lifted the lid, revealing the bracelet: slender, silver, and impossibly small. Two tiny charms lay side by side, a green wheelchair paired with a joyful dinosaur drenched in rainbow colors.

Emmett's gaze was steady, bright with meaning.

"Those are ours," he said. "Green for Marty. Rainbow dino for me." He showed her his arm, pointing to where Jerry's similar tattoo lived. "Dad has them. Now you do too. Because you're our mom ... even when you're not here."

He hesitated, then grinned. "But yours is cooler. Dinosaurs are better."

The ground seemed to shift beneath Scarlet, stealing her breath completely. Her hands weren't steady as she clasped the bracelet, the metal surprisingly warm against her pulse.

"Oh, Emmett," she breathed. He was in her arms before she even realized she'd opened them.

She hugged him tightly, and for the briefest second, grief wove itself through her joy. A whisper of longing for the child she had once imagined but never held.

It didn't dull the moment. It deepened it.

Because this, being chosen, being needed, was its own kind of motherhood.

When he darted off, sea-bound, Scarlet looked up to find Maggie watching her with that gentle, ancient look of quiet accounting.

Scarlet held it, unsure whether it comforted or unmoored her. There was love in it. But also a reminder: she was still becoming someone worthy of it.

"I don't know if I can accept this," Scarlet admitted quietly, touching the bracelet as if it might shatter beneath her fingers. "Not when ..." Her words trailed off, uncertain and fragile.

"When what?" Maggie prompted gently, shifting closer, her voice a soothing balm to Scarlet's frayed nerves. "You look like someone just handed you a gift and a burden all at once."

Scarlet exhaled shakily, tracing the tiny charms again, trying to find courage in their meaning. "Jerry and I ... we've felt disconnected lately. His calls are shorter. Texts have become logistics instead of conversations. I've started to wonder ..." Scarlet's voice wavered, her eyes welling. "Maybe he's realized it's all too much. Maybe it's all too complicated. That I'm not meant for this life."

Maggie paused, her thoughtful silence allowing the sea's rhythmic hush to soften the air between them. "Sweetheart, have you ever wondered why Jerry keeps so much of himself locked away?"

Scarlet looked up sharply, breath hitching, a small nod all she could manage. "I've tried not to push. I figured he'd open up when he was ready."

Maggie glanced toward Thomas, gently guiding Marty's hands through wet sand, Emmett splashing beside them with abandon. She took a slow, steadying breath, choosing her next words carefully. "Jerry and the boys have been through so much more than you realize. Their biological mother ..." She paused, clearly weighing the weight of truth against the delicacy of Jerry's secrets. "She walked away from them entirely. Abandoned them. Left deep wounds."

Scarlet nodded slowly, heart aching at the quiet strength behind Maggie's words. "Jerry has hinted before, but he's never really shared."

"And he might not, not easily," Maggie said gently. "What happened to him ... and especially to Marty and Emmett ... it broke something deep inside him. It's why he holds back, why he retreats. It's easier to guard himself, to expect loss instead of opening up to the risk of feeling it again."

Scarlet blinked back tears. "I can feel him pulling away. It scares me."

Maggie reached out, gently placing a reassuring hand on Scarlet's arm. "He's not pulling away because he cares less. He's terrified precisely because he cares so much. He's afraid that if he shows you all the broken parts, you'll leave too. That's his way of managing the fear, and deployment makes it worse when distance amplifies everything."

"I don't want him to carry this alone," Scarlet whispered fiercely. "I want him to trust me enough to share."

Maggie's eyes softened, reflecting years of quiet worry and guarded hope. "He will, Scarlet. I'm sure of it. If Jerry has brought you this far, if he's allowed his boys to call you 'Mom,' it means more than you can imagine. Trust isn't easy for him, but he's getting there. And when he finally tells you everything, when he opens that door, just listen. You don't have to fix the past for him. You just have to stand beside him as he lets it go."

The tears slid silently, the release sharp, almost shameful. "But I'm not their mother, Maggie. Not really."

"Scarlet," Maggie said firmly, gently cupping her cheek, forcing her to meet her eyes. "You have loved those boys more in these past months than their biological mother ever did. You have shown up for them every day, in the quiet ways that matter most. Biology doesn't measure love. What matters is how much you're willing to give, how deeply you're willing to care. You are already so much more their mom than she ever was."

Scarlet drew in a shaky breath, trying desperately to absorb Maggie's confidence, the truth she wanted so badly to embrace. "It just feels overwhelming, like I haven't earned the right yet."

"Love isn't something you have to earn, Scarlet," Maggie whispered, brushing away the tears on Scarlet's cheek. "Jerry's ex-wife had the title of mother, but never understood the meaning behind it. You already live it, every day. That bracelet isn't just about accepting them ... it's about accepting that you're already enough."

Scarlet turned again toward the ocean, where Thomas and the boys had paused to wave. Her heart lifted, fragile but suddenly lighter. "I'm so scared of letting them down."

Maggie squeezed her shoulder reassuringly. "The fact that you worry about that means you won't. Trust Jerry to trust you. When he's finally ready to open his past, hold space for him. Let him lay down the burden he's carried for so long. That's all he needs from you. Not perfection, just presence."

Scarlet nodded slowly, a gentle resolve settling deep in her bones. "I promise."

Maggie offered a soft, knowing smile. "Jerry doesn't need another person to rescue him. He just needs someone who won't leave when it gets hard. He needs someone like you."

They sat quietly, the sun warm against their backs, the sound of the boys' laughter mingling with the gentle whispers of the sea. After a long moment, Maggie gently nudged Scarlet's arm. "Let's take a video for Jerry. Show him exactly what he has to come home to."

Scarlet smiled softly, rising with Maggie and waving Thomas and the boys closer. As they all gathered around, Thomas draped an affectionate arm around Scarlet's shoulders, and Emmett launched into an excited retelling of their beach adventure, Marty's happy hums underscoring the scene.

The metal warmed against her skin, and she knew it wasn't from the sun. It was from staying.

She hadn't stepped into a role. It had grown up around her.

Maggie's words didn't echo. They landed.

You are already enough.

She hadn't planned to become someone's mother.

But it no longer felt like something that had happened to her.

It felt like a choice she kept making.

The simple statement carried acceptance from the entire Duncan clan, Maggie included. It settled around Scarlet like a protective cloak, warming her against the chill of uncertainty that had plagued her for weeks.

The afternoon stretched into evening, the beach gradually emptying as the sun began its descent toward the horizon. Marty had fallen asleep in his grandfather's arms, while Emmett's boundless energy had finally begun to wane, his sandcastle-building growing slower and more methodical.

"We should probably head back to the hotel," Maggie said, checking her watch. "Early boarding tomorrow."

"What time does your cruise leave?" Scarlet asked, helping to pack their beach supplies.

"Five, I think," Thomas replied.

"I wish I could see you off, but I've got that brunch with my family," Scarlet said, carefully dismantling the beach tent. "Mom would kill me if I missed it."

"Absolutely," Maggie agreed. "Mother's Day is sacred. Besides, we'll see you up in Utah again soon enough."

As they gathered their belongings and prepared to leave, Maggie slipped a small photo into Scarlet's palm. It showed Jerry with both boys, his smile unguarded, eyes crinkled with genuine happiness.

"He carries you with him too," Maggie said softly. "Even when he doesn't know how to show it."

Scarlet carefully tucked the photo into her wallet, next to her driver's license where she'd see it every day. She watched as Thomas carried a sleeping Marty toward the parking lot, Emmett dragging his feet in the sand beside them, Maggie following with the beach bag. The family she'd somehow found on a cruise ship, then chosen to build a life around despite deployments and diagnoses and distance.

The Mother's Day bracelet caught the last rays of sunset, the green wheelchair and rainbow dinosaur charms glinting like promises. Scarlet touched them gently, feeling something shift and settle within her. Whatever communication difficulties lay between her and Jerry, she knew what mattered most. The boys, their fragile trust, the family they were slowly building together. All of it was worth fighting for.

Her phone vibrated in her pocket. When she checked the screen, Jerry's name appeared with a message that seemed to bridge the distance between them.

Jerry

**Did they find you? Did they give you the gift?**

Scarlet smiled, the first genuine smile she'd felt at seeing his name in weeks. He'd been building walls lately, keeping his distance, surrounding himself with emotional armor. But despite all of that, he'd orchestrated this moment from across the world. Had been thinking of her, planning for her, even when his messages grew short and practical.

She typed her reply with renewed hope.

Scarlet

They did. It's perfect. I love it. I love them. I love you.

For the first time in months, she didn't stare anxiously at the screen waiting for his response. Instead, she tucked her phone away and followed the Duncans toward the parking lot, faith restored in the future they were carefully building, one difficult day at a time.

# Twenty-Seven

Light filtered in soft and deliberate, illuminating the kitchen with lines of brightness. One beam fell directly across the envelope waiting on the counter, cutting through its middle.

Scarlet worked with quiet efficiency: coffee grounds leveled, machine humming, her fingers betraying the calm in her face.

Twelve minutes until she had to be out the door.

And still, her gaze returned.

Jerry's familiar handwriting covered the page, those rigid capitals sloping gently right. It felt like a voice she hadn't heard in far too long.

Six months of reaching out into silence. Of giving without return.

And now this single envelope, arriving in the wake of a day that had cracked something open between them.

But she hadn't opened it. Couldn't bring herself to unseal whatever waited inside.

"I don't have time this morning," she told Storm, who watched her from his perch on the barstool, tail twitching with feline judgment. "I'll read it tonight."

Storm blinked slowly, unimpressed.

Scarlet glanced at her watch. Ten minutes. She needed to finish her makeup, grab her portfolio, and ...

Storm stretched languidly, then deliberately extended one paw toward the envelope.

"Don't you dare," Scarlet warned.

With elegant precision, Storm batted the envelope off the counter. It landed on the kitchen floor with a soft sound that somehow echoed in Scarlet's chest.

"Seriously?" She set down her coffee mug and scooped up the envelope. "I'm going to be late."

Storm merely yawned, mission accomplished.

Scarlet's fingers traced the edges of the envelope, a strange fluttering starting low in her stomach. The letter could contain anything. A deeper explanation for his emotional distance. News about a longer deployment. Or perhaps it would disappoint her with nothing more than logistics and pleasantries.

"Fine," she muttered, carrying the envelope to the couch. "But if I'm late, I'm blaming you."

She slipped her finger beneath the sealed flap, the tearing sound unnaturally loud in the quiet apartment. Inside was several pages of notebook paper, folded neatly, covered in the same blocky handwriting. Her heart stuttered as she unfolded them, smoothing the creases with shaking fingers.

*Scarlet*

*I don't even know where to start this. 4th try tonight. 5th? Lost count. Keep crumpling papers. Starting over.*

The rawness in those first lines stole her breath. This wasn't Jerry's measured voice from their recent calls. This was something else entirely. Unfiltered, unguarded.

*I counted them. All of them. All 23 letters you sent. I kept every single one even when I couldn't bring myself to read them. I laid them out last night. 23 letters and I sent back*

*Nothing. Not one fucking word. Just those calls getting shorter and shorter until I barely said anything at all.*

Her throat tightened. Even during those weeks when he'd withdrawn from her, when he'd seemed most distant, he'd kept them all.

*I'm sorry. God I'm so sorry. I don't even know if sorry means anything anymore.*

Scarlet pressed her palm flat against her chest, as if she could physically contain the emotion swelling there.

*That video my mom sent. Beach day. You and the boys. I can't stop watching it. Can't stop seeing that moment with Marty when the wave scared him and you just*

*You knew exactly what to do. Nobody told you. You just knew.*

*You were wearing the bracelet with their charms.*

Her fingers instinctively touched the silver bracelet on her wrist, the dinosaur and wheelchair charms warm against her skin. She hadn't taken it off since Mother's Day.

*I can't*

*Why am I like this? Why do I shut down? I don't understand it myself.*

*I've been AWOL. Not just Kuwait-gone. ME-gone. Pulling back. Shutting down. I kept telling myself I was protecting you but that's bullshit. That's what Vega said. Complete bullshit. I was protecting myself. Hiding. Like always.*

The confession landed like a key turning in a lock. Everything she'd felt, every distance she'd measured between them these past months, suddenly made sense. Not indifference. Fear.

*I'm seeing someone here. Oh God that sounds bad. I mean I'm talking to the chaplain. Grant. Started last week after Vega tore into me. He's helping me figure stuff out. Setting me up with an actual therapist in Virginia when I get to Belvoir. Says there's a PTSD program there. Specialized treatment. He thinks I need it. He's right.*

Her eyes widened. PTSD. The word hovered in her mind, suddenly making sense of things she'd noticed but never connected. His hypervigilance about locked doors. The nightmares he never discussed. The way he startled at sudden noises.

*I'm actually going to do it this time. Not just saying the words. Actually doing it. For real. I promised Vega. Promised myself.*

*I don't do this. The feelings thing. The writing it down thing. But I need to try because I don't want to lose you and I think I'm losing you and it's my fault.*

"No," Scarlet whispered aloud, tears forming. "You're not losing me."

*After the boys' mother left I just*

*Shut. Down.*

*Wake up. Feed boys. Work. PT. Therapy appointments. Sleep. Repeat. No room for anything else. No space for breaking because if I broke who would hold it all together?*

*But I am breaking. Been breaking for years. Just hiding it.*

The tears spilled over now, tracking silently down her cheeks. She'd suspected the pain behind his carefully maintained control, but seeing such raw confession from a man who never admitted weakness made her heart ache.

*There's stuff I never told you*

*My second deployment*

*Afghanistan patrol*

*Lost Hunter. My spotter. One minute walking point, next minute gone. Just gone. Not even pieces big enough to*

*God I need to stop*

Scarlet pressed her hand to her mouth, her vision blurring. He'd carried grief in silence, just as she had. Different shapes of the same ache, but grief nonetheless. And now, here he was, peeling it all back, asking to be seen. It wasn't just his healing that began here. It was hers, too.

*I still hear it. Still smell it. The nightmares didn't go away. I just got better at hiding them. Knife under pillow. Checking locks three times every night. Panic when I can't remember if I locked the door even though I checked already.*

*I keep having this dream where I can't find the boys. Like they're gone the way Hunter was gone. Just disappeared.*

*I never told you any of this because I didn't want you to see how broken I am.*

"Jerry," she whispered, tracing his name on the page as if she could reach through it to touch him.

*But I'm getting help. Real help. Chaplain says I need meds too. Probably right. I'm done pretending I'm fine. I'm not fine. Haven't been fine in years.*

*I'm talking to Vega every day. She's been where I am. Says I don't have to carry everything alone. Says it's the strongest thing I could do – ask for help.*

*I had no right to shut you out like I did. No excuse. None. You deserve better. So much better.*

She shook her head, as if he could see her denial. This wasn't about deserving better. This was about choosing him wholly and entirely, even the parts he kept hidden from the world.

*And then there's DC. Our orders. Fort Belvoir. It's a good spot. Great schools. Good hospitals for Marty. Programs for Emmett. Resources for me. It could be good. Really good.*

*But without you it's just*

*It's just another place I'm trying not to fall apart.*

Her breath caught, understanding what was coming even before her eyes reached the next line.

*Scarlet I want you with us. Not because we need you to fix anything. Not because I'm broken. But because I can't stop thinking about you. Every minute. Every second. Because when you're around, everything feels right. Because the boys light up around you in a way I've never seen before.*

*Because I want you. Not need. WANT. Want with everything in me.*

The distinction between want and need wasn't lost on her. She'd spent enough time around the boys to understand the profound difference between being needed and being wanted.

*You have your whole life in Miami. Your job. Your family. I know that. I shouldn't ask you to give that up. I know I shouldn't. But I don't know how else to say it.*

*I want you to come with us. Choose us. We would choose you. We DO choose you. Every day. In every way. Emmett asks about you constantly. Marty looks for you in every video call. And me? I'm so goddamn lost without you it terrifies me.*

Something shifted deep within Scarlet, barriers crumbling as a decision crystallized faster than she would have thought possible. Her apartment blurred through her tears as her world rearranged itself around this new certainty.

*You set something on fire inside me that I thought was dead. You make me feel alive in a way I'd forgotten was possible. When you walk into a room everything else disappears. When you laugh I can't think straight.*

*You see through every wall I put up. Every mask. Every bullshit excuse. You call me on it and I fucking love that about you. Nobody else does that. Nobody.*

A watery laugh escaped her. How many times had she challenged his stoic front, called out his deflections? She'd thought she was pushing too hard. Instead, it had been exactly what he needed.

*I want to build something with you. A home where I don't have to pretend to be fine all the time. Where I can finally let someone see me. All of me. Even the broken parts.*

*I keep seeing you there with us. Making coffee in the kitchen with your messy morning hair. Doing homework with Emmett. Rolling your eyes when I try to fix everything myself instead of asking for help. I can't stop thinking about you there. With us. Part of us. Completing us.*

The images he painted were so vivid she could almost touch them. She could see the home they hadn't built yet, the future that existed only in possibility. Yet it seemed more tangible than the apartment around her, more real than the job she'd devoted years to building.

*You said once you didn't know how to fit in a family that was already built but we're not built we're still just trying to figure out how to be a family and maybe that's what family actually is. Not some finished perfect thing but just people choosing each other every day especially when it's hard.*

Fresh tears spilled at the memory of that conversation. Her confessed fear that she'd always be an accessory to their established unit. His words now dismantled that fear completely.

*I'm going to be better. For the boys. For you. For me. I'm going to do the work. The therapy. The meds if I need them. All of it. And not just for a little while. For as long as it takes. Because I want to be whole again. Or at least less broken.*

*And I want you there. With us. Building something real.*

*I'm all over the place I know. Words coming out wrong.*

"No," she whispered again. "They're coming out exactly right."

*That morning on the ship. Last day. Sun coming up. You in that blue-green dress. Messy hair. You looked at me like you could see everything. All the shit. All the damage. And you didn't run.*

The memory crashed over her. The final morning of the cruise, watching sunrise together, knowing even then that something significant had begun.

*I want that Scarlet. I want real. I want messy and complicated and figuring it out together. I want your laugh first thing in the morning and your voice last thing at night. I want arguments and makeups and everything in between.*

*I want YOU. All of you. Not because we need a mother or I need someone to lean on but because there is no one else in this world who makes me feel the way you do. Like I'm more than I thought I could be. Like we could build something extraordinary together.*

She pressed the letter to her ribs, like it could hold her together from the inside.

Never before had she felt so clearly wanted for who she was. Not as someone filling a role or meeting an obligation, but as herself, completely and entirely.

*If you decide this is too much. If this letter makes you finally walk away. I'd understand. I know I'm asking for something huge. I know I've been gone - really gone - even before deployment. I know this might be the thing that makes you realize you deserve better than what I've been giving.*

*87 days until I'm home. Feels like forever.*

*I'm not asking you to fix me. I know I have to fix myself. And I'm trying. Really trying this time. But I'm asking if you'll be there while I do. If you'll be part of this weird unfinished family that would choose you in a heartbeat if given the chance.*

*I don't deserve a second chance. I know that. But I'm asking for one anyway.*

*Yours (if you still want me) Jerry*

By the time she reached the end, Scarlet was sobbing openly, clutching the pages as if they might disappear. All these months of uncertainty, of distance, reduced to simple, stark truth: Jerry loved her. Wanted her. Chose her. Not despite his damage but with it, alongside it, offering his whole self without pretense or protection.

A glance at her watch confirmed that she was already twenty minutes late.

In any other moment, she'd have been in a tailspin.

Now?

The idea of rushing back to spreadsheets and forced team-building felt irrelevant.

Jerry's words had shifted something. The office suddenly felt like the wrong place to be.

Storm approached, rubbing against her leg as if checking on her emotional state.

"I'm okay," she told him, wiping her eyes. "Better than okay."

The letter couldn't be answered in passing. It demanded presence. Intention. First, she had to make it through work. Then she'd give Jerry what he deserved: the truth.

She ducked into the bathroom and took one look in the mirror.

*SHIT!*

Ruined makeup. Raccoon eyes. Raw expression.

She cleaned it all off like shedding armor.

As she reapplied it, her mind refused to sit still.

Virginia. A new zip code. New neighbors. A future she'd imagined but never fully believed in.

Could she give up everything she'd built here for something so uncertain? Her home, her family, her job?

...

YES!

She didn't even flinch.

She left the house late. Chaos in her bag. Keys in hand.

She was forty minutes late, but for once, it felt like a small act of rebellion.

Driving through traffic, she didn't feel panic. She felt purpose.

Jerry's words hummed like background music: *We choose you. I want YOU.* Each repetition peeling back fear. Making room for hope.

The building rose ahead of her, all glassy detachment. She parked. Stared at it. Then walked in.

"There you are! Eric's been asking where you are for the past half hour. The Henderson clients are already in the conference room, and he needs those quarterly projections."

Scarlet nodded distractedly, making her way to her desk. The morning's revelation had created a strange filter through which she now viewed her workplace. It was like seeing a familiar photograph suddenly in sharper contrast, all the flaws more visible.

"Here," Maya appeared at her side, holding out a folder. "I tried to organize the Henderson materials, but there's something off with the third-quarter projections. Eric's freaking out."

Scarlet accepted the folder, immediately spotting the error in Maya's calculations. A mistake so basic it would have embarrassed a first-year associate, yet Maya had somehow been promoted over her.

"The depreciation schedule is wrong," she said, already reaching for her calculator. "Give me five minutes."

As she corrected the spreadsheet, a strange calm settled over her. This was how she'd spent years of her life, always fixing others' mistakes, steadying the ship, making everyone else look good while remaining invisible herself. Five months ago, it had been devastating to be passed over for promotion. Now, with Jerry's letter fresh in her mind, the entire situation seemed almost absurdly trivial.

"You're a lifesaver," Maya breathed, hovering anxiously. "Eric was about to throw me under the bus with the clients."

"Wouldn't be the first time," Scarlet muttered, without looking up from the calculations.

She finished the corrections and handed the folder back to Maya, who clutched it like a lifeline. "Thank you. Seriously. I owe you."

"Yes, you do," Scarlet agreed, surprising herself with the direct response.

She watched Maya hurry toward the conference room, elegant in her designer suit, completely unaware that Scarlet had just saved her career for the hundredth time. The familiar resentment stirred, but beneath it ... acceptance. Maya wasn't the problem. The system that consistently undervalued Scarlet's contributions was.

The firm had never seen her true worth. But Jerry did. Emmett did. Marty did. Even Maggie and Thomas did.

The thought sent her hands to her keyboard, impulsively logging into her online banking account. Her savings balance stared back at her: $75,842.19. Years of careful budgeting, of living beneath her means despite her success, had created a substantial cushion.

Enough to walk away. Enough to start over. Enough to choose differently.

The truth struck her suddenly and completely. She didn't need this job. She'd been telling herself that her career defined her, that professional success was the yardstick by which she measured her worth. But all along, she'd been building an escape hatch without realizing it.

"Bellari!" Eric's voice cut through her thoughts. He stood in the conference room doorway, face tight with irritation. "We need you in here. Now."

Scarlet looked up, seeing him clearly for perhaps the first time. A mediocre man who'd built his career on the competence of those beneath him, who never acknowledged the contributions of others. He'd passed her over even though everyone, including him, knew she was the best person for the job.

She stood slowly, straightening her skirt with deliberate calm. "I need a moment with you, Eric. In your office, please."

His eyebrows shot up at her tone. "The clients are waiting—"

"They can wait three more minutes," she replied, already walking toward his office with a confidence that surprised her. "Maya has the corrected projections."

Eric followed, clearly annoyed but unwilling to create a scene in front of clients. He closed his office door behind them, his expression carefully controlled. "What's so urgent that it couldn't wait until after the Henderson meeting?"

Scarlet took a deep breath, feeling strangely light. "I'm resigning. Effective immediately."

Eric blinked, momentarily speechless. "Is this about the promotion? Because if that's still bothering you ..."

"This is about five years of having my work attributed to others. About fixing Maya's mistakes while she gets promoted ahead of me. About being the go-to problem solver while never receiving appropriate recognition or compensation." The words flowed easily, years of carefully contained frustration finding precise, professional expression. "Frankly, it's about finally recognizing my own worth."

"Scarlet, be reasonable," Eric said, recovering quickly. "If this is about money—"

"It's not about money," she cut in firmly. "It's about respect. Something fundamentally lacking in how this firm operates."

Eric's face hardened. "If you walk out now, in the middle of the Henderson account—"

"Then maybe you'll finally see how much I've been carrying," Scarlet finished for him. "Maybe you'll notice that Maya can barely manage basic depreciation schedules without my help. Or that Simon has been quietly covering for your management gaps for years." She smiled thinly. "Or maybe you won't. Either way, it's not my problem anymore."

Eric stared at her, clearly struggling to process this transformation. This Scarlet was direct, uncompromising, free of the careful deference she'd maintained for years. "You can't just leave. There are procedures, transitions ..."

"I have eight weeks of vacation accrued," she replied calmly. "Consider this my notice that I'm taking it all, starting now."

"This is completely unprofessional," Eric snapped, color rising in his face. "I expected better from you, Bellari."

"Funny," Scarlet said, moving toward the door. "I expected better from you too. For years, actually."

She walked out of his office feeling ten pounds lighter, ignoring his sputtered protests behind her. The office had fallen unnaturally quiet, colleagues pretending to work while clearly listening to every word. Scarlet moved to her desk and began gathering what mattered most. The framed photo of her family went into her bag first, followed by her special pens and the dinosaur figurine that reminded her of Emmett.

Simon appeared beside her, eyes wide but mouth curled in a barely suppressed smile.

"Did you just—"

"Quit? Yes."

He let out a low whistle. "About damn time." He glanced around, then added in a lower voice, "That was the most beautiful thing I've ever witnessed in this corporate hellscape."

Scarlet laughed, the sound startling in its freedom. "Five years too late, maybe."

"Better late than never," Simon countered, helping her gather her things. "Seriously, Scarlet. Good for you."

She felt a ripple of grateful affection for the one colleague who'd consistently recognized her contributions, who'd quietly supported her through the disappointment of being passed over. "Thanks, Simon. For everything."

As she packed the last of her belongings into her tote bag, she noticed Maya standing frozen near the elevator, her expression a mixture of shock and what looked strangely like grief.

"You're really leaving?" Maya asked as Scarlet approached. "Just like that?"

"Just like that," Scarlet confirmed, pressing the elevator button.

"But ..." Maya glanced around nervously, then lowered her voice. "What am I supposed to do without you? You're the only one who ever helps me."

The unexpected vulnerability caught Scarlet off guard. She'd always seen Maya as entitled confidence personified, not as someone who might actually be struggling beneath the polished exterior.

"Maya, you've been doing this job for years," Scarlet said carefully. "You shouldn't need my help with basic functions."

"I know," Maya admitted, looking down. "I'm just ... I'm not good at the technical parts. I never have been. Everyone knows it, but they keep throwing me into deeper water because ..." She trailed off, shrugging helplessly. "Because I look the part, I guess."

"The pretty one," Scarlet supplied, recalling the familiar office narrative.

Maya looked up, eyes suddenly fierce. "Except you never treated me that way. You were the only one who acted like I could actually learn this stuff, not just smile and nod in client meetings."

The elevator arrived with a soft chime, but Scarlet didn't move. This Maya was different from the one she'd always known. Insecure, genuine, slightly desperate.

"I didn't realize you thought of me as ..." Scarlet hesitated, searching for the word.

"A friend?" Maya supplied, a sad smile flickering across her face. "Yeah, I guess I didn't make that clear. Too busy trying to seem like I had it all together."

Scarlet felt a surprising pang of empathy. How many women had she known who constructed elaborate facades to hide their struggles? How many times had she done it herself?

"You can learn the technical side," she said finally. "You're smart enough. You just need to stop letting them use you as the face of the firm and start demanding proper training."

"Is that what you're doing? Demanding what you deserve?"

Scarlet considered the question, Jerry's letter still echoing in her mind. "No," she said honestly. "I'm choosing what matters. There's a difference."

The elevator doors began to close, and Scarlet stepped inside, holding them open with one hand. "Stand up for yourself, Maya. You deserve better than being the pretty face they trot out for clients."

Maya nodded, her expression shifting from loss to something that resembled respect. "Where will you go?"

"Virginia," Scarlet replied, the word feeling right as soon as she said it. "To build something that matters."

The doors closed on Maya's surprised expression, and Scarlet leaned against the elevator wall, exhaling slowly. She'd just walked away from a secure, well-paying career without a concrete plan. The enormity of that decision should have terrified her. Instead, she felt nothing but certainty.

The doors spun closed behind her, sealing off the fluorescent quiet. Outside, June sunlight bathed her like absolution. Each step away from the building felt like exhale.

Her car waited in the lot, but the idea of going home felt too small. She needed sky. Movement. Salt.

Twenty minutes later, she reached the beach. It stretched wide and familiar before her, wind curling off the water in lazy strokes.

She kicked off her heels the moment her soles met sand, ignoring the stares. The grains clung to her stockings, her skirt tugged at her legs, but none of it mattered.

She walked anyway.

She found a quiet stretch near the dunes, dropped beside her shoes, and let herself sink down into the grit. The sand welcomed her like something that had been waiting.

For a long while, she did nothing but listen to the waves.

Then she lifted her phone, flipped the camera, and studied the woman staring back.

Hair tousled. Makeup flawless. But her eyes held something new, something different than before.

Resolve. Soft fury. A calm that came from choosing to feel everything and still stay upright.

Grief had made her cautious. Careful.

But love—*love*—was making her brave.

Scarlet pressed record, the waves crashing behind her.

"Jerry," she began, not softly, but with the kind of calm that follows clarity. "I got your letter today. Read it sitting on my couch while Storm watched, probably judging me for the makeup I ruined crying all over those pages." She smiled, blinking back fresh tears. "And then I went to work and quit my job. Just walked into Eric's office and told him I was done. Five years of putting up with being overlooked and undervalued, and it took your letter to make me realize I deserve better."

Her pause held reverence rather than hesitation. Reverence for the risk, for the truth. "I want you to know that nothing in that letter scares me. Not the PTSD, not the nightmares, not the challenges. Because it's you, Jerry. All of you. The broken parts and the whole parts together."

A further tremble in her voice wasn't weakness. It was the weight of every hard-earned word pressing into the next.

"And I choose you. I choose the boys. I choose us building something real together, whatever that looks like. So yes. A thousand times yes. I'll come to Virginia. I'll help you build that home where you don't have to pretend to be fine all the time. Where we can figure out family together, messy and complicated and real."

The ocean surged behind her, wild and constant, a rhythm that seemed to echo what had always been true beneath the doubt.

"I love you, Jerry Duncan. I love your boys. And I choose all of it … the beauty and the mess." She didn't brush away the tears. She let them fall, every drop a promise.

She ended the recording, then pressed send before she could overthink it. The video would take time to upload all the way to Kuwait, but eventually it would reach him. Jerry would know she was all in, completely and without reservation.

She set the phone beside her and leaned back, letting the weight of her body sink into the sand like an exhale she'd been holding for years.

No plans. No timelines. Just a decision that felt less like a risk and more like finally listening.

The sun warmed her skin and the sea offered its steady cadence, and for the first time, Scarlet didn't need to know what came next.

It was enough to feel the pull of something real, waiting.

# Twenty-Eight

The scent of her mother's guava pastries mingled with fresh coffee, filling the kitchen with the familiar aromas of Sunday morning. Scarlet arranged fresh-cut mango slices on a serving platter, glancing occasionally at her phone on the counter. Jerry's morning text glowed on the screen.





"If you check that phone one more time, it might actually grow roots into your hand," Elisa teased, sliding another batch of pastries onto a cooling rack.

Scarlet smiled, tucking the phone into her pocket. "Just making sure I didn't miss anything."

"Mhmm." Her mother's knowing look spoke volumes. "Since that letter arrived, you've been like a teenager with her first crush."

"It's not a crush when you're moving cross-country for someone," Scarlet pointed out, arranging silverware on the patio table.

"No," her mother agreed softly. "It's much more significant than that."

The doorbell chimed, interrupting whatever else Elisa might have said. Jade's voice carried from the foyer, followed by a deeper, unfamiliar tone that made Scarlet's eyebrows raise. Dave. This would be interesting.

"They're here!" Scarlet called to her father, who was pretending to read the newspaper while actually preparing his standard new-boyfriend interrogation strategy.

Jade appeared in the kitchen doorway, looking happier than Scarlet had seen her in months. The man beside her stood slightly taller, with kind eyes and a nervous smile. He clutched a bottle of wine like a lifeline.

"Everyone, this is Dave," Jade announced, her hand resting comfortably in the crook of his arm. "Dave, this is my mom Elisa, my dad Leo, and my sister Scarlet."

"The one moving to DC," Dave said, extending his hand to Scarlet. "Jade's told me all about your adventure."

Before Scarlet could respond, the back door swung open as Cami breezed in, arms laden with a tote bag clinking with bottles. "I come bearing liquid sunshine! Mimosas for everyone except Leo, who gets straight orange juice because someone has to drive me home."

The kitchen erupted in laughter and greetings, the initial awkwardness dissolving under Cami's characteristic energy. Leo emerged from behind his newspaper, sizing up Dave with thinly veiled interest.

"So, Dave," he began, "what exactly do you do?"

Jade rolled her eyes. "Dad, at least let him sit down before the Spanish Inquisition begins."

"Construction management," Dave answered easily, seemingly unfazed. "I oversee commercial projects downtown."

Leo nodded, clearly filing this information away for later evaluation. "Honest work. Good."

As they settled around the patio table, sunlight filtering through the bougainvillea overhead, Scarlet watched her sister with quiet fascination. The way Jade leaned slightly toward Dave when he spoke. How she used his actual name instead of her usual noncommittal "him" or the infamous "John" placeholder. Small signs of genuine investment that Scarlet hadn't seen before.

"Earth to Scarlet," Cami's voice cut through her observations. "I asked what decorating style you're thinking for the DC place. Please tell me it's not going to be all beige and practical."

Scarlet blinked. "I don't even have a place yet. Just some listings Jerry's sent from his housing allowance options."

"Show us!" Jade demanded, hand extended for Scarlet's phone.

Scarlet scrolled through her saved photos, displaying a modest three-bedroom townhouse near Fort Belvoir. "This is the one we're leaning toward. Good school district for the boys, accessible for Marty's appointments."

"Look at you, talking schools and accessibility like a full-blown mom already," Cami remarked, sipping her mimosa.

"That's because she is one," Elisa said simply, passing Dave a platter of pastries. "Those boys adore her."

Dave glanced between them. "So you're becoming an instant mom to two kids while moving across the country? That's ... significant."

"Terrifying is the word you're looking for," Scarlet corrected with a small smile. "But also right."

"When exactly are you leaving us?" Cami asked dramatically. "I need to start planning the Scarlet Farewell Tour immediately. We need beach days, dancing at Azúcar, one last shopping spree at Bal Harbour ..."

"I won't be moving until January at the earliest," Scarlet laughed. "We don't know the exact timing yet."

"That's only five months!" Cami protested. "We have to schedule everything now before your calendar fills with boring Virginia plans."

"Virginia's not boring," Leo interjected, surprisingly defensive. "Good fishing in the Potomac."

"Because that's what Scarlet will definitely be doing with her free time. Fishing," Jade teased.

"She might," Leo shrugged. "People change."

The simple comment hung in the air, carrying more significance than perhaps even her father realized. Scarlet felt it resonate inside her. The acknowledgment of how much she had indeed changed since Christmas. Since the cruise. Since finding a family she hadn't known she was looking for.

"Speaking of changing," Dave said, turning toward Jade, "your sister mentioned you've taken on that new sustainability account at work?"

Jade lit up, launching into an enthusiastic explanation of her marketing firm's newest client. Scarlet watched the conversation flow, noting how Dave asked follow-up questions that showed genuine interest in Jade's career. How different from Lucas, who had always redirected conversations back to himself.

"You know what I admire?" Cami said suddenly, interrupting a lull in conversation. "How you just … quit. Walked out of that soul-crushing firm and never looked back." She raised her glass. "I still want to hear the blow-by-blow of Eric's face when you told him."

"It wasn't that dramatic," Scarlet demurred, though the memory still brought a flicker of satisfaction.

"It was exactly that dramatic," Cami insisted. "You were their star player and you just … left. For love." She clutched her chest dramatically. "It's rom-com worthy."

"I didn't leave just for Jerry," Scarlet clarified, feeling the need to make this point. "I left because I finally realized I was worth more than being overlooked and undervalued. Jerry and the boys are where I'm going, but the decision to leave was about valuing myself first."

A moment of surprised silence followed her declaration.

"Well damn," Jade finally said. "When did my sister get so wise?"

"I didn't think you'd really do it," her father admitted quietly. "Quit the job. Move away." His voice softened. "I'm proud of you, Scarlet."

"Me too," Jade added. "Though I'll deny saying that if you ever bring it up again."

"And I'll visit constantly," Cami promised. "Your Virginia couch has my name all over it. I expect regular guest towels and a wine supply."

The table buzzed with laughter, familiar and easy. Scarlet breathed it in like the most essential oxygen, simple and life-giving.

It hit her all at once: no matter where she went, this would be the bedrock. The people who shaped her, still holding space for the woman she was becoming. "What will you miss most about Miami?" Dave asked, genuine curiosity in his voice.

Answers flowed from around the table:

"The weather," from Jade.

"The food," from Cami, patting her stomach.

"The coffee," from Elisa.

Then, unexpectedly, from Leo: "Our morning talks." When everyone looked at him in surprise, he shrugged. "What? I like when she explains her spreadsheets. Makes no sense to me, but I like how her brain works."

Scarlet blinked back sudden tears, reaching across to squeeze her father's hand.

Cami raised her glass. "To new beginnings that don't forget where they started."

"To new beginnings," everyone echoed, glasses clinking in the dappled sunlight.

Hours later, after the dishes were cleared and guests departed, Scarlet sat cross-legged on her childhood bed, surrounded by the strange juxtaposition of her past and future. Teen movie posters alongside printouts of DC school districts. Her high school trophy next to Marty's latest drawing.

She opened the small jewelry box on her nightstand, removing two bracelets. One held memories from her past: a delicate silver chain with a tiny palm tree charm from her high school graduation. The other represented her future, newer but already more precious, with small green wheelchair and rainbow dinosaur charms that Emmett and Marty had chosen for her.

Scarlet fastened the bracelet around her wrist, letting the charms catch the light. Then, after a moment's consideration, she added the palm tree bracelet alongside it, the charms clinking together softly.

Scarlet stared down at the bracelet until her vision blurred. She could still feel the echo of Emmett's arms around her waist on the beach, still hear the joy in his voice when he'd shouted *Mom* across the sand. Her heart clenched with something too big to hold alone.

She didn't hear her mother come in until the bed dipped beside her.

Elisa didn't speak. She never had to. Just sat there, like she'd done when Scarlet was twelve and had cried over her first heartbreak, or twenty and sick with finals and self-doubt. Present. Quiet. Steady.

Scarlet's voice was hoarse when it finally came. "There's something I never told you."

Elisa turned to her, but said nothing, giving her room.

"I was pregnant," Scarlet whispered. "Eight years ago. With Alex."

Elisa sucked in a quiet breath, but didn't interrupt.

"I didn't even tell him. I didn't tell anyone. Not Jade. Not Cami. Not you." Scarlet's voice cracked. "It was early … just a few weeks. And then … it was over. Just like that. I went to the ER alone, bled alone, came home and threw the sonogram in the trash. And the next day, I went to work like it hadn't happened."

The tears came hot and fast now. "I told myself it didn't count. That if I never said it out loud, I wouldn't have to mourn it. Wouldn't have to explain what it did to me."

Elisa's hand found hers, firm and anchoring. "Oh, mi amor …"

"I thought I was fine," Scarlet said, her words tumbling out in a rush now. "I thought I'd moved on. And then I met Jerry. And I met his boys. And I watched Emmett line up his dinosaur toys and Marty hum when I walked in the room. And something just … broke. Or maybe it cracked open."

She pressed the heels of her palms to her eyes. "I have this life now. This love. This *family*. And I'm so happy I can't breathe sometimes. But underneath it, there's this guilt. Like I left something behind. Like I'm betraying someone who never even had a name."

Elisa's arms wrapped around her before she could say more, tight, trembling, full of a grief Scarlet hadn't realized her mother had space for, too.

"You didn't betray anyone," Elisa whispered into her hair. "You survived something you shouldn't have had to survive alone. And now you're learning how to love again. That's not betrayal, Scarlet. That's resurrection."

Scarlet let herself sob then, deep and wrenching, the kind that shakes your ribs and steals your breath. The kind that only comes when you know someone will still be holding you when it's over.

After a long moment, Elisa pulled back just enough to look at her.

"You are not broken," she said fiercely. "You are *brave*. For carrying that secret. For choosing love again anyway. For showing up for those boys like they're already yours."

Scarlet wiped at her face, mascara streaking down her cheeks.

"I don't feel brave," she whispered. "I feel like I've been pretending to be fine for so long that I forgot how to actually be *not fine.*"

Her mother smiled through her own tears. "Then start here. Be not fine. Be messy. Be real. We'll hold you. I'll hold you."

Scarlet nodded, her throat too tight for words. She leaned into her mother's arms again, letting herself become the girl who had once needed someone to tell her it was okay to fall apart, not the poised woman packing for a new life.

# Twenty-Nine

Scarlet adjusted the collar of her navy dress for the tenth time, her fingertips smoothing fabric that didn't need smoothing. Fort Cavazos gymnasium had transformed into something between a rock concert venue and a high school prom on steroids. Everywhere Scarlet looked, glittering banners proclaimed "WELCOME HOME HEROES" while red, white, and blue balloons bobbed against the ceiling in patriotic clusters. A professional DJ booth dominated one corner, speakers taller than Scarlet herself flanking a mixing table where a grinning man in fatigues tested levels.

"Mom, are they here yet?" Emmett tugged at her hand, his voice slightly louder than usual as he compensated for the sound-dampening earmuffs that served as compromise headgear, allowing him to participate without being overwhelmed by the chaos. The dark blue headphones matched his carefully chosen "Dad's Coming Home" t-shirt, which he'd insisted on wearing despite Maggie offering three other options.

"Not yet, buddy," Scarlet replied, checking her phone again. "Any minute now."

Beside them, Marty bounced in his wheelchair with uncontainable excitement, his hands flapping joyfully at the sensory feast surrounding them. The wheelchair's wheels had been decorated with streamers that fluttered with his movements, making him look like a one-man parade float.

"He's going to spin himself right out of that chair," Thomas observed with grandfatherly affection, standing protectively behind Marty. "Never seen him this worked up."

Maggie nodded, her normally composed features softened by anticipation. "Nine months is too long. For all of them." Her eyes met Scarlet's with shared understanding.

Nine months. Two hundred and seventy-four days. Scarlet had counted each one, marking them off her calendar like breadcrumbs leading her back to Jerry. The first months had been the hardest, with his gradual withdrawal and the growing silence between them. Then had come his letter. Raw, honest, asking for a second chance and a shared future. Then her reply, without hesitation: *Yes. A thousand times yes.*

Now, after months of planning, of quitting her job, of packing up her life in Miami, the moment had finally arrived. In minutes, Jerry would walk through those doors. The thought sent a flutter of butterflies through Scarlet's stomach that had nothing to do with the thundering bass from the DJ's speakers.

"Look!" Emmett shouted, pointing at the massive digital screen that had been erected behind the DJ booth. It now displayed a live feed of buses pulling up outside. "The buses are here!"

The gymnasium, already buzzing with hundreds of families, erupted in anticipation. Children who had been running in circles froze mid-stride, heads swiveling toward the entrance. Mothers smoothed hair and reapplied lipstick. Fathers hoisted toddlers onto shoulders for better viewing. The energy shifted palpably from excitement to nearly unbearable anticipation.

"Places, everyone!" The DJ's voice boomed through the speakers. "Let's give our returning heroes a welcome they'll never forget! Make some noise!"

The crowd needed no encouragement. A wave of sound crashed through the gymnasium as families began cheering, clapping, stomping feet against bleachers. Scarlet felt the vibration through the soles of her shoes, the physical manifestation of collective joy.

Emmett pressed closer to her side, his eyes wide despite the protective earmuffs. Marty's bouncing intensified, his wheelchair nearly vibrating with excitement. Scarlet slipped one hand into Emmett's and rested the other on Marty's shoulder, steadying herself as much as them.

"You okay?" Maggie asked quietly, noting Scarlet's rapid breathing.

"Perfect," Scarlet replied, surprised to find it was true. Despite the nerves, despite the chaos, despite the uncertainty of what came next. She was exactly where she needed to be.

The DJ's voice cut through the noise again. "Ladies and gentlemen, are you ready to welcome home your soldiers?"

The answering roar was deafening.

"I said, ARE! YOU! READY?"

The crowd somehow found another level of volume, the sound becoming physical, tangible.

Scarlet barely heard the beginning of AC/DC's "Thunderstruck" as the music blasted from the speakers. The opening guitar riff was almost immediately swallowed by the crowd's reaction to the first glimpse of uniforms at the entrance.

The soldiers burst into the gymnasium like rock stars taking the stage, their entrance nothing short of explosive. They sprinted in formation, arms pumping, boots thundering against the polished floor. Smoke machines positioned at the entrance enveloped them in dramatic clouds, while controlled bursts of flame shot up on either side, framing their entrance in literal fire.

"Thun-der!" the crowd chanted with the music, fists pumping in unison.

Glittering confetti cannons detonated, showering the returning heroes in a patriotic storm of red, white, and blue. Children screamed with delight, adults shed unashamed tears, and the bleachers physically shook with the stomping of hundreds of feet.

Scarlet felt her heart pounding in rhythm with the music, her eyes scanning the incoming soldiers for Jerry. They formed up in disciplined rows, but excitement radiated from them despite their attempts at military bearing. Some couldn't resist pumping fists in the air. Others pointed to specific family members they'd spotted. One broke rank just long enough to catch a teddy bear thrown by a small child.

"Do you see him?" she shouted to Emmett, who had climbed onto a chair for better visibility.

"Not yet ... wait!" Emmett pointed excitedly. "There! Third row! That's Dad!"

Scarlet followed his finger, and her breath caught. She found him in the formation, standing taller somehow than she remembered, his face leaner but his posture strong. Even from this distance, she could see he was struggling to maintain his professional composure, his eyes already searching the crowd.

When their eyes locked across the gymnasium, the music and cheering and chaos all faded away. One silent moment of connection before the world rushed back in around them.

Colonel Sharp approached the microphone set up center court, raising his hands for quiet. The crowd reluctantly lowered their volume, though excited whispers continued to ripple through the space.

"Welcome home, Third Brigade Combat Team," he announced, his voice carrying impressively. "I know I'm supposed to give some long speech about duty and sacrifice ..." He paused, looking out at the crowd of expectant families, then back at his soldiers. "But I think we all know who you're here to see ... and it's definitely not me."

A wave of appreciative laughter rolled through the gymnasium.

"So without further ado," Colonel Sharp continued with a grin, "Soldiers ... dismissed!"

The formation exploded like a balloon popping, discipline dissolving into joyful chaos as soldiers broke ranks and families surged forward. The gymnasium became a sea of motion, bodies weaving through spaces, children darting between adults, tearful reunions blooming everywhere Scarlet looked.

"Come on!" Emmett shouted, tugging her forward. "Let's find Dad!"

But as they pushed into the crowd, Scarlet lost sight of where Jerry had been standing. Bodies pressed in from all sides, the noise level making it impossible to call his name. She held tightly to Emmett's hand, making sure Maggie and Thomas stayed close with Marty, craning her neck to see over the crowd.

"Scarlet!" A familiar voice cut through the noise.

She turned to find Mac grinning at her, his uniform crisp but his demeanor relaxed as always.

"There you are," he said, reaching for her arm. "Been looking all over for you."

"Where's Jerry?" she asked immediately, unable to waste time on pleasantries.

Mac's smile turned enigmatic. "That's what I'm here for. Need you to come with me."

"But we just need to find—"

"Trust me," Mac interrupted, already guiding her through the crowd. "You need to stand right here." He positioned her with surprising precision in a seemingly random spot near center court.

"Mac, what are you—"

"For once in your life, Red, stop asking questions," he teased, stepping back. "Emmett, bring Marty over here too."

Before Scarlet could protest further, she noticed something strange happening around her. At least ten soldiers had formed a circle, effectively walling her and the boys off from the rest of the celebration.

"What's going on?" she asked, confusion overpowering anticipation.

Mac winked. "Just wait."

The DJ's voice suddenly cut through the chaos. "Ladies and gentlemen, we have a special moment happening right now. Everyone give us some room in center court!"

The crowd noise dulled slightly as attention shifted to their circle. The pulsing rock music abruptly cut off, replaced by the unmistakable opening notes of "Lady in Red." A spotlight clicked on from somewhere above, bathing their small area in dramatic light.

"Mac?" Scarlet questioned, heart suddenly racing for a different reason.

Instead of answering, Mac nodded to the other soldiers. Like a perfectly choreographed theatrical reveal, they stepped apart in unison, creating a path through their human wall.

And there, kneeling in the center of their circle, was Jerry.

The sight stole Scarlet's breath. He looked up at her with eyes that contained everything they'd survived. Deployment, distance, his withdrawal, her patience, their gradual rebuild across continents. In his hand was a small velvet box, open to reveal a silver ring that caught the spotlight like a tiny star.

The gymnasium might as well have emptied. In that moment, Scarlet saw only him.

"Scarlet," Jerry said, his voice steady despite the emotion visible on his face. "I had a whole speech planned, but seeing you here ..." He shook his head slightly. "All I want to say is thank you. For waiting. For not giving up. For loving the boys like they were always yours."

She felt tears forming, but didn't try to stop them.

"You saw me at my worst," he continued, "and somehow still wanted me at my best. I don't know why fate put us on that cruise, but I thank God every day that it did." He took a deep breath. "I want to build a life with you. A real one, with all the messy, beautiful, hard, wonderful parts." His voice grew more certain with each word. "Scarlet Bellari, will you marry me?"

Time suspended itself for one perfect heartbeat.

"Yes," she whispered, then found her voice. "Yes. A thousand times yes."

Jerry rose to his feet, taking her hand and sliding the ring onto her finger. The metal was cool against her skin, but warmed immediately, as if it had always belonged there. His eyes never left hers as he stepped closer, one hand coming up to cradle her cheek, his thumb brushing away a tear.

When his lips finally met hers, the kiss contained everything: relief, desire, promise, home. Scarlet wound her arms around his neck, pressing closer, memorizing the feeling of him solid and real against her after so many months of absence.

The crowd's renewed cheers washed over them in waves as they remained locked in their embrace, the spotlight illuminating their reunion like a scene from a dream. In that moment, surrounded by joy and held in Jerry's arms at last, Scarlet knew with absolute certainty that she had found her way home.

# Epilogue

Sunshine filtered through the floor-to-ceiling windows of the Aphrodite Suite, catching the champagne bubbles in Scarlet's untouched glass. She stood still as Cami worked on her hair, weaving tiny white flowers through the loose waves that tumbled over her shoulders.

"So," Scarlet said, catching Cami's eyes in the mirror. "You disappeared pretty quickly after the bachelorette party last night."

Cami's fingers stilled for a fraction of a second before resuming their work. "I have no idea what you're talking about."

"Really? Because Mac texted Jerry asking if he'd seen you."

A smile played at the corners of Cami's mouth. "Pure coincidence."

"That you both vanished at the same time?"

"Precisely."

Jade snorted from her perch on the bed, where she was adjusting the strap on her heel. "You two are ridiculous. Just admit you've been circling each other since that first cruise."

"We have not been …" Cami began, then caught Scarlet's raised eyebrow in the mirror. "Fine. We ran into each other at the Celestial View lounge. And maybe we grabbed a drink. And maybe—"

"Spare me the details," Scarlet laughed. "Just don't ghost him this time."

"I prefer to think of it as creating an air of mystery," Cami replied, tucking a final flower into Scarlet's hair.

"Speaking of mystery men," Scarlet said, turning toward Jade. "Whatever happened with Dave? You never did tell me how that ended."

Jade rolled her eyes, though the action lacked her former bitterness. "The usual story. Great guy, wrong timing. He wanted more commitment than I was ready for after the Lucas disaster." She shrugged. "But at least I used his real name this time. That's progress, right?"

"Definite progress," Scarlet agreed.

"Enough about my non-existent love life," Jade said, popping a chocolate-covered strawberry into her mouth. "How's the non-profit treating Virginia's newest financial literacy guru? Still loving life in suburban military bliss?"

Scarlet's reflection smiled back at her, more relaxed than the woman who'd once boarded this ship looking for escape. "It's … surprisingly great. I never thought I'd love working for a nonprofit, but heading up the financial literacy program is actually using my skills for something that matters."

"And they promoted you after what, nine months?" Cami said, cleaning up the makeup station. "Some things never change."

"Program Director has a nice ring to it," Jade agreed. "Though I still think it's hilarious you went from tax strategy for luxury clients to teaching military spouses how to budget."

"What can I say? Turns out I'm good at translating financial jargon into human language." Scarlet turned slightly to see herself from a different angle. "And the flexibility is everything with the boys' schedules. I can be there for IEP meetings and therapy appointments without having to beg for time off."

"How is Marty doing with the new therapy center?" Jade asked, her tone shifting to something gentler.

"Amazing. They have this adaptive communication program that's been a game-changer. His eye-tracking device is letting him express so much more." A warmth filled Scarlet's chest. "You should see how his face lights up when he can tell us exactly what he wants."

"And Emmett? Still the little professor?" Cami asked, stepping back to assess her handiwork.

"More like an enthusiastic apprentice. Saturday mornings turn into a theatrical kitchen hour with him and Jerry, both of them doing voices and everything." Scarlet smiled. "Last weekend they made croissants. The kitchen looked like a bakery exploded in slow motion."

"I still can't believe Staff Sergeant Serious turned out to be such a softie," Cami said, reaching for the champagne bottle to refill Jade's glass.

"He always was," Scarlet replied. "He just needed permission to show it."

A gentle knock interrupted their conversation, followed by three distinct voices on the other side of the door.

"It's us," came Maggie's familiar voice. "Are you decent? We have some very impatient gentlemen here."

Jade crossed to open the door, revealing Maggie flanked by Emmett and Marty in his wheelchair, all three dressed in their finest. Emmett stood tall in his miniature tux, looking years older than the solemn six-year-old Scarlet had first met. Marty beamed from his wheelchair, the silver ribbons Mac had woven through the spokes catching the light with each movement.

"Mom!" Emmett exclaimed, his eyes widening as he took in Scarlet's appearance. "You look like a princess!"

Scarlet knelt carefully, mindful of her dress, to embrace him. "And you look incredibly handsome. Both of you do."

Maggie entered with quiet grace, her rose dress a perfect echo of the blush in her cheeks.

"The setup looks gorgeous. Your father's off with Thomas, trying to win his battle with the tie."

She turned to Scarlet, eyes misting. "Sweetheart ... you're breathtaking."

Scarlet held up a finger. "Nope. Don't you dare. One tear from you, and I'll lose it. And then Cami will stage a dramatic intervention with makeup brushes."

"I absolutely will," Cami confirmed, though her own eyes looked suspiciously bright.

Maggie composed herself, then turned to the boys. "Why don't you show Mom what Mac had made for today?"

Emmett stepped forward, proudly displaying a small white pillow attached to Marty's wheelchair tray. "Look! The rings go here, and Marty gets to carry them down the aisle. And I get to walk with you!"

His face grew serious. "I've been practicing walking slow. Mac says I have to match your pace."

"You'll be perfect," Scarlet assured him, touching the pillow gently. "Both of you will."

She moved to Marty's side, leaning down to his eye level. "Hey, sunshine. Look at you all dressed up." Marty's face lit up, his eyes communicating what his voice couldn't. He reached for her with both hands, and she leaned in closer, pressing her forehead to his.

The suite door opened again as Elisa entered, carrying a small velvet box. Her eyes immediately welled at the sight of her daughter surrounded by her chosen family.

"Oh, mija," she breathed, pressing a hand to her heart.

"Mom, I warned Maggie, and now I'm warning you ... no crying. Cami will have our heads."

Elisa composed herself with visible effort. "I brought you something." She opened the box to reveal a delicate gold bracelet with a single blue stone. "Your grandmother's. Something old and something blue in one."

"It's beautiful," Scarlet whispered as her mother fastened it around her wrist, just above the silver bracelet with the wheelchair and dinosaur charms that never left her arm.

"She would have loved Jerry," Elisa said, her voice soft with memory. "And these precious boys. She always said the best families are the ones we choose."

Scarlet swallowed the sudden lump in her throat. "And something borrowed?"

Jade stepped forward, slipping a pair of pearl earrings into Scarlet's palm. "These brought me luck on my first date with Dave." She smiled wryly. "It didn't last, but it was good while it did. Though you don't need luck today."

"And something new," Cami announced, stepping back from her handiwork to retrieve a small gift bag. Inside was a delicate anklet with a tiny silver wave charm. "To remind you how far you've sailed."

There was another knock at the door. "It's me," came Leo's voice. "Everyone decent?"

Jade opened the door to reveal Leo looking both uncomfortable and proud in his tuxedo. His eyes widened at the sight of his daughter.

"Wow, kiddo," was all he managed, his voice gruff with emotion.

"That's our cue," Cami said, scanning her phone. "Jade and I need to take our places. The captain's already there, and Mac says Jerry's on his way too."

She wrapped Scarlet in a quick embrace. "See you on the other side, warrior. Today's the easy part."

With Cami, Jade, and Maggie gone, Scarlet stood with her parents in the quiet pause before everything began.

She looked between them, the weight of everything that had led here suddenly rising all at once.

"You ready?" Leo asked, extending his arm.

She gave a nod, blinking back the lump in her throat.

Their path wound through familiar territory as each corner of the ship echoed a memory.

The bar where Jerry had first disarmed her.

The pool deck, where flirtation danced in the night air.

The promenade, where they'd walked without direction but with complete ease.

They paused just out of sight of the gathered guests, where Emmett waited solemnly to take over his special role. Leo's eyes grew suspiciously bright as he kissed Scarlet's cheek and placed her hand on Emmett's offered arm.

"You're in good hands," he said, stepping back to let them proceed.

"Ready, Mom?" Emmett asked softly.

She nodded, grateful beyond words for this boy who had so completely claimed her heart.

The melody shifted to something soft but certain, signaling their moment to begin.

They stepped forward together, greeted by a sea of familiar faces.

Mac stood beside Jerry, a grin stretching wide across his face.

Nearby, Marty sat beaming in his ribbon-adorned wheelchair, the ring pillow resting like a crown on his tray, glinting under the lights.

And there, waiting for her with eyes that had never looked so certain, was Jerry.

The same man who'd reluctantly boarded this ship two and a half years ago, who'd struggled to let himself want anything beyond duty and responsibility. The same man who'd opened his heart, his life, his family to her, piece by precious piece. He watched her approach with such obvious love that Scarlet felt her steps falter slightly, overwhelmed by the journey that had brought them here.

The man waiting for her wasn't the same one who had boarded this ship, shoulders tight with duty and grief. He was still healing. So was she. But they were doing it together. They'd both carried silent scars for too long, afraid to let anyone see what had broken them. And somehow, across deployments and distance and the chaos of parenting, they'd found safety in each other's open hands.

Emmett guided her forward with careful, measured steps, her heartbeat matching their deliberate pace. With each step, she felt the weight of every memory that had brought her here. Every choice, every moment that had led her to this man, these boys, this life she'd never imagined, this family that she couldn't imagine living without.

*I boarded this ship terrified of wanting too much. Of asking for more than my perfectly mapped life. I understood work, success, advancement. Those were familiar waters. Anything else felt like drowning.*

*I was so good at playing all my roles. The competent professional, the reliable daughter, the supportive sister. I excelled at being who everyone needed, but I'd forgotten how to just be. How to want things that didn't come with titles or promotions. How to stop measuring my worth by what I accomplished.*

*Then Jerry happened. With his quiet depth and unexpected honesty. He didn't perform. He just was. And somehow, with him, I remembered how to be too.*

*That night in the hot tub, I felt something crack open inside me. Some wall I'd built so carefully, I'd forgotten it was there. He saw through everything else to find me. Not my polish or my credentials or my carefully constructed facade. Just me. The woman beneath all the armor.*

*I fought it, of course. Tried to convince myself it was just a cruise fling, something to leave behind when real life resumed. But then he met my family, and I met his boys, and suddenly "real life" wasn't what I thought it was anymore.*

*When deployment came, I could have walked away.*

*It would have been easier.*

*My old self would have seen it as the practical choice. But the woman I'd become couldn't imagine choosing anything but them. Even with the hardship. Even with the distance. Even with the uncertainty.*

*So I learned. How to love a non-verbal child who communicates with his eyes and the most beautiful smile I've ever seen. How to support a brilliant, sensitive boy who notices everything and feels even more. How to navigate the world of adaptive equipment and accessibility. How to advocate in IEP meetings and find the right therapists and build a home where everyone belongs.*

*I learned that loving them didn't replace what I lost. But it made room for it. It gave me a place to finally grieve and to grow. I carried that secret pain for so long, believing it disqualified me from being a mother. But now, I know better. Love doesn't erase the past: it redeems it.*

*I spent so many years believing I had to earn love through perfection and achievement. Now I know the truth.*

*Love isn't earned.*

*It's chosen.*

*Every day. In a thousand small ways. In the chaos and the calm. In the mess and the magic.*

*Almost three years ago, I boarded this ship thinking I needed to escape. I had no idea I was sailing toward everything I never knew I needed. Every step down this aisle feels like finally arriving somewhere I've been searching for my whole life. Not because Jerry completes me, but because he, they, gave me permission to be completely myself.*

*For the first time, I'm not walking toward what I should want.*

*I'm running toward what I do.*

*And it looks like a man and two boys waiting for me at the end of this aisle, none of them perfect, all of them mine.*

*I used to think love was something that happened to you, an unpredictable wave that either carried you away or drowned you. Now I know it's the ship we build together, strong enough to weather any storm. And as I look at Jerry, at the family we've created, one truth fills me with absolute certainty.*

*I've finally found my home.*

# About the Author

I'm J.D. Harbor, a romance novelist drawn to love stories set on the high seas. A former military photojournalist, I discovered my writing voice through capturing real-life moments and now channel that same sense of intimacy and adventure into fiction. My novels invite readers aboard cruise ships filled with possibility, where love often arrives in unexpected tides.

The RomantiSea Serenades series began with Emerald Tide and Sapphire Seas and continues with Scarlet Wave and Golden Shores, companion novels that explore the same love story from two perspectives. These newest releases are loosely inspired by my own love story of meeting my wife at sea and finding a future neither of us had planned.

I now live in Central Florida with my wife and two kids, always dreaming up our next adventure on the open water. I believe the best love stories begin with self-discovery, because only when we truly know ourselves can we fully open our hearts to love.

## Set Sail with the RomantiSea Serenades Series: A Voyage of Love and Self-Discovery

RomantiSea Serenades is an ever-expanding world of love stories set aboard the luxurious Elysian Serenade cruise ship. Each novel is designed to capture the transformative magic of travel, connection, and the open sea. Whether it is through laughter at the pool deck or quiet moments under starlight, these books explore how love can be discovered when we finally give ourselves permission to be seen.

Every romance unfolds as a complete story told across a companion pair of novels, each one offering a distinct perspective on the same relationship. Readers can choose either side of the story or read both for the fullest emotional journey. In addition to these duet voyages, the series also features bonus standalone novellas that spotlight unforgettable characters and moments from the Elysian Serenade community.

While the novels connect through shared settings and cameos, each book stands entirely on its own and can be enjoyed in any order. The heart of RomantiSea Serenades is simple yet profound: new places, new faces, and the unexpected power of love to change everything.

## Golden Shores

Golden Shores is the companion to Scarlet Wave, offering his side of the same unforgettable voyage. Jerry Duncan has lived his life anchored by responsibility, carrying the weight of military service, single fatherhood, and the unspoken belief that good fathers do not get to want more. When his battle buddy convinces him to join a singles cruise, Jerry reluctantly agrees, unsure if he even remembers how to relax.

At sea, he meets Scarlet Bellari, a woman whose sharp wit and guarded confidence spark something he has not felt in years. Their connection grows slowly but deeply, tested by Jerry's instinct to hold back and Scarlet's fear of being truly known. Against the backdrop of Caribbean sunsets and newfound friendship, Jerry learns that wanting joy is not weakness but a form of strength.

Golden Shores is a love story about second chances, healing, and the courage it takes to step beyond duty into desire. Read on its own or alongside Scarlet Wave, it reveals the quiet power of choosing love not in perfection but in truth.

# Emerald Tide and Sapphire Seas

Emerald Tide and Sapphire Seas introduced readers to the sweeping world of RomantiSea Serenades with the unforgettable love story of Harper Brooks and Aidan Murphy. She is a driven New York advertising executive who has built her life on success yet feels hollow inside. He is an Irish chef who has sacrificed his own ambitions to carry the weight of family responsibility. Their chance meeting aboard the Elysian Serenade sparks a connection that challenges them both to question the lives they have accepted.

As their relationship unfolds, Harper and Aidan discover that love is not only about finding someone to share the journey but about daring to hope again. Together they awaken dreams they thought had slipped away, encouraging each other to imagine a future beyond the safe but unfulfilling paths they had been walking. Their story is tender, transformative, and filled with the promise of second chances.

Emerald Tide tells the story through Aidan's eyes, while Sapphire Seas offers Harper's perspective. Each novel stands on its own, yet when read together they reveal the full depth of two people learning that the truest love is the one that helps you grow into who you were always meant to be.

www.ingramcontent.com/pod-product-compliance
Lightning Source LLC
Chambersburg PA
CBHW060816120726
47909CB00006B/1947